Also by Grace Callaway

BLACKWOODS

One Kiss to Desire

Two Secrets to Surrender (May 2025)

LADY CHARLOTTE'S SOCIETY OF ANGELS

Olivia and the Masked Duke

Pippa and the Prince of Secrets

Fiona and the Enigmatic Earl

Glory and the Master of Shadows

Charlotte and the Seductive Spymaster

GAME OF DUKES

The Duke Identity

Enter the Duke

Regarding the Duke

The Duke Redemption

The Return of the Duke

HEART OF ENQUIRY (The Kents)

The Widow Vanishes (Prequel Novella)

The Duke Who Knew Too Much

M is for Marquess

The Lady Who Came in from the Cold

The Viscount Always Knocks Twice

Never Say Never to an Earl

The Gentleman Who Loved Me

MAYHEM IN MAYFAIR

Her Husband's Harlot

Her Wanton Wager

Her Protector's Pleasure

Her Prodigal Passion

"A spinoff from the Blackwoods was always going to be amazing, but after reading it, I'm even more convinced and can't wait to read the full set. Ethan and Xenia's story has so many fantastic tropes, it's hard to know where to start. Hidden identities, class differences, recovering from mutual trauma, and a ghost??? Perfectly done, a fantastic couple."
    -Jordan D., *Netgalley*

"Wonderfully written with lots of feels. I was totally immersed in the story."
    -Ruchika, *Goodreads*

"I really love [Ethan and Xenia] together because Ethan just needed someone to believe in him, same with Xenia... They really needed each other, and they pick each other up in kindness, care and passion."
    -Michelle, *Netgalley*

"Gorgeous romance, passionate and emotional."
    -AJ, *Bookbub*

"I loved the building of a new world of quirky secondary characters. And I also loved the Blackwood family dynamic."
    -Cindy, *Goodreads*

"I loved meeting Ethan and his siblings and getting to see his parents again. Xenia is a wonderful heroine with lots of tenacity and grit. She and Ethan are a terrific couple...a perfect mix of romance, steam and mysterious adventures."
    -Nancy, *Goodreads*

For everyone who's dreamed
of a better place;
and
for my readers who've campaigned
for more of the Blackwoods

ONE *Kiss* TO DESIRE

Blackwood Legacy

BOOK 1

GRACE CALLAWAY

USA TODAY BESTSELLING AUTHOR

Cover Art: Night Witchery

Formatting: Colchester & Page

PROLOGUE

Miss Xenia Loveday's next patron entered the confessional like a man who owed nothing to God, and this intrigued her. Of course, this was not a real confessional, and she was no absolver of sins. In fact, she was the opposite: a dispenser of iniquities.

She couldn't see much of her client through the silk screen that covered the hole between the two sides of the booth. The translucent window revealed only shadows, a unique arrangement that allowed the patron to receive his services anonymously. When she'd first proposed this diversion, her employer, who was known as the "Abbess," had seen its potential.

"*I like a woman with initiative.*" The Abbess's closely spaced eyes had gleamed with approval and avarice. "*You remind me a bit o' myself, dearie. When I first started this Nunnery in the middle o' nowhere, people said I was mad. Now bluebloods come from London to spend their blunt. I predict this new game o' yours will be the talk o' my brothel...no pun intended. Keep the ideas coming, dove, and you may find yourself rising through the ranks.*"

Rising through the ranks of the brothel wasn't Xenia's dream in life...but needs must. She was short on funds, and this job allowed her to make a good living without selling her body and exposing herself to a host of dangers, from diseases to pregnancy. Most importantly, she could keep her identity concealed, which was key to her survival.

Play your part well. If you earn a good tip, you could add to your savings...and maybe have extra left over for a meat pie.

Cheered by the thought of a savory pastry for supper, she took stock of her waiting patron. He'd turned down the lamp on his side of the confessional, rendering himself a flickering shadow. Like the other guests who attended the Nunnery's masquerades, he wore a mask to guard his privacy. Xenia's success stemmed from her ability to understand a customer and his deepest fantasies, and she discerned several details about the present fellow.

Limned by the dim light, he appeared fit...muscular without excessive bulk. The breadth of his shoulders and length of his torso suggested that he was tall, and his hair appeared short and thick. He had the posture of a gentleman who, from birth, has known his own worth. His stillness conveyed an uncommon degree of self-discipline. He did not fidget, nor launch into lustful demands. Instead, he waited with a quiet confidence that fascinated her.

What brought him here? What are his desires? What does he want from me?

By "me," Xenia was referring to her persona this eve, Sister Sirena. The angle of her patron's head indicated that he returned her scrutiny, and she knew what he saw. She'd worked on perfecting her silhouette, which was cast onto the silk screen by two bright lamps. As Sirena, she wore a dramatic wimple, beaded crucifix, and padded bodysuit that enhanced her curves and gave the illusion that she was as naked as the day she was born.

Her costume also provided protection. Back in London, she had let her guard down, and her past had nearly caught up to her. She'd learned her lesson. When she interviewed for this job, she'd done so under the alias of Mary Smith and altered her appearance with hair dye and face paint.

"Welcome to my confessional, sir," she said grandly. "I am Sister Sirena, the Salacious Storyteller. Tonight, I will enchant you with a tale woven from your deepest, innermost desires. As you listen to my voice, you will find yourself transported into another world. A world where pleasure is everything, and nothing is forbidden."

Although she'd given this introduction a half-dozen times this eve, her intimate tones made it sound like a secret between lovers. Her voice was her most prized asset, an instrument she'd learned to play with precision. She could tailor her tone, timbre, and accent to any role she played. She could sound like an eager wanton or a coy virgin; for the right price, she could be whoever the customer wanted.

"Nothing is forbidden?"

The stranger's query held a quiet intensity. Although his voice was muffled by the partition—he didn't project his voice the way she, a professional, did—his accent and manner confirmed that he was a blueblood. Her encounters with the breed had been far from sterling, but she was always willing to take their money.

"Tell me your desires, sir." She'd crafted Sister Sirena's voice to be an alluring mix of sultry and submissive. "And I will spin you a tale."

"What sort of tale?"

"That is up to you, darling," she purred. "Do you wish to hear about birching? A *ménage à trois*, perhaps? Or I could tell you about a dungeon where the most depraved acts imaginable take place..."

"None of that interests me," he said.

A picky toff. Just what I need.

She kept her tone sweet and cajoling. "What *do* you want, sir?"

He paused, as if contemplating his options. Was he hesitating because his fantasies were filthy? She could have assured him that she wasn't one to judge. She'd heard about every perversion under the sun and doubted his desires could be more depraved than those of the patron before him, who'd wanted a fantasy in which every orifice was filled and in simultaneous fashion. During the telling, she'd lost track of the body count and number of appendages; luckily, her patron had been too busy pleasuring himself to notice. His groaning climax had drowned out that of the tale.

"Discretion is my middle name," she said coaxingly.

"I thought it was '*Salacious*.'"

This fellow had wit. Interesting.

"I am salacious and capable of keeping a secret," she replied.

"Very well," he said. "I want something real."

Did he mean he wanted to tup? If so, he'd come to the wrong place.

"I am a storyteller, sir," she said. "If you're looking for another kind of diversion, the lovely novices downstairs will gladly—"

"I want you."

His statement set off a peculiar quiver at the center of her being.

"But I don't want to be peddled the usual drivel. I want your genuine responses—not what you think I want."

In the years Xenia had been doing this work, no one had asked her to be *herself* before. The proposal astounded her...and sparked a secret longing, which she snuffed. Her recent entanglement with a follower had demonstrated the futility of wanting to be desired for who she was. However, she was a professional. She could act the part of the genuine lover, and the toff across from her would never suspect she was playing a role.

"Of course, sir," she said in a flirty tone. "Now that you have me, I wonder what you desire of me?"

"I want you on my lap, your lips ready for mine."

At his demand, the tremor in her belly turned disconcertingly authentic. She didn't know why he affected her like no other patron had. Already, their encounter felt more titillating than her last conversation, which had involved six—or was it seven?—bodies and a great deal of thrusting. The passionate intensity she sensed beneath this fellow's restraint intrigued her. Her mind's eye filled in the details obscured by shadow and mask.

She pictured him as a handsome and charming faerie tale prince with golden hair and emerald eyes. He lived in a castle and had dozens of servants at his beck and call. Yet despite his life of privilege and command, something was missing...and he didn't know what. That was why he had come here, she concluded. He was searching for something—something real and intimate.

Although many would scorn her line of work, she took pride in the services she provided. She considered herself an artist, and her medium was sexual desire. In her confessional, guided by her creativity and imagination, clients were free to explore their deepest longings.

"I'm here," she said with soft invitation. "Waiting for you."

"I cup your cheek, and your skin is soft against my palm. When I press my mouth to yours, you tremble."

"Do I taste sweet?"

"Er, yes. You do, I suppose."

She imagined him frowning. She'd distracted him from his agenda, and maybe this was a good thing. Maybe challenging his self-control would allow him to discharge his primal impulses.

"I ate strawberries while I was waiting for you." She made her voice as sweet as the fruit. "Ripe, plump berries that stained my lips red to match my hair."

He cleared his throat. "You have red hair?"

She usually revealed as little of her true self as possible. Yet the image of scarlet berries, lips, and hair had flashed in her head, too delicious not to share. The way her patron was leaning subtly toward the screen, hooked on her every word, suggested that he had a preference for redheads. Since he'd started the fantasy with kissing, she suspected that he had a romantic streak as well—that he wasn't a poke-the-stick-in-the-hole sort of fellow—and she tailored her tale accordingly.

"Red as a flame," she said candidly. "I've left it loose because you like it this way. It flows over my sheer white peignoir edged with the finest lace. Sitting on your lap, I surrender to the masterful sweep of your tongue. I feel the thick ridge of your cock beneath my bottom, and it leaves me wanting more."

"I give you more." He took charge with thrilling dominance. "You're a naughty thing, wriggling your derriere against my erection, but I won't be rushed. I take my time enjoying your mouth before turning to your ear. I lick and suckle the plump lobe."

She felt the moist suction of his lips. Warmth rushed under her skin. Like any good artist, she let the fantasy sweep her up like a leaf in a flowing stream.

"It feels so good that I moan and arch my neck," she said huskily. "When you lick my ear, I feel that slick, hot sensation everywhere. Goose pimples prickle my skin. My nipples tighten—"

"I see them." The hypnotic cadence of his words penetrated the barrier between them. "Tight, rosy buds jutting against your robe. Your tits are round and full, tempting me to touch them."

Oh, he's good.

"I want you to touch me," she breathed.

"I tear off your peignoir and fill my palms with your soft flesh, using my thumbs to circle the tips. Do you like the way I'm rubbing your nipples between my finger and thumb?"

Her nipples throbbed. "Oh, yes. Do it harder."

"You want me to pinch them?"

"Yes, please."

"How do you react when I lick your nipples, suck them into my mouth?"

The ghostly tug of his lips drew a warm gush between her thighs.

"I slide my fingers into your hair." Her unsteadiness wasn't feigned. "I hold you close as you lick me. My breasts are glistening, heaving in the candlelight. When you draw on my nipple, I feel a delicious tug in my pussy."

"Is your pussy wet for me?"

"Yes." For once, she wasn't telling tales. "I need to touch you. I reach to untie the belt of your dressing gown and free your huge, hard—"

"I lift you off my lap. I deposit you on the carpet before the hearth and push you onto your back. I grab your hands and secure them above your head."

His authority sliced through the confessional, and it was electrifying. She realized that he'd been holding back. Now he was giving rein to his impulses and immersing himself in the fantasy with her.

"The carpet is silky-rough against my back as I gaze up at you," she said, giddy with triumph. "You've captured me, and I'm helpless to your desires."

"Your wrists are dainty within my grip," he said. "You give me the gift of your surrender because you know that I will take care of you. That no matter how wild and wicked we are together, you are always safe in my keeping."

She felt his powerful yet gentle grip holding her securely. She couldn't escape...and didn't want to. In her quest to uncover his desires, he was somehow baring hers.

"You want to belong to me, don't you?"

His question had a hint of arrogance, and she inhaled, intoxicated by his intensity. By the strength of his focus on her. What would it be like to be claimed by such a man? Would he see beyond her disguises and her past, and desire her for who she was? Would he demand everything of her and give everything in return?

"Yes," she whispered.

"Such a good girl."

His approval felt like a stroke against the neediest part of her, and she trembled.

"I reward you by taking my time. I taste every inch of your

skin. The pulse at your throat, the plump underside of your breast, the dip in your belly. Then I spread your legs and admire what is mine."

She felt branded by his possession. His need to claim was a lightning rod to her need to belong.

"My pussy is drenched," she confessed. "I need you so badly."

"I can smell your arousal." Satisfaction dripped from his voice like honey into dark, smoky tea. "When I part your little red nest, your juice coats my thumbs. You are ripe and ready to eat."

"Do you eat me?" she asked breathily.

"I savor you."

His cool correction made her squirm.

"I lick your slit slowly, up and down. You are a treat, soft and plump against my tongue."

"I like what you're doing. It feels like nothing I've ever experienced before." Which was the truth, since she was a virgin...in body only. In knowledge, she rivaled the most seasoned of harlots. "But I want you to lick me higher."

"Where?"

"On my pearl. Please."

"Since you ask so nicely. Do you want me to suck on it, too?"

Her pussy pulsed under his hot, greedy mouth. "Oh, yes."

"I think you need more. I think you crave something inside your empty little hole."

She knew the words he wanted, the ones burning on her tongue.

"Please fuck me," she breathed. "Take me with your big cock."

"I like that you're begging." A smile entered his voice. "But you're not ready for my cock just yet. I'm sliding two fingers into you, and even though you're dripping, it's a snug fit."

She squeezed her thighs together, feeling his touch and the way it opened her to sensation.

"I feel ready," she said.

"You're getting there. Especially when I stroke your needy little bud. You like that, don't you?"

"I love it, but I want more. I need your prick inside me. Please."

Desire swelled inside her as she imagined him leaning over her, a sweltering shelter of sinew and flesh. His green eyes pierced her, searching out her secrets. He was both safety and danger, and it was a thrilling combination.

"I fit my cock to your hole and push in. I do it slowly, watching you take me inch by inch." Pleasure roughened his voice. "You are hot and tight, made to take me."

"You're so thick and long, and even though you're stretching me, I want all of you."

"I plant myself deep. Claim you."

His possession sent a dizzying wave of pleasure through her.

"I've never belonged to anyone before," she admitted. "You fill the emptiness inside me."

"Christ." A note of strain entered his voice. "You're gripping me like a wet, slick fist."

"You feel so big and hard as you thrust inside me." Passion swamped her. "I lift my legs, circling your hips, wanting more."

"I give it to you. Everything you need."

"I want it harder."

"I hook your knees over my shoulders so that I can get deeper into your cunny. I'm pounding into you now, my stones smacking your wet folds."

"I want everything you have to give," she panted. "Take me, go deeper."

"I'm so bloody deep I hit your womb," he growled.

Bliss jolted her core just as a tapping sounded on her door.

"Sister Sirena, your next penitent has arrived."

Her employer's voice slapped her to her senses.

"Thank you for your patronage, sir," the Abbess went on.

"Upon leaving the confessional, please make a discreet exit using the door to your right."

Disoriented, Xenia tried to regain her bearings. To summon a farewell worthy of what had transpired between her and her client. He spoke first.

"My compliments, Sister Sirena." His muffled voice was composed, his passion leashed once more. "Your reputation was not exaggerated."

He exited the confessional, shutting the door behind him.

Chapter One

When it came to misfortune, it never rained but poured in Xenia Loveday's life.

Six weeks ago, she'd fled London after losing the man she'd thought she loved. Despair and self-doubt had nipped at her heels. No matter how diligently she worked, how hard she tried, her past always caught up to her and reduced her present to shambles. She'd forced herself to carry on, repeating her personal motto.

Pretend until it's true.

She'd felt hopeful when her motto seemed to be working. She'd found work at the Nunnery, and her performance as Sister Sirena was proving a success. She wasn't good at much, but she could spin a tale, and she had started to think that things might turn around. She might be able to save the money she desperately needed—enough to travel to and live on the Continent, where she'd finally be beyond her enemy's reach. Where she'd finally be free.

She ought to have known better.

The Nunnery had caught fire. Luckily, no one had been hurt, but the old church that had housed the brothel was now beyond repair, and the Abbess would have to reopen in a new location. Until then, Xenia was out of a job and the room and board that came with it. The bawd had generously offered ten pounds to tide her over...and to secure her promise that she would return as Sister Sirena once the business was up and running.

Even though a part of Xenia had hesitated—she didn't like to be in debt to anyone, least of all a cunning madam—she'd taken the money. It wasn't as if she had anywhere better to go, and she was tired of shuffling from one place to the next. Pastures always looked greener from afar, and whatever problems one thought one left behind had a way of following. During her childhood, her mama had dragged her from place to place, and trouble had greeted them everywhere. She'd never stayed anywhere long enough to make friends. Even if she had, her shady origins had guaranteed that she would be an outsider, respectable folk giving her and her kin a wide berth.

"You're lucky to be a part of my gang," Mama would snap, *"and you ought to focus on gaining some family talent. You're good for nothing—as worthless as your papa. I blame him for coddling you. For turning you into a useless twit who doesn't pull her own weight."*

Xenia shut out her mother's voice. She'd left that life behind for a good reason, and she had more pressing matters to deal with —namely, securing a roof over her head. The Nunnery had been strategically located near a cluster of villages where she could look for temporary lodgings and maybe even a job to build up her reserves. As it was a sunny summer day, she'd decided to investigate the two closest options on foot.

Ambling along the well-worn path, she tried to distract herself by whistling a bawdy tune. Even though she'd darkened her hair and concealed her figure with a shapeless frock, and she was on a country road surrounded by trees and rolling green hills, fear plagued her like a pesky insect. Would she ever be able to stop looking over her shoulder? Would she always be haunted by her past?

Will I ever feel safe?

Unbidden, her princely patron floated into her head. Although they'd only had the one encounter, he lingered in her awareness. He'd paid for the fantasy, yet their interaction had felt inexplicably...genuine. Real, as he'd requested. Even though they didn't know what the other truly looked like...or sounded like, for that matter. Nonetheless, for those rare moments, she'd let go of her worldly concerns and surrendered to her own desires.

And that is the danger of dealing in fantasy.

She told herself that what they'd shared had been a paid transaction. If she'd felt something, it was because she was lonely and still grieving the loss of Tony, the only follower she'd ever had. Not that Tony had been hers to grieve. While she'd fallen head over heels for his green eyes and writer's soul, he'd only been using her.

Back in London, she'd worked under the stage name "Scheherazade," and he'd charmed her into performing the erotic stories he'd penned. Because of her readings, his books had sold out several printings. Those tidy earnings hadn't been enough to save him, however. His debts had led him to take money from dangerous people. Although she'd tried to help, he'd ended up dead anyway, and she'd endangered herself.

She'd learned from her mistake. From here on, she was not getting attached to anyone or anything. She would focus solely on her own interests...namely, staying alive and out of her enemy's reach.

A shadow fell upon her. Startled, she looked up and saw that clouds had enveloped the sun. The breeze that stirred the tattered ribbons of her bonnet had a damp, warning chill.

Just my luck.

She hastened her pace as the sky turned stormy and grey. Cold droplets began to pelt her. Her worn soles slipped against the increasingly slick path, and she nearly missed the fork in the road. Panting and soaked, she had to dash water from her eyes in order to read the signpost.

The top sign pointed to the path on the right, the words "Chudleigh Crest" engraved in elegant lettering. The lower sign was angled to the left and, by her best guess, had once read "Chudleigh Bottoms." A mischievous hand had crossed out the second village's name in black paint, replacing it with "Chud-dums." The rebaptism was accompanied by a crude drawing of a derriere, a dollop of excrement beneath.

The last thing I need in my life is more poop.

Chudleigh Crest it was. As she was about to head down the right path, a boom sounded. The skies opened, releasing buckets of water. Sputtering, she cursed and gripped her sodden skirts, trying to hurry along, the mud sucking at her shoes with each step. Then a miracle appeared: an approaching carriage drawn by six noble chestnuts.

Surely any decent person would help a woman caught in a storm.

She waved eagerly, and the carriage came toward her...and sped by. Its large wheels churned up a wave of muck. She gasped as it engulfed her, coating her with cold, slimy mud.

An instant later, she recovered her wits.

Shaking her fist, she yelled, "Watch where you're going, you blooming idiot!"

The carriage pulled to a stop. A few heartbeats later, the door opened, and a tall figure dressed in black alighted. When he advanced toward her in a purposeful, long-legged stride, she didn't know whether to stay put or run. Her breath hitched when she saw him up close.

Odds bodkins, the stranger was...arresting.

He appeared to be in his thirties, and beneath the brim of his hat, his pale, stoic features looked sculpted from marble. His vivid gaze was the violet-blue of a flame yet gave the impression of coldness. His nose was straight, his mouth pulled into a taut line above the elegant knot of his neckcloth. He had thick raven hair which, paired with the dark scruff on his jaw, made him look like a rebel poet.

His double-breasted frock coat flaunted his broad shoulders and lean torso while his trousers accentuated his long legs. He wielded an umbrella in his gloved hand with masculine grace. Of course, it was easy to look graceful when one was not dripping wet and covered in mud. When one was shielded from the rain which, by the by, was deluging *her*.

He perused her, his expression brooding. "Do you require assistance?" he asked curtly.

The man was *unbelievable*. Anger swelled in her breast, and the sky seemed to agree with her, rumbling on her behalf.

"I did not need anyone's help," she said through gritted teeth. "Until you drove by in your blasted carriage and covered me with mud!"

"My apologies."

He did not sound sorry. He seemed irritated, his gaze focused on some point in the distance as if she wasn't important enough to warrant his attention. At the various jobs she'd held, she encountered her share of arrogant bluebloods, and she knew his sort.

"Well?" he said. "Do you want my help or not?"

I'd rather eat my shoe than take anything from you, you unfeeling lummox.

Yet she reined in her temper, hating that she couldn't afford the luxury of giving in to her feelings. Outrage was for the rich and free, not the poor and dispossessed. She had survived this long by keeping her head down. She was not about to risk the ire of some local toff who had the power to make her life miserable. In the past, her complaints to employers about rude and even abusive patrons had fallen on deaf ears.

As much as Xenia hated her powerlessness in this moment, she knew better than to make things worse. One day, when she had money and security, she would live on her own terms. She would tell this selfish, ill-mannered cove and others like him where to go. Until then, she would have to stand in the freezing rain and comfort herself with sarcasm.

"Thank you for your kindness." She aimed a saccharine smile at him while muddy rivulets slid down her face. "I would not wish to detain you from your obviously urgent business."

The tiniest of furrows marred the space between his straight brows. She had the fleeting hope that he might have discovered his humanity after all.

"Suit yourself." With a brusque nod, he turned and strode back to his carriage.

The callous nodcock!

Fuming, she watched as his driver smoothly navigated the equipage, taking the turn that led to Chudleigh Crest. After the carriage vanished from sight, she let out a yell of frustration that rivaled the boom of thunder. Picking up her heavy skirts, she stomped toward the other path, the one that led to Chuddums.

Chapter Two

Lord Ethan Harrington hated being coddled.

Coddling reeked of pity, and he wanted none of it, especially from his older brother James, the Earl of Manderly. James had a tendency to take charge, which Ethan, the younger by two years, had always found annoying but never more so than now. Ethan had come to this manor in the middle of nowhere for one reason: to be left alone. Yet there his older brother was, paying a visit and putting his nose where it did not belong.

From across the desk, James perused the study. "Your manor is, er, coming along, old boy."

"It's a rubbish heap," Ethan said bluntly.

Which is fitting, considering where my life is headed.

The familiar darkness welled inside him. Beneath his desk, he clenched his hands...or tried to. The damage in his left hand prevented him from forming a fist, reminding him of everything he'd lost. Of the man he'd been and who he was now. Three years ago, at eight and twenty, he'd been a rising piano virtuoso, hailed as the next Beethoven.

Now he couldn't use his left hand to wipe his own arse.

Ethan fought back the tide of rage and despair. After his injury, he'd been gripped by grief of such intensity that he'd feared he might drown in it. Nay, not feared—sometimes he'd *wished* it would kill him and end the torment. The anguish of waking up day after day, knowing that the one thing he was meant to do in life—the thing that had absorbed him from the time he played his first note on his grandmama's piano—was no longer a possibility.

Music had been his unrelenting obsession, his joy, his everything.

Now, there was only...silence.

The silence followed him like shit on his shoe. He couldn't bloody get rid of it. The sudden hush when he entered a ballroom. The anxious quiet of his parents and siblings, who tiptoed around him and treated him as if he were made of glass. The silence was even louder at night. He'd never been a good sleeper, and the only cure he'd found was playing. Beethoven's *Sonata quasi una fantasia* had always relaxed him, untangling him from the troubles of the day, but that was lost to him too.

Then there was the silence that had surprised him six weeks ago, when his fiancée had jilted him just before the wedding. That silence had doused his last spark of hope for normalcy and instead fed the demons of self-doubt and failure. It was a wonder he had any pride left. Yet he must have at least a shred because, as bad as things were, he refused to let his older brother condescend to him.

"Why are you here?" Ethan asked. "Did Mama and Papa send you to check up on me?"

James studied the perfect crease in his fawn-colored trousers.

Knowing him, he'd come because he felt duty-bound to look after his pathetic cripple of a brother.

"I came because I wanted to see how you were faring," James said. "After the...er, incident."

"By 'incident,' are you referring to my former fiancée running off with my former crony? Or perhaps you are inquiring after my shattered hand?"

"There's no call for sarcasm. As it happens, I was inquiring after the former."

"My engagement ended over a month ago," Ethan said curtly. "I've nearly forgotten what's-her-name. I'm fine."

James studied him for another moment, and Ethan returned his stare. There was a family resemblance in their height and the general shape of their features. However, James had inherited their papa's bronze hair, steel-blue eyes, and brawnier frame, whereas Ethan took after Mama with his black hair and indigo eyes. As boys, they'd gotten along in the way of brothers close in age: they had fought and bickered and competed over everything. They'd also defended each other, and woe to anyone who even dared to look askance at their younger brother Owen or their baby sister Georgiana, whom everyone called "Gigi."

The incident three years ago had changed everything.

Now the thought of Owen filled Ethan with emotions too volatile and painful to bear. At their last meeting, the tension between him and his youngest brother had erupted into a scene so ugly that they had avoided each other since. That had been over a year ago. All the while, the rest of the family continued the futile campaign of pretending things were as they once were, refusing to give up on anyone.

Ad Finem Fidelis.

Faithful to the End...that was the family motto.

Ethan had tried to live up to those ideals and look at where he was now at one and thirty: angry, aimless, and living in the manor he'd bought because he lost a bet.

"*Are* you fine, Ethan?"

James looked around the study, and Ethan knew what the other saw. Paper of an indeterminate hue was peeling from the walls and plaster crumbling from the ceiling. Woodworms had punctured the bookshelves. The rug was moss green, likely due to the clumps of moss growing upon it. Moth-eaten drapes framed the dirty windows that looked out into the garden, where a vine-covered gazebo looked like an ancient temple rising from a jungle.

The place was a dump. Yet it was still better than the glittering salons where polite society smothered him with pity and spitefully shredded Constance's reputation—yes, that was his ex-fiancée's name and the irony of it did not escape him. Although Constance had brought the situation upon herself, hearing the cruelty aimed at her and Armand Blake—his former friend and the fellow Constance had jilted him for—depressed him further.

Ethan didn't know whose betrayal angered him more. Then again, he didn't have to choose, did he? Being enraged with the world was becoming a habit.

"I am perfectly well." He picked up a pen, tapping out an irritable ditty. "I have been meaning to check up on this place and set it to rights."

"As I recall, you bought this manor because you lost a wager," James replied. "You and your cronies were three sheets to the wind and decided that whoever cast his accounts first would have to buy the most ridiculous property the lot of you could find. You lost—no surprise there, little brother, as you could never hold your liquor—and that is how you became the proud owner of the Bottoms House of Chudleigh Bottoms. Or, as your friends dubbed it in a fit of infantile inspiration, *Double Arse Manor*."

As lamentable as the tale was, Ethan almost missed those days. When he and his cronies, Parkhurst, Canning, and Blake, had been young and carefree. As second sons, they'd reveled in the unique freedom of being the spare. The fact that they all had artistic inclinations had strengthened their bond, and when Ethan's star had risen as a piano virtuoso, Blake, Parkhurst, and Canning had been there to cheer him on.

Until it had all fallen apart.

You despise pity, remember? So stop heaping it upon yourself.

"The manner in which this house came into my possession is

irrelevant." Ethan tossed the pen onto a tray. "It is mine, and it's high time that I did something with it."

"You don't have to do this, you know." James's gaze was steady. "If you don't want to be in London—and God knows no one can blame you for that—you could stay at Grove Hall. No one would disturb you there...except Evie. But the two of you have always rubbed along, and she values privacy as much as you do."

Grove Hall was James's country estate, but he seldom stayed there, leaving it to his wife Evie. In truth, if Ethan had wanted company, he wouldn't have minded staying with his sister-in-law, who was one of the few people who didn't act as if he were broken and held together by glue and spittle. She was also pretty and intelligent, and for the life of him he couldn't understand the bloodless arrangement between her and James.

However, Ethan was no hypocrite. If he didn't want James nosing around in his business, then he owed the other the same courtesy. He would leave the meddling up to their parents, who had a singular talent for it.

"I am undisturbed here," he said. "Since I moved in, no one has come around."

James arched a brow. "The local folk think this place is haunted by a ghost, you know. When I was in Chuddums, I heard them talking about some curse. They say the new owner had better watch his back."

Ethan nearly laughed. Truly, what further misfortune could befall him? He'd lost his ability to play piano—his one passion and purpose in life. He couldn't stand being in the same room as his youngest brother, and his relationships with his other family members were strained. Oh, and he'd been betrayed by his betrothed and his best friend.

Go ahead, ghost. Do your bloody worst.

"As the villagers also read fortunes from cherry pits," Ethan said, "I'll take my chances."

"You are going to need these cherry-pit-reading townsfolk to help you run this place. Do you have any staff? If memory serves, it was you who opened the door when I arrived."

And don't I regret it.

"My butler Brunswick recently hurt his hand," Ethan said tetchily. "And I am looking for help. The process cannot be rushed."

Although it *had* been two weeks, and he was getting nowhere. He'd found a cook, but she hadn't lasted long after supposedly spotting "Bloody Thom"—yes, the resident phantom came with a name—roaming the servants' quarters. Neither Ethan's reasoning that she'd had a nightmare, nor his bribe of higher wages could assuage her. She'd taken off, her wagging tongue scaring off potential candidates. The other staff member he'd hired, a footman by the name of Dobson Gill, had shown promise...until Brunswick had caught Gill with his hand in the silver cabinet. Gill had had the gall to become belligerent, threatening retribution when Ethan had tossed him out on his arse without pay.

As a result, Ethan's current staff consisted of his valet Mr. Valentine, his groom Spencer, and Brunswick. None of them had any talent in the kitchen; Brunswick had tried to cook...and promptly scalded himself. Ethan's diet consisted of burnt toast and rubbery boiled eggs, and he would do almost anything for a properly cooked meal. Anything but admit his desperation to his brother, that was.

"Lucky for you, I have come to help," James said.

"You?" Ethan scoffed.

Growing up, James had assumed the role of leader among their siblings. He'd commanded everyone and delegated everything. Ethan had been the artist and rebel who largely ignored him.

"I don't expect much will get accomplished," Ethan said, "since I don't take instruction well, and you don't enjoy lifting a finger."

"As it happens, I've already come up with a solution."

Before Ethan could tell James and his solution where to go, the doorbell rang.

"I'll get it."

Words, undoubtedly, that James had never uttered before. Despite his curiosity, Ethan decided not to scramble after the other like a damned puppy. He remained in his chair like he owned the place because he bloody did. When James returned, Ethan was forced to rise because of the female accompanying his brother.

She looked oddly familiar, but he couldn't place her. Then again, she would be easy to overlook. She resembled a dormouse with ash-brown hair bound in a topknot. Large spectacles magnified her dark eyes, and her pert nose twitched with the effort to hold them up. She was a tiny thing, likely a foot shorter than he was. Whatever figure she had was concealed by drab bombazine.

They stared at one another, and recognition dawned.

For both of them, apparently.

"It's *you*," she breathed.

Chapter Three

Can my luck get any blooming worse?

Xenia wanted to shake her fist at the sky.

It was *him*. The bastard who'd left her soaked and standing by the side of the road. There was no mistaking his devilish good looks or irksomely virile figure, which today was outfitted in a Prussian-blue frock coat, embroidered cream waistcoat, and pair of tan trousers. What made him truly distinctive, however, was his cold and brooding expression. He'd regarded her in just this fashion when he'd taken off in his warm and cozy carriage while she'd walked miles in the pouring rain.

"Are you two, er, acquainted?"

Seeing the Earl of Manderly's confusion, she composed herself. Yesterday, the earl had approached her when she had been inquiring about work at the Leaning House, a tea shop in Chuddums. Initially, she'd been wary of the attractive stranger...especially since he bore a passing resemblance to the princely patron of her imagination. His golden-brown hair and air of command had sent a quiver through her belly.

After speaking with the earl, however, she knew that he hadn't been in her confessional. He was too proper and straitlaced to have a mind as dirty as her prince's. Indeed, his offer turned out to be entirely respectable: his brother, Lord Ethan Harrington, was looking for a housekeeper and would offer generous wages for the right candidate. He'd invited her to come for an interview today. She'd been thrilled at the opportunity...at something good just falling into her lap.

I ought to have known better was becoming a refrain.

Seeing the earl and his brother together, Xenia saw more differences than similarities. While both had been blessed with good looks and virile physiques, the earl had an outgoing and agreeable personality. Lord Ethan, on the other hand, was grumpy and withdrawn. In all fairness, she couldn't blame herself for not realizing that the nice earl's brother was the bastard who'd left her in the rain. Who'd treated her like a nobody he couldn't be bothered with.

Resentment smoldered beneath her breastbone. She told herself there was no point in making an enemy of Lord High-and-Mighty when she had enough of those already. What she needed was a job and a place to stay. Since she'd taken the precaution of disguising herself as Jane Wood, respectable widow, she might as well act the part. She suppressed the sultry rasp of her voice, speaking in tones that were as dull and prim as her pseudonym.

"I met his lordship briefly," she said. "No introductions were made."

"In that case. This is Jane Wood, a candidate for the housekeeper position." The Earl of Manderly spoke to his brother, who still hadn't uttered a word. "Mrs. Wood, this is my brother, Lord Ethan Harrington."

To her surprise, Lord Ethan bowed. Apparently, His Uppityness had manners after all. Grudgingly, she dipped her knees in return.

"I see you survived the rain," Lord Ethan said.

No thanks to you.

Her retribution, however, would have to be achieved on the sly.

"I take constitutionals in any weather, my lord," she said blandly. "Exercise is not only good for one's health but improves moral character. *Never accept a ride when you can get there on your own two feet*, I always say."

"How profound," he muttered.

"Self-reliance is so important, don't you agree? On the list of virtues, I believe it falls only slightly under moderation as a precept. There is nothing so damaging as excess. One must always strive toward temperance and respectability..."

As Lord Ethan's eyes glazed over, wings of victory beat in her chest.

"I applaud your good character, Mrs. Wood." Lord Manderly came to his brother's rescue. "After that delightful recitation, we hardly need further recommendation. But you do have references, I assume?"

As many as I could forge in one night.

"Of course, my lord," she said diffidently.

Opening her battered satchel, she took out three envelopes. When she attempted to pass them to the earl, Lord Ethan intervened, snatching the letters.

Rude bastard.

She noticed that he wore gloves, the fine black leather tailored snugly to his long fingers. Were indoor gloves a new fashion amongst bluebloods? God knew they could afford to indulge any whimsy and hated getting their hands dirty. Lord Ethan opened the first letter, and she held her breath as he scanned it. When she was a girl, Mama had forced her to learn a trade that would be useful to the gang, and she'd chosen forgery as the lesser of evils.

"*Mrs. Wood can accomplish any task set before her,*" Lord Ethan read aloud. "*She is discreet, adaptable, and self-driven. In short, she is no trouble at all. Had my own circumstances not necessi-*

tated the reduction of my household, I would have kept her on, for she is worth her weight in gold. You will not regret hiring this exemplary woman who is the epitome of moral virtue."

He paused, studying her.

Had she poured it on too thick with the praise? She hadn't lied about her talents. She *was* good at keeping secrets, adjusting to any situation, and following her own instincts. Although the part about virtue might be a *teensy* stretch...

His lordship finished scanning the letters and tossed them on his desk. "These are remarkable references," he said.

His delivery made her question whether the compliment was, in fact, a compliment.

She raised her chin. "I take pride in my work, my lord."

"A commendable quality." The earl cut in, giving his brother a hearty slap on the shoulder. "Just what you were looking for in a housekeeper, weren't you, old boy?"

Lord Ethan ignored him, keeping his gaze pinned on her. "How old are you?"

"Seven and twenty," she replied.

Minus four years, but who's counting?

Since she was interviewing for the most senior female position amongst the household staff, she'd decided to age herself. Using face paint, she'd added subtle lines and shadows to her face. She'd also concealed her freckles and made her complexion pallid, like that of a woman who spent her life laboring indoors.

"Is there a Mr. Wood?" he pressed.

"Deceased, I'm afraid." She took out a handkerchief, lifting her spectacles to dab at her eyes. "We were only married a year, but my husband was a good man. He died saving children from a burning schoolhouse."

"I am sorry for your loss, ma'am," Manderly said sincerely.

Lord Ethan, however, stared at her broodingly.

Had she done it a bit brown?

"Come," he said brusquely.

He curled a finger at her…as if she were a *pet*. Before she could reply, he turned and prowled toward the door.

She remained where she was. "Where are we going?"

He pivoted. One dark eyebrow winged, accentuating his intense violet-blue gaze. "I assume you wish to see your new place of employ?"

Her heart thudded with a mix of surprise, irritation, and excitement.

She kept her composure. "Perhaps we should first discuss the terms of employment."

"Seventy-five pounds per annum, plus room and board. A yearly bonus if your work meets my standards. An evening off a week and half a day on Sunday."

The impatience of his reply did not negate the generosity of the offer. He was giving her the answer to her problems: a room and excellent wages to boot. Of course, her tenure would be temporary, but he didn't have to know that. This would tide her over until she could resume her work at the Nunnery. She could tolerate anything for a few weeks, even Lord High-and-Mighty.

"Coming, Mrs. Wood?" he asked.

Apparently, it was a rhetorical question, since he'd already headed out the door. She glanced at the Earl of Manderly and saw something flicker across his face. Sorrow, perhaps?

He inclined his head, his smile wry. "Good luck."

She curtsied, and huffing out a breath, hurried to catch up to her new employer.

Xenia had not been in that many manors. Well, except for the years spent in her mama's gang. Given the nature of those visits, she hadn't lingered to examine the surroundings. She forced herself to pay attention to Lord Ethan's issuance of demands as he led her to the entrance hall. Looking around her, she came to the obvious conclusion: this place was a dump. She didn't mind; having lived in dumps all her life, she knew how to make the best of things. Truth be told, she felt a kinship to the house. While circumstances beyond its control had brought it low, it remained standing.

She was reminded of the rumors she'd heard in Chuddums. For her, the possibility of a resident ghost added to the manor's charm. She'd always adored stories with a supernatural element.

"Have you seen the ghost, my lord?"

She directed the question at Lord Ethan's broad back.

"I have not." He didn't bother to turn, his footsteps clipping ahead. "Do you know why?"

"No."

"Because there is no bloody such thing as ghosts."

Not for those lacking in imagination, clearly.

"The rumors are nonsense." He twisted his head to scowl at her. "I hope you are not a silly and superstitious sort of female, Mrs. Wood."

She flashed to the salt she'd thrown over her shoulder this morning. The crack she'd avoided on the pavement. The spider in the cupboard that she'd painstakingly rescued in a cup and set outside, singing, *Be free, little friend. Be free!*

"Not at all, sir," she said.

His reply was a grunt.

No matter. She could ferret out information about the phantom on her own. Mrs. Pettigrew, the proprietress of the Leaning House tea shop, had seemed like a fount of information about Chuddums and its local lore. Inspiration percolated through Xenia.

Perhaps I could incorporate ghosts into my storytelling. Imagine what I could do with phantoms at an orgy...

They arrived at the entrance hall, which might have been grand at some point. The double staircase curved upward to the second floor, but several steps on the left side had rotted away, leaving gaps like rotted teeth. The floor was covered with grime, and the chandelier that hung from the high ceiling looked ancient, baptizing passersby with sprinkles of dust.

"I expect you will tidy things up," his lordship said.

His gesture encompassed...everything?

She was no authority on cleaning. Truth be told, she wasn't tidy by nature. She'd never given much credence to the adage concerning cleanliness and Godliness. She believed that neatness was a symptom of an uninspired mind, and while she had many failings, she never lacked for imagination. There were always more interesting things to do than tidy up, but she figured she could learn on the job. Just because she'd never kept a house didn't mean she couldn't do it. Although, given the manor's size and state of neglect, she would need help.

"How many servants do you have on staff?" she inquired.

"At present, Brunswick, the butler and Mr. Valentine, the valet manage the house. Spencer, the groom, oversees the stables."

Two servants in the house? Her eyes rounded. *And not a single maid or footman?*

"There is a mop fair in Chuddums next week, where you'll be able to hire as many maids as you wish," he added brusquely. "In the interim, do your best to make things presentable."

She nodded, relieved that help was on the way. Moreover, one could say that disguising things to make them look respectable was her specialty. The fact that this place was a mess might even work to her advantage. Who would notice smudges on the banister when half the banister was missing? Or a few footprints on the carpet when the entire surface was caked with mud? Maybe she wouldn't have to do much cleaning after all...

"Why are you smiling that way?"

Startled, she returned her gaze to Lord Ethan, who was giving her a surly look.

"No reason, my lord," she said hastily. "May I see the rest of the house?"

The tour continued. The manor was shaped like a rectangle, with the drawing room and morning room to the right of the entrance hall and the dining room and library to the left. At least she guessed the latter was a library due to the empty, cobweb-covered shelves spanning the length of the room. At present, the space was stuffed with furniture and trunks.

"I brought a few things from London," Lord Ethan said. "Brunswick will unpack and organize the books when he has time; in the meanwhile, clean around the trunks the best you can."

"Not a problem, my lord."

He either failed to notice her sarcasm or chose to ignore it. The tour continued to the row of rooms at the back of the manor, which included his lordship's study, a billiards room, and a music room, all with views of an overgrown garden. Upstairs, Lord Ethan showed her the six bedchambers and master suite. Crumbling plaster, scratched wood, and moth-eaten upholstery appeared to be the decorating motif.

Finally, he led her to the servants' wing. It occupied a separate building and was haphazardly attached to the main living area by an extension of the corridor that led to the study and music room. The kitchen was spacious and dirty, equipped with a large and rickety worktable, and the servants' hall and stillroom were likewise in need of cleaning. Below the kitchen were quarters for male servants. Above, in the sloped attic, were a series of small garret rooms for the maids and a larger suite designated for the housekeeper.

The latter was well, if shabbily, furnished with what looked like a prior owner's castoffs. Xenia discreetly pressed on the mattress, finding it surprisingly well stuffed. A faded chintz armchair sat by the small hearth, inviting one to curl up in it, and there was a small dressing table with a cracked looking glass. By some miracle, there was also an escritoire. One of the legs was wobbly, but she could fix it. She'd always wanted a writing desk and imagined herself outlining Sirena's tales upon it...

"Do you cook?" Lord Ethan asked.

"Yes," she said quickly.

He didn't ask if she cooked *well*, and there was no way she was losing the position now that he'd dangled this lovely room in front of her. At the Nunnery, she'd shared a tiny chamber with five prostitutes, and privacy had been a rare commodity. She couldn't explain it, but from the moment she'd entered this chamber, it had felt like...home.

Or, at least, a good stopping place.

Besides, how hard could cooking be? If she could work at a seedy London bookshop specializing in pornographic goods and perform as an erotic storyteller at various brothels, surely she could throw together a meal.

"Then you will be in charge of the kitchen until I hire a cook at the mop fair," he declared.

Although his expression remained brooding, she sensed he was pleased with the turn of events. Strangely, the feeling was mutual.

"Can you start tomorrow?" he asked.

With fluttering excitement, she nodded.

"Brunswick will show you the ropes and answer your questions." He removed a ring of keys from his frock coat. "You will need these. You have the run of the house, with one exception."

He pinched the last key on the ring. Smaller than the others, it had a patina of rust.

"This opens the room at the end of the corridor. Do not use it."

"Why not?" she asked instantly.

"Because you won't like what is inside. The door must remain locked. Surely you can follow a simple request?"

His grouchy countenance warned her not to argue. She

nodded because she wanted the job. The keys clanged as he dropped them into her palm.

"Good day, Mrs. Wood." With a stiff nod, he departed.

She resisted sticking her tongue out at him. Instead, she whirled around and giddily took in her new sanctuary. Her new home...for now.

Chapter Four

Walking up the oak-lined drive to Bottoms House the next morning, Xenia felt a renewed sense of optimism.

I've made the right choice.

Although this was only her second visit, there was a comforting familiarity to the surroundings. She guessed the manor was old, its limestone walls mellowed by the passing years. The gabled roof looked slightly newer, as did the three rows of sash windows. The size of the house was just right in her opinion: not too big or small. In Chuddums, people had spoken fearfully of the manor being haunted, but to her it seemed to offer shelter without pretension.

A sudden image flashed in her head: a traveler lost in a storm, whipped by rain and wind as lightning split the sky. Wet to the bone, she was out of options until she came upon this manor blazing in the darkness. Hope bloomed that it would offer temporary refuge, a respite from the evil that was pursuing her...

She blinked, and the image faded.

Your imagination is running wild. Focus, Xenia.

At the servants' entrance, she was met by Brunswick. The

butler reminded her of a mastiff with his wrinkled forehead and sagging jowls. Although he had a gruff manner, he was kind, insisting on carrying her sparse belongings to her new attic quarters despite the clumsily wrapped bandage on his hand. When she inquired about his injury, he admitted that he'd hurt himself preparing breakfast.

Since she had experience dealing with injuries—one of the few advantages of being a cutthroat's daughter—she offered to look at his hand. It was a good thing she did, for the wound needed proper care. After cleansing it, she applied a healing salve she'd concocted containing honey, rosemary, and calendula. Then she rewrapped his hand with clean linen.

Waving aside Brunswick's effusive thanks, she asked what tasks she ought to tackle first. He told her that the priority was to set up the delivery of foodstuffs from the village. When he gave her a list of the master's favorite meals, she tried not to let her trepidation show. She hadn't prepared most—all right, *any*—of the dishes before...but there was a first time for everything, wasn't there? Compared to the work she'd done, how difficult could it be to make blood pudding?

Pretend until it's true.

She gave Brunswick the smile of a woman who knew what she was doing and set off on the mile-long trek to Chuddums.

The first time she'd gone to the village, the rain had obscured her view. Today, the sky was clear, and as the path sloped downward to her destination, she saw Chuddums in its full glory...or, more aptly, with its warts and all. Situated on a low-lying riverbank of the Thames, Chuddums bore an unfortunate resemblance to a cesspit. The recent rains had turned the roads into muck. The village's ramshackle buildings sagged against one another like friendly drunks. The patching of cottage roofs reminded her of a tattered quilt that wasn't sufficiently large to cover all the important parts, leaving one's toes cold.

As she entered Chuddums, she was greeted with curious looks

and a few suspicious ones. Keeping her head ducked out of habit, she followed High Street to the village center, noting the mix of lodging houses, pawnshops, and public houses. Arriving at the square, she saw that the four main streets surrounded a village green...which was more brown due to the lack of grass and abundance of mud. A giant, bare-branched tree stood at the center. Around the square's border, only half the buildings boasted businesses; the rest were vacant.

"Hullo there!"

She turned to see a fellow wearing an old-fashioned top hat and checkered red coat waving as he approached her. Seeing that he relied on a cane and walked in shuffling steps, she met him halfway. Up close, he looked positively ancient...in his nineties, if he was a day. His wizened visage and lively black eyes reminded her of a turtle.

"Good morning, sir," she said politely. "May I help you?"

"Help *me*?" He chuckled. "No, dear Rosalinda. It's me, Wally."

"You must have me mistaken for someone else, sir." Seeing his confusion, she said gently, "My name is Jane Wood, and I'm the new housekeeper at Bottoms House."

"You are sure you're not Rosalinda?" he asked, frowning.

"Quite sure."

He sighed. "Sometimes I get muddled."

"We all do, from time to time." She smiled. "Regardless, it is nice to see a friendly face."

He perked up. "As the official guide of Chuddums, it would be my honor to escort you to your destination. Where to, Mrs. Wood?"

She consulted her list. "My first stop is the butcher shop."

"Then it's Mr. Bailey you ought to see. Follow me, follow me."

Xenia didn't have the heart to abandon Wally, even though his rheumatism kept them at a snail's pace. Her guide took his job seriously, however, pointing out highlights such as a newly installed lamppost and a flower box that had been savaged by Mrs. Elmwood's cat Fenwyck. According to Wally, the felonious feline had also knocked over rubbish bins and dug up Mrs. O'Hara's prized flower garden. Since Fenwyck was sneaky, he had never been caught red-pawed, and his owner staunchly maintained his innocence.

"If you catch Fenwyck in the act"—Wally wagged a finger at her—"be sure to let me know. I am collecting evidence against him."

"I will, sir," Xenia promised.

They arrived at a shop with a string of fowl hanging in the window. When Wally struggled to open the door for her, she did it herself, thanking him and reminding him of others who might require his services. Bowing, he hurried off...well, as much as Wally could hurry.

The interior of the butcher shop was shabby and cramped. The products appeared to be of good quality, however, and fresh sawdust covered the floor. Garlands of sausages adorned the walls, and a selection of meats was displayed on a counter. The butcher, standing by a row of joints, looked as if he'd been a prizefighter in his former life. Or maybe in his current life, given his shiner of a right eye. His substantial black moustache seemed to compensate for the lack of hair on his head, and his bare, bulging arms bracketed his leather apron.

"Welcome to my establishment, miss." His soft-spoken manner was at odds with his strapping exterior. "I'm Mason Bailey, butcher and purveyor o' Chuddums's finest meats. I ain't seen you around before. New in town, are you?"

Keep it simple. Tell him only what is necessary.

"I am Jane Wood, sir," she said. "The new housekeeper at Bottoms House."

Mr. Bailey raised his thick brows. "Are you indeed? Brave one, ain't you?"

She supposed working for a man like Lord Ethan Harrington

required a certain amount of pluck. Since he was supplying her with a generous salary and a roof over her head, however, she'd decided to let bygones be bygones.

"My master's bark is worse than his bite, and I'm grateful for the job."

"I ain't talking about the toff." Bailey raised his hands and wriggled stubby fingers. "I'm talking about Bloody Thom."

Oh, *right*. The ghost. Curiosity got the better of her.

"Has anyone actually seen the ghost?" she asked.

"To be sure." Bailey nodded vigorously. "Through the years, there've been multiple sightings, and one 'appened recently. Nelly Nettles—she was your master's last cook—woke up one night and saw an apparition standing in the doorway of her room. She said his face was white as snow, his eyes darker than midnight, and blood dripped from the corner of his mouth. Chains were wrapped around his body." The butcher shuddered. "He howled in pain before clanking off."

A delicious shiver ran through Xenia, the kind she experienced when reading her favorite gothic novels.

"Where did he go? What did he do next?" she asked.

"Nelly couldn't say since she fell into a dead swoon. When she came to, Bloody Thom was gone. She didn't 'ave a mind to linger herself and gave notice immediately."

"Why is the ghost named Bloody Thom? Has he...has he killed someone?"

"You don't know the story?" Bailey stared at her as if she'd confessed to not knowing the Lord's Prayer. "A rich bloke by the name o' Thomas Mulligan bought Bottoms House some eighty-odd years ago. According to legend, a witch sought shelter at his manor, and he turned her away. She cursed him, and not long after, he was found shot dead in his own home."

"Heavens," Xenia breathed.

"Since then, every owner o' Bottoms House has suffered

misfortune, and it got to be that no one would go near the place. It sat empty for years before your master moved in."

The tingle tiptoed up her spine. The only thing better than a ghost story was one that had a *curse*.

"There's more. When the villagers discovered the witch 'ad killed Mulligan, they tried to hunt her down. A local hero named Pearce—you'll see his monument in the square—led the charge and was found dead in *his* home."

Xenia gasped. "She killed two men?"

"Not only that, but she cursed the *entire* village. Before Mulligan's arrival, we had spas to rival Bath, but the springs began to dry up. Now there's only one spa left, and it's barely staying afloat. We used to produce some o' the finest fruit in the county, then all the crops failed. Our bustling market once attracted visitors from near and far. Now 'alf our buildings lay vacant or house disreputable businesses." He counted out the misfortunes on his sausage-like fingers, his expression glum. "To heap insult on injury, the village has been rechristened *Chuddums*. We're considered the latrine o' Berkshire. No one stays if they 'ave a way out."

"Why do *you* stay?" she asked.

Instantly, she chided herself for concerning herself with others' problems. That was how things had started with Tony: she'd wanted to help him with his writing career and his gambling habit. Not only had she *not* helped him, but she'd gotten her heart broken and exposed herself to her enemy. She'd been forced to flee London with her mama's lackeys snapping at her heels. If she hadn't managed to give them the slip...she shuddered at the punishments her mama might have meted out.

"My family's been here for three generations. No Bailey 'as ever left Chuddums, and I ain't about to be the first..."

When he trailed off, she followed the direction of his gaze. Two coves stood outside the shop window. Their dark caps with lowered brims and flashy neckerchiefs told her what they were.

Trouble.

"I'd best be filling your order, Mrs. Wood, and letting you get on."

In a blink, Mr. Bailey lost his affability, becoming anxious and twitchy. His transformation confirmed her hypothesis about the brutes lying in wait. Although a part of her wanted to ask if he needed help, she stopped herself.

You cannot afford to get tangled up in trouble. You have enough of your own. Move on.

She gave the butcher her ingredient list. He packed what she could carry, promising to deliver the rest, then nearly shoved her out the door. She hadn't gone but a few steps when the pair of cutthroats prowled inside.

She forced herself to continue with her errands.

A few doors down was Pickleworth's Produce, and the green-grocer was advertising his goods outside his shop. He had brown hair, twinkling eyes, and was a bit over four feet tall. He stood on a crate, holding a plate of sliced tomatoes.

"Ripe tomatoes," he announced in a rich, booming voice. "Come get your ripe and juicy tomatoes!"

As Xenia wasn't partial to tomatoes, she politely declined a sample. Unfortunately, the greengrocer took her refusal to try his fruit as a personal affront. To smooth things over, she went into the shop and arranged produce delivery with his wife, a pretty blonde who introduced herself as Loretta Pickleworth. Xenia went on to complete transactions with the cheesemonger, baker, and others.

Her errands completed, she was still worried about Mr. Bailey. She thought about checking in on him but abruptly changed direction, her heavy shopping basket banging against her hip. She took a shortcut through the village green to avoid the temptation of getting involved in the butcher's problems. Her extensive knowledge of cutthroats told her that she couldn't help him and would only risk her own hard-won freedom.

At the center of the square, she spotted the monument Mr. Bailey had mentioned and stopped to look. Sitting beneath the bare branches of a large, withered tree, the small slab of reddish stone bore a rusty plaque.

> In memory of Langdon Pearce
> Hero and Soldier of Justice
> May He Rest in Peace

An eerie sensation brushed over Xenia's nape. She took a hasty step back, nearly bumping into a glass-fronted box...the village notice board, where announcements were made. The pinned notices were all items for sale, most at steep discounts because the owners were moving in a hurry.

Mr. Bailey appeared to be right. No one stayed in Chuddums unless they had to.

Later that evening, Xenia flopped onto her new bed. She removed her heavy spectacles, rubbing at the indent on the bridge of her nose as she stared up at the ceiling. She was in that peculiar state of being both exhausted and wide awake.

She'd spent the last few hours preparing meals for the morrow. Cooking had proved harder than she expected. Unfortunately, Mr. Bailey had been out of blood sausage, her new master's favorite breakfast dish, which meant she'd had to make it from scratch. She'd located a volume of recipes at the village's only purveyor of books, a circulating library which, oddly enough, was called "Hatcherds." She didn't know if the name was an intentional misspelling of the famous London bookshop or merely a bit off-kilter, much like the village itself.

Sadly, her assumption that if one could read a recipe, one

could cook proved to be untrue. She had no idea how the blood sausage or other dishes she'd sweated over would turn out.

Edible, hopefully.

There was naught she could do about it now. Moreover, she had other worries, triggered by those cutthroats outside Mr. Bailey's shop. How many criminals operated in the village? Would any of them recognize her from the years she'd spent in her mother's infamous roving gang? Did the brutes draw the attention of the local constabulary? Would she be safe hiding in Chuddums?

Will I always be a fugitive from my past?

Memories ambushed her. The narrow, soot-filled chimneys her mama had forced her to climb down. *"Get inside and unlock the door, daughter mine, or you'll feel my wrath."* The abhorrent things she'd been required to do, the constant running and fear of being caught. The only safety had been her papa's arms...until he'd been ripped from her too. Xenia buried her face in the pillow, trying to shut out the memories, but they came at her like her mother's punishments, the blows she'd earned each time she'd tried to run away. Like the chains her mama had used to hold her captive, the starvation wielded to break her will.

"You cannot escape, you worthless, stupid girl. I will always hunt you down."

Xenia had escaped, but at what cost? The memory of Mr. Trelawney choked her with grief. The owner of the quaint Cornish bookshop had given her shelter and friendship, and how had she repaid him? She felt his blood oozing between her fingers, the shallow rise and fall of his last breaths. She relived the moment when his clear blue eyes went blank.

Guilt punched her in the throat, and she fought the hot push of tears. Crying changed nothing. Remembering changed nothing. Even hiding was futile, for where could she find shelter from the despicable life she'd led?

Yet she had to keep running. Had to escape her destiny.

Had to be someone other than who she was.

Pretend until it's true.

Scrubbing her eyes, she sat up and exhaled. She performed her ablutions at the washstand, then went looking for her hairbrush. Her one vanity was her hair; although she dulled its color out of necessity, she still brushed it one hundred strokes each evening to maintain its luster. Searching through her things, she was chagrined to realize that she must have left her brush behind at the Nunnery.

Perhaps the previous occupant left a few things?

Without much hope, she went to the dressing table and pulled on the drawer. It took a few tries as the sticky drawer refused to budge. When she succeeded, she squealed with delight at what she found inside: a hairbrush...and it was *exquisite*. The beechwood handle was smooth and designed to fit a lady's hand, and a beautiful rose design was carved on the back. Eagerly, she ran the brush through her hair, sighing at the luxurious prickle of the boar bristles.

She'd reached sixty-nine strokes when she heard a sound in the corridor. She paused mid-stroke, and the noise came again.

Thump thump thump.

Footsteps? Was someone approaching?

Setting down the brush, she hurried to the door and poked her head out.

Thump thump.

The sound was coming from the far end of the corridor. From behind the mysterious locked door. If those were footsteps...was someone locked in there?

"You won't like what is inside," Lord Ethan had said.

Was he hiding something? What kind of skeletons would he have rattling in his closet?

Her eyes widened as the realization struck her.

Maybe he isn't hiding skeletons but a ghost.

A chill snaked up her spine. Lord Ethan had insisted that ghosts did not exist, but according to Mr. Bailey, Nelly Nettles had seen Bloody Thom with her own eyes. Curiosity yanked at Xenia. If the manor *was* haunted, shouldn't she know about it...for her own safety? She could take a quick peek, and if anything was amiss, she would make a run for it.

Decision made, she grabbed her keys and headed to the forbidden room.

Chapter Five

"Pleasure is everything, darling." Sirena's husky timbre filtered into his side of the confessional. "Nothing is forbidden."

Her voice was hypnotic, unlike anything he'd heard. And he'd been around countless women—swived countless of them. During the height of his popularity as a virtuoso, females had mobbed him, offering every carnal diversion under the sun. Drunk on music and success, he'd taken what was given.

He liked wicked women and the games they played. But when fame deserted him, they did too. He'd told himself it was a good thing because, to be frank, none of them had been the sort of female a man would want for a wife. It was time to settle and settle he did: for a lovely widow whose very name evoked what he now needed.

If the few times he'd bedded Constance had been less than inspiring, he'd told himself he was a different man now. Life was no longer his oyster, and he shouldn't expect so much. The lack of a physical spark with his future wife didn't matter as much as her other virtues. Constance was well-bred and would preside over his supper table with grace. She accepted his moods, never argued with him, and gave him space. She was perfect for who he'd become.

He'd convinced himself of all this...and then she ran off with his crony.

The fury that swelled in him was all the greater because of the humiliation. Because of his changed circumstances, he'd been willing to accept a marriage far from his ideal. Before his injury, he would never have considered such a thing—would have never questioned whether he deserved true and ultimate happiness.

Now he questioned everything, and he was bloody tired of it.

He'd held himself back sexually with Constance because she'd made it clear that she expected him to be civilized in bed. His beastly moods she could tolerate, but when it came to coupling, it was lights off and clothes on. Any deviation from her idea of normal had made her cringe...which hadn't exactly been an aphrodisiac for him.

Well, he was done with Constance. Done with limiting his desires. He hadn't had a satisfying fuck in three years. Yet the damnable truth was that being publicly jilted had spooked him and made him hesitate to get back into the saddle again...which was where Sirena came in. She was safe, and she was naughty: the perfect way to ease back into the depravities of bachelorhood.

"Tell me your desires," she cooed. "Don't be shy. I'll do whatever you wish."

Lust pulsed in his veins, amplified by his residual anger.

"I haven't been shy a day in my life, wench," he said sternly. "I want you naked in front of me. Now."

The screen melted away, and Sirena emerged like Aphrodite rising from the waves. Her luxuriant flame-red hair tumbled over her creamy shoulders, matched by the fiery thatch between her thighs. Her rounded tits looked like they would fit his palms perfectly, her blushing nipples making his mouth water. She came to where he was sitting and struck a saucy pose.

"Like what you see, darling?"

Her smoke-and-honey voice heated his blood. He reached up and gripped her nape, dragging her onto his lap. She straddled him, her pussy pressing against his burgeoning erection. Devil and damn, she was wet. Her dew soaked through his trousers. He jerked her face close to his, and gazing into her eyes, he saw exactly what he craved.

Real desire. Feminine lust, raw and honest.

Her reaction burned away his self-doubt and misery. A fog lifted. He felt as if he were surfacing from a deep, dreamless sleep—and he awoke with a powerful hunger.

"I like what I see," he told her. "And I'll like touching it even more."

He clamped a hand on her rounded hip, guiding her cunny against his lengthening ridge. She clutched his shoulders, tossed her head back, and gave a throaty whimper.

"Look at me," he said.

Her lashes swept up. He took in her enlarged pupils and parted lips. Her breasts heaved, and against his throbbing prick, her cunny radiated needy heat. Her reaction gave him the same exhilarating satisfaction as an audience's thundering applause.

She wants me. She is mine to pleasure, to fuck...however I want.

He drew his fingers along her rear crevice. When he teased her little pucker, she shivered and arched her back, her breasts bobbing tantalizingly by his face.

"You'll give me anything I want," he said.

"Anything."

Her sweet submission enthralled him. He was hard as a rock as he drew his fingers lower. He circled the entrance to her pussy, pushing two fingers inside. The slick squeeze of her passage confirmed what he knew. The desire between them was real. Real and hotter than anything he'd experienced.

"Ride my fingers," he said thickly.

"Oh, yes."

She plunged downward, taking him to the knuckles. He urged

her on, thrusting his fingers while she impaled herself again and again.

"Touch yourself," he growled. "Play with your pearl, naughty minx."

Moaning, she diddled herself as she bounced on his digits. When he leaned forward and sucked her nipple into his mouth, her response was instant. She gasped, her pussy contracting around his fingers, her cream coating his palm. He couldn't wait any longer. He took her by the waist and lifted her off him. Twisting her around, he positioned her on the ground on all fours.

"I want you this way," he said.

She turned her head to look at him, her hair a spill of fire and her eyes even hotter.

"You can have me," she purred. "Any way you wish."

He unfastened his trousers, his rock-hard prick springing free. Palming her plump bottom, he fitted his bulging tip to her slit. He drove inside, groaning at the decadent friction, the heat and snugness of her pussy. Closing a fist in her silky locks, he withdrew, then hilted himself to the balls.

"Ask for it," he demanded.

"Fuck me, please," she breathed. "Take me with your big cock."

He obliged, pounding her cunny, which fluttered exquisitely around his shaft. He reached under, stroking her pearl as he swived her. Pleasure brewed at the base of his spine, and his cock swelled. He drove into her, about to blow like a cannon...

She let out a wail so loud that he jerked to a confused stop.

She screamed again, this time with full-throated fear.

He awakened with a start, panting harshly. He was...in bed? He rubbed his hands over his face. He was hot and perspiring, his bare skin damp against the sheets.

Devil and damn. I was dreaming.

His dream had felt enticingly real. Grimacing, he gazed past the twitching bands of his abdomen to the tented bedsheet. He considered taking matters into his own hands. It wouldn't be the first time since his injury...

A scream tore through his thoughts. He hadn't dreamed it? The likely cause of the sound slammed into him.

"Bloody hell," he muttered. "She opened the door."

Exiting his bed, he got dressed and stalked toward the servants' quarters.

I'm going to die. I'm going to die.

Darkness swarmed Xenia, a flapping shroud that muffled her screams. She hadn't been a good person, and this was a fitting end. Bitten to pieces, dying alone and afraid, unwanted and unloved...

"I've got you."

A strong arm hooked her around the waist. She was dragged out of the dark vortex. She felt her feet hit the ground, but her legs wouldn't work. She heard an oath; an instant later, she was hauled against a hard chest and carried with dizzying speed. A rectangle of light appeared, and they went through, their departure punctuated by a loud slam.

She blinked, panting. She was back in the corridor of the servants' quarters. A winged beast swooped by, and she squeaked, trying to duck from its path.

"Of the two of you, I wager the bat is more afraid."

The deep tones rumbled beneath her ear and jolted her back to her senses. Odds bodkins, she was in Lord Ethan's arms. She was huddling against his chest, her arms flung around his neck. Slowly, she tipped her head back...then back some more. Until she met her master's smoldering gaze.

Blooming hell.

He was looking down his noble nose at her, his sinfully handsome face as brooding as ever. Seeing the violet storm in his gaze, her belly sank. The consequences of her actions struck her.

Am I going to get sacked my first day on the job?

This was why she didn't deserve nice things. She always ruined them. Ruined everything.

"I can explain," she said weakly.

"That will be interesting."

He started moving, and seeing as he was carrying her, she had no choice but to go along. She didn't feel up to walking, and since she was about to get fired, she might as well enjoy the novelty of being swept off her feet. She'd always wondered what it would be like to play the role of the damsel in distress. Although she'd been in distress on numerous occasions, no one had ever treated her like a damsel. No one had thought her worthy of care and protection.

Except for Papa and Mr. Trelawney. And I paid them back by getting them killed.

Her chest tightened. Maybe she deserved everything bad that happened to her. Maybe it was her comeuppance for being a bad apple grown from a bad seed.

Nonetheless, when Lord Ethan nudged open the door of her bedchamber, exposing the warm and cozy space, yearning crept through her. This was the nicest place she'd ever stayed. She didn't want to give it up.

Her rescuer shouldered the door shut.

"To keep the bats out," he said.

She shuddered, not about to argue with his logic.

He carried her over to the bed. Through her threadbare night-gown, she felt the sleek bulge of his muscles surrounding her, and her tummy quivered. His scent was delicious: a mix of crisp, sophisticated spices and virile male musk. She stole another whiff before she found herself unceremoniously dumped onto the bed.

Lord Ethan towered over her, his hands braced on his hips. For some reason, he was wearing gloves. He was also wearing a black silk dressing gown that exposed a vee of his muscular chest, which had an enticing sprinkle of dark hair. His large feet were shod in fine velvet slippers.

"I am waiting."

She yanked her gaze up from his bulging, hair-dusted calves. "For what?"

"Your explanation," he bit out.

Oh, right. Think, Xenia, think.

"I heard a noise in the hallway," she said. "It came from behind the door. I thought it might, um, be a burglar or something of the sort. So I went to investigate."

His expression was stony. She had no idea if he believed her.

Then his eyes narrowed. "Is something wrong with your voice? You sound different."

Drat! She'd forgotten to disguise it. Now that the horse had left the barn, she decided it was too troublesome to keep up the prim tones.

"This is my usual voice, sir. If I sounded different yesterday, it was because I was recovering from a head cold," she said glibly.

"Hmm." He looked unconvinced. "Be that as it may, you disobeyed my direct order. I made it clear that you were not to enter that room under any circumstances. The infestation was discovered the day before you arrived. Until I can find someone to remedy the situation, I've kept the bats quarantined. Thanks to you, they are now loose in the house."

Eek! That's disgusting.

Wisely, she kept her reaction to herself.

"Since I caused the problem," she said, "I shall take it upon myself to rectify it."

He stared at her, not even bothering to voice his skepticism.

"I'll ask in the village," she clarified. "I am sure I can find help."

He crossed his arms.

"You needn't worry about a thing, my lord," she said stoutly.

Eager to persuade him (and keep her job), she rose and put on a brisk, the-housekeeper-will-take-care-of-it smile. She gave his arm a reassuring pat—which was a mistake. When her fingertips brushed the hard curve of his biceps, she felt as if she'd touched an electrifying machine. A charge buzzed through her, blood rushing to her cheeks and the tips of her breasts, which jutted visibly against the worn fabric of her nightgown.

Can he see my nipples? Her legs trembled.

As she jerked her hand away, his indigo gaze remained locked on her. Tension gripped the room. Her heartbeat measured out the seconds, his silence amplifying her anxious arousal.

"How did you intend to spot the burglar without your spectacles?" he asked.

Drat, again! Did the man have to be devilishly attractive *and* observant?

Her gaze shot to the escritoire, where she'd left her spectacles. Since her vision was perfect, she hadn't thought to wear them on her excursion to the forbidden room.

"I, um, only need them for reading."

As explanations went, she could have done worse.

"In the future," he said in ominous tones, "kindly refrain from risking your damned neck. If it were a burglar, I would expect you to lock yourself in your room and call for help. What do you think would have happened if you confronted a criminal? He would take one look at you and..."

He gestured at her, trailing off.

The unexpected flare of heat in his gaze shredded her composure. He was looking at her as if he were seeing her for the first time...and, she realized with a burst of nerves, perhaps he was. Without her spectacles, bulky frock, and face paint, she was far too exposed. At least her hair was still dyed.

Do not panic. Keep playing the part of Jane Wood.

"All's well that ends well," she said quickly. "I apologize again for disturbing your evening, my lord. Now, if you don't mind, I have an early day ahead."

He looked as if he might say something—argue with her, probably—but instead he regarded her for a long moment. She swallowed, feeling her knees wobble under the weight of his scrutiny.

With a slight shake of his head, he headed to the door. There, he paused, his hand on the knob.

"Keep your door locked," he said shortly. "The bats."

"Yes, sir."

After he left, she secured the door. Flopping onto the bed, she rolled over and buried her face in the pillow. She prayed that things would improve on the morrow.

At least they can't get any worse...can they?

Chapter Six

The next morning, Ethan set down his fork and looked at his hovering butler. "I don't suppose you had a hand in preparing this?"

Brunswick shook his head. "I cannot say that I did, my lord."

Ethan thought as much. With grim disbelief, he reviewed the contents of his breakfast plate. He poked at the eggs with his fork, and they pushed back with rubbery resilience. The sausages were burnt to a crisp on the outside, yet the insides were raw and pink. The toast, at least, held no surprises, being blackened through and through. As for the buns, the good news was that, if he were ever in need of doorstops, he now had a bountiful supply.

Good God, could the troublesome Mrs. Wood do nothing right?

First the bats, now this.

"She said she could cook," he said grimly.

Brunswick cleared his throat. "Did she say she could cook well?"

"That was implied." Ethan turned a hard stare upon his butler. "Get her in here."

"Are you certain that is wise, my lord? After all, it is Mrs. Wood's first attempt—"

"Are you defending her?" he asked in disbelief.

The old retainer's face turned ruddy. Bloody hell, he *ought* to feel embarrassed for acting like some knight errant. While Mrs. Wood lacked any detectable talent for housekeeping, she must have a hidden supply of charm if she'd won over Brunswick, who was a known curmudgeon.

With prickling unease, Ethan recalled his own reaction to her last night. Her spectacles had concealed more than he'd realized. Without them, he'd had his first good look at her, discovering to his shock that she was rather...pretty. More than rather. Her doe-like eyes were a warm, beguiling brown. They dominated her heart-shaped face, which also boasted a pert nose and cute little chin. She looked younger than seven and twenty, and her worn nightgown had clung to her nubile curves and perky nipples—

Do not go there. She's your employee, for God's sake. What kind of degenerate are you?

"As Mrs. Wood is new to her position," Brunswick said with quiet dignity, "I am merely suggesting that you give her a chance."

Ethan inhaled for patience. "I am not going to throw her out, if that is your concern. Go fetch her."

Before departing, the butler gave Ethan a look that he'd become accustomed to. Since his injury, the people in his life had frequently given him that look. As if they didn't trust him to behave like a civilized human being. It was infuriating...and embarrassing because he couldn't blame them. His mood *had* been beastly, driven by his rumination about his hand, his music, his family...everything he'd lost.

He would brood, brood, brood about the unfairness of it all.

Then emotions would ambush him. He could be riding in the carriage in a fine mood one moment, then shaking with rage the next. This very thing had happened before his first meeting with Mrs. Wood. Although she hadn't taken him to task for leaving her in the rain, he wasn't a complete idiot and knew that his behavior had annoyed her. The thing of it was, he hadn't intended to be unchivalrous: he'd left her for her own good—to protect her from his devil of a temper.

While he'd always been a fellow of strong passions, before his injury he'd had an outlet, pouring himself into his music. The lulling beauty of a sonata. The exuberance of a concerto. Even the practice of technique held pleasure: the absorbing rigor of scales and arpeggios, the demanding precision, the feeling that one was honing one's potential. Piano had always come easily for him, and unlike his siblings, he'd never complained about practicing. When it came to music, he had limitless ambition and self-discipline. In fact, his parents often had to pull him away from his instrument to prevent him from missing out on other things.

As much as his family loved him, they didn't understand what music meant to him. It wasn't a hobby or amusement. A vehicle for fame and fortune. Playing the piano had been who he *was*. When the keys had glided beneath his fingertips, he'd felt alive, powerful, unstoppable. He'd felt touched by destiny, by joy... by God.

Without his music, who was he?

Nothing and no one.

Which led to his present dilemma. He was in no shape to deal with an attraction to Jane Wood. Losing his ability to play had affected his overall confidence and, as lowering as it was to admit, the fiasco with Constance had made things worse, making him question his appeal to the opposite sex. He was on shaky ground all around. Moreover, he was not the sort of man who chased after housemaids. Papa had taught him and his brothers that gentlemen of honor respected women and never took advantage of those who were vulnerable.

Even at the pinnacle of his debauched youth, Ethan had taken lovers who were his equal. Experienced ladies who liked to play the same naughty games. Thus, how was he going to handle his unacceptable reaction to his housekeeper? Perhaps it was just a one-time thing. Perhaps her proximity last night and the fact that she'd interrupted his dream of Sirena had resulted in his sensual awareness of her.

Yet Mrs. Wood's effect on him was more than physical. The truth was she intrigued him. It was obvious that she had deliberately concealed her attractiveness. This led him to question why she'd done so. And what else she might be hiding. He suspected that all was not as it seemed with his housekeeper.

Brunswick ushered Mrs. Wood into the breakfast room. Ethan rose; despite her mousy appearance, she was the kind of woman who kept a man on his toes. She curtsied, then peered at him through the spectacles that were once again in place. It was too late, however. He saw her now: those big, brown eyes and thick lashes tipped with auburn, the sprinkle of freckles over her nose. The mouth that was a little too wide and much too sensual for a woman trying to pass herself off as plain.

"You, um, wished to see me, my lord?" she asked.

Her voice had a husky warmth that felt like a caress against his groin. Recovering from a head cold, indeed. The woman had more excuses than a cat had fleas.

He looked at his butler. "You may go."

On the way out, Brunswick bestowed a look of encouragement upon Mrs. Wood that made Ethan feel like an ogre. For God's sake, he was going to take her to task, not eat her. Out of nowhere, his wicked banter with Sirena surfaced.

"Do you eat me?" she'd asked.

"I savor you."

"What is this about, sir?"

Mrs. Wood's question dispelled the memory. She looked nervous, rubbing her palms subtly against her apron. Her clean, herbal scent teased his nose; he'd noticed it last night when he carried her.

He cut to the chase. "You said you could cook."

"You, um, didn't like the dishes I prepared?"

Understatement of the year.

He curled a finger at her. "Follow me."

Obediently, she accompanied him to the sideboard, where he uncovered the first dish.

"Eggs, overcooked and inedible." He removed the next dome. "Sausages, undercooked and inedible. Then there's this." He unveiled her *pièce de résistance,* a congealed blob the color of a fresh bruise. "I don't even know what the devil it is."

"Black pudding, sir," she mumbled.

So that was the identity of the mysterious glop.

"Did you not find it tasty?" she asked.

He handed her a fork. A challenge. "Why don't you see for yourself?"

She reached for the utensil. Her fingers feathered against his, and even though he wore gloves, the passing touch caused his gut to clench. He jerked his hand away the same time she did. Their gazes clashed as the fork clattered to the ground between them.

"P-pardon," she stammered. "How clumsy of me."

As she bent over to retrieve the silverware, the sensation in his gut traveled farther south. Devil and damn, his housekeeper had a nicely rounded bottom. When she straightened, he hastily raised his gaze, but when he saw her intent, he snapped his brows together.

"You are not going to use that, are you?" he said incredulously.

She paused an instant before the fork she'd retrieved *from the floor* touched the purple goop.

"Um..." she said.

"Christ." He braced a hand on his hip. "Were you actually trained as a housekeeper?"

"Of course, sir." She lifted her chin. "You have seen my references."

"Yet you find it acceptable to eat with a fork that has touched the ground?"

She drew herself up. Since she was a full foot shorter than him, she still had to tilt her head back to look him in the eye.

"As you have undoubtedly not received training in household management, your lordship," she said with admirable poise, "you are probably unaware of the Golden Rule of Housekeeping."

"What is this bloody rule?"

"It is taught in the finest households. Also known as the Rule of Five Seconds, it states that if an object makes contact with the floor for five seconds or less, it is perfectly acceptable to use."

He narrowed his eyes. "You are making that up."

"I assure you that I am not."

Her manner was bland and reasonable. Devil take it. As much as he doubted her sincerity, he had to admire her boldness and ingenuity.

"In my household, the Rule of Five Seconds does not apply," he said sternly. "Remember that in the future."

"As you wish, my lord."

Although she bowed her head, he suspected there was not a deferential bone in her body. Strangely, he liked that. Everyone else in his life seemed to be walking on eggshells around him, whereas she didn't seem the least bit cowed. Maybe she wouldn't be daunted by his temper. He wondered if she might be testing how far she could go with him.

Two can play at that game.

He grabbed a clean fork and handed it to her. "Don't think you are getting off the hook."

Shrugging, she accepted the fork and dug into the slop. Extracting a blob, she gamely shoved it into her mouth.

As she chewed, he found himself distracted by her lips. They had an appealing shape. Would they feel as soft and plush as they looked...?

She started gagging. He held out a napkin. Snatching it, she coughed into its folds.

"Well?" he inquired.

"It was dreadful," she admitted. "The worst thing I've ever tasted."

"You haven't sampled your eggs."

"The eggs were terrible too?" Her spectacles had slipped down, revealing a glimmer of worry in her velvety-brown eyes. "But I poached them exactly the way the recipe book advised."

"Don't believe everything you read," he said wryly.

"I tried my best." She lowered her head, speaking to the tips of her worn shoes. "Truly I did. I'm sorry I made a hash of things."

His enjoyment of their byplay faded. He felt as if he'd kicked a baby fawn.

"You made a bad meal," he said gruffly. "You haven't committed murder or some other unpardonable sin."

She bit her lip, her eyes wide.

He sighed. "Try to do better next time."

"Next time? You...you are not going to sack me?"

Hope flickered on her face, causing an odd constriction in his chest.

"Over the eggs and blood sausage? No."

"There was the incident with the bats too," she said in a small voice.

"Mistakes I can tolerate. The one thing I will not tolerate is being lied to," he said firmly. "If you lack knowledge in a certain area of housekeeping, I expect you to be honest. About your weaknesses and your strengths. Only then can we make the best use of your time here."

"That is very understanding of you, my lord."

Her gratitude made him uncomfortable. He hadn't offered much. She was still in charge of dealing with the filthy, tumbledown manor where he'd chosen to lick his wounds. She still had to deal with *him*. Damaged, short-tempered, and a shadow of the man he once was. Who was such a failure that his family fretted over him endlessly and his fiancée left him for another. Reality crashed over him like an ice-cold wave. He couldn't even find a proper housekeeper *and* entertained improper thoughts about the one he did have.

I'm a bloody wreck. This is why I need to be alone. I'm not fit to be around others.

"My lord?"

"What is it?"

He didn't mean to snap, and his lack of restraint shamed him. Luckily, Mrs. Wood did not seem hurt. Instead, she...brightened?

"I am good with books," she blurted.

He frowned. "I beg your pardon?"

"Before I was a housekeeper, I worked in a few bookshops."

Since her explanation explained nothing, he continued to look at her blankly.

"Your library needs to be unpacked," she reminded him. "You said to be forthcoming about my strengths, and, well, I could organize your books. In my spare time, of course, after I've dealt with more pressing household matters. And if I'm not stepping on Brunswick's toes."

After his boorish behavior, Ethan couldn't deny her earnest request. Truth be told, Brunswick would be grateful to be relieved of the task. Sorting out the room would give Mrs. Wood something to do...and even she couldn't wreak havoc with a bunch of books.

"Have at it," Ethan said. "And look for someone in the village to help with the cooking. Consult Brunswick, if necessary."

"I will. Thank you, sir. You shan't regret keeping me on," she promised.

She flashed him a smile that made him regret a lot of things. Mostly, he wondered what would have happened if they'd met under different circumstances.

If she wasn't his housekeeper.

If he had something to offer other than failure.

If he was the man he used to be.

If, if, if.

Chapter Seven

For the remainder of the week, a refrain played in Xenia's head.

Do not fail again.

She didn't know what was more terrifying: the bats she'd unleashed or the meal she'd cooked. Either way, she was in no danger of putting her best foot forward. She was fortunate that her employer had let bygones be bygones and was giving her another chance. Truth be told, Lord Ethan's compassion had surprised her, leading her to question whether she'd misjudged him.

Perhaps the day he'd left her in the rain had been an exception to his behavior rather than the rule. Everyone had a bad day, after all. And she couldn't forget how he'd gallantly rescued her from the bats. At night, tucked in her cozy bed, she relived the way he'd carried her as if she were a princess. Brooding, sleek as a panther in his black dressing gown, he'd been a tempting beast.

Her mind had roamed to wicked places. Her hands, too.

What if, after he tossed her on the bed, he'd torn off her nightgown? Shivering, she'd imagined him raking a possessive gaze over her naked flesh and laying bare her darkest fantasies.

"You've been a naughty girl," he said.

"I didn't mean to release the bats," she protested.

"Don't lie to your master. I see you, Xenia, the wicked and the good. You are mine."

As longing swelled inside her, he leaned over, anchoring her wrists above her head. He roughly kneed her legs apart, invading the cove of her body as if he had every right. His trouser-covered thigh pressed against her wet, quivering sex.

What happened next varied depending on her mood. Although she'd never lain with a man, she had a salacious imagination, fed by everything she'd witnessed in the brothels where she'd worked. Her dirty mind had helped her to earn a living, and now she used it for her own pleasure. She let her carnal creativity run wild, picturing the scenes that made her blood run hottest.

Her master would tell her to kneel and service his big, jutting cock with her mouth. Or he would toss her on a bed, claiming her virginity with a powerful thrust. Or he would make her ride him, and she'd skewer herself on his rod again and again while he fondled her breasts... No matter how they made love, his attention never strayed from her. His violet-blue eyes were focused on her, as if she were the only thing he saw.

"You're beautiful." His deep voice was the essence of desire. *"And you belong to me. Say it."*

"I belong to you," she breathed.

She'd touched herself, smothering her moans in her pillow.

She blamed her hot-blooded nature on her mother. Mama had changed lovers as often as undergarments...even when she'd been married to Papa. When it came to relationships—and life choices in general—Xenia refused to follow in her mother's footsteps. When she made love, she wanted it to be with someone special... someone she loved. This, along with pragmatic concerns about getting with child or contracting some horrid disease, was why she'd held onto her virginity.

But now she was three and twenty, randy, and the wrong man held her imagination captive. Even if Lord Ethan wasn't the grumpy bounder she'd initially believed him to be, he *was* her employer. His world was a stratosphere above hers, and he would never be interested in a servant. And what about her vow to avoid all attachments? She'd taken this job as a temporary measure, something to tide her over until she could return to the Nunnery.

It is just lust. Don't get distracted. Focus on your work.

For better or worse, she hadn't seen much of Lord Ethan. He'd cloistered himself in his study or bedchamber. She'd tried to ask Mr. Valentine if something was amiss, but the valet, a fastidious fellow with hair the color of marmalade, had made it clear she ought to mind her own business. Even the friendly Brunswick seemed reluctant to discuss their master.

"His lordship has his reasons for wanting privacy," was the most the butler would say. *"It's best to leave him be, Mrs. Wood."*

Whatever one could say about Lord Ethan, he'd apparently earned the loyalty of his longtime retainers. She pushed thoughts of him aside and concentrated on her duties. It had taken two days and an untold amount of elbow grease, but she'd managed to scrub off the grime coating the entrance hall floor. The effort had been worth it: the pink marble she'd uncovered was resplendent. The floor was so pretty that she resolved to fix up the chandelier so that its light could sparkle over the polished stone.

Brunswick had conveyed the master's decree that she had carte blanche to make improvements as she wished. She could open accounts at the village shops and hire servants at her discretion. The latter was proving difficult due to the fear of Bloody Thom. With the mop fair three days away, she was hoping that the sight of her, hale and hearty after a week's employ at Bottoms House, would entice others to join her.

Meanwhile, she'd found a temporary solution to take care of the meals. Chuddums had an inn named the Briarbush at the corner of High Street, and apropos to its name, the place offered few comforts, encouraging travelers to get back on the road. However, the establishment had one redeeming quality: its kitchen. Mrs. Thornton, the innkeeper's wife, was a temperamental genius who cooked a single dish a day. The menu depended on her mood, and she plunked her food in front of customers while sharing her philosophy on hospitality: "Eat it or starve."

Luckily, her hearty country fare was delicious. After much pleading (and a significant bribe) from Xenia, Mrs. Thornton agreed to send daily baskets to the manor. Since Xenia hadn't heard any complaints about the meals from Lord Ethan (and received ardent approval from the staff), she patted herself on the back for a job well done.

Thus, when her day off arrived, she rewarded herself by exploring the village. It was one of those glorious summer days when it seemed like the good weather would last forever. She trotted down High Street with the sun on her back, a gentle breeze stirring the frayed ribbons of her bonnet, and birds swooping and singing overhead.

She couldn't recall the last time she'd had free time and a bit of spending money. She planned to treat herself to afternoon tea and gossip with Mrs. Pettigrew at the Leaning House but made a quick detour to Hatcherds. On the way, she was waylaid by the ever-helpful Wally, who sported a yellow checkered coat today. When she presented him with a small pot of balm she'd made to ease his rheumatism, he thanked her with a wide, toothless grin.

"This will help me chase down that damned Fenwyck if I ever catch him in the act," the nonagenarian declared.

At the bookshop, Xenia's entry startled the wizened proprietor awake from his nap at the counter.

"If it isn't my favorite patron," Mr. Khan said, beaming.

Since she seemed to be his only patron—this was her third visit and she'd yet to see another customer in the tiny shop—she didn't let the compliment go to her head. She liked Mr. Khan. The friendly widower had wrinkles that rivaled those of a prune and kindly eyes that sparkled behind spectacles thicker than her own. His thick, white hair and eyebrows stood out like fluffy clouds against his skin.

"Good afternoon," she said with a smile. "Have any new books arrived since my last visit?"

Truth be told, her visit was prompted out of a desire to support the business rather than a need for reading material. She'd started going through the trunks in Lord Ethan's library, and it turned out that he owned *a lot* of books. So many, in fact, that it would take her weeks to unpack the trunks. Curiously, they shared a similar taste in reading material. She'd unearthed gothic novels and volumes of poetry. From *Frankenstein* and *Jane Eyre* to collections of verse by Keats, Wordsworth, and Blake, Lord Ethan's interest in the romantic was unexpected...and intriguing.

Men with artistic inclinations were, unfortunately, her Achilles' heel. She'd fallen for Tony after he'd told her about the novel he wanted to write. Unlike the stories he penned for coin, this story was about the common man's struggle, and the passion of his convictions—the way his green eyes had smoldered in his wan face—had hooked her like a fish. He'd only been her follower for a few months before his untimely demise. Her sorrow had dulled with time, but it was a reminder that forming attachments was dangerous. Especially for a woman like her, who would always be on the run. She could enjoy the moment, but she could never set down roots. That was the price of freedom.

"I set these aside, hoping you would come by."

As Mr. Khan bent to retrieve something from behind the counter, his bones creaked like a hinge in need of oiling. He straightened slowly, vertebrae by rusty vertebrae. Although Xenia had read the titles he set on the counter, she thanked him and paid the borrowing fee.

When Mr. Khan deposited the coin into his money box, it made a solitary clank.

"Business hasn't been flourishing of late," he said sadly.

By "of late," she wondered if he was referring to the last twenty years. The novels sitting on the shelves of the shop's single weathered bookcase were at least that old.

Not that it's any of your business, she told herself.

Nonetheless, she tried to cheer him up. "Perhaps this is a temporary slump, and business will improve."

"I've lived in Chuddums for over thirty years, Mrs. Wood, and things have only gone in one direction." Gloomily, he jabbed a finger downward to affirm the direction he meant. "Given the curse, I suppose there's nothing that can be done about it."

Despite Xenia's fanciful nature, she also had a practical streak. She wouldn't have survived her upbringing otherwise. The sensible part of her questioned whether everything bad that happened to the village could be attributed to a curse.

"Mr. Bailey told me about the legend concerning Thomas Mulligan," she said. "Do you think it is responsible for all of Chuddums's misfortunes?"

"I do, Mrs. Wood, and I'll tell you why. Every bad thing that has happened here has been foretold in an old poem about Bloody Thom. Have you heard it?"

She shook her head.

Clearing his throat, Mr. Khan intoned,

"Beware, beware the rattling chain
The flapping robes stained red and bold
Beware the moans and wails of pain
For 'tis Bloody Thom they do herald.

He brings death to all who cross his path
Be they creatures with feathers, fur, or skin
Green will wither and fortunes dwindle until his
    wrath
Is quenched by a true reckoning.

He plays a mournful ballad of blame
Shaking the manor with his ire
His cry for justice is like a flame
That scorches all with unholy fire."

"That is rather, um, dramatic." Xenia's eyes rounded. "Who wrote that poem?"

"No one knows, but it has been passed down for generations. All the schoolchildren know it." Mr. Khan shook his head. "Everything it predicted has come to pass. Crops have mysteriously withered, livestock perished. Businesses have closed, one by one. Take Hatcherds, for instance. When I first opened, I had eight full bookcases, and volumes were flying off the shelves. Now?" He shrugged. "If things don't improve, I shall have to close the store for good."

She couldn't bear to see him lose hope. Or for the village to lose its only source of books. Who would want to live in such a place then?

"Curse or no curse, there must be a way to turn things around," she said.

"I am open to suggestions." Mr. Khan peered at her hopefully.

She gnawed on her lip, surveying the shop. "Perhaps you could spruce up the place?"

He snorted. "If I had the money for that, I'd retire, and devil take the shop."

"It wouldn't require funds to make the space more inviting." If there was one thing she was good at, it was making do with whatever she had. "If you have a spare rug and pair of chairs at home, they would make that empty corner cozier, don't you think? It might encourage customers to come in and stay awhile."

"That is a capital idea, Mrs. Wood. I might have a few things upstairs." His excitement fizzled. "But my rheumatism makes it difficult to carry much."

She couldn't leave the elderly fellow to his own devices. The project was her idea, after all.

"I'll help," she offered.

As it turned out, Mr. Khan had more than a "few things" in his upstairs flat. He had a veritable museum of interesting objects he'd collected during his youthful travels. She learned that he'd once been a *sepoy* employed by the East India Army. Disillusioned by the shabby and inequitable way Indian officers were treated, he left the army and voyaged around India before making his way to England.

He'd brought a treasure trove of goods from his native land. Fascinated, Xenia learned about a pipe with a long stem called a *hookah*, and *ooh*ed and *aah*ed over an exquisite silk garment called a *sari*, which had belonged to Mrs. Khan. From a crammed storage room, she helped him unearth a blue rug decorated with vines and birds, a pair of carved rosewood chairs, and a small table. With her fledgling housekeeping skills, she polished up the items and arranged them in the shop. Mr. Khan also found a box of unused stationery items that he put out for sale.

It was nearing dusk by the time Xenia emerged from Hatcherds. Although she had missed afternoon tea at the Leaning House, she was stuffed to the gills because Mr. Khan had insisted on feeding her. The meal of curry, rice, and sweets spiced with cardamon and honey was one of the tastiest she'd ever had. At the doorstep, she returned her host's grateful thanks with her own.

"With any luck, our work will bear fruit," she said cheerfully. "I'm told the mop fair will bring an influx of visitors."

"We can hope, Mrs. Wood." Mr. Khan scrutinized the darkening streets. "It's getting late. Are you certain you won't allow me to escort you home? It isn't safe for a young lady to walk alone."

She was touched that Mr. Khan considered her a lady, but she'd lived in far more dangerous places than Chuddums. She could protect herself...better than he could, at any rate.

"I'll be fine," she reassured him.

"Be sure to avoid the east end of the village," he warned. "The riffraff gather at the docks."

After giving her promise, she set off for Bottoms House. At the deserted village green, she noted the huge shadow cast by the lifeless tree, its canopy of darkness cloaking the monument to Langdon Pearce. Shivering, she instinctively steered clear.

"Mary, dearie! Is that you?"

Xenia turned to see Alice Jenkins, a fellow employee of the Nunnery, heading toward her. A willowy blonde with plush lips, Alice was the brothel's most popular whore. She was a prima donna, yet she had been nice to Xenia—or Mary Smith, rather, the alias Xenia used at the brothel—and generously shared tips of the trade with her. Xenia had put Alice's knowledge to use in her stories.

"What are you doing here?" Xenia exchanged air kisses with her colleague. "I thought you'd gone to live with family in Cookham."

"I *was* staying with my aunt until her husband wanted more than money for rent." Alice rolled her eyes, as if such despicable behavior was to be expected. "Now I've need o' a place to stay until the Nunnery is up and running. As a matter o' fact, I've a lead on lodgings in Chudleigh Crest...say, you wouldn't be interested in sharing with me? The room is large enough for two."

"It sounds lovely, but I've found a place," Xenia said.

"Where?"

"Um, nearby."

Xenia didn't want to disclose more than necessary. Gossip had a way of traveling. The last thing she wanted was for Lord Ethan to discover that she worked at the Nunnery.

Alice wrinkled her nose. "You couldn't pay me to live here."

Xenia felt oddly protective of the village. She liked the residents she'd met. While they had their quirks, they were also accepting of others' foibles in a way she found charming.

"I find Chuddums to be quite respectable," she said stiffly.

"That's a pity," Alice drawled. "Since I came to find some *disreputable* distraction."

Xenia noted the saucy plume in the other's hair and the artfully applied face paint. Alice's strong perfume, Attar of Roses, tickled her nose. She'd wager that beneath that dark cloak, Alice wore one of her signature low-cut frocks.

"Are you working?" Xenia asked.

"Not tonight, dove." Alice winked. "A woman needs to let 'er hair down now and again. Why don't you share a pint wif me? Maybe we'll find somefing else to share too. A nice, brawny sailor wif stamina, eh?"

Xenia flushed. "I would like to, but I have, um, another engagement."

Alice pinched her cheek as if she were a cute tot. "Always the shy one, ain't you?"

"You ought to be careful at the docks." Recalling Mr. Khan's warning and the brutes outside Mr. Bailey's, Xenia felt a flutter of worry. "I'm told that ruffians gather there—"

"I like 'em rough and ready."

"Not this rough. If there's a gang in the village, it's best to—"

"I can take care o' myself." Alice waved off her concerns. "By the by, the Abbess is looking for a temporary place to host a masquerade. She says she'll be in touch through the usual manner."

As a condition of taking the Abbess's ten pounds, Xenia had promised to stay in contact. However, she hadn't wanted the bawd's messages to fall into the wrong hands at her new place of employ. Understanding the need for discretion, the Abbess had agreed to exchange messages via an anonymous box at the post office. In truth, Xenia ought to be happy at the prospect of returning to her previous job. The money she made as Sirena far surpassed her housekeeper's wages. Yet she was beginning to enjoy her life as Mrs. Wood...and she didn't want to give up her cozy attic room, either.

She forced a smile. "I look forward to it."

"You and me, dove. No work and all play is dangerous for women like us, eh?" With another wink, Alice sauntered off.

Bemused and worried, Xenia watched the other melt into the shadows. Then she hurried back to the manor.

Chapter Eight

The next morning, Xenia found herself alone in the manor. The Earl of Manderly had arrived, dragging his grumbling brother out for a ride. Brunswick was taking a well-deserved day off, and Mr. Valentine had gone into the village in search of an elusive grooming implement.

This left Xenia with rare solitude, which was a good thing since she wasn't at her best. She'd slept fitfully and blamed it on the eerie poem about Bloody Thom. While she couldn't recall her dreams, she'd awoken with a start...and a feeling that she wasn't alone. Panic and fear had bombarded her. Her pulse had raced as if she'd been running for her life, her knuckles throbbing as if she'd used her fists. Her throat was sore as if she'd been screaming.

She told herself it had been an ordinary nightmare. The kind she'd been having her entire life. Any ghostly presence she'd felt had been the product of her wild imagination. Nonetheless, unease clung to her like an invisible cobweb. To distract herself, she decided to take advantage of Lord Ethan's absence to clean his study. Tidying in his presence was an impossibility: she'd tried once and given up. It was like trying to organize the den of a growling, territorial bear.

But he's not here now, and what he doesn't know won't hurt him.

The curtains behind his desk were drawn. She pushed them open...and coughed. In the streaming sunlight, dust motes swarmed like angry insects from the velvet panels. The dirty floor-to-ceiling windows framed the dense jungle of a garden beyond. Creeping vines of ivy were everywhere and swallowed the gazebo in a far corner.

Turning, Xenia eyed the room from Lord Ethan's perspective —that is, from behind his cluttered desk. She took in the worn furnishings, pitted bookcases, and shabby carpets and wondered why a man of wealth and status would choose to live like this.

"A housekeeper's job is never done," she muttered.

She prioritized what she could do. The rugs would have to wait until there were footmen to carry them outside for a good beating. Dragging in a bucket of cleaning supplies, she set to work on the furniture. The combination of beeswax, lemon juice, and linseed oil did wonders, hiding scratches and giving the weathered wood new shine. Pleased with the results, she cleaned the floors around the rugs until they, too, were gleaming.

Next, she examined the bookshelves. Thanks to her mama's penchant for using abandoned properties as hideaway places, she was an expert at fixing woodworm damage. She would use vinegar to clear away any remaining infestation and then apply tinted beeswax to fill the holes. She followed the pockmarked trail to the cupboard door next to the shelves. When she tried to open the door to assess the damage inside, it wouldn't budge.

Odd. Why is the door locked?

She tried the keys on the ring Lord Ethan had given her. None of them fit. Perhaps she ought to move on; hadn't she learned her lesson with the bats? But her employer hadn't told her *not* to look in his closet. Moreover, she was on a legitimate mission to assess the extent of woodworm rot. On that well-reasoned note, she plucked a pair of pins from her hair. They were useful for keeping tresses in place and for getting her into places she wanted to be.

One couldn't grow up with the mama she had and not learn a few tricks of the trade.

The lock clicked, and she opened the door. What lay beyond wasn't a cupboard but a tiny antechamber that held the most stunning piano she'd ever seen. The grand instrument took up most of the space. Its black lacquer surface gleamed like a panther's skin, its smooth lines and robust curves like those of a prowling beast.

Why does he keep this magnificent piano in here?

The ancient piano in the music room looked like it had come with the house, and she wondered why he would display that one but keep this glamorous showpiece hidden. She traced her fingertip over the ornate gilt swirls that identified the piano maker as "Bösendorfer." Her gaze fell to the row of lustrous ivory keys. Her papa had been a musician. Some of Xenia's best childhood memories were of sitting on his lap as he taught her to play on a battered flash house instrument.

It had been a long time since she'd had a piano to play on, and never one as fine as this. She spotted the box that lay beneath the instrument. Opening the lid, she pulled out a sheaf of paper... music scores. One caught her eye: an unfinished piece labeled simply, "Sonata in C Minor." The title and notes in the margin were written in Lord Ethan's distinctive scrawl.

Had *he* composed this piece?

The trace of his spicy musk tickled her senses. Her heart thumped as she imagined him composing alone in this secret chamber. Was there anything more swoon-worthy than an artist in the passionate throes of creation?

I wonder what his piece sounds like.

Temptation gripped her. There was no one home to hear her. Peering out into the empty study, she made her decision and quickly sat in front of the piano. Her knees quivered at the thought of playing music her master had composed, of touching keys he'd touched.

Do I dare?

She pressed a key. The tone was beautiful, hypnotically expressive. As she warmed up with a few scales, she marveled at the keyboard's responsiveness, the way the keys seemed to flow beneath her fingers. When she was ready, she turned her attention to the score and played the opening notes.

With Brunswick off for the day, Ethan let himself and his brother in. He was glad that James had dragged him out of the house. Riding served to clear his head, and this hadn't changed after his injury, although certain accommodations had had to be made. He'd learned to ride one-handed from a Spanish instructor, who taught a method that involved a rein placed around the horse's neck. Ethan had trained his new Arabian, Legato, in this manner, and Legato gave him the smoothest ride of any horse he'd owned. The air and sunshine had dispersed Ethan's ruminative thoughts, carrying them away like dandelion seeds on a breeze. He felt better than he had in days.

"The ride was a good idea," he said gruffly.

James clapped him on the shoulder. "We'll do it again, old boy."

"Are you staying for tea?"

"It depends. Are you making it?"

"That is what I have a housekeeper for."

As Ethan said the words, he felt a sense of satisfaction. Even though he'd kept to himself this week, he was aware of the changes Mrs. Wood had made. His meals had improved, and his surroundings were noticeably cleaner. As he crossed the entrance hall, pink marble gleamed beneath his boots, and the chandelier cast a sparkling light. A vase bloomed with flowers, their fresh fragrance mingling pleasantly with that of wood polish.

When he first arrived, the only thing he'd wanted was to lick his wounds in private. Perhaps it was due to his improved sleep and eating habits, but after a few days of brooding, he'd concluded that things were not as dire as he supposed. Yes, he'd lost his true passion in life, and yes, he hadn't a clue what to do with himself. Thanks to his investments and an inheritance from his grandmama, however, he had the means to do whatever he wished—including nothing at all. He'd performed out of desire rather than necessity, a privilege that made him luckier than most musicians.

Another blessing was this estate, which he'd purchased because he'd lost a wager, but which was revealing itself to be a diamond in the rough. Again, he gave credit to Mrs. Wood. He'd contemplated his attraction to her, too, and decided that desiring her wasn't wrong if he didn't act upon it. In fact, maybe Mrs. Wood was a test of his self-discipline. Maybe by resisting her he was proving that he was returning to his normal, civilized self...the man he'd been before his injury.

"Mrs. Wood is working out, I take?"

Normally, James's smugness would have irked Ethan, but he supposed he owed his brother for dropping Mrs. Wood into his lap...

No, don't go there.

So much for his improved self-control. An image from last night's dream flashed in his brain: a female naked and on all fours, her pretty bottom jiggling as he swived her from behind. At first, he'd thought she was Sirena, but when she turned her head, her familiar brown eyes had captivated him with a mix of sweet innocence and heady feminine desire.

He'd spent in scorching bursts.

In the dream...and in reality.

By Jove, he was randy and in need of an outlet. His few encounters with Constance had never satisfied his carnal itch, and it had been ages since he'd indulged in his favorite kind of sexual play—the rough, raw, and real kind that would have caused his ex-fiancée to call for smelling salts. Was it any wonder that he was lusting after a young and attractive female in his proximity? The last thing he needed, however, was for his brother to glean on to his desire for his housekeeper.

He schooled his expression. "Mrs. Wood is proficient at her duties…"

He trailed off, his brow furrowing. He must be hearing things. Silence. And then…

The familiar notes made his blood run cold. An instant later, fury rushed through him.

"She wouldn't bloody *dare*," he bit out.

"Dare what?" his brother called behind him.

But he was already stalking to his study.

The piece was exquisite. Entrancing. A work, in truth, of undeniable genius.

As she caressed the keys, Xenia lost herself in the haunting melancholy of the melody.

"What the bloody hell do you think you're doing?"

A startled shriek left her, and she jumped up, whirling around.

She found herself facing Lord Ethan, and he embodied dark and terrifying rage. His face was an icy mask, his eyes burning with violet flames as he blocked the doorway. There was no escape.

Think, Xenia, think.

She racked her brain for excuses, but it was frozen in panic like the rest of her. Her limbs shook with the force of Lord Ethan's ire, which filled the chamber, choking out light and air.

"I…I'm sorry," she whispered.

"You're *sorry*? That is all you have to say?" he roared. "What kind of disrespectful, idiotic, *worthless* housekeeper are you?"

Worthless girl. Disobedient twit. Good for nothing.

She shut out the echoes of the past. Tried to focus on her explanation.

"I didn't mean to—"

"Didn't mean to barge into my private space? To use things that do not belong to you? To violate my trust and my property? Goddammit, woman, you've caused nothing but trouble from the day you started. I should have never taken you on—"

"Easy there, old boy."

The Earl of Manderly appeared behind his brother.

Perfect. Now she had an audience to complete her humiliation.

She curled her hands, fighting the surging heat behind her eyes. *Why do I always ruin everything? Why can't I do anything right?*

"I kn-know what I did was wrong," she said between hitched breaths. "I understand wh-why you're angry."

"You have no bloody idea why I'm angry!" Lord Ethan bellowed.

He raised a fist, and for a terrified instant, she thought he would strike her.

Beat her—like her mama had.

Instead, he grabbed the sheet of music from the piano rack. With savage motions, he ripped it to pieces. His gaze burned into Xenia's through the storm of falling confetti.

"I'm s-sorry for the trouble I've caused." She forced the words through her cinched throat. "I...I'll pack my things straightaway."

She edged toward the doorway. He glowered at her, unmoving, barricading the exit. She prayed that he would let her go—that he wouldn't hurt her. At the last possible instant, he stepped aside. She darted past him and managed to contain her sobs until she reached the servants' corridor.

Chapter Nine

At the knock, Xenia's heart hurtled into her chest. She stared numbly at her overstuffed valise. Her thoughts spun in a chaotic vortex.

I didn't pack fast enough. I shouldn't have borrowed those books from Mr. Khan when I knew my stay was temporary. I need to get out of here, but I have nowhere to go...

"Pardon, Mrs. Wood."

The door opened, and the Earl of Manderly entered. He had the same lord-of-all-he-surveys manner as his brother. He looked as if he'd stepped out of some blueblood's magazine in his green riding jacket, his trousers tucking into his tall, champagne-polished boots. His power and grandeur compounded Xenia's feeling of smallness and insignificance. Her pulse racing, she didn't know what to say. Didn't know if he expected an apology too.

"I am sorry to intrude." His tone was pleasant, the kind one might use when approaching a skittish horse. "I wanted to see how you were."

She found her tongue; it was the wooden object in her mouth. "I'm fine, my lord. I am almost packed. I'll be gone soon, I swear—"

"I hope you won't be."

She blinked at him, not comprehending.

"I came to apologize. On behalf of my brother," the earl clarified.

"That isn't necessary." She shook her head vehemently. "It was my fault. I shouldn't have trespassed, shouldn't have...have used things that weren't mine—"

"Be that as it may. You are not the only one to blame for what transpired."

Twin furrows formed between his brows, as if he were conflicted about what he was to say next. Which was interesting, because he struck her as the sort of man who seldom doubted his own judgment.

Unlike Xenia, who doubted herself all the time. And, obviously, with good reason.

This is why you do not deserve good things. You ruin them. Ruin everything.

Misery settled like an anvil in her stomach. It felt heavy and inescapable. A reality that even *"Pretend until it's true"* wouldn't change.

"I don't suppose my brother has mentioned anything about what happened. Before he came to Chuddums, I mean."

"No, my lord," she said blankly. "Why would he?"

Why would the earl think for a minute that Lord Ethan would talk to her about anything, let alone his past? She was just a servant. Not a very good one at that.

Disrespectful, idiotic, worthless.

Her fantasies about Lord Ethan only made her a bigger fool. Why would he have any interest in her? She had nothing to offer. The only follower she'd attracted was a fellow who'd used her to turn a profit. She'd thought she loved Tony, but for him, she'd merely been a means to an end.

"Right. Ethan's not one to take anyone into his confidence.

Even his own family...*especially* his family." The earl sighed. "And Brunswick and Valentine haven't said anything?"

She furrowed her brow. "About what?"

Instead of answering, the earl rubbed the back of his neck and muttered, "That was an asinine question. Of course those two haven't said anything. They're loyal to a fault."

"Beg pardon, my lord." She was getting more and more confused. "I don't understand what you are referring to. What haven't Brunswick and Mr. Valentine told me?"

During a long pause, the earl seemed to arrive at a decision.

"It has to do with my brother's past," he said curtly. "With what happened to him."

"What happened to Lord Ethan?" she asked.

Because really, who wouldn't?

"If you want to know, you must ask him yourself," the earl said.

"Blooming hell, you cannot bring up a topic and then just—"

She slapped a hand over her mouth to halt the flow of words. *You did not just swear at an earl and insult him.*

Manderly cocked his head. "I suppose I deserved that. Yet I'm still not going to answer your question, Mrs. Wood. If you are curious and brave enough, which I have cause to believe you are, then you will stay and discover what you want to know yourself."

She said nothing. She had no idea why the earl thought those things of her when she was just...herself. Nobody.

"If neither curiosity nor courage are sufficient enticement, then I hope this will be."

Manderly removed an envelope from the inner pocket of his coat, placing it on her escritoire.

She didn't need to look inside the envelope to know that it contained money. *Of course he thinks my compliance can be bought.*

"Lord Ethan doesn't want me to stay," she said categorically.

"You're wrong, Mrs. Wood. He does want you to stay. Needs you to, in fact."

"He said this himself?"

She didn't know why she was challenging the earl. Why she was looking a gift horse in the mouth when she ought to be relieved and grateful that the job might still be hers. Yet the anvil of despair suddenly flamed red-hot in her belly, filling her with unspeakable...anger.

At herself. At Lord Ethan. At the unfairness of it all.

"Not in so many words. But I know my brother, and I know he is sorry for...for overreacting. And for frightening you."

She hated that her fear had been so obvious.

"He wasn't always like this," Manderly said earnestly. "While I know your intention was not to provoke, hearing you play that piano stirred up memories for him. Unhappy ones."

Her resentment withered in the heat of shame. While Lord Ethan's reaction had been nasty, she had partly brought it upon herself. She *had* done all the things he'd accused of her doing, violating his trust and his property. And she'd done it without fully considering the consequences, not just for herself...but for him. She hadn't stopped to think that he might have a reason for keeping the instrument hidden away and that her actions might cause him pain.

He owed her an apology. But maybe she owed him one too.

Drat, drat, and blooming drat. Maybe I should go. Just leave this mess behind.

But how well was that philosophy working for her? While she'd made too many mistakes in life, she strived to be accountable —to herself and, where possible, to the party she'd wronged. For her, it was a point of pride...and what made her different from her mother.

"I will leave you to think things over," the earl said. "However, I can assure you that my brother expects and hopes that you'll accompany him to the mop fair tomorrow morning."

He was nearly at the door when she spoke.

"You left something behind, my lord." She caught up to him,

holding out the envelope. "I do not require an incentive to make my decision."

Smiling slowly, the earl tucked the envelope back into his pocket. "I thought that might be the case."

To her shock, he took her hand and kissed it respectfully before exiting.

Chapter Ten

The mop fair was a bustling event, and as Ethan's carriage pulled into the village square, he saw it was teeming with men and women looking for work. Those hoping to be hired wore emblems to show off their trades. Farmhands had straw tucked in their buttonholes, footmen dressed in old livery, and maids wore aprons over their frocks. Those who didn't have a specific skill carried mops as a sign that they were jacks-of-all-trades. The pool of available help boded well for Ethan's purpose, yet any optimism he felt was dampened by another emotion.

Guilt.

He slid a look at Mrs. Wood, who sat on the opposite bench, as far from him as possible. The morning light touched her mouse-brown hair, giving the illusion of fiery highlights. Her cheeks were pale, and her spectacles didn't hide the tired smudges under her eyes.

His chest tightened. He hadn't slept well either. After his temper ebbed, the undertow of remorse and self-revulsion had pulled him into their dark depths. He'd resisted the melancholy, however; he had to make things right with Mrs. Wood first. He knew he ought to apologize, but he couldn't think of a way to do so without exposing too much.

Without revealing what a bloody damaged bastard he was.

Mrs. Wood's gaze suddenly collided with his, and the hurt in her eyes sliced into his soul. He remembered her fear yesterday when he ripped up the copy of his sonata. The way she'd flinched, as if she thought he might hit her, made him suck in a breath.

You frightened her, you bounder. Caused her pain. Fix it.

The tension in the carriage grew suffocating. He had to say something.

"Thank you," he said.

Her gaze cut to his. "For what?"

For not leaving. For making my life better. For putting up with me.

"Er, for assisting with the hiring today."

Christ, he was an idiot. He wanted to bash his head against the headrest.

She looked out the window. "It is what you pay me for, after all."

If her reply was frosty, he couldn't blame her. Hell, she could call him all the names she wanted, and he would deserve it. Before his injury, he'd never been the type of man to take his temper out on others, no matter what they'd done. And what unforgivable offense had Mrs. Wood committed? She'd cleaned his study and, in the process, discovered his piano studio. Like any curious person (and musician, apparently), she'd played a few notes. She hadn't meant to cause harm.

She couldn't know what the piano meant to him...although he'd rather be drawn and quartered than talk about it.

"I am grateful, nonetheless." He cleared his throat. "For everything you've done for the manor. And for me. I hope...I hope we can put what happened yesterday behind us."

She pursed her too-plump lips, studying him, and he hoped

that she saw his sincerity. For what it was worth. Which, admittedly, wasn't much.

"As you wish," she said primly.

The carriage drew to a stop, putting an end to the awkward exchange.

"Here you go, Mrs. Wood." Mrs. Pettigrew peered anxiously at Xenia. "Taste it and tell me what you think."

They were standing outside the Leaning House. The three-story building was so named because of its visible tilt, a flaw in construction that turned out to be a happy accident as it drew curious customers. In fact, Mrs. Pettigrew played up her establishment's askew charm by painting each story a different color: pink on the bottom, blue in the middle, yellow on the top. Xenia thought the tea house looked like a layer cake created by a whimsical and slightly tipsy baker.

At present, Mrs. Pettigrew had set up a small table with a tray of samples, and she'd waved Xenia over to try her latest concoction. Dutifully, Xenia popped the bite-sized morsel of fried dough into her mouth. The sweet and fluffy concoction was the perfect mix of custardy softness and crispy caramelized edges.

"Well, what do you think? Be honest, now."

Beneath Mrs. Pettigrew's frilled cap, her light-blue eyes were wide. She was a comfortably curvy widow with eight grown children who were scattered across the county. To cope with her empty nest, she took newcomers like Xenia under her wing. She was a gossip, but a kind-hearted one, and Xenia had benefited from her knowledge about the village. Indeed, Mrs. Pettigrew had been the one who'd encouraged her to take up the Earl of Manderly's offer to interview at Bottoms House.

"Ghost or no ghost, an opportunity like that presents itself once in

a blue moon," Mrs. Pettigrew had declared. *"A person has to take risks once in a while if she's to get ahead."*

It turned out to be sage advice. By staying instead of running last night, Xenia had taken another risk. She hadn't seen Lord Ethan until this morning, and she'd braced herself for their encounter. She needn't have.

He'd been unfailingly polite. He'd even given her his version of an apology, which was probably more than most employers would have done. With a prickle of shame, she realized that she hadn't found the courage to admit her own wrongdoing. Confessing that she was a failure at her job wasn't the most pleasant task, especially since she'd been working hard at shedding that version of herself. At becoming a better person.

She had made amends in other ways. She had focused on the task of finding female staff, and by midday, managed to secure housemaids and a cook named Mrs. Johnson, whose references included the owners of two fine estates. A round-cheeked brunette with a cordial manner, Mrs. Johnson was eager to start. She helped Xenia select meats from Mr. Bailey, produce from the Pickleworths, and a flock of chickens from a farmer.

Lord Ethan had seemed pleased by Xenia's productivity. While his comment of "Well done, Mrs. Wood" couldn't be described as effusive, his approval had given her a warm, tingly feeling. Moreover, he'd given her leave to explore the fair while he and Brunswick worked on filling the roster of male servants.

Thus, Xenia had had the chance to wander amongst the colorful barrows and booths that had sprung up on the village green. Vendors offered everything from roasted chestnuts to potions guaranteed to cure a host of diseases. Intrigued, she'd been examining a red glass bottle shaped like a heart when the hawker, a woman with crinkly skin and a mass of ebony curls, startled her with a cackling laugh.

"That's a love potion, dearie," the woman said with a wink. "If you've a sweetheart who doesn't return your fancy, a few drops will change 'is mind."

For some reason, Xenia's gaze had searched out Lord Ethan. To her horror, he'd been standing a few feet away, looking straight at her. Her heart thudding, she'd shoved the bottle back at the seller and fled. She'd been flagged down by Mrs. Pettigrew, who was now awaiting her response.

"I am not certain what I think of this new dish," Xenia said.

Mrs. Pettigrew's face fell.

Xenia gave her an impish smile. "Another sample might help me decide."

With a relieved chuckle, Mrs. Pettigrew obliged. She placed her chapped hands on her generous hips as Xenia savored her second helping.

"Oh, you had me going there for a moment, Mrs. Wood. I must say I am relieved you're enjoying my Poor Knights o' Windsor pudding. It comes from an old family recipe, passed on from my great-grandmama, and I haven't served it before."

"It's delectable." Xenia licked sugar off her lips. "Why hasn't it been on your menu?"

"My great-grandmama's original recipe is for 'Bloody Poor Knights' pudding, a creation that made her famous countywide. She called it 'bloody' on account o' the sauce she drizzled over the pudding, made from a type o' cherry grown only in Chuddums. Used to be, the village was known as 'Chudleigh Blossoms' on account o' how plentiful the cherry trees were. Then all the orchards started dying."

Xenia drew her brows together. "What happened?"

"The curse, that's what," Mrs. Pettigrew said gloomily. "After Thomas Mulligan died, the cherry trees started to wither. Year by year, the orchards grew thinner, and the few trees that survived stopped bearing fruit. Many townsfolk lost their livelihoods. My grandma retired her mama's recipe because she said it weren't the same without the cherries...and only the Chudleigh Bottoms's cherries would do."

"Well, I am glad you revived it," Xenia said sincerely. "Cherries or no cherries, your pudding is delicious."

"Thank you, dear. Let's pray that it draws customers."

The proprietress narrowed her eyes as a trio of ruffians sporting striped neckerchiefs staggered by, bellowing a rude song and snarling at frightened villagers, who scrambled out of their way.

In an undertone, she added, "Let us also pray that the riffraff doesn't scare off the decent folk. If this keeps up, Chuddums will be filled with nothing but Corrigans."

"Corrigans?" Xenia asked.

"Not so loud." Mrs. Pettigrew glanced around nervously before replying. "The Corrigans are the gang that have taken over the docks. Their members wear those neckcloths with orange stripes, and make no mistake, they're a shady bunch. A cousin o' mine who works at the Redding constabulary says the Corrigans are suspected o' burglaries and other crimes, but the evidence and witnesses against them have a way o' disappearing. They're the worst sort o' trouble—take my advice and steer clear o' them, do you hear me?"

While Xenia doubted that the Corrigans could be worse than her mother when it came to villainy, she nodded. She had no intention of going anywhere near the gang.

"Now I must get to work. Enjoy the fair, dear." Mrs. Pettigrew straightened her shoulders, and hefting her tray, strode into the crowd. "Try my Poor Knights Pudding, fresh and tasty!"

Xenia continued her stroll around the square. She waved at Wally, who was happily giving tours to unsuspecting visitors. When she passed Mr. Bailey's and Mr. Khan's shops, she saw both men were busy with customers and did a happy skip on their behalf. At the Briarbush Inn, Mr. Thornton insisted on serving her a cup of cider on the house. She thanked him and bought one of his wife's golden-brown mushroom pies to enjoy away from the hustle and bustle.

She exited the square in search of a quiet spot. Turning right on a small street called "Spring Lane," she saw that it was deserted. Most of the storefronts were boarded up, and the few places open for business were empty, their half-closed shutters giving them a sleepy look.

A sudden shout snagged her attention.

"Let me go, you bastard!"

The female voice was familiar, and without thinking, Xenia dashed toward it. Two alleyways down, she spotted Alice. Her friend was being pinned against a brick wall by a large, menacing male.

"You weren't so hoity-toity last night, you stupid slut," he snarled. "I said I'll pay for the upright this time."

"I don't want your blooming money. Now get off me," Alice screeched.

The bastard grabbed her skirts, shoving them up as she struggled. "If you don't want to be paid, then I'll sample your bleedin' wares for free—"

"Let her go!" Xenia ran toward her friend.

The brute turned his head, and his lust-glazed eyes stopped Xenia in her tracks. He had dirty-blond hair, arrogantly handsome features, and the familiar, orange-striped neckerchief tied around his neck. He was drunk in a way that made him more, not less, dangerous.

His eyes slitted in a speculative manner. "If it isn't a little lost kitten."

Xenia's palms turned clammy, but she knew better than to show fear, which was an aphrodisiac to bastards like him.

"Let my friend go, and there won't be any trouble," she said evenly.

To her surprise, the ruffian released Alice. The latter stumbled, catching her balance on the opposite wall. Xenia noticed her friend's eyes were also bloodshot from drinking.

"I've let 'er go." The cad leered at Xenia. "What do I get in return?"

Xenia forced herself to stand her ground. "A clean conscience?"

"Ain't got no use for that. I'd rather 'ave some company."

He moved with shocking speed, grabbing her before she could get away. The next instant, she was shoved against the wall, sandwiched between brick and a heavy wall of muscle. A wave of panic crashed over her.

"Alice, help me!" she shouted.

Her friend stared at her...then took off down the alleyway.

Stunned, Xenia registered the trouble she was in. She opened her mouth, but the blackguard gripped her by the throat, strangling her scream for help.

"Now that the old slattern is gone, we can 'ave ourselves some fun." He oozed a noxious odor of spirits and sweat. "I've been hankering for some fresh meat."

When Xenia thrashed, trying to get free, he squeezed until stars floated in her vision. Darkness threatened to suck her under, but she continued to struggle, trying to push him off—

He flew backward, hitting the opposite wall with a loud thud.

She wheezed, filling her lungs with air.

Am I...am I stronger than I realize?

Then Lord Ethan stepped into view. He hauled the protesting ruffian up. The brute threw a sudden punch, and she gasped when it connected with Lord Ethan's jaw. The latter showed no reaction, and any wise person would find his stoicism foreboding. The brute, of course, didn't take the hint and swung again. This time Lord Ethan caught his fist, twisting it in a quick, controlled motion.

The brute yelped, holding his injured arm. "You're going to

pay for that! Do you know who I am? I'm Patrick Harlow, head o' the Corrigans—"

Lord Ethan drove his fist into the other's jaw. He pinned the ruffian with his left forearm, pummeling Harlow's face with savage right jabs. His technique was unique and effective, resulting in blood...a lot of it. When he was done, Harlow lay slumped in the dirt, moaning incoherently.

Lord Ethan looked down at his vanquished foe. "Touch my housekeeper again," he said with a soft snarl, "and I will finish you."

Then he raised his gaze to hers. She saw the primal blaze in his eyes, blood dripping from his gloved fist. Her rescuer was a beast of a prince.

She shivered, not with fear...but something far more dangerous.

Something she could no longer deny.

Chapter Eleven

"There is no need to fuss," Ethan said.

"I am the housekeeper. It is my job to fuss."

"I relinquish you of that duty."

"It's too late for that," she said. "I already went to the trouble of gathering the supplies from the stillroom. Now sit."

She pointed at the chair as if she were a governess and he a wayward schoolboy. Perhaps she felt comfortable asserting her authority because they were in the servants' hall. He decided to go along, mostly because he didn't wish to fight with her. The aftermath of violence still simmered in his veins, and he didn't trust himself to give rein to his emotions.

Especially where she was concerned.

As he sat, the image of that bastard Harlow groping her, *choking* her flashed in his mind's eye, and his insides tightened like a coil. She'd looked so small and vulnerable...though not powerless. Despite her assailant's grip on her throat, she'd fought like a wildcat. Thus, he'd discovered another fact about Jane Wood.

She had courage. In spades.

He tucked away the pebble of knowledge along with the others he'd collected. It had become a hobby, trying to figure out his housekeeper.

More like an obsession, and you know it.

She intrigued him, he realized. She was like Beethoven's *Grosse Fuge*: intricate, paradoxical, at times indecipherable. Although critics had panned the maestro's composition, Ethan loved it for its unapologetic embracing of chaos and complexity and all the tender moments in between. It was music that he would never grow tired of listening to.

Mrs. Wood fiddled with the objects she'd set on the table before turning to him. Given her petite stature, she barely had to bend to touch his jaw, examining the injury. Her scent wafted to his nostrils, herbal and feminine and clean. The gentle brush of her fingertips sent a sizzle to his loins; he inhaled sharply.

"Does that hurt?" Behind her spectacles, her eyes were that of a worried doe.

I ache like the devil. But not because of the scratch on my face.

"No," he said.

"Thankfully, the cut on your jaw looks shallow, but I'm going to clean it with witch hazel. This may sting."

What stung was how close she was, practically standing between his splayed thighs. What stung was how he burned to pull her closer and how he had to grip his thigh to prevent himself from doing so. The minuscule burn of the witch hazel?

That was nothing.

To distract himself, he said, "You seem to have experience dealing with injuries."

"They were...um, commonplace in my family."

He wondered why she'd hesitated in her reply. "Do you have brothers?"

"I have no siblings." She gazed at her handiwork. "That's much better."

She seemed satisfied; at least one of them was.

"Now I'll have a look at your hands," she went on. "Remove your gloves, if you please."

"That isn't necessary."

Her forehead pleated as she peered at his hands.

He wondered if she noticed that one was balled while the other was barely curled. In the time that she'd been working for him, he hadn't been around her all that much. During those times, he realized with a twinge of humiliation, he'd taken pains to hide his condition.

"I'll be gentle," she coaxed. "There is no need to worry."

"I am not worried," he said tightly. "I said I'm fine."

"You punched the living daylights out of that brute." Her voice had a new, husky edge...lingering nerves, no doubt. "No one has ever come to my aid in such a fashion. It was the most heroic thing I've ever seen."

Heroic? His chest expanded. At the same time, he was outraged that she'd gone this long without anyone to protect her.

"Why were you in the alleyway?" he said suddenly. "Did that bastard lure you there?"

"Not exactly. He was harassing an acquaintance, and I went to help." A quiver entered Mrs. Wood's voice. "But once she got free, she ran off and left me to fend for myself."

"No good deed goes unpunished," he said bitterly.

Bloody hell, how he understood the truth of that adage.

"In this instance, I cannot argue." She heaved a sigh. "But as your knuckles suffered for my folly, I ought to take a look at them."

He yanked his hands out of her reach. "Leave it."

"Why won't you take off your gloves..."

He saw the instant comprehension hit her. Her eyes darted to his left hand, and her lips parted. Fury surged, but it wasn't aimed at her. He was angry at himself—at his shame and inability to move on. Why in blazes did he bother hiding his injury? Why did he care that Constance had swooned the first time she glimpsed his hand without its glove? Or that the sight of it had once brought

Mama and Gigi to tears? Even Papa had had to clear his throat and look away.

Suddenly, Ethan was tired of concealing his disability. Tired of caring about how it affected others around him. Tired of pretending that he was like everyone else...that he was the man he used to be.

"You want to heal me?" he clipped out. "Have at it."

A perverse part of him wanted to strip off his left glove with dramatic flair...like a magician revealing a sleight of hand (a pun—wasn't he the clever one?). Instead, he had to inch the snug black leather off his stiffened fingers one by one. During Ethan's initial recovery, the physician had fashioned a glove to support his healing hand. He had continued to wear the covering, partially because the compression eased the contracture and aching, but mostly to keep away prying eyes.

In London, his ploy hadn't worked. Polite society stared at his hand anyway, whispering about his infirmity behind waving fans and in the private rooms of the gentlemen's clubs. Instead of hiding his changed state, the gloves became a magnet for curiosity and gossip. For scurrilous speculation about the nature of his damage and what had caused it.

To this day, only a few people—his physician, family, and trusted servants—knew how he'd injured his hand. Even Constance hadn't been privy to the full details. Since she'd never asked, he'd spared her delicate sensibilities.

He managed to remove the glove, and he saw with grim surprise that Mrs. Wood had been correct: during the fight with Harlow, he had wounded this hand as well. Due to his dulled sensation there, he hadn't felt the swelling or broken skin. Even though he'd punched with his right, in his rage he must have gotten in a few licks with his left too.

The torn skin was nothing compared to the permanent mutila-tion. Thick, pinkish scars welted his palm and the back of his hand. They were accompanied by the tracks of the stitches that had put him back together again. Like Humpty Dumpty of nursery fame, he was never again as he was before. His fingers were gnarled; he couldn't fully straighten them or move them with anything near his former dexterity. Parts of his hand were numb yet still ached. He couldn't grip, carry out fine movements, or play the piano.

The physician had told him that he was fortunate to have kept his hand. He knew he ought to be grateful, but at times he struggled. *Bloody hell*, he struggled.

Looking at his left hand, which felt like a dead weight, he saw more than mangled flesh and bone. He saw everything he'd once been. Everything he'd lost.

Xenia's throat clogged as the pieces came together.

Lord Ethan hadn't worn gloves to be fashionable. What she'd believed to be vanity on his part was, in fact, an attempt to conceal an injury. Looking at his damaged hand, it was obvious that he'd been in a dreadful accident. She thought of his hidden piano, that beautiful unfinished sonata... Her chest squeezed as she began to comprehend what the tragedy might have taken from him.

"My right hand bore the brunt of today's fight. If you wish to tend to it, I'll need help getting the glove off. The left being what it is."

His stoic expression made the anguish in his eyes that much more obvious.

"I'm sorry," she whispered.

"The last thing I want is your damned pity."

She didn't react to his snarl because she understood that she wasn't the target of his rage.

"That is not what I meant. I'm not sorry for your injury— though I am, of course," she said haltingly. "I'm apologizing because I made you remove your glove when it was not my place."

"You do not have the power to *make* me do anything, Mrs. Wood." He was testy now, and who could blame him? "Are you going to deal with the scrapes or not?"

But his wounds were more than the broken skin of his knuckles. More even than the damage done to his left hand. They went deeper, straight to the soul of a man who'd lost his ability to express his passion, his art...*himself.*

How I *would feel if I lost my voice and my ability to tell stories.*

Emotion overwhelmed her. Instinctively, she lifted his large hand in both of hers and brushed her lips gently over the scars. He jerked but didn't pull away. When she let go of him, his turbulent gaze locked with hers. In that moment, she saw how raw and exposed he was and couldn't let him feel that way alone.

"I'm sorry for playing your piano," she said, her voice serrated with emotion. "And your composition. I shouldn't have violated your privacy."

"Forget it."

"I can be impulsive, and I have a bad habit of not doing what I'm told to," she plunged on. "My mama wasn't one to give proper guidance, and my papa tried to teach me right from wrong, but he...he died when I was young. I had to figure things out on my own. Although I try to act the way a good and respectable person would, I make bad decisions all the time."

"We all make mistakes," he said roughly. "You are a good woman."

A pang hit her chest. "You wouldn't think that if you truly knew me."

If you knew I was lying about who I am. If you knew about my past and the things I've done. If you knew that people have died because of me.

If you knew...me.

"You are a woman who convinced servants to work here even though every idiot in the village believes this place is haunted."

"We don't know that Bloody Thom *isn't* real," she felt obliged to say.

He aimed his gaze heavenward before continuing.

"You're also a woman who villagers greet by name, even though you've been here less than a fortnight. You put yourself at risk to help others—something we will be discussing, by the by. And you win over grumpy butlers and even grumpier masters."

Her heart fluttered. She couldn't believe that he'd noticed these things. That he was *saying* these things.

"Brunswick isn't grumpy," she blurted.

Lord Ethan stared at her. Then he did something she'd never seen him do.

He smiled.

It wasn't a big smile and looked like it required effort. Yet it transformed him; in a blink, he went from broodingly handsome to utterly irresistible. His next words knocked her wayward heart farther off course.

"I'm sorry," he said gruffly. "For what I said to you when I found you at the piano. It was unpardonably rude, and I didn't mean it."

"I deserved it. I had no right to intrude—there or in the attic room."

"I had no right to tear into you like that." He drew a breath. "I can have a devil of a temper, but I hope you believe me when I say that I would never lay a hand on you. I would never do you harm."

"I believe you." She'd been around enough brutes to know that he wasn't one. "But I am at fault as well. In both cases, I should have known better than to trespass, but I did so anyway because I... I was so curious, you see."

"About what?"

She could have said that her curiosity had been of the idle sort. She could have lied and had done so for lesser reasons. Yet she couldn't bring herself to do so now.

"About you." Her cheeks warmed.

"What have you discovered about me thus far?"

The warmth in his eyes unraveled her good sense.

"To start, you are gallant and protective. You came to my aid with the bats even though I failed to heed your warning. Then you rescued me from that brute today. No one's ever defended me like that before," she said earnestly.

"Any gentleman would have done the same," he said dismissively.

Life had taught her that was untrue. She'd been accosted by more than her fair share of so-called gentlemen. Since she couldn't say that without giving away too much of her past, she kept the focus on him.

"I've also discovered that you are artistic and creative," she said. "A brilliant musician."

The warmth fled his eyes.

"Once upon a time that might have been true," he said starkly. "Now I can no longer play."

Her heart ached for him. "I cannot imagine how difficult that must be."

He scrutinized her, and she was careful to keep pity out of her expression. It wasn't what she felt, anyway. She felt for his situation, but she didn't feel sorry for him...not with his talent and abilities.

"The change hasn't been easy," he said wryly.

"But surely that shouldn't stop you from composing? That piece you began, it is lovely and full of such passion and feeling—"

"I don't wish to talk about it."

"You cannot allow your talent to go to waste," she persisted.

"My personal affairs don't concern you. Kindly drop the matter."

Even though she probably deserved it, the harshness of his tone hurt. *You're just a servant, a nobody. Your opinion means nothing to him.*

"I overstepped," she mumbled. "I'll, um, just leave you to—"

She took a step back, but he caught her wrist. Startled, she met his gaze. Frustration turned his irises a smoky violet, but there was something else there too.

Longing. It elicited a shivery, electric awareness in her.

"Devil take it, I'm sorry," he said hoarsely. "Don't leave."

Their eyes held.

In the next instant, he pulled her onto his lap. Stunned, she didn't react quickly enough when he removed her spectacles and set them on the table. She blinked, her heart racing as his gaze roved over her upturned face. When she tried to turn away, he caught her chin between his finger and thumb, holding her steady.

"You have freckles," he murmured.

Blooming hell, my face paint must have rubbed off.

Panic thrummed. "I, um, yes. I can't seem to get rid of them—"

"I like them."

Startled, she said, "You do?"

"I like a lot of things about you."

She gaped at him, no words emerging.

He cupped her cheek, his thumb sliding along the slope of her cheekbone.

Dazed, she said, "I...I, um, like you too, my lord."

"Ethan."

"What?" she asked.

She was distracted by the way he traced his thumb over her lips. Soft and tender, his touch conveyed a world of feeling. A musician's touch.

"I like you, *Ethan*," he prompted.

"Oh," she said shyly. "I like you...Ethan."

His nostrils flared, then he bent and covered her mouth with his. His kiss was everything she'd dreamed a kiss could be. Commanding yet courting, firm yet gentle. He gave even as he took, and her shock gave way to dizzying pleasure. So *this* was what passion felt like. This was why poets wrote sonnets and musicians composed songs. This was what she'd imagined when she spun her wicked tales.

Heat licked through her as Ethan deepened the pressure, his lips coaxing hers to open. His tongue entered her with a sensual authority that made it easy to yield. To melt. Her thoughts liquified like honey left in the sun, and she floated in the sweetness of his kiss. His flavor was rich and deep, his need undeniable. She was ravenous, too. When he licked inside her, she intuitively sucked on his offering.

His groan reverberated down her throat. His maleness made her quiver from head to toe, his spicy musk and bunching strength engulfing her senses. His mouth left hers, searching out her ear, and the hot, wet lick set fire to her blood. In theory, she'd known that the ear was a sensitive organ. But abstract knowledge did not prepare her for the reality of being suckled by Ethan. He flicked her lobe with his tongue, then drew it deep into his mouth, the moist tug seeming to pull at her core. Her nipples pulsed, her blood rushed, and she whimpered.

"You're responsive," he murmured.

That was one way of putting it. She would go out of her skin if he didn't kiss her again. So she kissed him. Throwing her arms around his neck, she smooshed her mouth to his. Hungrily, desperately. The world spun, and suddenly she was sitting on the table while he stood between her spread thighs. He tilted her head back, plundering her mouth while she clung to his rock-hard shoulders.

He cupped the side of her neck, running his palm over her shoulder and to her breast. He squeezed gently, and she gasped as her nipple rubbed against the stiff fabric of her corset. He did it again, the blissful sparks coalescing between her legs. The throbbing ache in her pussy grew, and she felt as if she might come apart if something didn't give.

"Please." She wetted her lips. "I want you."

His expression was dark with craving. "You'll have me," he vowed.

With thrilling dominance, he pushed her back onto the table—

Crack.

She felt something crumple between her shoulder blades.

The next instant, Ethan pulled her up again. Reaching behind her, he grabbed something...her spectacles. They were mangled, cracks spreading like spiderwebs through the lenses. He stared at them, and his expression hardened.

"Forgive me," he said in a low voice.

"It's nothing..."

The rest of her words died in her throat. Even her desire-fogged mind recognized the look in his eyes. They were no longer bright with passion but...disgust? Her breath lodged.

"This should not have happened." He clenched his jaw. "You work for me. You are my housekeeper."

She nodded, trying to breathe. To fight back the heat pushing behind her eyes.

He doesn't want you. Why would he? You're just a stupid, worthless girl no one loves.

"What I did was unpardonable. Especially after what you've just gone through." His gaze was locked on her spectacles. "I will, of course, replace these. As for the rest—"

"Do not concern yourself." She forced out the words. "Mistakes happen, my lord."

He might regret kissing her, a lowly servant, but she would hold her head high.

His eyes hooded. "It was a mistake. Right."

"We'll forget this happened," she said as briskly as she could.

"Is that what you want?"

"It is the sensible option, sir."

A crease appeared between his brows. "And you will stay? Be my housekeeper?"

Of course that is his priority. Having someone to manage his blooming house.

Even if she had somewhere to go, the fact was that she liked her current situation...except for the humiliating incident that had just taken place with the lummox across from her. An ember smoked beneath her breastbone. While she might not be good enough to be his lover, she had *earned* the right to keep his house.

She lifted her chin. "I am not going anywhere."

"I am glad to hear it," he said softly.

Needing to get away, she hopped off the table. Unfortunately, she'd used up her starch, and her knees wobbled. He caught her, and the contact with his hard length did not help her equilibrium *at all*.

"Have a care, Mrs. Wood."

"I'm fine." She pushed him away. "If you'll excuse me, I have duties to attend to."

She exited the servants' hall, feeling the burn of his gaze.

Chapter Twelve

"I'm sorry for running, Mary. I panicked."

Sitting at the scarred dressing table, Xenia met Alice's pleading gaze in the mirror. She had been putting on the last touches of her nun's costume when Alice found her. Resentment at the other's betrayal smoldered, and Ethan's words snuck into her head.

No good deed goes unpunished.

Not that she wanted to think about him. After their kiss, he'd left for London, accompanied by Mr. Valentine. He'd been gone a week, and Brunswick had no idea when he would be back. He hadn't left her any message...which was no surprise. He'd made it crystal clear that he regretted kissing her. That he saw her as his servant and nothing more.

Two could play at that game.

Henceforth, she would only think of him in professional terms. She concentrated on her duties, determined to prove how capable she was. Luckily, Daisy and Berta, the maids she'd hired at the mop fair, were there to help. Daisy, a robust brunette, was a bit domineering, but timid blonde Berta had an easygoing nature that balanced things out. They'd cleaned the manor from top to bottom and helped Xenia replace the moth-eaten curtains with new ones purchased from the village draper.

William and Fred, the new footmen, were young but progressing under Brunswick's guidance. William was shy, perhaps due to his unfortunate case of the spots. Xenia had given him one of her creams, which contained calendula to soothe his skin, and his complexion was on the mend. Fred was also a bit reticent, unless he was around animals. He was the only one who could manage the rooster Xenia had bought at the mop fair.

Dubbed "Brutus" by the staff, the bird strutted around the coop, his bright-red comb resembling an ancient Spartan helmet. Vigilant and bloodthirsty, Brutus attacked anyone he perceived as a threat to the hens. He made an exception for Fred, whom he graciously allowed into his domain to collect eggs.

In addition to the new household staff, Xenia had managed to retain the services of carpenters. Mr. Bailey had introduced her to his cousins twice removed, Thomas and Reggie Hirschfield. Expert woodworkers, the Hirschfield brothers had restored the double staircase and were fixing up the rest of Bottoms House. Day by day, Xenia could see her vision for the manor unfolding. As she knew from her experience living in dumps, a little care went a long way.

Give a house some care and attention, and it gives you what you need.

By the time Lord Ethan returned—if he returned—he would be in for a surprise. Xenia was going to stun him with her household management skills. She would prove to him that she was a consummate professional...and that she hadn't given their stupid kiss another thought.

She told herself that things had worked out for the best. She needed her independence, not some grumpy and uppity lover. Thus, when the Abbess had left word of this evening's masquerade, Xenia had jumped at the opportunity to resurrect Sister Sirena. The event was at a tucked-away manor several miles from

Chuddums. Until the bawd could secure a permanent location, the masquerades had to be impromptu affairs, but news had spread, and the crowd downstairs surpassed even that of the old venue.

It was the perfect opportunity for Xenia to add to her savings. But first she had to deal with her colleague.

"Forget about it," she said coolly as she adjusted her wimple.

"You can forgive me?" Alice's blue eyes shimmered with remorse.

Alice was the brothel's most sought-after light-skirt not just because of her sensual blonde looks. She was also a talented actress; she'd only shown her true colors when she'd abandoned the friend who'd come to her aid. While Xenia's mama had derided her for being weak and stupid, Xenia was not a simpleton and learned from her mistakes.

Fool me once, shame on you. Fool me twice, shame on me.

"I can move past what happened," Xenia replied.

"You're such a good sport, dear!" Alice hugged her, enveloping her in a cloying rose scent. "I swear on my mama's grave that the next time I'm at the docks, I won't give that bastard Patrick Harlow the time o' day."

Xenia's stare was incredulous. "You intend to return to the docks? Alice, after what happened—"

"Like I said, I'll steer clear o' Harlow."

"He's part of the Corrigans, you know. A notorious gang. You don't want that trouble in your life—"

"Ain't you sweet to care?" Alice cooed, patting her on the cheek. "But I can take care o' myself. Speaking o' which, I got gentlemen to entertain and so do you. I shall see you later."

The light-skirt sauntered off, leaving a trail of perfume.

As Ethan entered the masquerade, he wondered if his presence was a mistake.

In its prior incarnation, the Nunnery had offered a private entrance to see Sister Sirena, making it possible to avoid other guests. The promise of anonymous pleasure, with no physical contact, had led him to seek her out that first time. He'd gone in with little expectation and left with more than he'd bargained for.

Tonight, however, things felt...wrong.

There were too many people, for one thing. By the looks of the fashionable crowd, a goodly number of the attendees had come from London. Undoubtedly, this was due to the Abbess's discreet advertisements in a prominent London newspaper about her "revived entertainments." It was how he had learned about tonight's event. Even though he was masked, the last thing he wanted was to run into an acquaintance. While in Town last week, he hadn't ventured to his clubs or any of the places where he would have to endure polite conversation and pitying looks.

He'd needed time to himself...and time away from Jane.

Recalling how he'd smashed Jane's spectacles, he felt his chest tighten. The sight of her mangled frames had brought him to his senses: in his damaged state, he had no right to get involved with her. Moreover, she'd just survived an assault, *and* she was his employee...and there he was, pawing at her. It didn't matter that they'd shared the hottest, most carnal kiss he'd ever experienced. He had acted no better than the bastard he'd dispatched in the alleyway.

He realized that Jane was the main reason his presence here felt wrong. Yet he was hardly betraying her: at best, their relationship was professional, and at worst...God, he hoped she didn't hate him, though he'd earned her enmity. In fact, he'd come tonight to discharge his lust—so that he wouldn't give in to his filthy impulses toward his little housekeeper. Talking with Sirena would distract him, give him something else to fantasize about. Something other than kissing Jane again, bending her over his desk, and plowing her until she screamed his name.

He consulted his pocket watch. As he had time before his appointment with Sirena, he might as well circulate. He followed the crowd toward the public rooms. He didn't know how the Abbess had managed to secure the country house for her event, but she'd transformed it into a Bacchanalia, a celebration of the god of wine and ecstasy. Vines of plump grapes were draped along the corridor, and the air was heavy with incense.

In the drawing room, festivities were in progress. A dozen light-skirts were dancing to the clapping and whistling of the masked guests. Ethan guessed they were supposed to be Maenads, their bodies draped in filmy veils. They whirled through the room, teasing the audience by shedding their coverings piece by piece. Once naked, they proudly displayed their wares, pushing up their breasts and bending over to show their pink folds glistening with oil. They whipped the crowd into a frenzy, men shouting out bids for the pleasure of their company.

A pair of naked blonde doxies sauntered up to Ethan and flanked him. The one on his left was tall and slender, the other short and voluptuous.

"Looking for company, sir?" The taller one spoke through rouged lips. "I'm Alice, and this is Annie. We're sisters."

He didn't think they were sisters any more than they were true blondes. As neither feature held any particular appeal for him, he politely declined.

"Are you certain, luvie?" Annie pressed her generous breasts against his arm. "Double the pleasure, double the fun."

The women leaned in, their mouths meeting in front of his. Although his brows elevated at the acrobatic agility of their tongues, that was the only part of him to rise.

He extricated himself. "I have a prior engagement."

"'Ere to see Sirena, are you? She 'as a talented tongue, that's for certain. But so do I." Annie winked. "Take me into the room wif you, and when she gets to the climax o' the story, I'll get you to a real one, eh?"

"Or take me," Alice cooed. "I'm at my best on my knees."

While he didn't doubt the light-skirts' claims, he didn't want to share his time with Sirena. The intimacy he'd felt with her, even though it wasn't real, was the reason he'd returned.

"Good evening, ladies."

He bowed and walked away, leaving behind the pouting pair. As he made his way deeper into the masquerade, the lighting dimmed, along with the crowd's inhibitions. In the music room, a prostitute was playing the piano—badly, in part because she was also bouncing on a guest's lap. She pounded on his prick and on the keys, and it was clear which was her true skill. Ethan cringed as she massacred blameless arpeggios. Her audience was less discerning. Sprawled in chairs, masked men were watching her, their fingers clenching in the hair of the kneeling whores whose heads bobbed in rhythm to the clamor that approximated music.

Ethan continued to the ballroom, which had been transformed into a Roman hall...an appropriate setting for the orgy that was taking place amidst the plaster columns and lush potted palms. Guests were taking full advantage of the long banquet table, upon which whores had arranged themselves like a carnal feast. A brunette on all fours took a fellow in her mouth and from behind. Next to her, a sandy blonde sat astride a guest while frigging two others.

Draped over the far end of the table, a group of five were connected in a writhing chain. The head of the line, a redhead lying on her back with a hirsute fellow thrusting heavily into her, smiled and crooked a finger at Ethan. He shook his head and moved on. The surrounding carnality, while provocative, did little to stir him. He craved something else...something more. And it was nearing time for him to have it.

He exited the ballroom and mounted the steps to the next floor. A footman directed him to Sirena's "confessional," which turned out to be a bedchamber at the end of the hall. The attendant at the door bade him to wait. A few minutes later, the door opened, and a patron strolled out, his smile satisfied beneath his demi-mask.

Ethan felt a hot stab in his chest. It was stupid, he knew. Sirena made her living seducing men with her stories. Intimacy was an illusion she wove.

Nothing about this is real.

He didn't know if he felt relieved or disappointed.

"Your turn, guv." The footman smirked. "Enjoy your confession."

Inside the chamber, a white curtain hung from ceiling to floor, dividing the small room in half. Ethan's pulse quickened when he saw Sirena. Although she was still a shadow, the fabric barrier revealed more of her than the window of her old confessional. Reclined upon a chaise, she presented a tantalizing silhouette. She wore her trademark wimple with paganistic wings and appeared otherwise naked. Her back was arched, her breasts perfect globes with jutting tips. One of her legs was bent at the knee, the other lying straight. While her legs weren't long, they were shapely, leading to a nicely rounded bottom.

In fact, he realized with a trickle of heat, in shadow she could pass for a more voluptuous version of Jane.

"Welcome to my confessional, sir."

Although her voice had captivated him during their last encounter, the original confessional must have muted its power. Her sultry tones poured through the fabric partition, and he inhaled, feeling as if he'd downed a snifter of brandy. Hot, smoky, and potent, her words swirled his blood and whetted his appetite.

"I am Sister Sirena, the Nunnery's sensational and salacious storyteller. Tonight, I will enchant you with a story woven from your deepest, innermost desires. My voice will transport you to a world where pleasure is everything, and nothing is forbidden."

"Nothing is forbidden?" he asked.

She gave a visible start, sitting up straight.

Did she remember him? He'd only come to her that one time, weeks ago, and she must have countless clients.

"You...you were here before."

He was absurdly gratified that she'd remembered.

"Yes," he said.

"It was *you*," she breathed. "You're the fellow. The one who... who wanted something real."

While he was pleased to have made an impression, her words had an odd inflection that he didn't understand. Her posture was upright, and he felt the heat of her stare through the curtain. He wondered uneasily if returning had been a mistake. If his memory of their prior encounter had been idealized. Then she relaxed, reclining against the chaise and curling toward him like they were having an intimate *tête-à-tête*.

"I hoped you would visit again, sir."

Her sultry register wove its usual spell on his senses. He was drawn back to the moment. Back to the world of fantasy where he could have whatever he wanted.

"You made an impression the last time," he said.

"The feeling is mutual, darling. What kind of story do you desire from me today?"

Her purring words coaxed the truth from him.

"Tell me one about a housekeeper," he said.

CHAPTER THIRTEEN

Lord Ethan was my princely patron.

Now he's back and wants a fantasy...about a housekeeper.

About me?

Xenia didn't know which of those discoveries shocked her the most. During their first session in the confessional, she'd pictured her patron as a golden-haired prince whose sensual dominance had seduced her utterly. Then she'd met Lord Ethan, and he'd seemed the opposite: dark and aloof, arrogant and unfeeling...with a beastly temper to boot. She supposed it wasn't surprising that she hadn't put two and two together.

Sitting across from him now, with only a curtain separating them, she had no doubt that her shadowy patron *was* Ethan Harrington. While the old confessional had muffled his voice, his deep tones penetrated the fabric clearly. He was seated in a wingchair, and there was no mistaking his virile silhouette, nor the fact that the hands that lay on the arms of the chair were gloved. Yet her certainty about his identity came from her primal awareness of him...an awareness that had flourished since she'd been in his employ.

Emotions clamored in her chest. Joy and fear. Giddy delight.

He wants me. And I want him too.

The wall she'd erected around her heart crumpled like paper in a fist and left her exposed to a host of conflicting desires. While she couldn't deny her attraction to him, she had to proceed with caution. If he knew that his housekeeper was also an infamous brothel worker, he would throw her out on the spot.

Never mind that Jane Wood wasn't even her real identity.

Yet Lord Ethan hadn't been entirely forthcoming either. If he wanted her, why had he rejected her so soundly? Why had he left for London without a word? Was she reading too much into his request for a fantasy about a housekeeper?

I must discover his true desires.

Determination filled her. Not for the first time, she thanked the Lord for the gift of her voice—the instrument she could play with such precision. As Sirena, she sounded entirely different from herself...and she needed to keep it that way.

"Once upon a time," she said in honeyed tones, "there was a young woman named Ella. When her papa died, she was left in the care of her stepmother, who was beautiful but cruel. The step-mama fancied herself a lady and treated Ella like a servant, beating and berating her. Our heroine did her best to perform the chores that were asked of her. The work was awful and demanding, leaving her covered in cinders and dirt—"

"I think I know this story," Lord Ethan said.

"You haven't heard this version," Xenia said confidently. "Ella's situation grew so unbearable that, one day, she ran away. In need of money, she found a job as a housekeeper. Ella's employer was a man named Mr. Prince."

"How fitting."

"Mr. Prince was the sort of fellow Ella had dreamed about. He was tall, dark, and handsome. Unfortunately, he could be surly."

"And she still liked him?"

His wistful words tugged at her heart.

"She did," Xenia affirmed. "Because she knew he was a gentleman at heart. He appreciated her housekeeping efforts and treated her with respect. When burglars broke in one night, he fought them off and protected her. Moreover, he confided in Ella and made her feel special, like no one else ever had. She found herself falling for him...which was a bad thing."

"Why?" He sat up straighter in the wingchair. "Why was it bad?"

Exhaling, she let out the truth. "Because she knew that she wasn't good enough for him."

"He wouldn't care about their differences in station," he said dismissively. "Not if he was the gentleman she believed him to be."

His reply made Xenia both giddy and anxious. While Lord Ethan might not care about their class differences, he didn't know how depraved her background was. Being a servant was her biggest claim to respectability.

Reminding herself that she was Sirena at present, she continued her tale.

"Ella couldn't stop thinking about her master. Despite her drab appearance, she was a hot-blooded woman. When he walked into a room, her heart would thump, her skin warming with a flush. Her nipples would stiffen and tingle. And she would find it difficult to breathe, as if his nearness tugged on the strings of her corset."

"She was aroused whenever her master was near?" he asked hoarsely.

"Even when he wasn't." With her imagination lighting the way, Xenia led them down the dark path of fantasy. "She couldn't stop having depraved thoughts about him. One time, when he was out, she was supposed to be cleaning his study but couldn't resist sitting in his desk chair. She inhaled his lingering scent, imagining the firm leather beneath her was his lap. She grew so hot and wet between her legs."

"What did the naughty little thing do about it?"

"She ran her hands over her bosom, imagining it was her master's hands tracing the curves of her breasts." Inspired, she acted out what she described, letting her hands wander over her padded bodysuit. "She squeezed her aching mounds, playing with the straining tips, pretending that he was the one rubbing her nipples with demanding strokes."

Her shadowy, erotic show achieved its purpose, for his next words were serrated with lust.

"Are your nipples hard now?"

It was so easy to slip fully into make-believe with him. Her script faded away, and it was just the two of them, creating their own story.

"Yes," she sighed.

"I would tease you, circling toward those needy peaks but not touching them. I would watch your nipple get flushed and swollen for me. Only when you squirm in my chair and beg to be touched would I rub the pad of my thumb over that velvety tip. Back and forth. I might lick my thumb, so it feels like a tongue working over your engorged bud. Are you imagining how that feels while you touch yourself?"

Blooming hell, I am now.

"It makes me so wanton that I throw caution to the winds. Even though I can hear the servants in the distance and know I could be caught, I draw up my skirts. I find the slit in my drawers and a whimper leaves me when I touch my pussy."

She let one of her hands fall between her legs. Since she didn't trust herself to masturbate and keep up the tale, she stroked the crease of her thigh instead. In silhouette, however, she knew it would appear like she was doing something far naughtier.

"You're dripping, aren't you?" His voice was thick with anticipation.

"I'm so wet that I've soaked the linen of my drawers."

"Tell me how you touch your cunny."

As she painted the tableau with precise strokes, she mimicked the motions.

"I pet myself, pretending it is you parting my slick, swollen folds. My cream coats your fingers as you explore my juicy slit. You know just how to touch me, what I like best. You find my pearl and rub it, shooting pleasure through my veins. I beg for more."

"At first, I caress your bold nubbin gently. When you beg nicely, I do it harder, frigging you roughly. Which way do you prefer?"

The truth made her pussy clench.

"I like it rough," she said breathlessly.

"That is what I thought," he said with growling satisfaction. "You like it so much that you sling a leg over the arm of my chair, giving yourself full access to your hungry pussy. You lose yourself in the fantasy of being frigged hard by your master. Even knowing that you could be caught, you play with your cunny like the naughty wanton you are."

Pulse racing, she had to resist the urge to do what he described. To touch herself in truth. She squeezed her thighs together and felt how slippery she'd become.

"Your eyes are closed, and your head is flung back," he went on. "Your hand works furiously between your splayed legs. Pleasure is building and building..."

"Oh, *yes*."

The smoldering heat in his voice mesmerized her. She arched against the chaise, pretending-but-not-pretending that she was losing herself in pleasure.

"You are so lost in your fantasy that you don't hear the door open."

Her breath puffed from her lips.

"By the time you have the presence to open your eyes, I am standing there before you. I see you sitting in my chair, your legs spread, your fingers tangled in your wet thatch. Your cheeks are flushed, and your beautiful brown eyes are those of a doe who knows she has been well and truly caught.”

Brown eyes...his fantasy truly is about me.

Her heart stuttered. “Now that you’ve caught me doing wicked things, what do you do to me?”

“I give you what you deserve, pet.” His voice was deliciously stern. “I punish you like the naughty little housekeeper you are.”

Christ, she is delicious.

Her filthy story and writhing, voluptuous form tested the limits of Ethan’s tailoring. His cock formed a visible ridge in his trousers. He knew it was a dangerous game he was playing, pretending Jane was on the other side of the curtain. Yet he reasoned that no harm could come of indulging in a fantasy. In fact, discharging his lust this way would protect her from his worst impulses. His desire to ravish his housekeeper while she begged him for more like the sweet, filthy girl she was.

Moreover, with Sirena, he could give rein to his darkest impulses. He could return to who he’d been before his failed engagement, before his injury. Anticipation roiled: he was a free man, and he could do whatever he wished. *Everything* he wished with his fantasy housekeeper, his Jane.

“What...what happens next?” she asked breathily.

Arousal seared him as the forbidden scenario unfolded in his mind’s eye. Walking in on his housekeeper sprawled in his chair, her skirts tossed up. She was pink-cheeked and trembling, caught in the desperate act of masturbating.

“You try to cover yourself,” he said thickly. “But I don’t allow it. I can see how needy your pussy is, how lewdly you treat yourself when you think no one is looking. I tell you to confess that you’re a wicked minx.”

"I'm not wicked. At least, I try not to be," she amended. "I try to avoid trouble, but somehow I end up running straight into it."

Her protest was perfection, a mix of innocence and guile. The fact that she believed what she was saying was endearing. It was as if she didn't realize that mischief-making was part of her nature. That she enjoyed playing games as much as he did. That she was a provocative little vixen through and through.

"You have been caught, young miss," he said severely. "And I shall be doling out your punishment."

"Oh, sir. Please don't punish me."

Her coy reply made his erection leap and strain the seams of his trousers.

"The time for protestations is over," he said. "You've been a naughty wench, frigging yourself in my chair. Now every time I sit there, I will remember the sight of your wet, pink pussy, and it will distract me from important matters. In fact, you've made me hard right now. As you are the cause of my condition, you ought to be the one to relieve it."

"Please don't sack me, sir," she beseeched. "I'll do *anything* you say."

That was Jane to a tee, submissive yet full of cheek. Even as she surrendered to his dominant tendencies, she would tease and challenge him. His pulse was a rapid staccato, his stones tautening at the carte blanche she offered. The invitation to indulge his darker desires.

"Get on your knees in front of me," he said.

To his depraved delight, she rose from the chaise and knelt in a graceful motion. With her tits bobbing and generous bottom nestled against her heels, her silhouetted profile was the definition of sensuality.

"I am here, sir," she said meekly. "Kneeling penitently before you."

"What do you see?"

"Oh, sir. I'm not sure how to describe it."

"Perhaps you need a closer look."

He couldn't resist going to the curtain. He faced her, lining his groin up with her piquant profile. Even though they were separated by the curtain, their merged shadow made it look as if he was standing right in front of her.

"It looks like you have a cricket bat stuffed down your trousers," she said playfully.

While she may have exaggerated his size, she wasn't wrong about one thing: he was harder than wood.

"It's a cockstand, naughty minx. Surely you have seen one before."

"Not up close. It's true that I have wicked thoughts about you, but I haven't had a lover."

At her bashful confession, a drop of pre-seed leaked from his cock. He gave in to the lust pounding in his veins, reaching for the fastener of his trousers. "It's time to get a good look, then," he said. His cock sprang free, and he grunted as he fisted the thick, throbbing length.

"Oh, sir," she squeaked. "Your member is even bigger than I imagined...and jutting straight at me. What shall I do?"

He pictured Jane on her knees, gazing at him with wide brown eyes. Rimming her plump lips with her tongue like the tease she was. He bit back a groan as more pre-seed wetted his throbbing crest.

"Put your hands on my thighs, Jane." Her name slipped out, but the fantasy was so enticing he didn't even care. "You're to keep them there until I tell you otherwise."

She positioned her hands so that, in their combined shadow, it looked like she'd done as he instructed.

"Oh, your cock looks fearfully large from this angle. The tip is so thick and wide...and you're dripping onto the carpet. I do hope the stain comes out."

Her irreverent wit and commitment to her housekeeper's role made his lips twitch.

"You talk too much," he rebuked. "Luckily, I have a remedy for that. Open your mouth and put your tongue out for me."

Shadowy Jane parted her lips, poking out her tongue to receive whatever he gave her.

"I put the tip of my cock on your tongue." As he spoke, he positioned his prick to her profile. "It's a nice resting spot, wet and soft. I push inside, and you take every inch."

"Mmm hmm."

Christ, she sounds like she has a mouthful of prick.

His chest heaving, he thrust his shaft into his fist, imagining it was her mouth.

"Even though you've never had your mouth swived before, you are a natural at sucking cock. You know how to relax for me, to let me all the way into your hot little hole."

"Mmm mmm," she moaned.

"I give you more. I tangle my fingers in your tresses as I thrust between your lips. You are such a good girl, taking what I give you. As I plant myself deeper, you sputter, and I pull out so you can catch your breath..."

"But I want you inside me." She gasped out the words as if she'd been deprived of air, and she'd *liked* it. "I want to pleasure you. To be yours."

Bloody hell, yes.

He jerked his fist along his cock, his glove slick with pre-seed.

"You are mine," he growled. "When I take your mouth again, I am not gentle."

"I don't want you to be."

"I push so deep I can feel your throat."

"Yes, please," she breathed.

"You want to swallow my cock, do you, minx?"

"I want whatever you give me."

"Does the idea make you randy?"

"Oh, yes."

"Do you need to pet your pussy?"

A pause. "May I?"

It was the perfect response. A make-him-explode sort of answer.

"You may."

"Thank you, sir."

"Are you diddling yourself, Jane? Whilst I fill your hungry mouth?"

She made a whimpering sound. "Yes, sir. I have my hand between my legs. My pearl is so slippery and I'm rubbing it, faster and faster. Then you drive your cock even deeper, and I need it, I need everything..."

Heat seared his gut as he lost himself in the fantasy, drilling his prick between Jane's lips. Even as he fucked her mouth and she rubbed her cunny, her brown eyes shone with a pure and vibrant passion. A passion that made the filthiest of desires feel like the sweetest of longings. The realization stole his breath, and suddenly, he was right on the razor's edge. There was no stopping the inevitable...and he didn't want to.

"I'm going to spend," he gritted out.

She moaned. "Me, too."

"Come with me, then. Pet that sweet pussy. Make it purr."

"Oh, it feels so fine. I...I'm going to come..."

Her silhouette trembled, and she gave a husky cry. In response, his stones swelled, heat pulsing up his shaft. He groaned as his release shot from him, splattering the floorboards. In that moment of agonizing bliss, clarity struck him.

The fantasy of Jane was not enough.

As wrong as it was, he wanted more of her. To know her...the *real* her.

But does she want me?

Chapter Fourteen

"Come in."

Xenia's heart beat a nervous pitter-patter as she obeyed her master's summons. The sight of Lord Ethan standing by his desk weakened her knees. He'd returned to the manor an hour ago, and this was the first she'd seen of him since their scorching encounter last night.

Since he'd used her name in his fantasy.

"Put your hands on my thighs, Jane. You're to keep them there until I tell you otherwise."

His depraved command had twisted her insides with yearning. To be desired by her brooding-yet-protective master was the most potent of aphrodisiacs, and moreover, he'd tapped into her naughtiest fantasies: to surrender to a powerful lover and belong to him fully. To service him while he watched with a proud gaze that declared, *You are mine.*

Lord Ethan had said those exact words. Better yet, he had *growled* them.

Of course, he didn't know that *she* knew of his feelings. Or that she wanted him just as badly. Last night, their passion had turned from make-believe to real, and she still couldn't believe that she'd made herself climax in front of him. Or that he'd done so in front of her. After he departed, the lingering scent of his pleasure had filled her with satisfaction.

She had to face the truth: Lord Ethan Harrington was the lover she'd been waiting for.

She would give anything to have an affair with him...including undoing some of her deceptions. To that end, she'd lightened her use of hair dye, allowing some of her natural red to show through. Recalling that Ethan had expressed a preference for redheads during his first visit to Sirena, she hoped he would like the new shade and her looser, more flattering chignon. She'd also left off her face paints, allowing her real complexion to show, freckles and all.

"Good morning, Mrs. Wood."

Lord Ethan met her halfway, and her breath hitched at his resplendence. He was in shirtsleeves, his sapphire-blue waistcoat accentuating his vivid eyes. Beneath his freshly shaven chin, his grey silk cravat was knotted with casual elegance, and his buff-colored trousers hugged his sinewy legs.

She wished she had something prettier to wear than her drab bombazine.

Stop being a wilting violet. You've never worn anything fashionable around him, and by some miracle, he wants you. Don't make excuses...it's now or never.

"Good morning, sir," she said.

"You look different today." He studied her, his head tilting.

"I, um, tried something different with my hair."

"Ah. Well, the new style suits you. And the color is quite... becoming."

The violet smolder in his gaze heated her cheeks. He did like redheads, after all. Her gaze darted behind him to his chair, and she flashed to the scenario they'd dreamed up together. Of him discovering her doing a naughty deed and delivering the delicious punishment she'd taken on her knees. Desire fluttered, warmth leaking from her core.

Focus. Say something, you ninny.

"I have something for you."

She blinked because they'd said the words simultaneously. She realized that their postures mirrored one another, and they both had one hand behind their back.

"May I go first?" he asked.

Entranced by his tentative smile, she would have agreed to most anything. She nodded, and he revealed what he'd been hiding: a rectangular case made of black leather. The words *C. W. Dixey & Son* were embossed on the smooth surface.

"This is for you," he said. "I picked it up while I was in London."

Slipping her gift for him into her apron pocket, she took what he offered. Inside the velvet-lined box was a pair of polished gold spectacles. The frames were delicate, with a round feminine shape. In a separate compartment was a matching chain with intricate links and dark topaz beads. The set was finer than any jewelry she owned.

"This is for me?" She looked up at him in wonder.

"I owed you a pair of spectacles," he said gruffly. "These ones are lighter; I ordered thinner lenses since you said you only need them for reading."

She felt a prick of guilt since she, in truth, didn't need spectacles at all. They were merely part of her disguise. But the fact that he'd paid attention—that he'd given her this marvelous present— filled her with giddy delight.

"This is the finest gift anyone has given me," she said. "I shall wear them with pride, my lord."

"Ethan, remember?"

"Ethan," she said shyly.

Saying his name somehow felt more intimate than all the erotic words she'd used with him. Probably because she'd been Sirena then, and their steamy banter had been part of a fantasy. In this moment, however, she was Xenia...she was *herself* in a way she'd seldom allowed herself to be. From the start, he'd had a way of eliciting her genuine reactions, and while she couldn't share her past, she didn't want to keep up all the false pretenses either. Thus, she'd decided to compromise.

I'll be as honest as possible, but I won't put either of us at risk.

"I, um, have something for you as well."

Setting the beautiful spectacles on a table, she removed his present from her pocket.

He took the glass jar with a puzzled look.

"It's a salve." She was aware of how paltry her gift was compared to his. "I made it specially for you. It contains some healing herbs."

"So this is the salve Brunswick keeps talking about." Ethan's mouth curved faintly. "He swears it performs miracles."

"This is a different formulation. One that I thought might, um, help with your hand."

She bit her lip, wondering if she'd made a mistake. With good reason, he was prickly about his injury, and she'd already angered him by repeatedly poking her nose where it did not belong.

Yet here you are bringing up his wound again. Are you a glutton for punishment?

She held her breath when he studied her with inscrutable eyes.

"There is one way to find out," he said. "Will you apply the salve, Mrs. Wood?"

Relief flooded her, along with elation.

"I would be pleased to," she said softly. "If you would call me Jane."

As Ethan led the way to the sitting area, he noted the improvements Jane had brought to his life. The carpet was clean and a lustrous sage green, the windows sparkled, and lemony polish scented the air. The oak surround of the fireplace gleamed; with the dirt removed, a delicate, leafy pattern had emerged along with the elegant Tudor roses affixed to the panel. The leather sofa had been buffed to a shine.

"You've worked miracles in my absence," he said.

He could tell his compliment pleased her. As they sat on the sofa, her eyes sparkled, and her cheeks were flushed. Her skin had the dewy ripeness of a fresh peach. Recalling her comment about her freckles, he concluded that she'd probably tried to conceal them with powder, which explained her formerly pallid complexion.

Today, she looked young and fresh. Her hair seemed brighter and glossier, the reddish gleam beneath the brown raising his temperature several notches. He'd always been partial to red hair. Jane was already temptation itself, but if she had fiery locks too...

He warned himself to slow down. He knew what he wanted, but he had to make certain that she wanted the same thing. If she did indeed return his interest, then he had to figure out a way to put them on equal footing. For he refused to take advantage of a woman in his employ—a woman who, he thought with a jolt of anxious arousal, now looked younger and more innocent than a typical twenty-seven-year-old widow.

"Shall I help you with your gloves?" she asked.

He nodded, for no reason other than a yearning to feel her touch. He watched her expression as she stripped off the casings of leather. Constance had tried to mask her revulsion the few times she'd seen his hand, and looking back, he would have preferred her honesty. It was mortifying to realize that he'd been willing to accept his former fiancée's politely averted gaze and martyred expression because he hadn't felt he deserved better.

Jane, however, showed no sign of pity or disgust as she worked off his left glove. Her touch was efficient and gentle as she bared his monstrous hand and placed it on her lap. Opening the jar, she scooped out some salve with her fingers. When she applied the creamy white ointment to the back of his hand, he felt a cooling sensation.

"It tingles," he said.

"It's supposed to. That means the peppermint and lemon balm are working. When I rub in the salve, it should dull the ache and improve circulation as well."

Her head bent over the task, she held his hand in both of hers, massaging his contracted muscles with soothing strokes. Despite his dulled sensation, he felt the pressure of her touch. She pressed into knotted tendons and stiff flesh, easing the contracture of his fingers.

"That feels nice," he admitted.

Her gaze flew to his, and a smile tucked into her cheeks.

"I'm glad." She hesitated. "I know it's not my place, and you don't have to answer if you don't wish to but—"

"You want to know what caused the injury."

Outside of his family, no one had directly asked him the question—out of politeness or fear, he didn't know. Even Constance hadn't inquired, likely because she didn't want to be privy to grisly details. Her preference had always been to sweep unpleasant things under the carpet, and truth be told, he'd thought he wanted that. He'd liked that she never pushed him, that they never fought, that she would abandon him to his moods, returning only when he'd battened down the hatches on his emotions.

"I shall return when you are ready to be a gentleman again," she would say in cultured tones.

He'd never blamed her. Who wanted to be around some snarly beast of a fellow who wasn't good for anything? Who would understand what it was that he'd lost? Who wanted to sit with him when he was swamped with self-pity, rage, and anguish?

His family was the exception. They *would* do all those things, but he couldn't unburden himself without causing them pain. His animosity toward Owen threatened to destroy everything the Harringtons held dear. *Ad Finem Fidelis* felt like a curse. How could he be loyal to a brother who'd ruined his life? Yet how could he make his family members choose between him and Owen, who'd suffered his own unspeakable tragedy?

Ethan couldn't do either of those things. Instead, he withdrew.

"Forgive me." Jane's tremulous voice brought him back. "I shouldn't have asked."

"It's all right." He forged on before he could regret it. "I injured my hand during an altercation with my brother."

"With the earl?" she asked, wide-eyed.

"No. My younger brother, Owen. He...he's troubled."

"How so?"

Jane's matter-of-fact tone, combined with her relaxing massage, permitted him to continue.

"Owen was part of the 44th Regiment, which served under the command of Major-General Elphinstone in Kabul."

Seeing the horror in Jane's eyes, he didn't say more. He didn't need to. Everyone knew about the retreat from Kabul, one of the worst military defeats in British history. Of the 16,000 British and Indian soldiers and camp followers who'd tried to make the disastrous journey from Kabul to a British garrison in Jalalabad, only a handful had survived; the rest had been killed or taken hostage by local Afghan tribes. Ethan recalled his desperate fear for his younger brother and his grief when Owen had gone missing and was presumed dead. Then his indescribable relief and joy when Owen was later discovered alive and brought home.

"Your poor brother," Jane said softly. "I cannot imagine what he must have endured."

Shame constricted Ethan's chest because she was right. Intellectually, he knew that Owen could not be held responsible for his actions after everything he'd suffered. Yet there was also no denying the damage Owen left in his wake.

"Since his return, Owen hasn't been himself," he said starkly. "He drinks too much. Gets into fights and other bad situations. Then he disappears, causing the entire family panic."

"Was it during one of the fights that he injured your hand?" she asked keenly.

He concentrated on the kneading motions of her hands. The way she was locating the knots and loosening them. Words rose inside him, emerging in a rush.

"Since Owen's return, Papa, James, and I have had to take turns bailing him out of trouble. That night, I was the one who found Owen at a gaming hell. He'd lost a fortune already and was sinking into debt with moneylenders. I forced him to come home with me. He was drunk—drunker than I'd ever seen him—and belligerent too."

Remembering Owen's red, militant face caused acid to churn in Ethan's gut. The scene was like a nightmare he used to have. One in which he was performing before an adoring crowd. He was on stage, and he played each note with crisp precision. Yet as the crescendo built, his fingers gained their own momentum. They began striking the wrong keys, moving at an uneven tempo...and he lost control. The audience began to boo and hiss, but he couldn't stop himself—couldn't stop the approaching disaster of the coda.

"I tried to reason with Owen," he said tightly. "Tried to calm him down. But when he insisted on leaving, I physically restrained him. *He just needs to sleep it off,* I thought to myself. I wrestled him away from the door, and he suddenly pulled out a pistol."

Jane gasped. "He...he shot you?"

"I don't know that he meant to."

That was the truth, which didn't torment him any less than if Owen had intended to shoot him. Maybe it tormented him more. If Owen had done it on purpose, then Ethan would have been utterly justified in his rage. Instead, he found himself in limbo: he had to come to terms with the fact that his brother had taken everything away from him...by accident.

"Owen was drunk and shaking like a leaf." His jaw clenched, and he had to force the words out. "Even when sober, he's not always in his right mind. He startles easily, seeing danger where there is none. Most likely, he pulled the trigger by accident."

"But he shot you. In your hand. And you are a pianist."

The tears that welled in her eyes brought heat to his own. Ashamed, he blinked away the moisture and drew a calming breath.

"My brother lost himself fighting for our country," he said. "I lost the ability to play an instrument. How is it fair for me to blame him...especially when he didn't do it on purpose?"

"Even if your brother did not intend to hurt you, don't you dare minimize what happened," Jane said fervidly. "Playing music is not a trivial matter. To an artist, making art is *everything*."

Her understanding smashed through some inner dam, and the truth burst from him.

"I cannot be angry at Owen," he said roughly. "But I cannot *not* be angry at him either."

The conundrum had eaten at him for the last three years. Even now, he saw no solution. No way to reconcile his love and rage toward his sibling.

Jane sighed. Then she shrugged. "Family is complicated," she said with feeling.

He stared at her.

"Why are you looking at me in that fashion?" She returned his gaze like an inquisitive doe. "Am I wrong?"

She wasn't. In three words, she'd summed up the problem that had consumed him for years—that had turned him into a brooding, grumpy bounder because he'd felt no one could understand his experience. But somehow *she* did, and her empathy made him feel almost...normal.

The rumble started deep inside him. It traveled from his gut to his chest and up his throat, emerging as a shout of laughter. He couldn't stop, the guffaws coming out of him until tears ran from his eyes. Jane went from looking puzzled to giggling, and then she was laughing too. She looked so sweet and adorable that he couldn't resist kissing her.

She kissed him back.

He clenched his hand in her hair, tilting her head back so he could ravage her as he wished. She whimpered, pulling him closer, parting her lips for him like the wanton girl she was. He thrust his tongue inside her, and she let him, moaning into his mouth. When she sucked on his tongue, he went hard as a rock.

He pushed her back onto the sofa, his hand going up her skirts. Her stockinged legs were enticingly curvy, and when he touched the slit in her drawers, he groaned aloud.

"You're drenched," he rasped.

She bit her lip. "I want you."

Her honesty unraveled him. Burgeoned him with pride and desire.

"Devil and damn, how I want you, Jane."

He kissed her, lingering when she sighed. He couldn't help fingering her a little, marveling at her passionate response to him. She was slippery and hot, her moans making his cock throb with anticipation. By Jove, he wanted to make love to her.

But...he couldn't.

Not until they had settled some things.

Inhaling for control, he lowered her skirts and pulled her into a sitting position. His fingers glistened with her dew. Despite his own advanced state of arousal, he hid a smile at how dazed she looked.

"If we are to move forward, there are matters we must discuss." He tucked a stray curl behind her ear. "You are in my employ, and I will not take advantage of you, Jane."

"I know you won't. I make my own decisions, and I want this as much as you," she said earnestly. "I am fully aware that our affair will not come with commitments: anything that happens between us will be temporary, with no strings attached."

Even though he'd been about to propose a casual liaison, her reply annoyed him.

"Why do you assume that?" he asked.

"You're a peer, and I'm a housekeeper." She shrugged. "We come from different worlds."

"I don't give a damn about that."

"Not when it comes to a temporary affair, perhaps. But for a permanent relationship?"

She lifted her brows knowingly, and he felt...trapped. He hadn't been thinking about marriage. But not for the reason she supposed. Having recently been jilted, he wasn't considering matrimony again...with anyone. As he was trying to figure out an explanation that didn't expose his mortifying rejection, Jane chuckled.

"Rest easy, my lord," she said. "I'm not about to spring the parson's mousetrap on you. I have no interest in marriage."

"Because you've been married before?"

She averted her eyes. "Because I cannot commit to a permanent arrangement. There are things you need to know—"

A scream from the hallway cut her off.

"It's Bloody Thom! Lord have mercy, he's on the rampage again!"

Chapter Fifteen

Shortly thereafter, Xenia, Ethan, and the staff gathered in the courtyard outside the kitchens, which served as an extension of the servants' working space. A few clotheslines, planters of herbs, and a large chicken coop occupied the gravel-lined area. Daisy, a stout brunette with blunt features, pointed at the wood-and-wire enclosure.

"See, my lord? It is like the curse foretold: *He brings death to all who cross his path, be they creatures with feathers, fur, or skin.* Bloody Thom slaughtered the chickens!"

Xenia made the sign of the cross as she examined the scene of the crime. Blood was grotesquely splattered over the coop, the bodies of its feathered occupants littering the ground. She counted five dead hens, which left Brutus and another hen unaccounted for. She prayed that they'd survived the attack and escaped.

"When you hired us on, you told us there weren't no ghost, Mrs. Wood."

Daisy waved her arm out to include the other maid, Berta, and the footmen, William and Fred. Mrs. Johnson, the cook, gripped her apron, tension lining her plump features. Ethan stood with his three longtime retainers at his back.

"I told you I hadn't seen Bloody Thom," Xenia corrected. "That is the truth."

"Nelly Nettles saw 'im," Berta said in her wispy voice. "She said 'e was terrifying. 'E were in shackles, dripping blood, and moaning in pain."

Despite her slight stature, the diffident blonde did the work of three maids. Worry crept over Xenia. She could not afford to lose Berta...or any of the servants. Even Daisy, who liked to tell tales and stir the pot, was an integral part of the small staff. Together, they'd made excellent progress on Bottoms House, and Xenia couldn't bear to let the hard-won gains slip away because of a possible phantom.

While ghosts were unnerving, she didn't believe they were all bad. In the gothic novels she'd read, even the scariest spirits usually haunted for a reason. Maybe they had unfinished business they needed to attend to or some truth they wished to make known. If Bloody Thom did exist, she needed to understand what he wanted...and how to make him leave.

Xenia turned to Daisy. "Did you actually see Bloody Thom?"

"Sure, I did." Daisy raised her dimpled chin. "When I came out this morning, I saw all 'em chickens 'e murdered and the bloody trail 'e left behind."

She pointed again, this time at the bloody footprints that marked the gravel leading out of the coop. With a chill, Xenia saw the footprints continued a few paces then stopped.

As if the owner vanished into thin air.

"That is not the same as seeing him," Ethan said.

While everyone—including Xenia—was on edge, he remained composed. He had his arms crossed and didn't seem perturbed by the talk about the ghost. Truth be told, he played the lord of the manor splendidly, and his confidence aroused her. She felt a quiver between her legs, where she was still wet from his petting.

Daisy slapped her hands on her hips. "Then 'ow do you explain the murdered chickens?"

"I would start with a rational explanation," Ethan said coolly. "For instance, perhaps a fox got into the coop."

William, the lanky footman, brightened. "Mr. Hodgins, who lives down the road, did mention that a fox has been stealing his chickens. It could be the same fox."

"Precisely, William. A mundane explanation is often the accurate one."

At his master's praise, William blushed, the color blending away his spots.

"That doesn't explain the footprints," Daisy argued. "The *disappearing* footprints."

"Did you enter the coop, Daisy?"

She drew herself up. "I did, my lord. To check if any o' the chickens were alive."

"Would you mind showing us the bottom of your shoes?"

With obvious reluctance, she complied. The worn soles were streaked with dried blood. A collective sigh of relief went up from all of them...except Daisy, who looked sulky.

"You made those tracks," Ethan said. "The reason they 'disappeared' is because the blood had either dried or worn off."

"I caught a glimpse o' Bloody Thom, I'm telling you!" Daisy directed her appeal to her fellow workers. "When I was in the coop, I saw the flutter o' his robe from the corner of my eye. I turned just as 'e vanished."

"You saw something white flutter?"

"That's what I said, my lord," Daisy said triumphantly. "All I saw was a glimpse—but a glimpse was all I needed to know who it was."

"You are certain that the flash of white you saw, out of the corner of your eye, was not that?"

Ethan gestured at one of the clotheslines, to which a bedsheet was currently attached. On cue, a breeze blew through the courtyard, causing the white cloth to give an eerie flutter.

"There is no ghost," he stated.

"I'm telling you, it *was* Bloody Thom," Daisy insisted. "I 'ave a feeling in my bones that something ain't right 'ere—"

"If you wish to collect your things and leave, do so." Clearly, Ethan was at the end of his patience. "If you stay, I will hear no more talk of this Bloody Thom nonsense. This applies to everyone. Do I make myself clear?"

"Yes, my lord," the staff chorused.

Seeing Daisy's chin wobble, Xenia knew the maid was debating between her pride and more pragmatic concerns. How often had she, herself, made that same calculation? Admittedly, Daisy's behavior was misguided and stemmed from a need to be right. Nonetheless, Xenia understood the maid's predicament and wanted to give her an easy way out. A way to stay without damaging her pride.

Mrs. Johnson beat her to it.

"Come along, Daisy and Berta," the cook said. "We'll have a nice cup of tea before we get back to work."

Xenia sent Mrs. Johnson a grateful look as the other ushered Daisy and Berta back inside. While Brunswick gave orders to William and Fred to clean up the coop, Ethan took Xenia aside.

"We have unfinished business," he murmured. "Will you come to me tonight?"

Her pulse raced. "I look forward to it, my lord."

"As do I, Mrs. Wood." To any observer, his manner was formal, yet the warmth in his eyes made her heart flutter. "Until then."

After he departed, she took it upon herself to hunt for the missing chickens in case they had managed to escape the predator. She headed toward the gardens, where she would go if she were a chicken. As Ethan had yet to secure a gardener, weeds carpeted the path, and the towering hedges allowed only a glimpse of the gazebo in the far corner.

Xenia made friendly clucking noises, hoping to attract the chickens. To her delight, the missing Dorking hen poked its head out from the hedge. Its single comb and silver-grey feathers were a trifle askew, but it appeared otherwise unharmed.

"There you are, poor thing." Xenia approached slowly, not wanting to frighten the hen, who watched her with wary eyes. "I'm so glad you escaped the fox."

Bending, she picked up the hen, and with a sigh, it cuddled against her.

"There, there," she murmured. "Everything's going to be all right. Let's see if we can find Brutus, too."

With the hen tucked under her arm, she was about to continue the search when a movement caught her eye. She went over to the hedge and plucked the object from the branch. Her blood chilled when she realized what she was holding.

A strip of ancient white cloth...tattered and stained with blood.

"Do you really want to spend our time discussing this?" Ethan drew his brows together. "A ghost that does not exist?"

Xenia had arrived at his bedchamber shortly before midnight. She'd taken the precaution of using the servants' corridor, which opened into his room via a panel in the wall. Taking in his room, she'd had a moment of professional pride. The mahogany frame of his tester bed gleamed in the corner. In the sitting area, the chester-field he'd brought from London had been buffed to a soft sheen, and the wingchairs, reupholstered in a lovely midnight-blue damask suggested by Mr. Duffield, the village draper, perfectly matched the new velvet drapes.

Ethan had been waiting for her, looking magnificent in a burgundy smoking jacket and loose trousers. He'd left off his gloves, a sign of intimacy that squeezed her heart. His long, hot kiss of greeting intensified her swoony feeling. She wanted to kiss him again...wanted to do more than kiss him. But first they had a hefty agenda to get through.

In addition to Bloody Thom, there were the facts about herself and her past that she could no longer, in good conscience, conceal. If she and Ethan were to embark on an affair, then she owed him the truth. He deserved to know the essential facts so that he could decide whether he wanted to be the lover of a woman like her.

Although cowardly, she'd decided to start with the least daunting topic...which happened to be the vengeful spirit haunting the manor.

Facing Ethan in the sitting area, she held up the bloody cloth. "We cannot ignore this," she averred.

"I am not suggesting that we ignore it. But we needn't make a mountain out of a molehill."

"A ghost is not a molehill."

"A scrap of fabric is not evidence of a ghost."

"You heard Daisy. She said she saw a fluttering white robe—"

"According to Brunswick, Daisy has a penchant for telling tales. Her various claims include being related to a viscount, surviving being struck by lightning not once but twice, and seeing Herne the Hunter riding near Windsor Forest." Ethan cocked his head. "Come to think of it, lightning strikes would explain some things about her."

Xenia rolled her eyes. "While Daisy may not be the most reliable source, how do you explain the bloodstained cloth?"

"A previous gardener cut himself and lost the bandage. An animal found an old handkerchief and carried it into the garden. A passerby was wiping his bleeding nose, and the wind blew it out of his hands—"

"All right, all right." Xenia wrinkled her nose. "You win."

Ethan quirked a brow. "Are you certain? I could list other rational explanations."

"You are an artist. Shouldn't you be more creative than rational?"

"That is a general misunderstanding about artists." He sounded exasperated. "Creativity matters, yes. But one's creativity only gets a chance to soar through discipline and hard work. A piece might sound spontaneously expressive when one is performing it, but that effortlessness took untold hours of practice. The more seamless the playing, the more the musician rehearsed."

That made sense, of course, and suddenly reminded her of Tony's struggles. While he'd been fervent about discussing his ideas, he'd been less committed to sitting at a desk and writing them down. He'd waited for inspiration to flood him; instead, it had come in drips and dribbles. This had led to his frustration and sulking; when she'd tried to console him, he'd retorted that she didn't understand the struggles of a true artist.

That had hurt, especially since she worked hard at her craft. While many wouldn't consider storytelling an art, she did...and she took it seriously. She'd spent hours practicing and preparing for her performances, wanting to create the most compelling fantasy possible. Yet she'd allowed Tony's jibe because she'd been desperate for affection...even if it had been an illusion.

"Is my discussion of art boring you, Jane?"

At Ethan's polite inquiry, she shook free of the past and felt a burst of gratitude for where she was now. With a man who desired and appreciated her.

"You are being rather sensible," she teased. "I thought musicians were more passionate—"

She broke off with a gasp when he hooked her by the waist and maneuvered her onto the chesterfield. The next instant, his mouth clamped over hers, his hard length pushing her against firm, tufted leather. She arched her neck as his kiss claimed her breath and her thoughts.

"I am not passionate enough for you, hmm?" His breath coasted against her ear, making her shiver. "Do you need more proof of my impetuous nature, pet?"

The way he was touching her made her *feel* like a prized pet.

He stroked her cheek and neck with his long fingers, and she nearly purred. His heavy erection pressed through the layers of her skirts. Yet there were things they needed to discuss. The affair with Tony had been disastrous in part because she'd been afraid to ask for clarity about his intentions. She'd allowed him to string her along, and it was a mistake she would not make again.

"Yes," she said. "After we talk about our, um, arrangement."

"Now who is being sensible?"

Ethan gave an exaggerated sigh, but he helped her to sit up. He slung his arm around her shoulders, and she settled into the solid harbor of his body, marveling at how natural it felt to do so. Tony had not been the sort of fellow to cuddle.

"Shall we start where we left off?" Ethan said. "You were about to tell me why you were averse to relationships of a permanent nature."

She was not fooled by his casual tone. "Was I?"

"You said it wasn't because of your prior marriage," he prompted.

His intent look and the fact that he'd listened gave her courage.

"That is true." She drew in a breath. "Because, you see, I was never married."

Chapter Sixteen

Ethan angled himself to face her.

"You said you were a widow," he stated.

"I know." She tried to control the tremor in her voice. "I needed the job and thought that being a widow would be an advantage. That it would make me seem older and more respectable."

"To be clear." He pinned her with his gaze. "There is no Mr. Wood."

She gave a small nod.

"Are you seven and twenty?"

She shook her head. "I am three and twenty."

His brows formed an ominous line. "You lied. About everything."

"Not about everything—"

"You've never been a housekeeper before, have you?" He surged to his feet, glowering at her. "I *knew* those bloody references were too good to be true."

"I'm sorry. I just needed the work so badly—"

"That gave you the right to lie to me?"

His rage chilled her to the bone.

"No, what I did was wrong." Her throat tight, she tried to explain. "I didn't know you then. At least, not the way I know you now. After our first meeting, when you left me in the rain, I thought you were an arrogant blueblood. When I ended up interviewing for the job, I didn't feel I owed you anything—"

"Least of all the truth." Icy flames leapt in his eyes. "Why are you telling me this now?"

"Because...because things have changed. For me, at least."

Her heart hammering, she rose and reached for him. He stepped away. Looked at her as if she were something he'd found stuck to the bottom of his shoe.

"I have no tolerance for liars," he said.

"I'm sorry," she whispered. "I know I've made a hash of things, but the primary purpose of my disguise wasn't to spite or deceive you. It was to protect myself."

"Right. You had *no choice* but to pull the wool over my eyes."

His bitterness made her shrink inside.

"I had a choice," she admitted. "And I made the wrong one. I told you before: I have a habit of making bad decisions."

"I suppose you'll blame me for that. For giving you no option but to deceive me."

"No." She frowned because the notion hadn't occurred to her. "The decision was mine alone, and I regret deceiving you. In the past, you see, I've worked in places where being myself put me at risk, and I thought—"

"What happened?"

She blinked at the ferocity of his question. "I beg your pardon?"

"Did some bastard make advances on you?" he bit out.

Which bastard are you referring to?

When one worked in seedy establishments, unwanted attention was a way of life. She flashed to Wallace's Bookshop, her last place of employ in London. She saw the sneering, aristocratic face of her assailant, felt his smothering weight, tasted the blood in her mouth as she'd tried to fight him off. She felt the overwhelming, paralyzing terror.

"Recently?" Ethan asked, as if he'd read her mind.

"A few months ago." She exhaled, shaking off the past. "Luckily, another patron came to my aid before the assault could progress."

"Did you report the bastard?" he demanded.

"The assailant was a gentleman. I was a shopgirl," she said tonelessly. "Who would listen to me?"

Seeing the revulsion in his eyes, she knew it was over. He saw her for who she was: a nobody. A woman who was beneath him in every way. The fact that she'd made a living as a shopgirl wasn't the worst of it, not by far. He didn't know about her work as Sirena. Or about her mama and the people who'd been hurt because of her...she hadn't scratched the surface of her ugly past.

You don't deserve him. You don't deserve happiness, and you never did.

It wasn't the first time she'd watched her dreams go up in flames, yet she couldn't recall it hurting this much. Like a razor blade slicing across her heart, hope bleeding out cut by cut. She needed to get out of here before she fell apart.

"Again, I am very sorry for deceiving you." She willed back the heat surging behind her eyes. "I wish I had done things differently. I'll pack my things and be gone on the morrow."

She'd almost made it to the servants' door when his voice stopped her.

"Is your name really Jane?"

She didn't trust herself to turn around.

"No," she said. "It's Xenia...Xenia Loveday."

His quiet footsteps fell like thunder in her ears. She sensed him standing behind her. He was close enough for her to feel his heat, to smell his virile scent. She clasped her hands together, fearful that she might reach for him and make a fool of herself.

"Xenia." His breath caressed her ear. "Was all of it a lie?"

Too scared to hope and too scared *not* to, she squeezed her eyes shut and surrendered what she could no longer keep inside.

"Not the part about you. About us," she said hoarsely. "When I met you, I thought you were handsome...in a grumpy, unfeeling sort of way. But then you turned out to be gallant and kind. When you rescued me from the bats, I was attracted to you, but I resisted the feeling because I knew nothing could come of it. Then you risked your life to save me from that cutthroat and shared about your past, and my feelings became undeniable. I want to have an affair with you more than I've ever wanted anything. Even though I know that you're better than me."

She lowered her head. It didn't happen often, but she was out of words. He turned her toward him, tipping her chin up, and she gazed into his storm-filled eyes.

"I am not better than anyone, least of all you," he said. "I am brooding and grumpy, and I'm sorry I left you in the rain."

Her breath lodged in her throat.

"But I won't countenance being lied to, Xenia. For any reason."

"I understand," she said tremulously. "I know I don't deserve your forgiveness, but I swear I didn't intend for my deception to go on for as long as it did."

"If we are to continue on the path we're on, you must be honest henceforth," he said sternly.

"Continue?" She stared at him, her heart pounding. "You mean you...you still want me?"

"Give me your word that you won't lie to me."

It would be so easy to agree, and her past self might have done so.

But Ethan deserved better.

"I can promise that I won't deceive you from now on," she said. "But there are things about my past that I will not share. I am not a good or respectable woman, Ethan, and I won't let my past affect you. I won't. I will leave before I let that happen." Her voice shook with the force of her emotions. "I have little to offer you. I am nothing special. I don't have wealth or looks—"

"Stop, Xenia."

She couldn't, though. She had to get through this, or she would regret it for the rest of her life.

"I am reckless and prone to bad decisions. I knew I shouldn't fall for you, but I let myself do it anyway. Even though you deserve more. Now I've made a hash of things—"

"Be quiet," he growled.

Before she could speak again, he gathered her against him and covered her mouth with his.

Ethan didn't care if he was making a mistake. He'd made plenty in the past, and at least this time he was going in with open eyes. His initial anger at Xenia's deception had subsided when he realized that she wasn't like his former fiancée.

Yes, she'd lied about who she was. But she'd done so for reasons he could understand. Well, not entirely—he'd never been in her situation. He'd never needed to work to survive, never been a vulnerable young woman who'd had to protect herself against the predators of the world. The thought of what she might have gone through seized his gut, and he wanted to tear every bastard who'd mistreated her limb from limb.

How could he hold her deception against her? She'd worked hard to improve his manor and the quality of his life. Her presence had upended his existence but in a good way. She made him look beyond his misery and self-pity. Hell, because of her, he was even thinking about trying his hand at composing. A long time ago, before his injury, he'd given writing music a go; he'd started a sonata but gave up on it...had forgotten about it, in truth, until Xenia had played it on the Bösendorfer. Now he couldn't stop thinking about the piece and had even made another copy, with what he thought were improvements.

Xenia reminded him that life was worth living. And despite her ruses, she hadn't lied about her feelings for him. She took responsibility for what she'd done. Of her own volition, she had told him the truth *before* they'd started their affair—unlike Constance, who'd betrayed him with his friend and jilted him right before the wedding.

Xenia had to have known the risk she was taking, yet she'd done it anyway. Her behavior was nothing if not consistent. She was impulsive, troublesome, and brave. She called into question her own morality, yet she clearly had her own sense of honor. From the start, he'd been intrigued by her contradictions...her resilience and vulnerability. He couldn't deny his desire to defend her, his housekeeper who thought far too little of herself.

Then and there, he decided to discover Xenia's secrets. She might tease him for being rational, but as an artist, he'd learned to trust his instincts. He knew that she wasn't capable of malice. Mischief, yes, but her heart was too tender for any true wrongdoing. Whatever she was running from—for clearly, she *was* running —he would help her with it. He would keep her safe.

Once he made the decision, everything else became clear. He'd experienced this before when learning to play a new and complex piece. As daunting as the score might be, once he'd decided to tackle it, he would. No matter how much patience and effort was required. The same held true where Xenia was concerned. He was going to discover the intricacies of who she was, including her past, and he was going to protect her.

Ergo, it made perfect sense to kiss her as if she belonged to him.

She melted against his chest, soft and eager. That was another thing about her: when it came to passion, she was charmingly candid. Her mouth parted hungrily beneath his own, and she clutched the lapels of his smoking jacket with such exuberance that he would have to think of an excuse to tell Valentine in the morning. He loved her enthusiasm, her taste, the soft sounds she made while he licked inside her.

Despite her delightful alacrity, her confession had triggered a question he needed answered. Reluctantly, he broke from her sweetness.

"We need to talk," he said.

"Again? Haven't we talked enough? Can't we move on to other things?"

At her dismay, he had to stifle a smile. He enjoyed her artlessness. Despite Xenia's disguises, she was far more honest than most ladies of his acquaintance.

"This is important," he said. "I need an honest answer from you."

"All right," she said warily.

"Are you a virgin?"

Her cheeks turned pink. "Does it matter?"

"It does to me."

"If we are speaking in technicalities, then...yes."

Her reply gave him a jolt of primal satisfaction. It was stupid, he knew, because her innocence was going to make things more complicated. If she'd been a widow, he could give full rein to his desires, knowing that they were on equal footing in terms of experience. With a virgin...well, he'd never been with a virgin before, but his honor told him the rules were different.

"But I am not without experience," she said hastily. "I've had a follower and, um, done some things. Just not *the* thing. I know what goes on between a man and woman...I *am* three and twenty, after all, and practically on the shelf. You needn't be concerned on my behalf. I know what we're about to do, and I *want* to do it with you."

As usual, she had a unique way of tying him up in knots. Her lack of the usual female modesty about sexual matters amused and beguiled him. At the same time, he tensed at her blasé reference to her "follower."

Who was this bloody cove with whom she'd done "some things"?

The bite of possessiveness stunned him. Constance had complained that he hadn't seemed to care when men flirted with her—that he was more likely to get jealous if someone touched his piano. She hadn't been wrong.

But with Xenia, things were different.

"Unless you don't want to have an affair with me because I lack experience?" As was her wont, Xenia struck upon a notion that was both fanciful and ridiculous. "Rest assured that I have not led a sheltered existence. I consider myself a woman of the world. Moreover, I have an active imagination. While I have not engaged in relations per se, I have *thought* about it. Excessively. I am a quick study and—"

"You needn't list your qualifications for an affair," he said wryly. "You are not interviewing for a position, you know."

"Aren't I?" Her eyes sparkled, and she raised her brows. "Perhaps even for *several* positions?"

It took him a moment to realize that she had made a warm jest. Bemused, he had to acknowledge she wasn't maidenly in the least. His tension eased. She was a rare jewel: a woman whose body was untouched but whose mind was delightfully wanton. Wicked yet sweet, she was the lover he'd been searching for all along...and she wanted him back.

By Jove, when did he get to be such a lucky bastard?

"Getting rather ahead of yourself, aren't you, minx?" he murmured. "Talking about variations when you haven't done it the usual way."

"I don't want you to think that I'm innocent. I know what I want," she said with endearing conviction. "I fantasize about you constantly."

"Do you, now?" He tried not to let his smugness show, but damn, it felt good to be desired. "What do you fantasize about?"

"One time, when I was making your bed, I imagined being in it with you," she said dreamily. "We were naked, and you were on top of me, your weight pressing me into the mattress. You were kissing me, touching me everywhere..."

The notion that she'd entertained such wicked thoughts while doing her chores heated his blood. Christ, she was naughty—a perfect little vixen. He took her hand, leading her to his bed.

Her eyes shone. "Are you going to make love to me?"

"To a point," he replied. "Until we make decisions about the future, I will not do anything irrevocable."

"But there is no future for us." She gnawed on her lip. "Our affair can only be temporary—"

"For the moment, let us agree to disagree." He lifted his brows. "Now, do you want to argue or make love?"

A pause.

"Make love."

He hid a smile at how torn she looked.

He took her hand. "I was hoping that would be your answer, pet."

Chapter Seventeen

Thoughts of the future vanished from Xenia's head as Ethan took her to his bed. There was only now, this moment she'd been waiting for. Truth be told, she felt nervy and bashful, which she told herself was ridiculous. This was what she wanted. She was finally going to experience lovemaking with the lover of her dreams.

And it was as she'd said: she was a virgin in body only. She had a light-skirt's knowledge of sex, which, combined with her imagination and lusty nature, meant she'd entertained detailed fantasies about Ethan. There was no need for her to feel shy and uncertain. What she was about to do she'd done in her head countless times before.

Yet nothing prepared her for the desire carved on Ethan's elegant visage. He made her feel beautiful and special, heightening her arousal. Her nipples were tight buds, her knees quivering as they stopped by the side of his massive bed.

When he reached for her, she trembled in anticipation. He slid his fingers into her hair, and as he plucked out her pins, the faint pings as they hit the ground built her tension. She couldn't have imagined how intimate this felt: a man letting down her hair for the first time. The heavy strands tumbled, falling over her shoulders and down to her waist. Her breath quickened as he captured a tress between his long, elegant fingers.

"This isn't your real color, is it?" he said.

"No," she admitted. "It's a more brazen shade, I'm afraid."

Hunger flared in his eyes. "I want to see you in your natural state."

Even desire couldn't stop the pulse of worry. Her bright red hair made her more recognizable...and amplified her resemblance to her mother. Whenever the papers wrote about Mama, they mentioned her delicate features and "hair as red as flames," characteristics that were incongruous with her occupation as a cutthroat.

"Perhaps one day," Xenia said cautiously.

"There is no perhaps about it." His nostrils flared. "You cannot hide from me, minx. One day, I shall see all of you."

Their intimate banter reminded her of their exchange at the Nunnery, and she felt another anxious stab at her sin of omission. However, she'd promised not to lie *from now on*, and she'd been forthright, telling him she would not discuss her past. Revealing that she was Sirena would open the Pandora's box of her past, and she wasn't willing to risk exposing Ethan to her demons. She couldn't bear the thought of his rejection—or, even worse, of him coming to harm because of her.

Besides, she was willing to lay Sirena to rest for the duration of her affair with Ethan. The instant he had taken her hand, she'd known that she would do anything to be his lover...and that included retiring her money-making persona. While it wasn't the most sensible decision, she didn't want to sell fantasies to other men while being with Ethan.

She resolved to inform the Abbess of her decision and return the ten-pound note. When her liaison with Ethan ended—and she knew that it would—she could resurrect Sirena elsewhere. For now, however, she'd earned her dream, and she was going to savor it for as long as it lasted.

"Turn around, pet," he said.

Shivering, she did. When he started undoing her buttons, she felt a moment's concern for his limited dexterity. She needn't have, she realized dryly. The man had a talent for undressing women, even one-handed. She trembled as he stripped her layer by layer. Soon she stood in only her stockings and garters, discarded garments pooled at her feet. Being naked in front of a fellow was a first for her, and she instinctively folded her arms over her chest.

"Don't hide your loveliness," he murmured. "Let me see you."

Slowly, she let her arms fall.

Firelight flickered over his sinfully handsome features, his male admiration making her heart hammer against her ribs. No man had ever looked at her thus. As if she were the only thing worth looking at in the world. As if she belonged to him. As if, standing exposed in her own skin before him, she was the safest she'd ever been.

His eyes locked on hers, he cupped her cheek, and she shuddered at the contact. He touched her as if she were a fine instrument he was playing for the first time. His caress was not tentative but exploring. He stroked his fingertips over her lips, her chin, the leap of her throat as she swallowed.

"Sit on the edge of the bed for me," he said. "Up you go."

When she perched on the mattress, her legs dangled above the ground. He stood between them, spreading her further. He took his time, looking his fill before he touched her again. Her pulse quickened as he traced the slope of her collarbone, brushing his knuckles against the swell of her breast. When he drew his thumb over one throbbing nipple, she couldn't hold back a needy whimper.

"Beautiful."

His approval melted her insides.

"Touch me," she whispered. "Please."

His eyes holding hers, he brought his thumb to his mouth and moistened it.

I might lick my thumb, so it feels like a tongue working over your engorged little bud.

Then he was doing it, rubbing his damp thumb over her nipple, sending sizzles of bliss through her veins. He smothered her moan with his mouth, kissing her as he played with her breasts. He cupped and molded them, teasing the tender tips. She'd talked about this with strangers, even done this to herself...but it had never felt like this. This was no fantasy but the real thing.

With Ethan, the pleasure was more than physical. The sense of belonging she felt was intoxicating and unraveled her inhibitions. She squirmed against the mattress, desperate for relief. He wedged his thigh deeper, pressing against her throbbing pussy.

"Go ahead, Xenia," he said thickly. "Rub yourself against me."

Shamelessly, she took him up on his offer, sliding her mound against his sinewy limb. The friction sent heat blazing through her limbs. She was so slick that she made embarrassing sounds, but he urged her on with hot eyes and even hotter words.

"Such a lovely wet pussy," he crooned. "Come on my leg, there's my good girl."

He pinched her nipple, twisting it. The sensation pushed her over the edge, and she came with a gasp, the pleasure intense and bone-meltingly sweet. Breathlessly, she sank onto the bed and watched dreamily as he shed his clothes. In her line of work, she'd seen naked men, but Lord Ethan Harrington was in a class of his own.

Muscles rippled as he tossed aside his shirt. The taut skin of his broad shoulders gleamed, and his chest was a stack of chiseled blocks with a sprinkling of dark hair. Pushing down his trousers, he revealed narrow hips topped with a sinewy vee, long, muscular legs, and...

Oh, my.

His cock was big. As magnificent as the rest of him. Long and girded with veins, the thick shaft jutted from a dense black nest, the rosy swell of his stones visible beneath.

"You are beautiful," she said wistfully.

He swept a possessive gaze over her, lingering unabashedly between her legs.

"And you," he said with a wicked smile, "are a true redhead."

The mattress dipped as he put a knee on the bed. Then he was on top of her, and they both inhaled sharply at the feel of skin against skin. She couldn't have guessed how much this would arouse her, the sensation of a lover's body against her own. Since he was supporting himself on one arm, she wasn't taking all his weight, yet the feel of him pressing her into the mattress thrilled her. He kissed her mouth, her ear, her neck. His hard chest abraded her nipples, setting off sparks of pleasure.

She couldn't believe that this glorious man was *her* lover. She felt as if she were in a sweets shop and didn't know what to sample first. She ran her palms over his wide shoulders, the flexing expanse of his back, marveling at his honed strength. When she reached the high, hard swell of his arse, she gave him a greedy squeeze, trailing her fingertips along the tight crevice between.

"If you are done playing," he muttered, "it's my turn."

He closed his mouth over her nipple. The things he did with his tongue made her gasp and arch her spine. He flicked and teased and sucked on her aching bud. She felt a corresponding pull between her legs as he drew on her nipple. The pulsing ache in her pussy grew and grew.

"Oh, please," she begged. "I need you to touch me."

"Where, pet? You know the word for it."

Truth be told, she knew a great many words for it. But she gave him the one he'd used.

"My pussy," she said obediently. "Please touch my pussy."

She didn't know what was more wicked: the glint in his indigo eyes or the curve of his smile.

"Actually," he said. "I have another idea."

"Odds bodkins," Xenia gasped as she spent yet again.

Odds bodkins, indeed.

Raising his head, Ethan found himself smiling as he licked her cream from his lips. He didn't know which was the better view: her glistening slit framed by fire-red curls, or her heaving breasts topped with ripe, plump berries. What he did know was that Xenia, in her crisis, was the prettiest sight he'd ever seen. She tasted like a treat too, her wanton flavor making him harder than a pike.

Her responsiveness astounded him. While he'd been with randy women, she was unique. Sweetly voracious. With her, he felt a connection that went beyond lust...beyond anything he'd felt before. She was both wicked and adorable, allowing him anything and wanting it all.

The things I am going to show her...

He nipped her silky thigh. "I knew you would like it."

"I more than *liked* it. Oh, Ethan, I never knew..." She lifted her head, gazing at him with rapturous eyes. "Is it always this splendid?"

He crawled over her so that they were face-to-face.

"Only with me," he said sternly. "Don't get ideas about anyone else."

To his surprise, he wasn't teasing. This strange proprietary urge still confounded him. Since nothing was normal around Xenia, however, he supposed he would have to get used to it.

"Why would I even think of anyone else when *you* are my fantasy?" she asked.

Her sincerity expanded his chest and his cock. His erection

jammed into her soft belly. He'd played the gentleman and made sure she came first (three times, actually, but who was counting?). Now his own hunger was demanding to be satiated, and he could wait no longer.

Adjusting their bodies, he slid his shaft against her pussy. He groaned as her plump folds enveloped him, slick and satiny-soft. He drove against her plush flesh, and when his thick head butted against her pearl, she moaned.

"Do you like my cock rubbing against your pussy?" he rasped.

"You feel so fine," she panted. "Don't stop."

He thrust harder. Pleasure sizzled down his spine as her dew coated his shaft and balls. The urge to hilt his cock inside her was nearly overwhelming...but his honor wouldn't allow him to take her virginity. Luckily, there were many paths to pleasure. Leaning on his left forearm, he used his good hand to grip her bottom, pulling her tighter against him. He rocked against her, driving his cock against her cleft, the slippery friction making him grunt.

"Wrap your legs around my hips," he instructed.

When she did, they both moaned at the improved angle. He drove his rod against her engorged pearl, mashing his stones over her tender lips. She dug her heels into his flexing arse and then she stiffened, her cry shattering his restraint. He arched his neck as bliss erupted from him and left him shuddering.

When he leaned down to kiss her, her mouth curved.

He lifted his head. "What is so amusing?"

"I am not amused. I'm happy. Thanks to you."

Xenia's flushed cheeks and tangled hair supported her claim. Only she could manage to look thoroughly debauched and cute. It was a look he could get used to.

"Your happiness is my reward," he said gallantly.

"I think you had your own reward."

Reaching down, she touched a finger to the sticky mess he'd made on her belly. When she twirled her finger in his seed and giggled, renewed heat flickered in his loins.

Devil and damn, that was a quick recovery. Even for him.

He lifted his brows. "Allow me to fetch you a towel, then I'll make you happy again."

"So soon?"

At the lusty sparkle in her eyes, he made an easy decision.

"To hell with the towel," he muttered.

He closed his mouth over hers.

Chapter Eighteen

Drawing a breath, Xenia approached Ethan's study. She felt unaccountably nervous. She'd last seen him when she'd left his bed and returned to her own room. The image of him on his stomach, a bedsheet draped over the taut curve of his buttocks and his sculpted back rising and falling as he slept, sent a lovely shiver through her.

Last night, he had shown her the difference between swiving and lovemaking. What they'd done together had felt intimate, even the wicked parts. The fact that Ethan didn't take her virginity, even though she would have given it if they took precautions, demonstrated his respect for her.

In short, Ethan Harrington had been a fantasy come true.

Even the most wondrous dreams suffered in daylight, however, and she felt a frisson of anxiety. What would things be like between her and her aristocratic lover this morning? Obviously, they had to keep up appearances around the other servants. The notion of addressing one another as "my lord" and "Mrs. Wood" felt strange now that they'd made love, but perhaps they'd save endearments for their next rendezvous.

Will there be a next rendezvous?

They'd made no promises. Although she had been the one who'd insisted on a casual affair, the undefined nature of their relationship gnawed at her. She told herself that, with her past, she could not ask for more, and she ought to be satisfied with finding happiness where she could.

That's the problem with happiness. A taste of it is never enough. One always wants more.

She missed Ethan already. Since she knew his routine, she knew he'd been up for a few hours, and when he made no effort to find her, she came up with an excuse to see him.

She knocked, and when Ethan bid her to enter, she saw that he was meeting with Brunswick.

"Yes, Mrs. Wood?" Ethan asked. "Was there something you wanted?"

He looked and sounded the way he had when they first met. Remote and haughty, like he couldn't spare her the time of day. The effect was chilling, and her self-confidence wavered.

"I, um, finished organizing the library," she said haltingly. "I thought you might want to take a look. When you have time."

"I have time now."

They left the study, Ethan stalking behind her. They didn't have far to go, but the tension between them made it feel like miles. Panic played with her thoughts, twisting and tying them into knots.

Does he regret last night? Is that why he is acting distant? Have I done something wrong... Odds bodkins, what if he hates what I've done with the library?

As they reached their destination, Xenia whipped around and barred the door.

"I have changed my mind," she said. "The library isn't ready to be seen."

"I am sure it's fine."

While his words were terse, his eyes had a familiar, brooding look.

"Are you…" She searched for the right words. "Is everything all right?"

"Why wouldn't it be?"

He was definitely grumpy.

Because he wishes he hadn't made love to me?

Pain seized her, but if he had changed his mind about her, she had to know.

She looked both ways down the corridor before whispering, "Is this because of last night? Do you…do you regret what we did?"

He drew his brows together. "No."

"Then why are you cranky?"

"I'm not."

"You are. You're grumpy and brooding." Suddenly, she was annoyed, too. "If you've changed your mind about us—"

"I haven't. Open the bloody door, and we'll talk inside."

"No, I want to know now—"

Quick as lightning, he reached for the doorknob. The door swung open, and she stumbled backward with it. He caught her, herding her inside and spinning her around. She was once again up against a closed door, only this time he was leaning over her, a hand next to her head.

"You left," he said.

Her head whirled from the sudden movements and his oddly accusatory manner. "Are you referring to this morning?"

He jerked his chin, his gaze ominous.

"Then I did," she said slowly. "I couldn't risk Mr. Valentine seeing us together."

"That is the only reason?"

She furrowed her brow. "What other reason would there be?"

"Maybe you're the one with regrets this morning."

When she stared at him, he stared stonily back.

He's…serious?

"Of course I don't regret last night." She was shocked that he could harbor any doubts in that regard. "Being with you was the most beautiful experience of my life."

"Then why did you leave without waking me?"

"Because you looked peaceful sleeping, and I didn't want to disturb your rest."

"And nothing else prompted your stealthy departure?" he pressed.

Pondering the matter, she realized there was another reason.

"I suppose...I suppose everything seemed so perfect last night, and I didn't want that to change." She expelled a breath. "I wasn't sure how things would be between us in the light of day. When we were back to being Lord Ethan and Mrs. Wood. If we might be awkward with one another, or if things would be different. Maybe...maybe I was scared to find out."

"You should have woken me." His tone softened. "We could have talked about it."

"You could have summoned me this morning," she countered. "We could have had a discussion then."

"You're right," he said after a pause. "We're a pair of fools."

"Do you..." Her throat cinched. "Do you think what we did was foolish?"

"Probably." He leaned closer, and her heart thumped when she saw passion flaring in his eyes. "But I don't give a damn because it was the most sensual experience of my life."

"Truly?" she breathed.

"How could you doubt it?" He outlined her mouth with his thumb. "We set the bedsheets on fire, you and I."

"It was like that for me too. But I didn't know if you felt the same way."

"The morning-after jitters. It happens to everyone."

"You included?"

"Me included." He cupped her cheek, his gaze intense. "May I ask a favor?"

"Anything," she said promptly.

"In the future, don't leave my bed without waking me."

He's referencing the future...which means he wants to be with me again.

Feeling giddy, she said, "I won't."

"Thank you."

His slow smile felt like a gift. Then he kissed her, courting her mouth as if he could do it all day. Her toes curled, her eyes closed, and she clutched at his shoulders, drowning in sensation.

"By Jove, you tempt a man," he murmured. "But we should save this for bedtime. For now, let's have a look at the library."

Her lashes flew open.

He was already striding into the heart of the room, examining her handiwork. She'd left the curtains open, and the sunlight from the sparkling bay windows illuminated the high ceilings and bookshelf-lined walls. Because of the woodworm damage, she'd asked the carpenters to patch the holes and paint the shelves dark green. She'd thought the color went well with the carpets, which, after repeated cleanings, were revealed to be deep sage and patterned with flowers and leaves. The floral motif was echoed in the plasterwork on the ceiling, now restored to a pristine white.

The only thing she hadn't been able to fix was one of the fireplaces. Despite multiple cleanings of the brick firebox, it had spewed smoke and ashes. Since there was another hearth to warm the room, she'd decided to cover it up. At her behest, William and Fred had transported a cabinet from the morning room; the mahogany showpiece had beautiful relief carvings and scrollwork. The lower half of the cabinet was deeper, with drawers which she'd used to store knickknacks. The upper part was narrower and had two glass display cases where she'd placed interesting objects, including a chunk of crystallized mineral, seashells, and figurines.

Lord Ethan wandered down the length of the library, his hands clasped behind his back. She didn't know what he was thinking as he walked along the shelves, gazing at the neat line of volumes. She followed him, her stomach aflutter.

"You sorted the books by color," he remarked.

She cursed herself for following her silly impulse. During her stint as a clerk at Wallace's Bookshop, she'd rearranged the books by shade and size because she thought it looked better and helped her to locate volumes. No one had complained, but since the business had catered to those looking for erotic materials, the patrons had tended to keep their heads down.

"The books are still categorized by subject," she said in a rush. "I can re-organize them alphabetically if you wish—"

"I like what you've done."

"You do?"

"You've transformed the library. Given it a unique and warm appeal."

She basked in his approval the way a cat basks in the sun.

"Thank you, Xenia." He took her hand, brushing a kiss over her knuckles. "For everything you've done to make this manor a home."

"You're welcome," she said softly.

"This should probably wait," he said, "but I find myself impatient to discuss our arrangement."

"I was wondering about that too," she admitted. "How will we keep our relationship a secret? The other servants cannot know—"

"I concur. Your reputation must be protected at all costs."

"I was more concerned for yours." She hitched her shoulders. "No one cares about what I do. I'm nobody—"

"Don't say that. You are someone—someone special, Xenia."

His ferocity clogged her throat.

"No one has ever said that to me before," she said in wonder.

"You had best get used to hearing it."

For once, his preemptory tone didn't bother her in the least.

"You're mine now, Xenia. Upon my honor, I will take care of you. Do you believe me?"

"I do." Her heart swelled, but she'd promised not to lie to him. "But we both know this affair cannot last—"

"Why?"

She wetted her lips. "Why...what?"

"Why do you insist on a condition that need not be true?" His gaze pierced her. "What are you afraid of, Xenia? Whatever you are running from, I can help you—"

"You can't."

Fear oozed through her, the memory of her papa's weary and determined face.

"Don't be afraid, poppet. I won't let her hurt us any longer. We're going to leave this life behind us—start afresh."

He'd been confident up until the moment Mama and her lackeys had charged into the cottage where they'd been hiding.

"You'll be all right, poppet. Put your hands over your ears."

Those had been his last words to her before Mama's brutes dragged him outside.

She'd done as he asked, but she heard it anyway—his cries of pain, that single ringing shot that pierced her own heart. When she'd tried to run to him, Mama had blocked her way.

"Those who betray me don't survive, so let that be a lesson, daughter mine."

That was a lesson Xenia refused to learn. She'd run and run from her mother's cruelty, willing to accept the consequences. Finally, she thought she was free, but danger shadowed her to Mr. Trelawney's cozy bookshop. It knocked over his shelves, smashed his money box, and sliced his throat wide open.

Safety was an illusion.

Even here. Even now.

Even with the man she was falling in love with.

The realization of her feelings did nothing to alleviate her fear. In fact, it made it worse. This affair with Ethan was pure selfishness on her part. Even if he could accept her past, her presence in his life put him at risk.

"If you run again, daughter mine, I will find you." Mama's vow had terrified her more than the beatings, more than being chained

like an animal. *"I will always find you—and you won't like it when I do."*

"Xenia."

At Ethan's gentle shake, she snapped out of the past.

"Tell me what is troubling you," he said intently.

"I can't," she whispered.

"Does it involve debts? I can help you—"

"I will not take your money." As uncertain as she was about everything else, she was sure of this. "I am not your whore."

He stiffened. "I never implied that you were."

Seeing the tight line of his mouth, she regretted her harsh words. He was only trying to help, but he couldn't—no one could. When the past caught up to her, as it always did, she had only one choice, and she promised herself she would make it.

No matter how hard I fall for Ethan, I will leave to protect him.

"Forgive me," she said miserably. "You asked for honesty from me, and this is the truth: I cannot promise you anything but the moment. I know that's not worth much—"

"Christ, Xenia. You've no idea of your own worth, do you?" He pulled her into his arms.

Held by his solid strength, she realized she was trembling. He pressed her cheek against his chest, and she didn't resist.

His voice was like rough velvet against her ear. "One day, you are going to trust me."

"It's not about trusting you—"

"I disagree."

Lifting her head, she managed a wobbly smile. "Can we agree to disagree?"

He regarded her for a moment. "It depends."

"On?"

"Whether you can distract me."

Relieved to see the crinkles of humor around his eyes, she was leaning up to kiss him when the door flung open. They sprang apart, and Xenia stared as a young lady blew into the library like a spring breeze. Silk flowers fluttered on her bonnet, the skirts of her lavender gown frothing with her haste. The newcomer was stunning: raven-haired and slender, she had sculpted features worthy of a cameo, familiar violet eyes, and an air of well-bred confidence.

Her lively gaze locked on Ethan, whose jaw slackened.

"Gigi?" Surprise laced his words. "What the devil are you doing here?"

"Oh, my dearest brother," Gigi wailed. "I'm *ruined*."

With that, she dashed over and flung herself into Ethan's arms.

Chapter Nineteen

With one shoulder propped against the display case, Ethan observed his sister through narrowed eyes. Gigi, being Gigi, showed no sign of being discomfited by his hard stare. She occupied the settee, sipping tea and exclaiming over the delicious scones. Xenia had brought in a tray earlier, then promptly fled before Ethan could make more than cursory introductions.

Given the tension in the room, he didn't blame her.

Flanking Gigi were her escorts, who happened to be Ethan's estranged cronies. Simon Parkhurst, a stylish rake with a mop of copper locks, sat in the wingchair to her right, and Cyril Canning, dark-haired and somber-looking, occupied the one to her left. Ethan was grateful that the pair had looked after his sister. While he suspected their actions were not solely prompted by their loyalty to him—Gigi had a habit of wrapping males around her finger—he was relieved that they'd insisted on accompanying her here.

Truth be told, he also felt guilty. After discovering Constance's perfidy with Blake, Ethan had cut off not only Blake but also the rest of the group, which included Parkhurst and Canning. At the time, the two had claimed that they had no knowledge of Blake's betrayal, but Ethan had been too angry to care. He'd lashed out and accused them of being traitors.

There would be time to apologize...after he dealt with his sister.

"Tell me what happened, Gigi," he said flatly. "Every detail. Leave nothing out."

Sighing, Gigi set down her cup. "I got into a bit of a scrape, that's all."

This did not come as a surprise. He'd been bailing Gigi out of scrapes for the past twenty-one years. Spirited and willful, his baby sister had a tendency to do as she pleased. In fact, she and Xenia had that in common, and he suspected that they would get along like a house on fire. The idea of his sister and his lover getting acquainted probably should have concerned him, but for some reason it didn't.

Gigi hadn't liked any of the ladies who'd flocked to him during the height of his fame. She'd been particularly disapproving of Constance, no matter how hard his ex-fiancée had tried to win her favor. He used to think Gigi was a brat. Now he considered that she might be an excellent judge of character.

"If it is just a scrape," he said, "why did you say you were ruined?"

"Because Society is stupid."

Since he couldn't argue, he waited, brows raised.

"It was nothing," she insisted. "I was at a ball two nights ago, and it was a dreadful bore, so I decided to get some air in the garden—"

"You went to the garden unchaperoned?"

"There's no need to raise your voice," Gigi said primly. "If I wanted a lecture, I would have gone to James. Anyway, I didn't think I needed a chaperone since I only intended to be out there for a minute or two. Unfortunately, I ran into Sir Fenton."

Ethan's chest tightened at the mention of the corpulent fortune hunter.

If that bastard tried to lay a hand on Gigi, I am going to call him out.

"What happened?" he asked grimly.

"At first, it was the usual nonsense. He was pouring on the butterboat about my looks, my genteel disposition—clearly, he doesn't know me well—and so forth. He spoke at an atrociously loud volume, probably hoping that we would be discovered. Then I would be compromised and have to accept his offer. I could not let that happen...so I made a run for it."

At the idea of his sister having to flee from Fenton, scarlet splattered Ethan's vision.

"I'm going to kill him," he decided.

"*No.*" Gigi's violet eyes widened with her first show of concern. "You are not to murder anyone. And calling out the bounder will only draw attention to what happened—the very thing I was trying to prevent by fleeing."

"You cannot expect me to do nothing when the bloody bastard *chased* you—"

"Sir Fenton didn't chase me. In case you haven't noticed, he is at least five stone overweight and lethargic at the best of times. Simply put, he was too *lazy* to pursue me. He didn't cause the harm to my reputation—a stick did."

Ethan strove to control his temper. "Explain."

"I tripped. Over a dashed branch." Gigi huffed out a breath. "I had the bad luck to land in a rosebush, and the thorns ripped my bodice and one of my sleeves. I didn't realize the extent of the damage until I returned to the ballroom and noticed the stares and whispers behind fans. I tried to explain that I'd slipped outside—"

"Where were Mama and Papa?" Ethan asked the obvious question.

"Um, they could not make it." Gigi bit her lip, her gaze darting briefly to the side. "They were out of town, and Lady Darby was acting as my chaperone."

A friend of the family, Lady Darby was a gentle widow and no match for Gigi's antics. Mama and Papa ought to have known better than to leave Gigi in her care...then the realization hit him.

"They were taking care of Owen, you mean," he said starkly.

Gigi gave a small nod. "Owen had another, um, episode, and they took him to recover at the family seat. I wanted to stay in London, so they left me with Lady Darby."

Bloody Owen. Of course this is his fault. He causes trouble for everyone...even if he cannot help it.

Resentment and concern were a confounding mix, and Ethan took a steadying breath.

"Since they're occupied, I came to you. You'll let me stay, won't you?" Gigi wheedled. "Until the scandal blows over?"

She was staring at him with beseeching eyes...eyes that they'd both inherited from their mama. Of the four siblings, they were the closest in looks and temperament; perhaps that was why she'd always come to him first when she was in trouble. At least, until his injury. With gnawing shame, he realized that of late he'd been so wrapped up in his misery that he'd failed to be a proper big brother.

He addressed Parkhurst and Canning with a nod. "How did the two of you get involved with my sister's mess?"

"I was at the ball," Parkhurst replied.

He was, as usual, dressed in the latest fashion with a stylishly knotted cravat and frock coat, his copper curls in artful disarray. He was an aspiring painter, and despite his boyish looks, an exceptional rabble-rouser. Indeed, his drinking prowess had caused Ethan to lose the bet that made him the owner of Bottoms House.

"I heard the talk, but Lady Gigi had already left," he went on. "When I went to call on her the next day at Lady Darby's, I, er, saw her leaving. Out a back window. I offered to escort her wherever she was going."

"*Et tu*, Parkhurst?" Gigi muttered.

"I was with Parkhurst since I'd heard about the incident at the club," Canning added.

Dark-haired and lanky, Canning had an air of earnestness. Although he came from noble stock, his family's changing fortunes made it necessary for him to have a career. However, his true passion was writing. As far as Ethan knew, he'd been working on the same novel for years. The fact that he'd heard about Gigi's latest escapade at his club was bad news.

"I didn't need either of you," Gigi said sulkily. "I was going to travel with my maid Colette."

"You are fortunate Parkhurst and Canning saw you safely here," Ethan clipped out. "Have you informed our parents about the incident and your whereabouts?"

"I wrote them, and I left a note for Lady Darby."

Ethan turned to his friends. "You have my gratitude."

"Think nothing of it," Canning said. "You would do the same for us."

"We also wanted to see how you were getting on with the Double Ar...with, ahem, your new abode." Parkhurst cleared his throat, clearly remembering that a lady was present. "I must say you've done wonders with the place, old chap."

"The credit goes to my housekeeper, Mrs. Wood," Ethan said with pride.

"She seems lovely," Gigi said brightly. "She's young to be a housekeeper, isn't she?"

He didn't like the speculative glint in her eyes. While he didn't mind if she and Xenia got to know one another, he needed to settle things with his lover first. To convince Xenia that she could trust him with whatever she was running from. In the meantime, he didn't want his madcap sister scaring her off.

"James found her," he said noncommittally. "She came with excellent references."

"Speaking of James, could we invite him and Evie over for

supper?" Gigi asked hopefully. "I haven't seen Evie in ages and miss her dreadfully."

"Get settled first." Ethan shook his head. "Then we can talk about supper parties."

"And this is why you are my *favorite* brother!"

With a happy squeal, Gigi threw her arms around him. He stilled. Gigi had always been affectionate, yet in recent years he'd pushed her away, along with everyone else. He realized now that he missed their closeness. He returned her hug before letting her go.

Turning to his friends, he said, "You are both welcome to stay. The manor isn't fully restored but—"

"We would enjoy the country air." Parkhurst came over, slapped him on the back.

Canning smiled slowly. "It will be like old times."

"Without the drinking contests," Ethan said with feeling. "One tumbledown manor is all I can manage."

Chapter Twenty

"I love you, my dearest rose. But are you certain you want this?"

She gazed into her lover's eyes, the pure blue of heaven, and knew she had found her place of belonging. She'd been running for so long, and now she was finally safe.

"Yes, I want you. Take away my fear. Show me how love is meant to be."

"Then I will love you. I will always love you..."

Xenia stirred. She kept her eyes closed, wanting to linger in the voluptuous passion of her dream, the safety of her lover's arms and his sweet promises of love.

"Christ, pet. You get wet for me even in your sleep."

Her eyes flew open. It took her a moment to register that she was in her bed, lying on her side...and Ethan was there. He lay behind her, nestling her against his hard form. She twisted to look at him, and his eyes glinted, reflecting the moonlight coming through the dormer window.

"What are you doing here?" she whispered. "I thought you were entertaining your friends."

According to Brunswick, whenever Ethan got together with

his old cronies, they stayed up all night carousing. Xenia hadn't expected to see Ethan tonight.

"I missed you," he said.

His simple words sent a thrill through her. Or perhaps it was his hand, which was doing wicked things between her thighs. Her nightgown was bunched at her waist, and when he caressed the slick crease of her pussy, a moan scraped from her throat. He covered her mouth with his own, swallowing the sound, and she tasted fine whisky mingled with his own delicious flavor.

"Shh," he murmured. "We'll have to be quiet. The walls are thin, and we can't wake the others."

She couldn't believe that he'd come to her in the servants' wing. The risk of discovery added to her dreamy excitement, especially when he uttered a command in a low, guttural voice.

"Take off your nightgown, and show me what's mine."

Shivering, she sat up and did as he asked. The moonlight turned to molten silver in his eyes.

"By Jove, you're beautiful," he said.

Beneath his proprietary gaze, she felt beautiful. Beautiful *and* lucky because he rose from the bed and gave her a show as she reclined on her side. He stripped off the casual attire he'd worn for a night in with friends. Covetous need coursed through her as she took in his long, sleek lines and sectioned chest, the grooves and hollows of his splendid arse. Then there was the raring instrument between his legs. When he took his meaty cock in his fist, giving it a deliberate pump, she felt an answering flutter in her pussy.

He came to the edge of the bed, bringing his erection toward her face. She wetted her lips, not out of nerves but excitement. She'd seen her colleagues perform fellatio on a regular basis—heard them exchanging tips of the trade, too. For reasons she couldn't explain, this act had always titillated her, and she couldn't wait to try it with Ethan.

The wide crest of his cock glistened with his essence. When he swiped his head gently over her lips, she understood he was giving her the choice of whether she wished to proceed with this naughty deed. In response, she licked up his salty maleness and hummed with approval.

"Good girl," he said. "Now take more of me."

He fed her his cock with slow, arousing insistence. Recalling the advice she'd picked up, she kept her teeth out of the way and tried to relax her jaw. His size made it a challenge, but she loved the feeling of his thick, bold manhood claiming her mouth. Breathing through her nose, she tried to take more of him.

"You're a natural. Christ, the way you're sucking me..."

The strain in his voice made her redouble her efforts. She wanted to please him more than she wanted her next breath. She relaxed her muscles even more, letting the proud heat of him go deeper and deeper still. He released his cock, his hand clenching in her hair as he swived her mouth. His harsh breaths and the slick sounds of his thrusting inflamed her. When he went a bit too far, the muscles of her throat clenched around him.

"Devil and damn." He pulled out, even though she didn't want him to. "Love, I'm sorry—"

"I'm not," she whispered. "I liked that."

He groaned, bending to kiss her passionately before flipping her onto her stomach. She trembled as his lips seared the ladder of her spine, winnowing pleasure from each rung. Suddenly, he gripped her by the hip, raising her bottom high in the air. Her pulse thrummed at the lewd position, especially when he nudged her knees farther apart.

"Look at you," he murmured. "Swollen and juicy as a ripe peach. Shall I eat you, pet?"

Her cheek burned against the mattress. "Yes, please."

"Then you'll have to be a good girl and stay quiet while I feast."

At the heated slide of his tongue up her intimate crack, she whimpered and bit her lip. He took his time as if she were his favorite meal, his soft grunts of enjoyment adding to her tumultuous pleasure. When he circled her pearl with his thumb, she couldn't hold back a gasp.

"Quiet, love," he said. "Unless you want everyone to know you're a naughty minx who likes to have her pussy licked."

His admonishment scalded her insides. He'd given her an impossible task, for he was playing with her bud, showing her the nuances of bliss with his musician's touch. He tapped lightly, rubbed roughly, circled and stroked up and down. She became his willing instrument, every fiber of her being resonating with pleasure. He began licking her again, his mouth like wildfire, burning her up. Suddenly, his tongue delved between her folds, driving steadily *inside* her, and her muscles clenched.

"One day soon," he said with a low growl, "you're going to trust me, Xenia. When you do, you'll be getting more than my tongue. And I cannot wait to fill this beautiful, tight pussy of yours with my cock."

She had just enough time to grab a pillow, smothering her cries as she went up in flames.

Xenia woke with a start. It was still dark, and she was alone in her bed.

For an instant, she thought it'd been a feverish dream: sucking Ethan's cock and spending as he ate her pussy. She'd twisted her neck to watch as he'd risen behind her like some pagan god, pumping his huge rod in his fist, groaning as he'd sprayed his hot pleasure on her back. Even then, they hadn't been satiated. They'd made love again, face-to-face, the friction of his steely shaft against her pussy bringing them to ecstasy together. In the lovely aftermath, he'd cuddled her close and whispered the sweetest things.

Relief filled her when she heard a rustling and saw Ethan getting dressed in the darkness. She hadn't dreamed the searing intimacy. Sitting up, she was about to speak when she heard sounds...the unmistakable notes of a piano.

"What on earth?" she whispered.

"It woke me up," Ethan said tersely. "I'm going to investigate. Stay here."

He cracked open the door. After a quick glance down the hallway, he exited, his steps stealthy. She leapt out of bed, threw on her robe, and counted to ten before leaving her room. She followed the eerie tune, which raised goose pimples on her skin. As she reached the main house, the music suddenly stopped. At the same time, she saw Lady Gigi standing there in a voluminous night rail, her eyes huge in the flickering light of her lamp.

"You heard the music too, Mrs. Wood?" she said.

"Yes, my lady." Xenia resisted the urge to check her hair, hoping to God she didn't look like she'd been doing the mattress jig all night with the lord of the manor. "I, um, came to see what was going on."

"It doesn't sound like my brother playing. His touch is far more refined."

Xenia knew better than anyone how refined Ethan's touch was.

"Well, the music has stopped." She tried for a reassuring smile. "I'm sure it was one of the other guests—"

"What the devil?"

Ethan's exclamation came from the music room. Xenia exchanged startled glances with Lady Gigi, and then they were both dashing forward. Xenia reached the music room first, and through the doorway, she saw Ethan at the far end of the room. He had his back to her as he stared at the piano. Someone must have left the windows open, for the drapes were swirling, framing him in a ghostly fashion.

Aware of his sister's presence, Xenia spoke in what she hoped was a housekeeper's tone.

"Is everything all right, my lord?"

Ethan turned to her, a storm brewing in his eyes.

"No," he said grimly. "It's not."

He moved, and her breath hitched when she got a clear view of the piano. Blood splattered the ivory keys. A sheet of music was propped on the stand, the notes obscured by bold red letters:

Leave my home...or die.

Chapter Twenty-One

"Nothing has been touched, my lord?" Constable Rawlins asked.

"Nothing," Ethan confirmed. "I instructed the staff to leave everything as I found it."

"Very good, sir. That will make my job easier."

Chuddums shared a constabulary with a cluster of villages, and Rawlins had come from several miles away. The constable was greying and rumpled, with heavy bags under his eyes. Despite his sleepy appearance, his gaze was keen as he examined the piano.

Also present in the room were Gigi, Parkhurst, Canning, and Xenia. The latter, Ethan noticed, was a bit twitchy. Since she'd fallen prey to the notion that Bloody Thom was haunting the manor, he supposed her nerves weren't surprising. His rational explanations did little to sway her...or some of the others. Daisy had given notice first thing this morning. Good riddance, as far as he was concerned. Yet rumors had a way of spreading, and Ethan wanted to nip any talk of a vengeful spirit in the bud.

"Do you see any clues, Rawlins?" he asked.

"To begin with, whoever made the bloody handprints was

wearing gloves." Rawlins pointed at the keyboard. "There are not the usual lines and whorls associated with fingerprints."

"Unless the handprints were made by a ghost," Gigi chimed in.

Ethan shot an exasperated look at his sister. She and Xenia were standing side by side, birds of a fanciful feather. All morning they'd been thick as thieves, discussing what Bloody Thom might be after and using their favorite gothic novels as reference. They'd debated scintillating topics such as whether a specter could cause changes in the material world. Yes, they'd decided, because the ghosts they'd read about tapped on windows, opened doors, and played mournful tunes on instruments in the dead of night. Ergo, they'd concluded with trembling excitement, Bloody Thom could have left the bloody handprints and the note.

Rawlins lifted his thick grey brows. "You are referring to Bloody Thom, my lady?"

"Precisely," Gigi said eagerly. "From what Mrs. Wood, here, has told me of the legend, Thomas Mulligan was killed in this manor, and his murderer was never found. Isn't it possible that he might be haunting the place because he wishes justice to be served?"

Ethan aimed his gaze at the ceiling. "No, it's not."

"It seems unlikely." Rawlins's reply was more diplomatic. "In my experience, it is best to consider rational explanations first."

Parkhurst cleared his throat. "But there have been sightings of the ghost, have there not?"

"Christ," Ethan muttered. "You too, Parkhurst?"

"Sorry, old chap." Parkhurst ran a hand through his mussed curls, looking sheepish. "Mrs. Wood mentioned that a previous cook saw Bloody Thom, chains and all—"

"And there was the incident with the slaughtered chickens," Gigi added. "There were only two survivors, Brutus the rooster and a hen...if only chickens could talk. Mrs. Wood, didn't you also find a piece of tattered, bloody cloth in the garden that could have come from Bloody Thom's robe?"

Xenia gave a hesitant nod.

"You don't say?" Canning looked intrigued. "This has the makings of a novel."

"Good God, is silliness catching?" Crossing his arms, Ethan glowered at the group. "This is not the work of a ghost, but some living, breathing blackguard who has carried out this hoax to spook me."

"Quite right, my lord. We should proceed to a review of human suspects," Rawlins said easily. "Unless you have anything to add, Mrs. Wood? We have yet to hear from you, and it seems you are the resident expert on Bloody Thom."

At the constable's inquiry, Xenia visibly started. "I have nothing to add, sir," she said quickly.

"You seem well-versed in local lore. Are you perchance related to Mr. Wood who owns the smithy in Chudleigh Crest?" Rawlins's manner was friendly. "He fixed up my horse when it threw a shoe."

"No, I'm not a relation." She wetted her lips. "I came from London recently and heard about Bloody Thom during my visits to Chuddums."

"Ah, well. That explains it." The constable turned to the group. "May I suggest we have a seat and discuss other possibilities?"

They arranged themselves in the seating area. As Gigi distributed the tea, Ethan considered how he could maneuver her out of the room. The last thing he needed was for his sister to get embroiled in the situation.

"Forget it, Ethan." Gigi's gaze remained on the cup she was filling with expert precision. "I'm not leaving, and if you make me, I will eavesdrop."

Since he was not one to fight a losing battle, he decided to let the matter go.

"Now, my lord." Rawlins took out a notebook. "You were

saying you believed someone might have perpetrated this hoax. Do you have a suspect in mind?"

"More than one," Ethan said grimly. "I'll begin with the bounder who accosted Mrs. Wood ten days ago at the mop fair."

"How frightful." Gigi gasped. "Are you all right, Mrs. Wood?"

"Nothing happened," Xenia assured her. "His lordship arrived in time and beat the bounder to a pulp."

The admiration in her pretty brown eyes puffed out his chest. He'd been the object of female adulation before, when his piano playing had made him a celebrity. But he'd never experienced a woman adoring him for being *himself*. Although Xenia was undoubtedly acquainted with his flaws, she still looked at him as if he could hang stars in the sky for her...and it made him want to do it.

To be her hero—to protect and cherish her.

He cleared his throat and looked away, afraid of giving away too much.

"The blackguard threatened to make me pay for my interference," he said.

Rawlins's pencil was poised. "Do you have his name?"

"Patrick Harlow. He claimed to be the head of the Corrigans."

Rawlins's gaze sharpened. "You've made a powerful enemy, my lord. The Corrigans run the docks in Chuddums and specialize in everything from extortion to robbery. We also suspect they're behind a rash of house burglaries and the theft of a fortune in jewels, but we've never been able to pin anything on them. Slippery as lampreys, they are."

"I will not be intimidated by a bunch of ruffians," Ethan stated.

"Harlow, in particular, has a ruthless reputation," the constable warned. "It's rumored that he instigated a coup against the former gang leader, a fellow named Vickery. A few months ago, Vickery disappeared and has never been seen again."

"If Harlow has a problem with me," Ethan said, "I will deal with him man-to-man."

"Are you certain that's wise?" Canning aimed a meaningful glance at Gigi.

"There's no shame in retreat, old chap," Parkhurst murmured. "Maybe you ought to return to London until the trouble blows over—"

"This is my goddamned home, and I'm not leaving." Ethan bristled at the idea of being chased from his own estate. "I will, however, hire some guards from London. Round-the-clock surveillance ought to take care of any further mischief the Corrigans might have planned. As for Gigi—"

"I am not leaving either." His sister lifted her chin. "I will not abandon you in your time of need, and you cannot make me. If you send me away, I will only sneak back. *Ad Finem Fidelis.*"

He exhaled through his nose. The idea of Gigi traveling on her own was too terrifying to contemplate, and she wasn't one to make idle threats.

"If you stay, you will obey me," he told her.

"Of course, brother dear." Her smile was that of an angel. "Your word is my command."

He snorted.

"Allow me to investigate the Corrigans' involvement, my lord," Rawlins said. "I must advise you not to confront them directly. For your own safety."

"I will not approach the bastards. But if they bring the fight to me, I will not back down."

"Understood. Now, you mentioned you had more than one potential culprit in mind?"

"Yes, there's a fellow named Dobson Gill. He worked here briefly as a footman, but my butler caught him stealing. I sacked him without pay, and he wasn't happy about it. He issued some threats but left when I threatened to summon the constables."

"Can you provide a description of Mr. Gill, my lord?"

"Fair, with a burly build, five feet and nine or ten inches tall. He claimed he'd worked as a footman in several local homes. Brunswick will have the details."

"Very good, sir." Rawlins jotted some notes. "Are there any other candidates who come to mind? People with whom you have had recent conflict...who might wish you ill?"

Ethan hesitated as another name suddenly surfaced. One he hadn't considered until Rawlins phrased the question that way. But he didn't wish to discuss the person in front of the others.

"No," he said.

"Then I've no further questions." Rawlins closed his notebook. "If I may have a word, my lord?"

The others left, leaving Ethan alone with the constable.

"Now that we have privacy, would you care to add anything else?"

Since the constable was as acute as Ethan had suspected, he went with his gut. "I do not think this amounts to anything," he said, "but I had a recent falling-out. With a fellow who used to be a friend."

"What was this disagreement over?"

"He had been carrying on with my betrothed."

In speaking of the betrayal, Ethan was surprised that he felt less of a burn now and more of a sting. He realized that he had, in fact, dodged a bullet. If he'd married Constance, he would not have met Xenia. He would not have discovered the difference between contentment and happiness. Although things were far from settled with Xenia, being with her made him feel happy, lighter, and more optimistic about the future...more like himself again.

This awareness allowed him to relate his past matter-of-factly.

"Right before our wedding, my fiancée left me a note calling it off because she was in love with my friend. This friend paid me a visit a few days later. Apparently, my former betrothed couldn't bear the pain of the scandal and being called a jilt, and he begged me, for her sake, to make it publicly known that the decision to end the engagement had been mutual. I refused to lie, and things got...unpleasant."

"*You're a selfish bounder, Harrington.*" Blake's righteous anger blazed in Ethan's head. "*For years, you've been wallowing in self-pity and taking Constance for granted. Can you blame her for turning to me for comfort when you gave so little? All I am asking now is that you lessen her pain...but you won't even do that. Well, I hope you reap the suffering you've caused a thousandfold, you bloody ungrateful sod.*"

Blake had broken a few things before slamming his way out.

"What is this gentleman's name?" Rawlins inquired.

Despite the bad blood, Ethan felt loathe to give it. To betray Blake, which was rich. Yet he could not fathom his former crony stooping to staging a haunting...and for what purpose? To scare Ethan? Make him feel as unsettled as Blake and Constance were in their new life together? The pieces did not quite fit.

"It is of no consequence," he said.

"But my lord—"

"If I have cause to believe this friend is responsible, I will let you know."

Rawlins acquiesced. "As you wish. I will keep you apprised of developments concerning Harlow and Gill. In the meantime, I must urge you to take precautions for your safety and those of your guests. Vigilance is key."

"I will secure the manor and the safety of those in it," Ethan vowed.

Chapter Twenty-Two

Three days later, Xenia passed one of the guards in the corridor. He, along with four others, had arrived the day before from London. Ethan had hired them to do round-the-clock surveillance of the estate, and they worked in shifts, taking turns sleeping. Although the men were friendly, Xenia felt as nervous around them as she had the constable. Her upbringing had given her a fear of police, guards, and others who upheld the law that she could not shake.

A part of her briefly considered leaving. But she couldn't, of course. She was falling in love with Ethan more and more each day. She couldn't abandon him in his time of need, and she wanted to help him with his troubles. Thus, she'd resolved to stay as long as she could...until she had no choice but to run.

Maybe Mama won't find me this time. Maybe I can find a way to be safe.

"Good morning, Mrs. Wood."

The guard, a ginger-haired fellow named Jim Ferris, was built like a brick house. He gave a courteous nod, and she reminded herself that he wasn't the enemy. On the contrary, he'd been hired to protect her.

"Hello, Mr. Ferris." She hid her nerves behind a smile. "You're early for your rounds, aren't you?"

"Yes, ma'am. His lordship's guests are playing croquet in the garden, and 'e wanted us out there to keep watch."

With Lady Gigi and the others outside, Xenia would have more privacy to speak with Ethan. They hadn't managed to be alone since his visit to her room, which felt like three years rather than three days ago. Ethan had been busy securing the manor, and the omnipresent guards made sneaking around at night more challenging. She missed him...and needed to talk to him.

She stopped by his study first. The door was cracked open. When she peered inside, he was at his desk, his head bent as he scribbled something.

"I'm sorry to interrupt," she said softly. "Shall I come back later?"

"No." Ethan rose, hastily shuffling papers. "Is there something you wanted?"

"It can wait if you are busy."

"I am never too busy for you."

Limned by the light of the windows, he looked like a virile god, and a part of her marveled that he was her lover. His imposing grace did make the purpose of her visit more difficult, however. Since the piano incident, he had forbidden her—and the others—from leaving the estate. She knew he was only being protective, but enough was enough.

She went over to him. "I need to go to Chuddums."

"No," came his predictable reply.

"Nothing is going to happen," she insisted. "I have business to attend to in the village. If I don't find a replacement for Daisy, Berta is going to quit too. She was in tears this morning; she's simply stretched too thin. I also need to replenish our supplies, arrange deliveries, and—"

"I said no."

She threw up her hands. "You cannot keep me trapped in this manor forever..."

Her breath whooshed from her lungs as he caught her by the waist. Her bottom hit his desk with a soft thump. Her hands planted on the blotter as he stood in the vee of her dangling legs.

"Shall we wager on that?" Wicked challenge glinted in his eyes. "You are important to me, Xenia. I won't let anything happen to you."

His words transformed her heart into a swarm of butterflies.

"I know you won't," she said tremulously. "And that is my point—you've taken every precaution. You've had locks installed on the doors and windows and arranged a constant patrol of guards. If someone did stage the scene with the piano, they are unlikely to strike again."

"There is no 'if' about it: the hoax *was* perpetrated by a flesh-and-blood bastard, and I'm going to see that justice is served." His gaze was piercing. "In the meantime, I know what you mean to do, and I forbid it."

Her pulse raced. "Um, forbid what?"

He snorted. "The purpose of your visit to Chuddums isn't for housekeeping. You want to find out more about Bloody Thom. You think that if you can understand why he is 'haunting' the manor, you can stop him from causing more trouble."

Odds bodkins. He can read my mind.

"But your plan won't work," he said. "Do you know why?"

She sighed. "Because there is no such thing as ghosts?"

"She proves that she is capable of learning."

She narrowed her eyes. "He, however, has yet to prove that he can have an open mind. Has it occurred to you that there is more than one way to cook an egg?"

"I wasn't aware that you could cook an egg." He cocked a brow. "In any fashion."

She huffed. "My point is that even if it is not a ghost behind these incidents—"

"It's not."

"Even if the culprit is human, he or she is using details from the legend of Bloody Thom to try to frighten you. Have you heard the verse about him and his curse?"

"As I am not a child, I do not listen to nursery rhymes."

"Well, you should. Because this one is unfolding before us."

Taking a breath, she recited,

> "Beware, beware the rattling chain
> The flapping robes stained red and bold
> Beware the moans and wails of pain
> For 'tis Bloody Thom they do herald.
>
> He brings death to all who cross his path
> Be they creatures with feathers, fur, or skin
> Green will wither and die until his wrath
> Is quenched by a true reckoning.
>
> He plays a mournful ballad of blame
> Shaking the manor with his ire
> His cry for justice is like a flame
> That scorches all with unholy fire."

"Don't you see?" she concluded breathlessly. "The robes and chains, the murdered creatures with feathers, the mournful ballad. It is all happening like the poem says."

"A bit of verse doesn't prove that the ghost is real."

"I realize that," she said patiently. "But the events predicted by the poem are happening, which means the more *we* know about the supposed curse, the more we can anticipate what our adversary —be they spectral or human—might do next."

After a moment, Ethan said grudgingly, "That is sound logic."

"You needn't sound so surprised."

"I am not surprised. I'm impressed."

"Really?"

"Yes. You presented a rational case to justify finding out more about a ghost."

"The truth is..." She exhaled. "I *have* felt a...a presence in the manor."

"That is just your imagination, pet."

"No, it's more than that." She tried to piece together what she'd been sensing. "When I first arrived, I felt like I had been here before. Like the manor was...was almost waiting for me to return."

"Perhaps the house knew how desperately it needed a housekeeper."

"Very amusing." She wrinkled her nose at his smirking visage. "I am just trying to explain why I cannot discredit the possibility of a supernatural cause. Are you afraid to discover that I am correct, and you are wrong?"

When he bent toward her, she tilted her head back and gazed into his gleaming eyes.

"If you're trying to goad me into allowing your scheme, it won't work. I do have an alternative proposition, however."

A proposition. Now that sounds promising.

"What were you thinking?" she asked coyly.

He leaned closer, his spicy scent filling her senses. Anticipation quivered through her when his lips brushed the curve of her ear.

"We make a trade. A favor for a favor. I agree to let you pursue this Bloody Thom business, and in return, you give me something that I want."

Her nipples tightened into throbbing points, and her pussy dampened. "What do you want?"

"I want..."

When she wetted her lips, his gaze followed the path of her tongue. She recalled the wicked delight of taking him in her mouth. Would he ask her to do it now? Would he command her to kneel while he took out his big instrument and pushed it between her lips—

"I want you to tell me something about your family."

She blinked. "Um, what?"

"A few details about your parents, whatever you wish," he coaxed.

Although she thought about denying him, she wanted to grant his small request. To share more of herself with him—the sorts of things that a normal person could share without a second thought.

What harm will a few details do?

She sifted through her ignominious past and settled on a few safe facts.

"My papa was a musician who taught me to play the piano. He was also an excellent storyteller." She smiled wistfully. "Since we traveled a lot, we didn't have a place of our own, but wherever we ended up, he made it feel like home. He had this laugh that rumbled out of him...that made everyone around him laugh too."

"His passing must have been difficult for you," Ethan murmured.

You have no idea.

She remembered her father's hope that last week they had together. When they'd believed they had escaped Mama's clutches and would be starting a new life, a good life. He'd talked about her going to school and making friends, never living in fear again. She remembered him saying, *"You'll be all right, poppet"* and his agonized cries before he was killed.

Fifteen years of living with the loss—with the grief and guilt of her papa's sacrifice—allowed her to say quietly, "It was."

"And your mama?" Ethan prompted.

Nothing about her mother felt safe to share. Long ago, when she was a child, she'd yearned for her mother's approval...but that desire had died the day her papa did. Anger, resentment, and even hatred had smoldered in its place. Eventually, though, even those emotions burned out. After Mr. Trelawney's death, she'd recognized the truth: the woman who'd birthed her was not her mother in any meaningful sense. To her mind, she was an orphan...one who had the misfortune to be the only offspring of a heartless female cutthroat.

When she'd chosen to be Xenia Loveday, she'd emancipated herself emotionally from her mother. If only she could be free of the woman in reality as well. Yet her mama refused to let her go, was determined to control and punish her—to turn her into a cautionary tale.

"My mother and I never got along," Xenia said neutrally. "I left home when I was sixteen and haven't looked back."

Except in fear...always in fear.

Ethan stroked his thumb across her cheek. "Now I understand where your resourcefulness comes from. You've been taking care of yourself for a long time, haven't you?"

All my life, it seems.

A lump rose in her throat, and she couldn't speak.

"But now you have me, Xenia. Trust me. Let me in."

Her heartbeat accelerated, but she couldn't give in to her dangerous yearning. When she tried to protest, he swooped down. His kiss was scorching yet intimate. The urgency of their passion transported her into another realm, one where she felt safer than she ever had. When he broke the kiss, she was pressed against him, her arms wound around his neck as if she never wanted to let him go.

"I think I got the better end of the trade." His eyes held a smile. "Go get ready, and I shall escort you to the village."

"Hold up." She shook off the haze of desire. "You are coming with me? Why?"

"While you are looking for your ghost, I will be looking after you."

He kissed her nose, pulling her up. Papers clung to her skirts and swirled to the floor like dried leaves. Automatically, she bent to pick them up.

"Leave the papers." Ethan crouched beside her. "I'll get them—"

She looked at the sheet in her hand, recognizing it immediately. It was the sonata she'd found by his piano—the one she'd played, eliciting his wrath. He must have made another copy. A wise woman probably would have returned the score to him without another word...but when had she been wise?

"Have you been working on this?" she asked curiously.

He tried to snatch it from her, but she was too quick, keeping it out of his reach as she rose. Scanning the notes, she hummed the melody. The tune was as soulful and elegant as she remembered, and there were new bars that added an interesting shift to the melody.

"If you're quite finished." He held out an imperious hand. "Give it here."

When she complied, he shoved it under a pile on his desk.

"Why are you hiding your composition?" she asked. "It is beautiful."

"Do you think so?" His tone was gruff. "You are not saying that to be kind?"

"The melody is unique, both restrained and passionate," she said candidly. "It lingers like a memory one can't stop thinking about. I've caught myself humming it a few times since I, um, played it..."

Really, Xenia? Did you have *to remind him that you violated his privacy?*

He sighed. "I haven't properly apologized for my outburst, have I?"

"You have. And it was my fault as well—"

"Then it's an explanation I owe," he said. "After the damage to my hand, I thought music was lost to me forever. You were right when you said that playing the piano is not a trivial matter—to me, it was everything. But I was a performer, not a composer, and the sonata you found...it was my first and only attempt at writing music. Something I'd started as a lark before my injury and forgotten about. Hearing you play the piece brought back memories...mostly of everything I'd lost. I took my anger out on you, for which I humbly beg your forgiveness."

His sincerity made her heart flutter.

"You are forgiven," she said sincerely. "And I hope I am as well."

"Not only are you forgiven, but I may also owe you thanks." He hesitated. "Because you unearthed that sonata, I started wondering if I could...well, perhaps if I could give composing a go again. A real go, this time. It's not the same as performing, but..."

He gave a self-conscious shrug.

"But you would still be making music," she said excitedly. "Oh, Ethan, I think it is a *brilliant* idea. How is it going so far?"

"Slowly," he admitted. "I keep telling myself that if Beethoven could compose his greatest work without his hearing, then surely I can manage with one hand. But not being able to play the melody and accompaniment together is a challenge."

"I could help if you'd like. Play the part of the left hand."

"You would do that?"

The heated intensity of his gaze made her pulse race.

Don't you know, Ethan? I would do just about anything for you.

She cleared her throat. "Most definitely."

"I am a novice at composition," he warned. "I am not sure I have a talent for it."

"May I share a bit of hard-earned wisdom?"

He cocked his head.

"Pretend until it's true," she said. "Act as if you know what you are doing and soon enough you will."

When he looked skeptical, she added, "The method works. I didn't know how to be a housekeeper, but I acted as if I did. Eventually, I figured it out...and I even fooled you."

"You didn't fool me." He snorted. "From the time you shared your 'Golden Rule,' I knew you'd never been in service."

Perhaps not her grandest moment.

She tipped her head. "Then why did you let me stay on?"

"Because I like you." He pulled her close. "Thank you, Xenia. For your encouragement."

"You're welcome."

His kiss was tender and sweet, leaving her lightheaded.

"I kept you on for another reason too," he said.

"Oh? What reason was that?"

"You're a naughty minx, and I like the games you play." He gave her a playful swat on the bottom. "Now go get ready for our outing."

She squeaked with mock indignation before hurrying off. A smile played on her lips...because she liked the games he played, too.

CHAPTER TWENTY-THREE

When Lady Gigi got wind of the trip to Chuddums, she insisted on going. Misters Canning and Parkhurst promptly joined the entourage. None of them seemed to mind that they were accompanying a servant on an errand to the village. Ethan insisted on bringing a pair of guards, who followed on horseback. Despite all that, the carriage ride over was jolly and full of easy conversation, and Xenia found herself relaxing.

She particularly enjoyed the banter between Ethan and his sister. Having no siblings of her own, she observed their closeness with a wistful pang. Ethan was the epitome of a big brother, protective and a bit overbearing. Lady Gigi held her own with spirited verve, displaying her clever wit and independent mind. She and Xenia had a fun chat about their shared love of novels.

Upon arrival in Chuddums, Ethan declared that Xenia would be their guide as she was most familiar with the village. She accepted her role with grace, wanting to share the charms she'd discovered. She began the tour at Hatcherds, where the group received an effusive welcome from Mr. Khan. His success at the mop fair had motivated him to expand his offerings, which now included a bigger selection of books, stationery items, and bric-a-brac he'd gathered on his travels.

In the cozy new reading area, he presented them with sweets he'd made himself. After tasting one of the syrup-soaked, cardamom-spiced treats, Lady Gigi asked for another, much to his beaming delight. The party continued to browse, and Xenia took the shopkeeper aside.

"Has there been talk about what happened at the manor, Mr. Khan?" she said in an undertone.

He glanced at Ethan, who was a brooding presence behind her.

"I would consider it a favor if you would speak freely, sir," Ethan said.

"In that case." Mr. Khan pushed up his spectacles and lowered his voice. "A certain former employee of yours has been palavering about Bloody Thom to anyone who will listen. She says she saw him slaughter a flock of chickens with her own eyes. Then she claimed he hosted a ghoulish ball at midnight, and when his lordship interrupted, Bloody Thom erupted into a temper and cursed everyone in the manor."

If nothing else, Daisy is creative.

Xenia exchanged looks with Ethan, whose jaw had a grim edge.

"That report is more fiction than truth," Xenia said. "In fact, the so-called haunting might be a hoax."

The wrinkles on Mr. Khan's forehead deepened. "Why would anyone play such a horrid trick?"

"A constable is looking into the matter. In the meantime, whoever is behind the scheme knows a lot about the local folklore. Thus, we are trying to learn more about Bloody Thom. Other than the poem, is there more you can tell us about him?"

"Off the top of my head, I cannot think of anything." Mr. Khan scratched his ear. "But you should ask Mrs. Pettigrew. Her family has been here for several generations, and she has grown up with tales about the ghost."

Thanking Mr. Khan, Xenia waited for the group to make their

purchases, then led the way to the Leaning House. She was pleased to see that the tearoom was bustling. Mrs. Pettigrew greeted them with a respectful bob, looking flustered by the noble guests.

"What a charming establishment, ma'am," Lady Gigi enthused. "And how original that you've eschewed conventions of symmetry."

"Thank you, my lady." Mrs. Pettigrew appeared starstruck by the glamorous debutante. "My grandpapa built the shop at an angle by accident. Since his mistake drew customers, he didn't bother to change it."

"As I am often a trifle askew myself," Lady Gigi confided, "I shall feel right at home."

Her quip led to laughter all around. A smiling Mrs. Pettigrew seated the party at her best table, which had a view of the village green. After the food arrived—pots of strong Assam tea and plates of sandwiches and cakes—Xenia slipped away to find the good lady, who was in the kitchen, putting the finishing touches on a familiar dish.

"Is that Poor Knights of Windsor pudding?" Xenia asked.

"Indeed, it is." A smile tucked into Mrs. Pettigrew's generous cheeks. "Since the mop fair, it has become my signature dish. I do hope his lordship's party will enjoy it. And I must thank you again for bringing them to my humble establishment."

"You're most welcome. The truth is I have another purpose for coming today as well."

"Oh?"

Xenia repeated what she'd told Mr. Khan. "If you can tell me anything else about Bloody Thom, I would appreciate it."

"I don't know what else to add." Mrs. Pettigrew tucked a stray curl beneath her cap as she mulled over the matter. "But you ought to pay a visit to Henrietta Sommers."

Although Xenia had passed Mrs. Sommers's dress shop on several occasions, she'd never had reason to go in.

"Her grandpapa, Old Man Walford, lives with her and

knows Chuddums better than anyone," Mrs. Pettigrew went on. "You might have seen him in the square wearing a checkered coat."

"You mean Wally?" she asked in surprise. "The gentleman who gives directions?"

"I see you've met him," Mrs. Pettigrew said fondly. "Mr. Walford is in his nineties now, and his faculties aren't what they used to be. However, he was the mayor at one time and might have the information you are seeking."

It did not take much convincing on Xenia's part to add the dress shop to the group's agenda.

"There is a dress shop in Chuddums? Why didn't you say so earlier?" Lady Gigi moaned. "We should have gone there *before* I stuffed myself with Mrs. Pettigrew's pudding."

Ethan arched a brow. "If you wish to skip the visit—"

"Skip the dressmaker's?" The raven-haired beauty looked at her brother as if he'd suggested that she somersault off a bridge. "I think not. I shall simply do what every lady does in such a situation."

"You'll choose a looser style?" Parkhurst ventured.

"Heavens, no. I'll tighten my corset strings."

Lady Gigi rolled her eyes at Xenia as if to say, *Gentlemen don't know very much, do they?*

On the way, they lost Misters Canning and Parkhurst to a store displaying pocket watches. Mr. Pickleworth also stopped them, barring their way like a highwayman with his platter of cut tomatoes. As usual, Xenia declined, but in contradiction to her earlier concerns, Lady Gigi sampled several slices and purchased some to take home with her.

"These are the most delightful tomatoes," she exclaimed.

"Exactly, my lady." Mr. Pickleworth handed her the bag while giving Xenia an *I-told-you-so* look. "Ripe and juicy, like I said."

When they finally entered Mrs. Sommers's shop, Xenia gazed around with professional admiration. Despite the small space, everything was neat as a pin, with no clutter anywhere. A line of fashionable frocks was displayed on dressmaker's dummies. Cabinets containing unmentionables and accoutrements were tucked along the wall for discreet browsing. Looking glasses were spotless and counters polished to a dust-free gleam.

The dressmaker came to greet them. Dressed in black, she was small in stature and as tidy as her shop. Hastily, Xenia smoothed a wrinkle on her skirt.

"Good afternoon. I am Mrs. Sommers." The dressmaker curtsied. "May I be of assistance?"

"I hope so," Lady Gigi said brightly. "I am visiting my brother from London, and in my haste to see him, I did not pack sufficiently. I am in *dire* need of a wardrobe."

Truth be told, Lady Gigi looked like a fashion plate in her stylish pink-and-white striped carriage dress, bonnet trimmed with matching ribbon and silk flowers, and dainty shoes. Like any wise businesswoman, however, Mrs. Sommers's response was a deferential nod that said the customer knew best...especially when said customer had ample coin to spend. An assistant seated Lady Gigi in a comfy chair and brought her tea while Mrs. Sommers proceeded to show her examples of the latest silhouettes to use as inspiration for her own gown. The assistant brought over bolts of fabric for Lady Gigi to inspect.

Lady Gigi narrowed the choices down to two. "Ethan, which color do you prefer?"

Ethan, who had been idly examining a display case of gloves, looked over at the bolts. "They are both blue."

"One is mazarine blue," Lady Gigi said patiently. "The other is cornflower blue."

He aimed his gaze heavenward. "Get dresses made in both colors. And whatever else you need."

"This is why you are my favorite brother!"

When Lady Gigi went to a dressing room to have her measurements taken, Xenia hovered nearby, hoping to speak with Mrs. Sommers when the lady had a moment. As she waited, a frock caught her eye. It was cut from taffeta the shade of tender spring leaves. The dress had a modest square neckline and puff sleeves, the fitted bodice flowing into full skirts. A bit of lace at the sleeves and hem finished the creation.

It was probably the plainest dress in the shop, but Xenia loved it.

"See something you like?"

Ethan's deep voice startled her. She snatched her hand away from the dress.

"I don't need anything," she said.

"That is not what I asked."

The look in his eyes ruffled her, and her cheeks warmed. To be caught wanting what she couldn't afford embarrassed her. She was poor, but she had her pride. Of course, he wouldn't understand because he was a man who could buy whatever he wished.

She was saved from replying by Mrs. Sommers, who emerged through the back curtain.

Ethan took the lead. "Mrs. Sommers, if I might trouble you for a moment?"

"Certainly, my lord." Mrs. Sommers's manner was obliging to her well-paying client. "How may I be of assistance?"

"I am interested in some local history," he said. "Mrs. Pettigrew suggested that I speak to your grandfather. Is Mr. Walford available?"

"He usually is, but he's gone to stay with my sister in Manchester for a month. Is there anything I might help you with? Having lived in Chuddums all my life, I'm quite familiar with its history."

"It has to do with my property," he said. "Certain rumors about a ghost have made the retention of staff difficult. Thus, I would like to understand more about the local lore."

Xenia admired his tact.

"I see. Well, rumors about Bloody Thom have been around longer than I have," Mrs. Sommers said matter-of-factly. "They seem to have worsened in recent years, much like the fortunes of the village, I suppose. If you ask me, it's a bunch of nonsense. There is no such thing as ghosts."

"On that, we agree," Ethan said.

"But there are plenty of superstitious folk in the village, and the reports of so-called sightings don't help. Especially when those reports are, shall we say, embellished."

"You have heard Daisy's account?" Xenia guessed.

"Who hasn't?" The dressmaker snorted. "If you ask me, you're better off without her."

Xenia sighed. "It does leave the staff shorthanded, however."

"If you are looking to hire maids, Mrs. Wood, I have a gaggle of nieces in the next village looking for work. I'm certain they'd jump at the opportunity."

"I'd be much obliged," Xenia said gratefully. "And even more in your debt if you can think of anything to tell us about Bloody Thom beyond the rhyme and curse."

"I don't know if this will help." Mrs. Sommers pursed her lips. "But once, when I was a girl, my older sister decided to play a trick on me by dressing up in a tattered sheet stained with berry juice. She woke me in the middle of the night, and I screamed so loud I woke the house. I was scared to sleep for days. Finally, my grandpapa took me aside and asked if I could keep a secret. He told me I needn't be afraid of Bloody Thom. While others believed that Bloody Thom was a ghost story, he said that it was actually a love story."

"A love story?" Xenia echoed. "How can that be?"

"According to Grandpapa, the witch of the story wasn't a terrifying hag but a beautiful young woman. He said that she and Thomas Mulligan were in love."

"I don't understand. What about the curse?"

"I'm afraid that is all I can recall. It's possible that my grandpapa made this up to soothe me, but you can ask him when he returns. Hopefully, he will remember." Mrs. Sommers's smile was poignant. "He is the last of his generation in Chuddums, and when he goes, so will much of our village's history."

Chapter Twenty-Four

"I have to go," she said.

Even though she knew this was the right thing to do, her heart twisted at the thought of leaving him. Her beloved. Her knight in shining armor.

"No, my darling." He held her against him, his heartbeat steady and strong. "You must stay. Trust me to protect you."

"I am nothing but trouble," she said fretfully. "I will not be a burden to you."

"You could never be a burden. You, my sweet rose, are my salvation."

His kiss was gentle and convincing. Even as she lost herself in their passion, a shadow fell over her soul. She looked out the window and saw her nightmare coming up the drive. Terror welled as she saw moonlight glinting off a pistol. Then came the violent pounding on her beloved's door...

"Xenia?" Ethan looked up in surprise when she entered his bedchamber through the hidden servants' corridor. "I wasn't expecting you tonight."

That much was obvious. He was ready for bed in his dressing gown, his hair damp and curling from a bath. Already out of breath from rushing here, she felt her lungs strain in part because of his splendid virility...but mostly because he was alive and breathing. The terror of her dream propelled her into his arms.

He caught her against him, holding her tight.

"What happened, love? Why are you so frightened?"

His voice rumbled beneath her ear, as did his steady heartbeat. *Thank God.*

"I had a dream," she said shakily.

He stroked her hair. "A bad one?"

She nodded against his chest, feeling muddled. The nightmare had been so convincing, so real. Her pulse was racing, her skin damp beneath her nightgown. She'd been in such a panic to make sure he was all right that she hadn't changed before rushing here. It was only by chance that she'd evaded the guards.

"What was the dream about?" he asked gently.

"I don't know," she said.

"You don't remember the dream?"

"I'm not sure it was a dream."

"What was it then?"

She lifted her head to look at him. "You are going to think I'm mad."

"I won't. Tell me."

Drawing a breath, she said, "It felt almost like...like a memory."

"It isn't unusual to dream about things that have happened to us."

"But it wasn't my memory. I think...I think it was someone else's."

Ethan's brows winged. "Whose?"

"I don't know. But she was like me." Xenia bit her lip. "I told you that I've felt a presence in the manor, and now I think it's her —the woman from the dream. She and I...we're alike. She is trying to leave her past behind. And she doesn't want to be a burden to her lover."

"You could never be a burden..." He trailed off. "Why are you looking at me that way?"

"He said those exact words," Xenia whispered.

"Er, who did?"

"The lover from my dream. He said, *'You could never be a burden. You, my sweet rose, are my salvation.'* But someone was coming after her, and she was frightened because now he was in danger too. This good man who was trying to protect her. It felt so real, and I...I thought it was you, so I had to come see..."

"I'm fine, pet." Ethan cupped her cheek. "But I think I know what the problem is."

Having spoken her fears aloud, she knew how batty they sounded.

"Do you think I have a screw loose?" she said in a small voice.

"I think you are overtired," he said firmly. "With Daisy gone, you've had more on your hands, and you've had to train the new maids as well."

True to her word, Mrs. Sommers had sent over her nieces Molly, Mary, and Millie, and Xenia had spent the day getting the trio on board. The girls were young and a bit flighty. On the bright side, their boundless energy and tendency to flirt with the footmen gave the staff something to talk about other than Bloody Thom.

Xenia bit her lip. "You don't think it's, well, *strange* that I feel as if I'm having someone else's memories?"

"This is because of what Mrs. Sommers said, isn't it? About Thomas Mulligan and his supposed lover? You think you are dreaming about her memories?"

Beneath his shrewd gaze, she gave a small nod. "The lover in my dream, who could be Mulligan, calls her *his sweet rose*," she said hesitantly. "I think...I think that might be her name: *Rose*. When I first arrived, I found a beautiful hairbrush in my room, far too expensive for a servant to own, and there's a rose carved on the back. I think maybe it was a gift from her lover. Oh, and the first time I went into the village, Mr. Walford greeted me by the name 'Rosalinda'—"

"Do you think it's possible that you are more observant than most and making connections between coincidental events?" Ethan spoke without judgment. "Building on tales that you've heard?"

It *was* in her nature to do those things. She was a storyteller, after all. Moreover, she couldn't deny that the dreams she'd been having had a lot in common with her own past and fears.

"It's possible," she admitted.

"All jests aside, I do want to keep an open mind. While I do not believe that my enemy is supernatural, I do trust your instincts," he said earnestly. "If you believe the history surrounding Thomas Mulligan and how he died is somehow relevant to what is going on presently, then perhaps we could obtain the address of Mrs. Sommers's sister in Manchester and write Mr. Walford. Perhaps his reply will shed light on the matter."

She adored him for taking her seriously, even though he might not agree.

"Thank you," she said softly. "That would ease my mind greatly."

"With all this talk of ghosts and curses, it's no wonder you are on edge. I am too."

"You are?" She studied him. "One would never know. In fact, you seem to be rather sure of yourself and what needs to be done."

"It's a trick I learned when I was performing. Never reveal your nerves to the audience."

"Pretend until it's true," she said sagely. "But you don't have to hide your nerves from me."

"I know." His gaze was as warm as the firelight. "You are one of the few people I can be myself with, Xenia. All evening, when I was with the fellows, I found myself missing your company. I am glad you came to me, and I want you to know that you always can."

His sincerity caused her heart to pitter-patter. Wordlessly, he took her hand and led her to the chesterfield. He went to pour them glasses of port, then sat beside her, putting his arm around her shoulders. She snuggled against him, sipped the sweet, fruity spirit, and felt much more the thing. She was grateful that the master suite was down the hall from the guest chambers, affording them some rare privacy.

"You heard about my day," she said after they set down their glasses. "How was yours?"

His lips curved, as if he, too, appreciated being able to share a mundane moment. He told her about Rawlins's report. Apparently, the investigator had spoken to Harlow, who denied going anywhere near Bottoms House. Rawlins had advised Ethan to leave things be for now. On a more positive note, the Hirschfield brothers had finished renovating the stables and gazebo, and Ethan had hired a groundskeeper.

"I also worked on my composition," he said casually.

It was so like him to save the most important news for last.

"How is that going?" she asked.

"Could be better, could be worse." He paused. "I was hoping you might assist me tomorrow. If you have time in between your duties."

"I think my employer will allow it," she said, smiling.

He raised his brows. "He might even give you a raise. There is a lot of work to be done."

"Getting started is the hardest part. I am certain it will go easier once you are back at it."

"Canning said the same thing. We're in the same boat, he and I. His novel has been stalled for years, and he wants to really give it a go and finish it."

"It must be nice to have friends who are also artists," she said wistfully.

"Yes. We've supported one another through the highs and lows. Back in the day, the fellows attended my concerts, and I went to their exhibitions and readings."

While Xenia had eyes only for Ethan, she could imagine that the three handsome gentlemen must have stolen more than a few hearts.

"You must have been popular," she teased.

"We were."

No false modesty there.

She couldn't help but inquire, "With the ladies especially?"

He arched a brow. "Are you asking about my past lovers?"

Admittedly, she was curious. Of late, she'd found herself thinking about the relationships he'd had in the past...and whether he'd been in love.

"Was there anyone you were serious about?" she asked tentatively.

"I had casual liaisons. Nothing lasting. I was also engaged, but that ended when we discovered we did not suit."

As she digested that information, he asked, "Why don't you ask the question that is really on your mind?"

"What question is that?"

"You want to know if I have been in love."

She took the bait. "Have you?"

"No," he said solemnly. "Not yet."

His emphasis on "yet" and the way he squeezed her shoulders made her toes curl.

"My parents, you see, have always been unfashionably and madly in love," he went on. "Their relationship sets a high bar for the rest of us. One day you'll meet them, and you'll see what I mean."

I am going to meet Ethan's parents?

Yearning and fear wrung her insides. On the one hand, she

wanted to meet the rest of Ethan's family...to know the people who were closest to him. On the other, she was his servant, and they were having an illicit affair. While they'd managed to hide their relationship from his naïve young sister, his parents might not be as easy to fool. They would undoubtedly disapprove of her and might even insist Ethan break things off.

Why are you worrying about Ethan's parents? You'll probably have to run before you get a chance to darken their door. Don't fool yourself into believing that this affair can last.

"What about you?" he asked.

She blinked, so absorbed in her inner conversation that she'd lost track of the actual one.

"My parents fought constantly and if they were ever in love, it didn't last—"

"Not your parents, pet. You. Have you been in love?"

She hesitated, but their intimacy felt so good that she didn't want it to end.

"I thought I was in love once," she admitted.

"With that follower you mentioned?" he asked intently. "Tell me about him."

"He was, um, a writer. I admired his passion for his craft and wanted to help him succeed." She glossed over the details of how Tony had asked her to perform his erotic stories. How he'd used her and how she'd willingly let him do it. "But he had troubles... vices he couldn't escape. He owed money to some villains, and the long and short of it is that he was eventually found dead."

"By Jove." Ethan tipped her chin up, looking into her eyes. "I'm sorry for the pain that must have caused."

"He was too young to die," she agreed sadly, "and he left behind a brother who grieved for him. I wish I could have helped him—"

"When a man is in the grip of vice, no one can help him but himself."

Ethan's jaw was taut, and remembering everything he'd gone through with his brother, she laced her fingers with his.

"I've come to accept that." She released a breath. "And the fact that while I was infatuated with him, he wasn't interested in me. He just liked being admired."

Her cheeks burned with humiliation at her own folly. Would another man's indifference make her seem less worthy in Ethan's eyes? Would it make him realize that she was no one special?

"He was a fool," Ethan said.

Relief heated her eyes. "I was a bigger one."

"You are not a fool." He thumbed away a tear wending down her cheek. "What you are is too tender-hearted for your own good."

"I realize now that I was in love with the *idea* of being in love. All that novel reading, I suppose." She tried for a smile. "I promise I have learned my lesson. I shan't be silly where you are concerned."

I may be in love with you, Ethan Harrington, but I'll keep it to myself.

"I don't want that promise from you."

Her breath jammed. "You...you don't?"

"I want you to be *you*, Xenia." His intensity was spellbinding. "Your brave, sweet, and naughty self. I don't want you to hold anything back with me. Your follower might have been blind, but I'm not. I see how special you are, and I want to know you, not just in the biblical sense. I care about you, and for my part, I don't want to limit what is happening between us. Do you trust me, pet?"

Her heart pounded against her ribs, but it was a sweet pain.

"I trust you more than I've trusted anyone," she said.

"Then I need to teach you to trust me completely. To show you that you are, and will always be, safe with me. No time like the present for a lesson."

At his dark, seductive tone, anticipation unfurled.

"What sort of lesson is this?" she asked coquettishly.

"What did I just say about trusting me?"

Odds bodkins, she loved it when he got stern.

"Now stand up and undress," he said. "But do it slowly. I want a show."

With a shiver of arousal, she rose. He remained where he was, with one arm across the back of the sofa, sleek as a panther in his black dressing gown. He played lord of the manor with such arrogant veracity that she would have been intimidated if not for the playful glint in his eyes. His expression dared her to participate in his naughty game, and she'd never been one to back down from a challenge.

As she was wearing a shapeless nightgown, giving a sensual performance wasn't the easiest. Yet if she excelled at anything, it was making do with what she had. Having observed how her light-skirt colleagues titillated audiences, she resolved to do the same. She began by lifting her hair above her head, letting it fall slowly. His gaze followed the strands where they landed, caressing her breasts and hips. Seeing that she had his attention, she smoothed her palms over her chest, cupping her mounds through the worn flannel.

"Are your nipples hard, pet?"

His casual tone made them harder.

"Yes. I wish your hands were on me."

"I shall be touching you soon enough." He sat back, comfortable as a king on his throne. "Carry on."

She obeyed, running her hands over her rib cage and the indentation of her waist. She traced the flare of her hips and the curves of her thighs and bottom. Bending, she reached for the hem of her gown.

"Pull it up slowly," he ordered. "Reveal one beautiful inch at a time."

Somehow he made her *feel* beautiful. As if she wasn't a housekeeper lifting a shabby nightgown but a siren shedding silken veils for her master. She drew her hem up bit by bit, her blood thrumming as his sensual commentary continued.

"Such pretty toes," he said. "And those calves, they gripped my hips so nicely when I rubbed my cock against your slit. Did you like that, pet?"

Her hands trembled at the memory, and she almost lost her grip on her nightgown.

"Very much," she said truthfully.

"Keep going, love. Show me what a fortunate man I am."

Her heart racing, she raised the material higher. When she exposed her sex, his eyelids lowered halfway, and his voice had a guttural edge.

"By Jove, you're a tempting piece. I can see your dew on that lovely red hair of yours. It makes my mouth water. Do you know why?"

Blood rushed under her skin; she felt hot all over. "Because you want to taste me?"

"More than taste," he chided. "Pet, I am going to eat you like you are my last meal."

Blooming hell. When she squeezed her thighs together, she felt the slickness of her arousal.

"You like that idea, I see." His eyes had a wolfish gleam. "We'll get to that once I finish enjoying my show."

The sizeable bulge in his lap confirmed his appreciation. Knowing that she'd brought about his aroused state emboldened her. She turned around, giving a saucy wiggle of her bottom. When he let out a ragged breath, she felt a heady rush of accomplishment. Unbuttoning her nightgown, she drew it over her head and let it fall on the ground. She kept her back turned to him, covering her chest with her arms, throwing him a flirty glance over her shoulder.

"My naughty girl is showing off," he said with approval. "You know how beautiful and special you are, don't you?"

Her throat swelled. "I feel special when I'm with you."

"You are special always," he corrected. "Turn around, please."

She did, letting her arms fall to her sides. She'd never felt more exposed, yet when he raked his flame-hot gaze over her, she didn't feel embarrassed or shy…she felt *coveted*. As if she belonged to Ethan, and he to her. The intensity of the feeling blocked out everything else.

"You are a feast for the eyes," Ethan said. "You know that, don't you?"

I do. Because of you.

"Yes, sir," she replied demurely. "But the only eyes I care about are yours."

"Such pretty words." He crooked a finger at her. "Time to see what else that talented mouth of yours can do."

Chapter Twenty-Five

Xenia walked to him like Aphrodite emerging from the sea. Her tresses played peekaboo with her mouthwatering curves, and her eyes shone with beguiling new confidence. There was also a hint of mischief in her smile...that of a minx who was discovering her own sensual power. Under normal circumstances, Ethan found Xenia irresistible. At present, his rampant erection threatened to push through the panels of his robe.

His pulse broke into a staccato when she halted in the vee of his legs and started to kneel. Christ, he liked the way her mind worked. However, he wouldn't last if she put her mouth on his cock, and he wanted to draw out the pleasure.

"Hold that thought, pet." He circled his fingers around her wrist, dragging her onto his lap. "I want to taste your mouth first before I enjoy it in other ways."

Given that she was naked and straddling him, it seemed impossible that she could look innocent. Yet she turned a charming shade of pink that turned *him* into a territorial beast. He couldn't believe that this sweet girl had fallen into his lap—figuratively as well as literally—and he burned to claim her as his. Although she insisted their affair had no strings, she was wrong: their bond was growing stronger day by day. She'd trusted him enough to talk about her follower, and she'd come to his room, panicked by a dream of him coming to harm. He could discuss his family and his music with her—the fears and hopes that were too tender to share with anyone else.

Each kiss, each touch—hell, each argument they had—deepened their relationship. He'd never been this intimate with any woman before, and he hadn't even made love to her fully. While he had much to learn about her past, he nonetheless knew *her*—the woman she was, the woman...

The woman I am falling in love with.

The knowledge soared through him like a Bach hymnal. With Constance, he'd envisioned a calm and conventional future. With Xenia, he didn't know what the future would bring, but he didn't care...as long as she was in it.

"Kiss me," he ordered.

He slid his fingers into her hair as she pressed her lips to his. She tasted of port and her own sweetly intoxicating flavor. When he licked inside her mouth, she licked him back, making his cock jerk against her bottom. He curled her hair around his fist, holding her still while he drove his tongue deep. His blood rushed when her pussy dampened the fabric over his cock.

His little minx liked a bit of roughness, did she?

He yanked harder on her hair, exposing her throat. He set his mouth on the vulnerable arch, kissing and sucking, increasing the pressure. When she squirmed, he experimented with his teeth, and her excited little gasp told him everything he needed to know.

Christ, she's a wild one. Absolutely, bloody perfect.

He cupped one enticing tit while putting his mouth on the other. He teased her nipple with his tongue, flicking then sucking. He went back and forth, pausing to bury his face between her plump mounds, inhaling her clean, womanly scent.

Her breathless pleas drove him wild. He traced the supple

curve of her spine down to her crevice. He feathered over her forbidden rim and noted her little shiver...another thing to explore later. He brought his fingers lower, and satisfaction rolled through him at the lushness of her response. With Xenia, he always knew where he stood.

"You're soaked, minx. We can't let that cream go to waste, can we?"

He brought his dew-slicked fingers to his mouth. Her eyes got even bigger when he licked his middle digits. The devil inside him wanted to push her a little.

"Your turn." He offered her his fingers.

Blushing to the roots of her hair, she hesitated before taking a tentative lick that he felt in his balls. When he shuddered, her expression turned impish. She closed her lips around him, applying suction. He growled, pushing his fingers into her saucy mouth. Her naughtiness and the velvet pad of her tongue unleashed his basest urges. He gave a few rough thrusts before pulling out his digits and bringing them to her pussy. He pushed a finger into her slowly, and she clutched his shoulders, gasping.

"You're so tight," he said. "And you're squeezing my finger. Do you want more?"

"Yes." Her cheeks were flushed, her eyes dazed. "Give me more."

Her dew eased his way. As he impaled her to the knuckle, a feeling of *déjà vu* stirred. A fragment floated into his consciousness...a dream he'd had of Sirena. Of her riding his hand just like this. He pushed the thought aside, not wanting to spoil the moment. Xenia deserved his full attention. She was his fantasy come to life.

"Can you take more?" he asked.

At her moaned reply, his cock jerked, pre-seed wetting his dome. He added another finger, gritting his teeth at the exquisite stretch, imagining those untried muscles gripping his cock. He pushed all the way in, letting her adjust before retreating. He repeated the motion, and when she started to wriggle, he knew she was ready for more.

"Ride my fingers, pet," he said.

Bracing her hands on his shoulders, she rose up, her eyelids fluttering as she sank down. She did it again and again with sensual grace. Her pussy made slick, squelching sounds...the most enchanting music. Yet it was the way her gaze stayed locked on his that took him to the edge. She was looking at him as if he were the epicenter of her pleasure...of her everything.

The need to bring her over blazed through him. He didn't have sufficient dexterity in his free hand to diddle her pearl, but he could do something else with it. Lifting his left hand, he spanked her bottom. She squealed, her pussy clenching his fingers. He spanked her again, and she rode him harder. The third time he swatted her blushing arse, she chanted his name and came.

Christ, did she ever. Savoring her full-body spasms, he gave her languorous kisses. A few moments later, he suspected that she was no longer trembling from the aftermath but wriggling against him with renewed purpose. She confirmed this by untying his robe and sliding her pussy over his turgid shaft. His chest heaved as she painted him with her lush folds.

Christ, if her pussy feels this good on the outside, how will it feel once I'm buried inside her?

His cock twitched as temptation once again beckoned. Until she was ready to trust him fully—to consider a future with him— he wouldn't give in to it. Not all the way, anyway.

He cocked a brow in challenge. "Shall we try it this way, pet? Can you make both of us come by rubbing your sweet cunny against my cock?"

Desire had never looked more beautiful to him than it did now, shining in her eyes.

"I shall put forth my best effort, sir," she said.

She was a cheeky one, all right.

And he was one fortunate bastard.

"What do you think?" Xenia asked.

As promised, she'd come to his study this morning, and they were sitting side by side at the Bösendorfer. She'd played the left hand to his right. Hearing the parts together had set the cogs turning in his head.

"The exposition needs something more," he said. "It is too simple."

Her brow pleated. "I think what you have is elegant."

"You say elegant, I say boring. I need to modulate to another key. Something like this."

He played a few notes for her, and she nodded slowly.

"That is more interesting," she admitted.

He experimented further, transitioning from C minor to E-flat major and reworking the progressions. He made notations, working so quickly that he smeared the ink.

"All right, I think this is better," he said. "Let's try it this way."

She gave him a demure look. "That is what you said last night."

The memory burst into his head: of her sitting in his lap and squirming against his cock, rubbing her wet pussy against him until they both exploded. The saucy wench had thought they were done, but he proved her wrong by eating her on his chesterfield, feasting on her until she sang her release again. He'd reached his second finale by pumping his cock, spraying his seed over her breasts while she watched with worshipful eyes.

"Minx," he growled. "How am I supposed to finish this sonata with you distracting me and making me hard?"

"All right," she said with a laugh. "No more flirting. Let's give it another go."

He wanted to give *her* another go, but he also wanted to keep working on the piece. With Xenia beside him, composing music— and life in general—felt less daunting and more fun. She was supportive yet honest, and while she didn't have much in the way of formal training, her innate musicality allowed her to give useful feedback. She was everything he hadn't known he needed...and he found her utterly irresistible. Cupping her jaw, he pulled her in for a quick kiss. Somehow their tongues got in the way, and when they broke apart, they were both panting.

"Now who is being distracting?" she asked breathlessly.

Seeing the smudge on her cheek, he smiled and reached for his handkerchief. "Hold still," he murmured. "I've left ink on you."

As he wiped off his fingerprint, she gazed at him with a tenderness that constricted his chest.

"Ethan, are you in here?" Gigi called.

His sister burst into his inner sanctum. Her dark ringlets swung as she gazed first at Xenia, who'd jumped up like a thief caught red-handed, then to Ethan, who rose at a less incriminating pace.

"Am I interrupting anything?" Gigi asked.

"No," Xenia said.

"Yes," Ethan said at the same time.

Gigi was obviously trying not to laugh. "No, yes...which is it?"

"I was working on a composition and wanted to hear it played," Ethan said with as much dignity as he could muster. "Mrs. Wood was helping me."

"But we're, um, finished, my lady," Xenia blurted. "And I must get back to my duties. If you'll both excuse me."

She fled the room, leaving him with his sister.

"You're composing?" Gigi's eyes shone. "Ethan, that's wonderful news!"

"Don't get too excited," he muttered. "I haven't made it past the exposition. Now, was there something you wanted?"

"As a matter of fact, yes. Let's talk over tea."

They went to sit in his study. One of the giggly maids—Millie, Molly, or Mary...he couldn't for the life of him distinguish between them—brought in a tea tray before he rang for one. His chest warmed at Xenia's thoughtfulness, at the grace notes of her presence in his life.

"These scones are divine." Seated in a wingchair, Gigi dabbed a buttery morsel with clotted cream and jam. "If this were London, someone would have lured your cook away in an instant."

He couldn't deny that Mrs. Johnson was a find. The fare she produced could compete with the best in London, and it was a miracle that Xenia had found her in Chuddums. Then again, his minx had a way of performing miracles.

"Mrs. Wood found her," he said.

"What would you do without Mrs. Wood?" Gigi said airily.

The possibility chilled him, and he didn't want to contemplate it.

"Was there something you wished to discuss?" he asked.

"Actually, we are discussing it: Mrs. Wood."

Instantly, he was wary. Had Gigi guessed the nature of his relationship with Xenia? While they'd tried to be discreet, the scene Gigi interrupted had smacked of intimacy. Moreover, his sister was uncommonly perceptive. Since she was a girl, she'd been the first to pick up on tensions and intrigues within their family. At heart, she was a peacemaker who wanted everyone to get along...which had made things difficult for her these last few years.

"It is about the gift you asked me to order for Mrs. Wood," Gigi explained.

He'd taken a calculated risk, asking his sister to order the dress for Xenia. But having observed Xenia's soft, covetous expression when she'd touched the frock, he'd been determined to give it to her. Of course, he couldn't buy a dress for his housekeeper without causing talk, and Xenia had so much pride that she might not accept it from him. Thus, he'd hit upon the plan of asking his sister to buy it.

Pulling Gigi aside, he'd told her that he saw Mrs. Wood eyeing the green dress and wanted to reward her for her excellent service. Gigi, being Gigi, picked up on the dilemma immediately. She offered to purchase the dress for Mrs. Wood—with Ethan's funds, of course, since she was a sieve with her pin money. The situation had worked out well...or so Ethan had thought.

"Is there a problem?" he asked.

"No. But the dress just arrived, and I was wondering what you want me to do with it."

"Give it to Mrs. Wood," he said. "Like we discussed before, tell her it is a gift from you."

Gigi gnawed on her lip, then blurted, "Mrs. Wood is very sweet, and you mustn't hurt her."

He stilled. "I beg your pardon?"

His sister's cheeks reddened, but she met his gaze squarely. "I am not a dummy, Ethan," she said. "It is obvious from the way you look at one another when you think no one else is watching that there is something going on."

He grew uncomfortably warm under the collar. "If you are implying—"

"I am not implying anything. I am saying it directly because you are my brother, and I care about your happiness." She took a breath. "And you haven't seemed happy, not for a long time. Not since...since the accident."

He was momentarily stunned. While his family tended to be oversolicitous about his injury, they rarely addressed the subject of how he'd received it. They had their reasons. His parents and siblings didn't want to upset him...and they feared widening the rift between him and Owen. Since the rift was more of a chasm, however, he didn't think they could do further damage. Nonetheless, why would Gigi, the pacifist, bring up a topic she normally avoided like the plague?

"I didn't think Constance helped matters," his sister said, wrinkling her nose. "But when she broke things off, I was worried that *how* your engagement ended would make everything worse. You wouldn't talk about it with the family, and then you came here, to a manor in the middle of nowhere. Bottoms House of

Chudleigh Bottoms, for heaven's sake. I was dreading the state I would find you in."

"You needn't have worried, Gigi. I am fine," he said gruffly.

He was surprised to realize that this was true. He was in a different frame of mind now than when he'd left London...than he'd been in a long time, in truth. He had to credit the change to Xenia.

"I see that." His sister smiled. "While the country air might agree with you, Ethan, I also think your improved mood has to do with Mrs. Wood."

"She has been of great help. She's made the manor habitable—"

"And she's made *you* much more comfortable to be around. You are far less brooding than you were, brother dear."

"Is there a point to this analysis of my mood?"

"It is simply this: as relieved and overjoyed as I am that you are feeling better, I don't wish it to be at the expense of Mrs. Wood."

"I don't follow," he said.

"For years, I saw you surrounded by an adoring female horde. Even after your injury, when you avoided the public eye, Constance managed to worm her way into your sphere. I am not saying you encouraged any of this, but you are used to female attention, Ethan, and have always taken it as your due. But Mrs. Wood...she's different from the others."

His sister's insights both disturbed and alarmed him. "How do you mean?" he asked.

"Mrs. Wood is not after your fame or wealth, for starters. And unlike Constance, she's not using you to establish herself as some Paragon of Womanly Virtue."

"Constance wasn't using me..."

He trailed off, drawing his brows together at his sister's unsettling supposition. Was that why Constance had pursued him after his accident? He'd thought it was because she was compassionate and willing to take on a damaged fellow like himself. Christ, he'd been grateful for her unending patience when it came to his brooding and irritability.

"Wasn't she?" Gigi curled her lip. "I didn't dislike Constance because of some childish whim. I disliked her because of the way she treated you. Like you were some damaged rake who needed to be reformed by her righteous guidance. If I had a penny for every time she told me that I should be more patient with you—give you space and leave you to your moods—I would be rolling in pin money. She wedged herself between you and not only our family, but the rest of the world. She indulged your worst tendencies and acted as if she was the only one who could understand you."

Reeling, Ethan said, "If you believed all that, why didn't you say something sooner?"

"I *tried*. Countless times." Gigi balled her hands in her lap. "But you wouldn't hear a bad word against Constance and got angry if I brought it up. I feared putting a strain on our relationship, so I stopped."

He remembered being annoyed with Gigi. He'd thought that she was being a spoilt brat—that she was jealous of Constance for being the paragon that she wasn't.

In reality, did I shoot the messenger?

"I'm sorry," he said with prickling awareness. "I should have listened."

"Apology accepted. As long as I may say *I told you so* as many times as I like."

At that, he narrowed his eyes.

"Fine. I shall only say it on holidays and special occasions." Gigi's expression turned serious. "But I hope you will heed me when it comes to Mrs. Wood. Trust me when I say she is unlike other dalliances you've had. To you, she may be a convenient distraction, but you could hurt her if you are not careful."

Ethan did not know what appalled him more. That his sister was speaking of his "dalliances" or that she believed that he would use Xenia for his own selfish ends.

"I have no intention of hurting Mrs. Wood," he said brusquely.

"Are your intentions honorable?"

"My private affairs are none of your business—"

"Didn't we just establish that they are? After all, if you'd listened to me about Constance..."

He gave a disgruntled sigh. Gigi was never more annoying than when she was right. Which, unfortunately, was often. Truth be told, he wanted to discuss the notion that had seeded itself in his brain with someone who knew Xenia and his family. Someone whom he could trust to give their honest opinion. While he wished that someone was not his baby sister, he did not have many options.

"If Mrs. Wood were to become a permanent fixture in my life, how would you feel about it?" he said carefully.

Gigi tipped her head to one side. "By 'permanent,' do you mean she would be your mistress or your wife?"

"Devil take it." He scowled at her. "Of course I meant I would marry her. Do you think I would discuss the matter with you otherwise?"

"There is no need to be cross. I wanted to be sure. And to answer your question: I would very much like having Mrs. Wood as my sister-in-law."

Even though he'd suspected as much, some of his tension eased.

"And the rest of the family?" he asked. "How do you think they would react?"

"We are not a bunch of snobs, as well you know. Nor are we sticklers for propriety...well, with the exception of James," she said thoughtfully. "He's a bit of a stick-in-the-mud when it comes to duty. Ultimately, I think that what he and the rest of us care about most is your happiness. If you and Mrs. Wood love one another, then why shouldn't you get married?"

Put that way, it seemed so simple. While he and Xenia had not made professions of love, he could not deny that he was falling for her. He was reasonably certain she was falling for him too. Xenia's inability to hide her feelings from him was one of her most endearing qualities...even if she harbored secrets.

Her past was a barrier he'd yet to surmount. However, he was chipping away at her defenses, and she'd disclosed some facts. Enough for him to know that she'd been making her own way in the world for a long time, without the support of family, friends, or even a lover. It explained a lot about her resourcefulness and insecurities about her self-worth.

He was proud of her strength and resilience. Proud that such a woman wanted him.

Now all I have to do is win her trust.

"The decision is not mine alone," he said slowly. "Mrs. Wood does not wish to make any commitments. Something happened in her past that has her running scared. She refuses to talk about it."

"She does seem skittish." Gigi brightened and sat up straighter. "However, I have a plan."

Because he knew his sister, he asked with suspicion, "What sort of plan? You are not to engage in any of your harum-scarum schemes—"

"Don't worry about a thing." She bounced up, making a beeline for the door. "I know what I'm doing."

"I mean it, Gigi. Do not meddle in my affairs."

"When have I ever meddled, brother dearest?"

Gigi shot him a guileless look before hurrying out.

He groaned.

Bloody hell. I am doomed.

Chapter Twenty-Six

"I've changed my mind, Lady Gigi," Xenia said nervously. "I should have an early night—"

"Nonsense. You look too pretty to spend the night in your room," Lady Gigi coaxed. "You don't want Colette's efforts to be wasted, do you?"

"Um, no."

Xenia was still befuddled over how she'd ended up allowing Lady Gigi's maid to dress her and do her hair. It had started with Lady Gigi summoning her to her chamber after supper. She'd thought the other needed help with something. Instead, Ethan's sister had presented her with a gift: the beautiful green dress from Mrs. Sommers's shop.

To be seen as worthy of such a magnificent gift had overwhelmed Xenia. While she suspected that Ethan was behind the scheme, Lady Gigi was obviously in on it too, and she'd choked out thanks, fighting back tears. She'd also tried to refuse the generous present, but Lady Gigi would hear none of it. The lady had insisted she try on the dress—which fit like a glove—and maneuvered her into a chair. Before she knew what was happening, Colette had descended like a whirlwind.

While the lady's maid worked her magic, Lady Gigi had distracted Xenia with chitchat.

"You must keep me company in the drawing room," Ethan's sister declared. "Parkhurst and Canning are making mincemeat of my toes, and another female dance partner is required to even the balance."

"I don't belong with the guests, my lady," Xenia protested.

"It's a small and casual gathering," Lady Gigi said airily. "There will be no sticklers to tell us what we can and cannot do. We need not stand on ceremony, and to that end, I must ask that you call me Gigi. I shall call you Jane, if that suits."

"I couldn't, my lady." Then Xenia heard herself blurt, "But you may call me Xenia, if you wish."

"Xenia?" Lady Gigi looked puzzled. "I thought your name was Jane."

What was it about the Harringtons that made Xenia want to unburden herself? While she couldn't confide her secrets, she did the next best thing.

"Xenia is what my friends call me."

Lady Gigi gave her arm a squeeze. "Then Xenia it is."

For the next little while, they chatted like bosom chums. Xenia discovered that she was only two years older than Ethan's sister. Lady Gigi was charming and witty, brimming with amusing anecdotes. Xenia forgot to protest over Colette's ministrations as Gigi related stories from her childhood. The ones involving Ethan captivated Xenia.

"Did Eth—his lordship, I mean, truly run away when he was ten?" Xenia asked.

"Yes," Lady Gigi confirmed. "I was a babe at the time, so I don't recall any of it. According to Mama, he and Owen had gotten into one of their usual tiffs, and Ethan got blamed for picking on his younger brother. Well, he got so angry at the unfairness of it all that he filched one of Papa's valises, filled it with food from the kitchen, and took off."

Xenia felt a twinge of empathy for Ethan's younger self. Although she was an only child, she imagined being born in the middle couldn't have been easy. One would have to deal with domineering older siblings and pampered younger ones.

"Did anyone go after him?" she asked.

"No."

She felt indignant on his behalf. "Why not?"

"Because the valise wasn't big enough to fit the piano," Lady Gigi said with a twinkle. "And everyone knew he wouldn't go far without it."

Xenia couldn't help but laugh. "Was his lordship always fond of the piano?"

"One of my earliest memories is of Ethan playing. Even though he was introduced to the piano relatively late—he was eight or nine, I think—he was an instant prodigy. Our grandmama, the dowager marchioness, was especially proud of his musical prowess and insisted on hiring famous maestros to teach him. She was a harridan, but Ethan was her favorite and she loved to hear him play. That Bösendorfer in his study was a gift from her. When he hurt his hand..." Lady Gigi's voice got a bit choked. "I think it broke Grandmama's heart. She died that same year."

"I'm so sorry," Xenia whispered.

"It was a hard time for our family," Lady Gigi acknowledged. "Which is why I am grateful you entered Ethan's life. Because of you, he is finally getting better."

At the other's knowing look, panic tiptoed up Xenia's spine.

"You misunderstand, my lady. I'm just his housekeeper—"

"And a very fine one you are," Lady Gigi said warmly. "You've made my brother's house into a lovely home, and now he's making music again. I cannot thank you enough."

"You don't have to thank me—"

"But I already have," Lady Gigi said gaily. "Come take a look."

The younger woman took Xenia by the hand, leading her to the full-length looking glass.

"Blooming he—" Xenia caught herself in time. "Colette, what have you done?"

"You don't like it?" the maid said anxiously. "When I was arranging your hair, I noticed the dye had already faded. I used a little paste to remove the rest, and I think it looks better, *non*?"

"You look *resplendent*," Lady Gigi declared. "Red suits you so much better, Xenia, and that shade in particular is stunning. The dress sets off your natural coloring to perfection."

Staring dazedly in the mirror, Xenia had to admit that she'd never been in better looks. She didn't even recognize the lady in the mirror with her fancy hair and clothes. Vanity got the better of her, and she went with Lady Gigi to the drawing room.

Now that she was here, however, she was having second thoughts.

I don't belong with this rarefied group. What if Ethan doesn't want me here? What if he is embarrassed by me? What if others suspect that we are having an affair? And now that my hair isn't dyed, I am far too exposed...

"Mrs. Wood?"

She froze as Ethan emerged from the drawing room. Her hands curling at her sides, she met his gaze. His eyes widened...and then his entire expression changed. The admiration—and hungry possessiveness—on his face gave too much away, but she couldn't bring herself to care. In that moment, she wanted his claim— wanted the world to know that she belonged to this magnificent fellow. And he *was* magnificent: there was no other way to describe the way he looked in his elegant blue tailcoat and trousers, a white silk cravat knotted elegantly beneath his chin.

"How lovely you are," he said huskily.

He took her hand and brushed his lips over her trembling fingers. His indigo gaze remained locked on her while he addressed his sister.

"Is this what you were up to, Gigi?"

"You are welcome," his sibling said brightly. "But do not think to monopolize Xenia. She is my guest, and for once I shan't be so dreadfully outnumbered by males. Come along, dear. I want to show you that novel I was telling you about."

As Xenia was pulled into the drawing room, she looked desperately behind her.

Ethan raised his brows, mouthing, "Xenia?"

She gave a bewildered shrug and saw a smile tug at his lips.

A moment later, he followed.

Admittedly, Ethan had a preference for redheads, and he'd known that Xenia in particular, with her creamy complexion and velvety-brown eyes, would look splendid with red hair. Yet even he hadn't guessed quite how stunning her transformation would be. Her hair wasn't just any red: it glowed like fire. It was parted in the middle and styled into shining wings that framed her lovely face. Fresh flowers added simple adornment to her chignon.

He'd also never seen her in anything but dull colors, and in the leaf-green taffeta, her beauty hit him like the lush heat of summer. The cut of the frock, while relatively modest, made him realize how much her usual dresses hid. The square neckline displayed the rounded tops of her breasts, which gave a tantalizing jiggle when she laughed. Her nipped-in waist invited a man to span it with his hands. Compared to Gigi's ruffled blue dress, Xenia's was plainer, but its simplicity suited her, allowing her elemental beauty to shine through.

On an ordinary day, Xenia made him hard. Seeing her now, he felt like a cross between a pirate and a troglodyte. He wanted to haul her over his shoulder, take her to his cave, and ravish her until she was hoarse from screams of pleasure. Unfortunately, he wasn't the only one captivated by her charms. Parkhurst and Canning were taking eyefuls too, practically tripping over themselves to get closer to her.

He downed another shot of whisky to prevent himself from going over and driving his fist into Parkhurst's charming visage as he partnered Xenia in a polka while Gigi accompanied on the piano. Unused to the bite of jealousy, Ethan couldn't say he liked it. His sister hadn't been wrong when she said that he'd once taken feminine interest as his due. In the past, when women had flocked to him, he'd enjoyed the interludes but hadn't much cared how long they stayed. With Constance, he'd felt a certain complacency because he thought she was too perfect to err out of passion... which showed how much he knew. When Constance left, she'd taken a chunk of his self-confidence with her.

Being with Xenia had restored his faith in himself. While he didn't doubt her loyalty, he couldn't say the same about his cronies. To be fair, Canning and Parkhurst were unaware that Xenia belonged to him...but, dammit, they ought to know better than to lust over his housekeeper. The fact that he couldn't cut in without raising suspicion frustrated him to no end. As it was, he'd already interrupted a few times to take her for a turn around the drawing room. Fear of discovery had limited their conversation, but her sparkling eyes and shy smiles had made him feel like the luckiest bastard alive.

Since his discussion with Gigi, he'd started thinking about marriage to Xenia as less a question of *if* and more a question of *when*. The bottom line was that Xenia *did* make him happy... happier than he'd ever been. With a certainty that he'd only felt about music, he knew she was his destiny. If his sister was right, his family would pose no barrier to their union, and beyond them, he didn't give a damn what anyone else thought.

This meant that the only real obstacle was Xenia herself. How could he get her to agree to marry him when she wouldn't even commit to staying? How could he prove to her that he would protect her against whatever she was running from?

As he sipped whisky and brooded upon the matter, he saw that Canning was now monopolizing Xenia's attention. They were standing close—*too close*—together, and Canning had one arm propped on a bookshelf while he bent his dark head toward Xenia. A gentleman used this debonair posture to convey his interest and display himself to an advantage. Ethan knew this because he'd adopted that exact bloody stance himself with Xenia.

"Fine evening, eh?" Parkhurst settled into an adjacent chair, two glasses in hand.

Taking the fresh drink, Ethan threw it back and set the empty glass next to the others.

Parkhurst arched a brow. "Are we having that drinking contest after all, old boy?"

"I have learned not to accept challenges I cannot win."

"Mayhap we should have a different sort of wager then?"

Seeing the wicked grin on Parkhurst's face, Ethan rolled his eyes. "If this involves a brothel, prizefight, or dice, the answer is no. When it comes to debauchery, you are unbeatable."

"We must all have our talents." Parkhurst patted himself on the shoulder. "Very well, I shall have to come up with another kind of distraction. Although, come to think of it, maybe we should enjoy the peace and quiet. God knows there's been enough brouhaha of late. Any news from the constable?"

"The latest is that Rawlins is tracking down Dobson Gill, the footman who worked here. Gill seems to have gone missing. Although he paid a month's rent, no one has seen him at his boarding house in Cookham for days."

"Interesting." Parkhurst sipped his drink. "You don't think that Gill or that Corrigan fellow is truly dangerous, do you? This is all a bit of mischief?"

"I don't know what to think."

Through narrowed eyes, Ethan watched Xenia nod enthusiastically at something Canning said. At her animated response,

Canning drew out a pencil and notebook from his pocket and jotted something down.

"But you do think we are safe here?" Parkhurst pressed.

"The guards offer security, but I cannot guarantee anything. If you wish to leave—"

"No, no. It's not me I am worried about."

Parkhurst glanced at Gigi, who was massacring a Mozart serenade.

"I'll look after Gigi..." Ethan trailed off. "What in blazes are those two talking about?"

"Canning and Mrs. Wood?" Parkhurst glanced at the pair. "I've no idea. Something related to writing, probably, since that is all Canning cares about. As I was saying, if you need someplace to go, I do have that cottage in the Cotswolds..."

Ethan lost track of the rest, stuck on what Parkhurst had said about Canning and writing. Didn't Xenia mention that the follower she'd been head over heels for had also been a writer? Ethan felt something burn in his gut, and it wasn't just the whisky he'd consumed. It was a feeling of intense and uncomfortable *déjà vu*.

This exact scenario had happened to him before.

Constance and Blake had always been friendly. In fact, they'd had a shared love of poetry, and Ethan should have guessed his ex-fiancée's true feelings when he found her reading a volume of Blake's love sonnets, looking uncharacteristically flustered. She'd said that she found Blake's work a bit too earthy, and Ethan, fool that he was, had believed her.

Fool me once.

Ethan set his glass on the table, with enough force to make the other glasses rattle.

"Is something amiss?" Parkhurst asked.

"Everything's fine," he said curtly. "Since I left London, what has Canning been up to?"

Looking puzzled by the non sequitur, Parkhurst replied, "The usual. He works by day and carouses by night."

"Is there anyone in particular he carouses with? Females, I mean."

Is the bastard setting his sights on my lover? On my future bride?

"You know Canning," Parkhurst said. "His equanimity acts like a magnet when it comes to the ladies. They believe he will take to domesticity like a fish to water, not realizing he's as rakish as the rest of us."

Was Xenia attracted to Canning's steady temperament? She'd described Ethan as "grumpy" and "brooding," and Canning was neither of those things. Maybe she wanted a fellow who didn't have moods. Who had full functioning use of his body. Maybe she'd only been settling for Ethan until someone better came along. Maybe that was the real reason she refused to commit to a permanent relationship.

"Speaking of jaded...I hesitate to bring this up, but Blake is in the neighborhood."

That got Ethan's attention. "How do you know that?"

"When I paid a visit to Chudleigh Crest today, I bumped into him and his, ahem, new wife." Parkhurst's face turned ruddy. "Apparently they've taken up residence at a cottage not far from here, waiting for the scandal to die down."

The hairs tingled on Ethan's nape. "Do you know when they arrived?"

"They've been here a fortnight, I think."

While Ethan didn't think Blake was responsible for the Bloody Thom hoax, he couldn't rule out his former friend, especially now that he knew Blake had been in close proximity.

"Did Blake say anything?" he demanded.

"He wanted to know how you are faring." Parkhurst had the look of a reluctant messenger. "He said he wanted to...to apologize. For everything."

"It's too bloody late for that."

Fuming at Blake's audacity, Ethan glanced over at Xenia...and his breath jammed in his throat. Canning was *touching* her, his hand gliding against her cheek. Even from a distance, Ethan could see that she was blushing.

Bloody fucking hell.

His vision turned scarlet, a rush sounding in his ears. He was beside Xenia in the next instant. Planting his hand on Canning's shoulder, he gave the other a shove.

Canning stumbled back and lost his balance, toppling onto his arse.

Xenia gasped. Gigi stopped mid-passage.

Ethan's roar shattered the sudden hush.

"Get your hands off her, you bastard. She's *mine*."

CHAPTER TWENTY-SEVEN

"I looked everywhere for you," Xenia said softly.

Although Ethan heard her enter the stall, he didn't turn at her approach. He was in his shirtsleeves, his coat and cravat tossed over a nearby bale of hay. His hair was damp from the dunking he'd given himself in the trough to sober up. He continued to brush Legato, who gave Xenia a nicker of welcome.

"You've found me," he said tonelessly.

"Everyone was worried—"

"They needn't have been." Self-derision sharpened his words. "By now, they ought to be used to me acting like a lunatic."

"No one thinks you are a lunatic. Just that you overindulged with the whisky."

It was a ready excuse, but he felt like a coward taking it. He knew it hadn't just been the drink. What he didn't know was if he wanted to share the truth. As far as he was concerned, there'd been enough humiliation for the evening. Trapped between bad options, he chose to remain silent, moving the bristles through Legato's shining coat.

"You weren't actually jealous, were you?" she blurted.

One of the things he liked about Xenia was her directness.

When it came to their interactions, she called a spade a spade. She would never tread on eggshells around him because of his infirmity or anything else. It was relieving, even though it put him on the spot. If he admitted to jealousy, he would have to provide context and disclose facts about his relationship with Constance that, frankly, he would rather not.

"Mr. Canning wasn't flirting with me," Xenia went on. "I ate one of the cakes and got icing on my face. Out of courtesy, he tried to remove it for me. That was what you saw."

The explanation made Ethan sink lower in his own esteem.

"I acted like an idiot," he said with disgust. "Let's leave it at that."

"Perhaps it wasn't your finest moment," she said candidly. "But we've all been guilty of misunderstandings at some time or another. After you left, Mr. Canning was horrified that you had arrived at the conclusion that he and I...that there was anything going on. We were merely discussing his novel. He was stuck, and I had some ideas. You know, because of all my novel reading."

"I know nothing was going on," Ethan bit out. "It was...it was just me. Being an idiot. I will apologize to Canning in the morning. Now, you should get some rest. You must be tired after the debacle of the evening."

"I am not leaving until I know why you are angry." She stood her ground, her hands clenched by her fluffy green skirts. "Did you not want me there this evening? If so, you should have told me."

"Of course I wanted you there." He gave up on grooming Legato, irritably tossing the brush into a box.

"I understand, you know." She lifted her chin. "What happens in private is one thing, in public another altogether. We may be lovers, but that doesn't change the fact that I am your servant and not from your class. I do not belong amongst your family and friends. Perhaps seeing me there tonight brought home that fact."

"Christ, Xenia." He stared at her, dumbfounded by the

conclusion she'd arrived at. "You think that I'm in a devil of a mood because you did not *fit in* this evening?"

"It was not my idea to be an interloper, you know," she shot back. "It was your sister's. She said she wanted female company this eve and gave me this dress which, by the by, I'm certain was actually from you. Her maid dressed me and ruined my hair—"

"Your hair isn't ruined. It's bloody perfect," he said in exasperation. "I hope to God you never dye it again. In fact, I insist upon it."

"You don't have a right to tell me what to do with my hair." She was working herself into a fine rage. "Not when you cannot be honest. Just admit it, Ethan: you don't want anyone knowing about us. Maybe seeing me in that dress made you realize that fine feathers do not make the bird and that I'll never belong in your world. Something *I* knew from the start, which is why I never asked for commitments or promises—"

"Christ, I am not angry at you," he exploded. "I am angry at my *own bloody self.*"

"Why?" she retorted. "Because you stooped to dally with your housekeeper?"

There were so many things wrong with her statement that he didn't know where to start. His temper snapped.

"No, I'm furious because I didn't know that my ex-fiancée was sleeping with my best friend," he said savagely. "And because I was foolish enough to propose to her in the first place."

When Xenia lost her temper, which wasn't often, she typically took awhile to wind down. Not this time. Ethan's admission was like a pile of ashes dumped on her anger.

"Uh..." was all she could think to say.

"You want to know about the woman I was engaged to," he said curtly.

Right. Yes. She most certainly did. While he'd mentioned being engaged before this, he'd obviously glossed over a few details. He'd said the relationship ended because they "did not suit," which was a far cry from "my betrothed did the mattress jig with my best friend."

"Who...when?" Xenia managed.

"Her name is Constance. She was a widow, and I met her shortly after I was injured. We were engaged for two years, and things ended a few weeks before my arrival in Chuddums."

He was with this woman for two years? And their relationship barely just ended?

"I was never in love with Constance, but I thought we suited," he went on. "She was well-bred and accommodating. She didn't seem to care that I lost my ability to perform as a virtuoso and my short-lived fame along with it. When I had my moods, she was patient and kind."

Xenia's insides plummeted. Constance seemed like the perfect lady. The opposite of Xenia, who'd accused Ethan of being grumpy, got herself hired on false pretenses, and pestered him about ghosts, curses, and making music again.

"I don't understand," she said in a small voice. "Why would such a perfect lady commit infidelity—"

"She only sounds perfect." Ethan raked a hand through his hair. "Like I said, I was foolish enough not to see the truth...but Gigi did. She never liked Constance, and recently, she told me why. She said Constance needed to be seen as a paragon, and I was the perfect foil: a damaged rake who she could reform with her virtue."

"You are *not* damaged," Xenia said fiercely.

"You didn't know me then." His violet-blue eyes were tormented. "After my injury, I was a bloody wreck. I was so *angry* —at Owen, at the loss of my music and my life as I knew it. Constance did seem like an angel at first. She buffered me from the people and things that triggered my rage and encouraged me to withdraw when I wasn't fit for company. What I didn't realize until Gigi pointed it out was that Constance was, in fact, also reinforcing my worst tendencies."

"What tendencies?"

"Instead of sorting things out with Owen and my family, I avoided them. Instead of accepting my physical limitations and looking for different ways to pursue my passion, I wallowed in self-pity and rage and gave up music altogether. Instead of managing my moods, I would lock myself in my study and brood for days. I am not blaming Constance: I, alone, am responsible for my behavior. However, being with her did not bring out the best in me, and I am only now realizing it."

"But if she was getting what she wanted from the relationship," Xenia said slowly, "why did she betray you?"

"I tortured myself for weeks asking that exact question." He braced his hip with his good hand, his gaze studiously on the hay-strewn floor. "At first, I thought it was because I did not satisfy her...physically, I mean."

Xenia snorted. "That seems unlikely."

She said the words without thinking, but she was rewarded by Ethan's searching glance, an easing of the lines around his eyes. It astounded her that this dashingly virile fellow could harbor any concerns about his sexual appeal or abilities. Yet that was the insidiousness of self-doubt. Until Ethan had come into her life, she hadn't realized the extent to which she struggled with her own self-worth.

"I am glad you think so," he said with a trace of a smile. "But things between Constance and I were nothing like what you and I have. She and I only went to bed a few times, and at the risk of sounding ungentlemanly, the occasions were less than memorable. A few days before our wedding, she left a letter telling me she was eloping with Armand Blake, my close friend."

"Odds bodkins," Xenia murmured.

She suddenly recalled his request during his first visit to the Nunnery: *I want something real.* After being betrayed so horribly by the woman he'd intended to make his wife, no wonder his fantasy had involved genuine emotion. Genuine passion and connection.

"Odds bodkins, indeed." Ethan's mouth curved wryly. "I think I see now why she broke off our engagement. Not because of bedroom matters, but because I was changing. I was slowly but surely coming back to myself. My moods were far from perfect, but they were improving. Except for Owen, I started seeing more of my family again...and I didn't need *her* as much. I recall now that we even fought about it. She called me ungrateful—said I didn't value the sacrifices she'd made. I even felt guilty about it."

"You weren't the guilty party," Xenia said crisply. "Did Constance marry your friend?"

"Yes. Since he's the biggest rake of our group, she will have her hands full."

She tilted her head. "You don't sound too distraught about it."

"First of all, I was never distraught over their betrayal," he said. "I was furious. There's a difference."

The fact that he can split hairs has to be a good sign.

"Second, and more importantly, I realize now that everything worked out the way it should have."

Ethan came closer, close enough that he could touch her. He didn't, however. He looked steadily into her eyes, as if he wanted her to see he wasn't hiding anything.

"If Constance hadn't jilted me, I wouldn't have come to Bottoms House. And I wouldn't have met you. The woman who reminded me that life is worth living—who showed me the difference between merely existing and being happy."

Her heart thumped in a giddy rhythm. "Nonetheless, I am sorry you went through what you did. Why didn't you tell me about this sooner?"

"I was embarrassed." Ruddy color washed over his cheekbones, making his irises appear even more vivid. "Being jilted is not something a fellow takes pride in. I did not want you to think less of me."

"I understand, you know. I felt the same way when I told you about my infatuation with Tony."

He cupped her cheek. "I would never think less of you because someone was foolish enough to let you go."

"Likewise."

They smiled at each other, and he was pulling her into his arms when she stopped him.

"Don't forget we need to figure out an explanation," she said. "To tell the others."

"I will make an apology to Canning and everyone else in the morning."

"Yes, but how will you explain what you said?"

He lifted his brows. "Which part?"

"The part where you said I'm yours."

"I will tell them it's true."

"You can't..." She bit her lip. "We agreed to keep our relationship a secret."

"*You* want to keep it a secret. *I* want us to discuss our future together."

"Our *future*?" Her jaw slackened. "I thought I made it very clear that I cannot commit—"

"Gigi likes you," he said solemnly. "She thinks my family would like you too, and she's usually right about these things."

"You spoke to your sister about me? About *us*?"

The very idea made her start to wheeze.

"Take a deep breath, pet."

"I can't. *We* can't..."

She couldn't fight the surge of panic, the sense of impending doom. If Ethan had talked about her with his sister, the future he was referring to could only mean one thing. A permanent, marriage sort of thing. That he thought her worthy of such an honor made her feel a bit weepy...but she could never accept.

I will always find you—and you won't like it when I do.

Mama had proved those words time and again. But this time, Xenia had more to lose than her freedom. She couldn't let what had happened to her papa and Mr. Trelawney happen to Ethan.

"Tell me what is going on in that head of yours," he said keenly.

She wanted to—had never been so tempted to disclose her secrets. With Ethan, she felt safer than she ever had in her whole life. Yet telling him about her past would be the ultimate act of selfishness. She knew the sort of man he was, knew that he would insist on trying to defend her against her mother...like her father had tried to. And Mr. Trelawney.

Look how they had ended up.

I love Ethan.

The realization constricted Xenia's chest. This was no infatuation. She'd fallen completely and incontrovertibly in love, and she would never, ever allow Ethan's blood to be shed because of her.

"Xenia? What is it? Tell me."

He was looking too closely, seeing too much. She needed to buy time to think. To figure out if and how she could be with the man she loved without endangering him.

"I...I want you, Ethan," she whispered.

It was *a* truth, if not the main one burning in her heart. From the flare in his eyes, she'd succeeded in diverting him. To distract him further, she rose on tiptoe and pressed her mouth ardently to his.

CHAPTER TWENTY-EIGHT

While Ethan suspected that Xenia was employing a Fabian tactic, he didn't care. In fact, she was welcome to distract him with kisses whenever she wished. She was only delaying the inevitable: he was going to get to the truth about her past sooner or later. Whatever secret she was hiding terrified her, and he could afford to be patient. Especially when she offered such delightful diversions.

After his idiotic behavior with Canning, he probably didn't deserve the sweetness of her lips against his. Yet Xenia had made his disclosure far less painful than it might have been. She understood him in a way no one had before. He knew that their future would not be without conflict. They would challenge each other and make mistakes, but if it always came back to this—their mouths fused and tongues twined, their bodies pressing to get closer— then he knew everything would be all right.

"I wanted to do this all night." He nuzzled her ear, inhaling her herbal-fresh scent. "Do you know how beautiful you are?"

"It's the dress. Thank you for buying it for me, by the way."

She arched her neck as he kissed his way down the soft column.

"You're welcome, but you're wrong. It's not the dress—it's *you*, Xenia." He caressed her jaw, gazing into her blinking brown eyes. "If I were asked to describe the perfect woman for me, I would describe you."

He saw that his declaration affected her. She swallowed unsteadily, but her response was teasing.

"Even though I am troublesome?"

"You know very well I like how naughty you are," he said. "Stop fishing for compliments."

She pursed her lips, then that saucy twinkle he loved came into her eyes.

"Speaking of naughty, there is something I would like to try again." She fluttered her lashes at him. "If you don't mind."

"As it happens, I'm in the mood to be accommodating," he drawled. "What do you have in mind?"

His blood simmered when she sank gracefully to her knees. He didn't know how Xenia managed to tap into his deepest fantasies, but their desire was even more intense because of the way it was shared. In the mellow glow of the stable lamps, he saw the flush of arousal on his siren's cheeks as she unfastened his trousers. The fact that she fumbled with the fall made her actions even hotter. By the time she managed to free his cock, he was hard and ready, falling with a slap into her waiting palms.

She used both hands to stroke him. He loved her touch, even though it was torturously gentle.

"I love the way you feel," she breathed. "So hard, big, and vital against my palms."

"You touch me so well, pet," he said huskily. "Do it harder, yes?"

Immediately, she tightened her grip, and pleasure blasted up his spine as she jerked his rod with her little fists. Christ, he loved what a quick study she was. She pumped him while watching his face, her lips parted with concentration, and that image alone was enough to make a drop of seed bead on his dome. Her gaze flitted on the glistening pearl, then back to his face, seeking the sweetest permission.

"Lick it up," he said. "There's a good girl."

She leaned forward and laved his tip. The sight of her tongue swirling around his bulging crown was enough to bring forth another droplet. She took that one too, lapping it up like an eager kitten. He thanked his lucky stars that she had a passion and native talent for fellatio. Time to push her further. He fisted her hair, admiring the fiery ribbons wound around his fingers.

"Did I tell you how much I adore your natural color?" he asked.

"Only about a hundred times this evening." Her smile held a hint of smugness.

"Saucy wench," he admonished. "If you cannot accept a compliment without it going to your head, then I shall give you something else. Open wide for my cock now."

She did, and he pushed his prick through the lush hole of her lips. His spine bowed as her kiss engulfed him, the perfect blend of heat, wetness, and suction. He pulled out and pushed in, this time deeper, savoring the velvet cushion of her tongue.

"Devil and damn, I love your mouth," he growled.

Her hummed reply was muffled by his plunging cock. Her lips formed a tight seal as he plumbed her lush depths, her eyes watering with proof of her effort, her palms quiescent against his bulging thighs. When he tightened his grip in her hair, giving a slight twist, she moaned around her mouthful. Every moment he shared with Xenia made way for new discoveries, new avenues to explore. Their passion was untamed and visceral, erotic beauty in its purest form. *This* was the connection of his deepest fantasies, and it unleashed a primal urge to mark and claim what belonged to him: his wanton minx and lover...his future wife.

His Xenia. *His.*

His burgeoning conviction drove him deeper into her kiss. The shining trust in her eyes brought a sting to his. She overwhelmed him: with physical pleasure, yes, but so much more. Emotion surged through him like the finale of Beethoven's Ninth, jubilation that was all the greater for the suffering that went before it. His hips bucked, his cock lodging in his beloved's throat, but her gaze only mirrored his own wild joy.

Being held by her, desired by her, for nothing more than being himself, brought him right to the edge. With his last ounce of self-possession, he tried to pull free...only to feel her hands slide over his arse, holding him in place. Her squeeze signaled a decadent offer that made his vision darken with lust.

"Are you certain, love?" he said harshly. "You have me so lathered up that I will fill up your sweet mouth. I'll come so hard you'll have no choice but to swallow me down."

Her needy moan pushed him past the boundaries of civility and self-control. Grunting, he thrust deeper and deeper still, taking everything she had to give. The climax rumbled through him, and he buried himself in her throat, his stones pulsing against her lips as he exploded. He shouted her name as bliss jetted from him. He came and came, his release so copious that she gagged and sputtered, the lovely music wringing him of his last drop.

Chest heaving, he withdrew, and his heart stuttered at her expression. Her eyes were soft and dreamy, her sinfully red hair tousled by his hand. She looked like a sleepy angel...except for the sheen of his seed on her swollen lips. Astoundingly, he was still hard, and from the way his cock twitched, the road to recovery would be short. In the meantime...

He helped her up and tipped her head back.

Smiling, he said, "Your turn."

"Oh, Ethan." Xenia rocked her head back and forth. "I can't, not again."

She was lying on a waist-high bale, Ethan's jacket buffering her from the prickly straw. Not that she would have noticed it: her nerves were too saturated with pleasure to feel anything else. She was floating, her bones dissolved by too many climaxes to count. Ethan wasn't done, however. He had her legs slung over his muscled shoulders and was eating her pussy with wicked voraciousness.

"You can, pet." Raising his head, he licked his glistening lips. "I want to feel you come again for me."

To punctuate his request, he drove two long digits into her passage. She was so wet that he slid in easily, pressure morphing into pleasurable fullness. She whimpered as he kept her impaled on his touch.

"Feel how you're squeezing me," he said. "This hungry little mouth needs to be fed, doesn't it?"

"Yes."

Her reply came out as a gasp because he'd started stirring his fingers, opening her up to even more sensation. She thought nothing could feel better than what he was doing. Then he proved her wrong by curling his fingers, stroking some exquisite place inside her that set off blissful tremors. He kept doing it, rubbing and rubbing that spot. The climax started at her core, rippling outward in deep, ecstatic waves. Her entire body shook as she came.

"By Jove, you're incomparable," he murmured.

He pulled her up, only to spin her around. With a hand between her shoulder blades, he pushed her down until she was bent over the bale. Her nipples chafed against the straw where it wasn't covered by his coat, but she liked the abrasion. Then she felt his cock nudging her rear crevice, and she liked that friction even more. He gripped her by the hip, holding her steady as he slid his erect length along her crack.

"I can't get enough of you." His tone was deep and guttural. "I wish you could see what I see."

Twisting her head, she gave him a saucy look. "You could describe it to me."

"My cock is dark and engorged, sandwiched by the pale cheeks of your bottom." Lust thickened his voice. "I'm thrusting my shaft against your crack, and your back arches every time I do it. Like you cannot get enough."

"It feels so naughty," she breathed.

He thrust harder, his steely length stimulating forbidden nerves. With each incursion, his bollocks collided with her swollen sex, the weighted smacks rumbling up her spine. The sounds of their mating agitated the horses, who seemed restless, whinnying softly.

"But you like it." Ethan's look was wickedly knowing. "You're drenching me. I think I know what you would love even more."

She felt the wide head of his cock lodge against the entrance of her pussy. He didn't push inside, just teased her by rubbing his tip up and down her slit. Pure want poured through her. She needed to know what it would be like to be fully possessed by him. To hold the man she loved inside her body.

"Do it." She met his gaze, letting him see her desire. "I want you inside me, Ethan."

His pupils flared with arousal. "Not until you and I discuss our future."

Frustration knotted her insides. "There cannot *be* a future between us."

"Why? Tell me, Xenia. *Trust me.*"

At the same time, he pushed. Not all the way, just enough for her to feel how huge he was, how his cock would stretch her and fill her and take away the emptiness. Just enough to make her burn even hotter...wait.

Burn. Is something burning?

She straightened, sniffing the air. "Ethan, do you smell that?"

"Yes. Smoke. Something's burning."

Brows drawn, he pulled away, quickly donning his clothes and helping her with hers. A grey haze was filtering into the stables, the horses whinnying and stamping in agitation. Ethan rushed out of the stables with her at his heels. In the far corner of the garden, a blaze lit the night.

"The gazebo," Xenia said in shock.

The structure was engulfed in flames, the cupola flickering like a candle.

"Sound the alarm and alert the others," Ethan ordered.

He was already running toward the inferno.

By morning, all that remained of the gazebo was a charred section of railing. The rest had been reduced to ashes, which blanketed the nearby hedges like dirty snow. On the bright side, they'd managed to contain the damage, and Xenia made note to remind Ethan of that as she approached him. He was speaking with the Hirschfield brothers, the three men surveying the smoldering ruins with somber expressions. Tension was carved into every rigid line of Ethan's lean form, and for once even he had shadows under his eyes.

The Hirschfields nodded politely at her before departing.

"I didn't mean to interrupt your meeting," she began.

"We were done." Ethan looked at her, then raised his brows. "Do you have something to tell me?"

"Would you prefer the good news or the bad news first?"

"There is more bad news?"

Given the situation, she was glad that he was still capable of dry humor.

"Berta left," she said. "She is convinced that Bloody Thom means to destroy the manor and everyone in it. She thinks that the burning of the gazebo was part of the curse—the part where '*his cry for justice is like a flame, scorching all with unholy fire.*' Nothing I said could dissuade her."

After a pause, Ethan asked, "Do *you* think it was Bloody Thom behind this?"

"In this instance, no."

"Why not?"

"I can't explain it, other than to say the arson doesn't feel supernatural." She drew her brows together. "I'm not discrediting the notion that Bloody Thom exists, but my instincts tell me that it was a flesh-and-blood foe who set fire to the gazebo."

"As it happens, there is evidence to corroborate your instincts," Ethan said grimly. "The Hirschfield brothers were using the old gamekeeper's cottage to store their equipment, and when they went by today, they saw that someone had taken the supply of linseed oil. They think someone doused the gazebo with the oil to increase its flammability."

"Odds bodkins," Xenia said, eyes wide. "Do they have any idea who did it?"

"No." Ethan's expression was stark. "Last night, I had guards posted at the front and back gates of the manor. They did not see anyone enter or leave the property. Which leads me to an unwelcome conclusion."

"It was someone who was already inside the manor," Xenia said, stunned.

"I cannot think of a more likely explanation. It was around two in the morning when we noticed the fire, which means someone exited the manor, fetched the linseed oil, then set the gazebo on fire."

"Wouldn't the guards have noticed?"

"They are more focused on potential intruders coming *in* than getting out. And if the culprit is indeed someone currently in the manor, they will have observed the guards' schedule and routine. They could figure out a way to sneak around without being seen."

"Who do you think is responsible? One of the staff...or one of the guests?"

Thinking of Ethan's recent betrayal by those close to him, she felt a spreading chill.

"I have no idea." The ice in his voice conveyed that he, too, was contemplating duplicity. "I sent word to Rawlins. Everyone who was in the manor last night must be treated as a potential suspect —except you, Gigi, and my longtime retainers."

Xenia wondered if Rawlins would agree with Ethan's exceptions. The constable would probably want to interrogate everyone with no exclusions. Dread percolated through her as she thought about him digging into her past. What if he unearthed her connection to her mama?

Should I tell Ethan everything?

Indecision churned her insides as she contemplated telling him the truth: that she was the daughter of Joanna Wardell, the infamous cutthroat dubbed "Lady Jo" because of her elegant beauty and manners, never mind that she would murder you for the right price. Or just for fun. Lady Jo led her roving gang wherever there was a fortune to be had, lurid accounts of her crimes filling the newspapers. Her ability to evade the authorities was legendary.

Would Ethan cast Xenia off because of her family connection? He would have every right to. Strangely, it wasn't his rejection she feared the most but the opposite: if he wanted to protect her, he would be guaranteeing his own doom. She'd promised herself that she wouldn't allow her past to hurt him—that she would run before she let that happen.

Yet how can I run now when he's dealing with a secret nemesis?

As she gnawed on her lip, debating her options, Brunswick approached.

"My lord," the butler said. "You have visitors."

"Rawlins and his men are here already?" Ethan said. "That was quick."

"It is not the constable."

Xenia didn't understand Brunswick's guarded look.

Ethan cocked his head. "Who is it, then?"

"The Marquess and Marchioness of Blackwood, sir, and the Earl of Manderly." The butler inhaled like a messenger who didn't wish to deliver the news. "And Lord Owen as well."

CHAPTER TWENTY-NINE

If someone had told Xenia that she would be having tea with a marquess, marchioness, and an earl, she would have laughed and asked for the punchline of the joke. Yet the event had somehow come to pass. When Xenia had brought in the tea cart—thank goodness for Mrs. Johnson who, despite last night's fracas, had managed to bake her delectable scones—she'd planned to deposit the refreshments and leave.

Ethan had had a different plan, however. He'd blocked her path, taking her by the elbow and turning her to face his entire family.

"Everyone," he'd said calmly, "may I introduce to you my housekeeper, Xenia Wood? Mrs. Wood, these are my parents, the Marquess and Marchioness of Blackwood. My younger brother, Lord Owen Harrington. You already know my other siblings."

"It is, um, an honor." Xenia had curtsied and stammered. "A true, um, pleasure to make your acquaintances."

Ethan's parents had exchanged a look that made her cheeks warm. However, they and the rest of his family greeted her with nothing but politeness, as if Ethan introducing his housekeeper to them was a perfectly normal thing to do. Then, before she could make her escape, Lady Gigi hopped aboard Ethan's train of madness.

"Do come sit with me, Xenia." Lady Gigi had patted the seat next to her on the settee. "If things get boring, we can finish the discussion of *Jane Eyre* we started last night."

Xenia had no way of knowing if Ethan's sister meant anything by referring to the novel about a forbidden romance between a gentleman and his servant. Seeing no polite way to refuse, however, she went and sat. As Ethan's family did her the courtesy of not gawking at her, she tried to return the favor. It wasn't easy. Seeing the Blackwood clan together was akin to looking into the sun: they were a physically dazzling bunch.

Xenia saw that Ethan and Lady Gigi had inherited their looks from their mama, Lady Pandora Harrington, who occupied the chaise across the coffee table. Although she must be in her fifties, the Marchioness of Blackwood's glamorous beauty was ageless. Her upswept raven curls were lustrous and rich, the few streaks of silver adding dramatic flair. Her tip-tilted eyes were a familiar stormy violet-blue, and her delicate features had a few lines to honor the passage of time. She wore a smart cerulean carriage dress which accentuated her voluptuous figure.

Standing behind her chair was the marquess, Lord Marcus Harrington, who'd obviously passed his looks to his eldest son and heir, Lord James, the Earl of Manderly. The men shared the same bronze-colored hair, grey-blue eyes, and brawny build. The Marquess of Blackwood's hawkish countenance was pleasantly weathered, and he had the kind of upright bearing that Xenia associated with military men.

Sprawled in an adjacent chair was Lord Owen Harrington. He combined his parents' traits, having his father's blade of a nose, his mama's full mouth, and eyes that appeared to range from grey-blue to grey-violet, depending on the light. Yet he also possessed characteristics entirely his own. His skin was darker, tanned from exposure to a strong sun. His gaunt face held shadows that looked as if they'd been inked on by exhaustion. Although his build appeared naturally rawboned, he was nonetheless too thin. The same height as Ethan, Lord Owen probably weighed three stone less.

The frequency with which he ran a hand through his shaggy brown hair suggested this was a nervous habit. He was fidgety in general. The reason for Lord Owen's agitated state was obvious to Xenia: his eyes kept darting to Ethan who, on the other hand, assiduously avoided the other's gaze. Because she knew Ethan, she knew that he was not unaffected—quite the opposite. Despite his indolent stance by the fireplace, he was struggling to maintain his composure, and his earlier words came back to her.

"I cannot be angry at Owen. But I cannot not *be angry at him either."*

She wished with all her heart that she could ease Ethan's torment. Even though she did not know Lord Owen, she felt a welling of compassion for him too. He seemed to mirror Ethan's emotions, but he was far worse at hiding his pain. A cloud of dark energy seemed to surround him, letting out lightning flashes of anger and shame.

If it hurt Xenia to witness the tension between the brothers, she couldn't imagine how it felt for their family members. What she did know was that there was no shortage of love in the room. It was there in the way Lord Blackwood kept a proprietary hand on his wife's shoulder, as if he craved a physical connection with her and this small gesture was what propriety allowed him. The way she looked up at him, with the adoration of a newlywed despite their years of marriage. The way they both looked at their children, with pride and anxiety and fierce protectiveness.

Seeing the familial closeness reminded Xenia of her old longings. There'd been a time when she yearned for her mama's love and approval. She could have endured Mama's beatings and tongue-lashings...but Papa's murder had been the last straw. That horrific act had made her realize that her mother was a monster from whom she wanted *nothing*.

Yet even good and loving parents had their crosses to bear. Despite their wealth and power, the marquess and marchioness could not change what had happened to Lord Owen in the war. Or what happened between Lord Owen and Ethan afterward. Or the losses Ethan had sustained while trying to help his brother. The ongoing tension between the Blackwoods' sons yanked and thrashed like a fish caught on a hook, straining the bonds between all the family members who were simply trying to hold on.

Standing by the fire, Ethan felt none of its warmth. Cold rage spilled through his veins, triggered by his brother's presence. He didn't know what Owen was doing here—why their parents had thought having them in the same room together was a good idea after the last time. In that instance, Owen had been drunk while the rest of the family, as usual, made excuses for his behavior. Resentment had swelled in Ethan, overwhelming his self-control. Before he knew it, he'd dragged Owen out of his chair, throwing him against a wall.

"You're a selfish wastrel," he'd roared in his brother's face. *"Destroy yourself, if you must, but have the courtesy of not taking the rest of the family along with you. I've already lost everything because of you. Isn't that bloody enough?"*

"I didn't ask for your help or anyone else's," Owen had shouted back. *"You should have left me alone!"*

Seeing red, Ethan had thrown the first punch. Owen had fought back, and it had taken Papa and James to break them apart. Mama's weeping echoed in Ethan's head now as he surveyed his younger brother. At least Owen didn't appear soused. Conflict twisted Ethan's gut as he realized that his brother looked like shite...like he wasn't eating or sleeping properly. Was Owen still up to his old vices? Was he drinking, gambling, and whoring?

What Owen does is none of your damned business. Because of him, you lost your ability to play and perform. How much more are you willing to sacrifice?

His chest heaved, and he instinctively looked at his hands...his uncovered hands. After exposing his scars to Xenia, he'd worn the gloves less and less and now rarely did so when he was at home. Gigi hadn't commented upon this change, but he knew that she'd noticed and the rest of his family noticed too. He saw the hope in his parents' and James's expressions. And he saw Owen looking at his damaged hand while pretending not to.

Ethan didn't know how he felt about any of that.

He looked over at Xenia. The understanding in her eyes felt as soothing as her balm. In truth, he'd maneuvered her into staying for two reasons. The first was that she was an important part of his life, and he wanted her and his family to meet. The second reason was purely selfish: with her by his side, he felt calmer and better able to deal with his brother. She had liked that he'd protected her, but what she didn't realize was that, in her own way, she protected him too. From his temper and tendency to brood on the past.

"So." As usual, James took charge, breaking the awkward silence. "The rumors of the ghost are proving more than rumors, then?"

Ethan held on to his patience. "There is no bloody ghost."

"But Gigi wrote us a letter informing us of a curse. That is why we came with such haste, dearest." Mama gazed at him, her brow pleating. "Gigi wrote about slaughtered chickens, a piano covered with bloody fingerprints, and a sighting of a specter in chains. And now your gazebo went up in flames? Clearly, *something* is going on."

Despite her ladylike appearance, Mama had a spine of steel. She'd been a loving and indulgent mother, but she was no pushover. Ethan and his siblings had discovered this the hard way.

"The sighting was not verified," Ethan replied. "A former cook was the only one who supposedly saw the ghost. At any rate, I am taking care of the matter. There is no need for interference on your part." He narrowed his eyes at Gigi. "Or anyone else's."

"Don't glower at your sister, dear," Mama said. "She was only trying to help."

"I *was* only trying to help." Gigi nodded righteously. "As you haven't made inroads into finding the culprit, it wouldn't hurt for you to accept assistance, would it? There's no need to be stubborn."

"I am not being stubborn," Ethan retorted.

Unfortunately, he was, and he didn't know why. Perhaps it had to do with the time immediately following his injury, when his family's desire to help him had felt too much like pity. Perhaps it was his pride and desire to show them that, despite his altered condition, he was still his own man and could handle his affairs.

"Perhaps your family could help review possible suspects?"

The suggestion came from Xenia, of all people. All gazes swung in her direction, including Ethan's. He didn't hide his annoyance, but she only raised her brows as if to say, *If you didn't want my participation, then you oughtn't have plunked me in the middle of your family gathering.*

He supposed she had a point.

"What suspects?" Mama asked intently.

Sighing heavily, he provided a summary of the suspect list, including Patrick Harlow and the Corrigans, former footman Dobson Gill, and his new suspicion arising from last night's fire.

"This is serious business, son." Papa frowned. "And you have cause to believe that whoever committed the arson is amongst the staff?"

"I think the arson was committed by someone in the manor," Ethan corrected.

It took an instant for the others to grasp what he was saying.

"You don't think Canning or Parkhurst was involved?" Incredulity laced Gigi's voice.

His cronies had gone into the village to give him and his family time to catch up. With a prickle of guilt, he wondered if their ears were burning.

"I don't *want* to think that either of them is guilty," he said. "But it would not be the first time I was betrayed by someone close to me."

He'd been referring to Blake, but he saw Owen flinch. Guilt and self-recrimination lined his brother's haggard features, and once again, Ethan felt a violent internal tug-of-war. A part of him recognized what the battlefield had done to Owen and wanted to forgive him and ease his pain. A smaller, meaner part wanted Owen to suffer.

Shouldn't Owen feel remorse over depriving me of my passion and destiny?

"What motive would Canning or Parkhurst have to do such a thing?" James asked.

Grateful for the distraction, Ethan exhaled. "I don't know. Last night, I had a misunderstanding with Canning, for which I take full blame. I apologized to him right before he left for the village, and he seemed receptive. Truth be told, the business with Blake hurt my friendship with both Canning and Parkhurst, but they seem to have let bygones be bygones. And they proved themselves to be loyal friends when they escorted Gigi here after her latest scrape."

"Speaking of that 'scrape'"—Papa aimed a stern gaze at Gigi—"your mama and I will have a discussion with you shortly, young lady."

"Yes, Papa." Gigi sighed.

She shot Ethan a look of pique; he gave her a smug smile, enjoying the tit for tat.

"You've discussed revenge as a possible motive for that gang leader, Harlow," Mama said. "And also for that disgruntled footman, Gill. What about the other staff? Do they bear you ill will or have other reason to resort to mischief?"

"Obviously, I can vouch for Brunswick, Valentine, and

Spencer," Ethan said. "They've proved their loyalty through the years. As for the rest...well, Mrs. Wood can speak to that better than I can."

Although Xenia looked nonplussed to be at the center of his family's attention, she recovered splendidly.

"I hired the original maids, Daisy and Berta, at the mop fair over a fortnight ago," she said. "Both grew up in the area and had good references, although a previous employer found Daisy's personality 'irksome' because of her need for attention. Anyway, she was convinced Bloody Thom was behind the dead chickens and quit after the piano business. Apparently, she's been spreading tales about the ghost, which hasn't helped in finding her replacement. Berta, on the other hand, is Daisy's opposite, mild-mannered and hard-working. But she gave notice this morning; the destruction of the gazebo frightened her off, and I can't say I blame her."

"Neither have reason to act against my son?" Papa asked.

Xenia shook her head. "Not that I am aware of, my lord. As for the three remaining maids, they are the young nieces of the village dressmaker. I cannot see them participating in mischief either."

"Other than the kind involving a fellow, that is." Gigi's eyes twinkled. "According to Colette, they are obsessed with gaining a follower. Apparently, they have taken to chasing the footmen."

"They can be a bit silly," Xenia allowed. "But they are hard workers and good girls, even if poor William and Fred have to hide from them."

"William and Fred are the footmen, I presume?" James inquired. "What do you know about them?"

"They are sensible lads from local families," Xenia said. "William has twelve siblings and counting, and he works to support them. He can be shy, but since he started using the spot-reducing cream I made him, his confidence has improved. As for Fred, if you assign him a task, he will see it done. His true talent is with animals; in fact, he's the only one who can manage Brutus, our resident rooster. I am trying to convince Lord Ethan to give Fred a shot at working in the stables."

James gave Ethan an amused look. "I think your housekeeper is a soft touch."

Ethan smiled faintly. "She is."

"I am not," Xenia protested. "But I cannot see anyone below-stairs participating in these hoaxes. The only person we haven't discussed is the cook, Mrs. Johnson. And she's a godsend: steady as a rock and always ready with a cup of tea when anyone needs it."

"What is Mrs. Johnson's background?" Mama asked.

"She is a rather private person," Xenia admitted. "She's never spoken of a husband; the 'Mrs.' is an honorific. She did, however, have glowing references from two homes she worked at—one in Lincolnshire, the other in Devonshire, I believe. And her scones speak for themselves."

She gestured at the tiered serving plate, which now held only crumbs.

"Did you correspond with her prior employers?"

Xenia drew her brows together. "There wasn't time, my lady—"

"It isn't Mrs. Wood's fault, Mama," Ethan cut in. "As I was tired of subsisting on Brunswick's cooking, I told her to hire someone at the mop fair. Mrs. Johnson was the most qualified candidate by far, and because she is not from the area, she was not frightened off by the rumors of the curse. We had to make do, and we did."

"Hmm," Mama said.

"What are you thinking, my love?" Papa asked.

"That we ought to find out more about Mrs. Johnson."

"Where was everyone last night when the fire happened?"

The question came from Owen, who'd been silent until now. He flicked his gaze around the room, tapping his fingers idly against his thigh.

"Good question, son," Papa said. "Perhaps we ought to have started there."

"I was in bed," Gigi piped up. "Colette can vouch that she helped me get ready."

"No one needs to vouch for you, Gigi." Ethan rolled his eyes.

"If we are going through everyone's alibis, it's only fair that I supply one too," his sister said blithely. "As for Canning and Parkhurst, after you, um…decided to have an early night, they stayed up and played cards. Xenia and I left them to it. Did you go straight to bed afterward, Xenia?"

"N-no," Xenia stammered. "Not quite yet."

"Forgive my curiosity, Mrs. Wood." Although Mama's tone was pleasant, her gaze held a familiar shrewdness. "It was mentioned that you were the first to notice the fire around two in the morning. Was there a reason for you to be up at that hour?"

Seeing Xenia freeze like a cornered doe, Ethan recognized her dilemma. She didn't want to lie to his family. But she couldn't tell the truth either: that she had been having a late-night rendezvous with him.

"Mrs. Wood was with me," he said.

Speculative glances darted through the room. Xenia stared at him, wide-eyed.

"I had overindulged," he clarified. "Mrs. Wood wanted to make sure I was all right and found me in the stables. Good thing she did, too, as she was the one who noticed the burning smell. If it hadn't been for her, the damage would have extended beyond the gazebo. She has my full trust."

The lines eased around Mama's eyes.

"If that is the case, then you have mine as well, Mrs. Wood," she said softly. "And my gratitude."

A knock sounded, and Brunswick entered. "Pardon, my lord, but the constable has arrived. Shall I have him wait?"

"No, bring him in," Ethan said.

Rawlins was ushered in, looking as rumpled as ever. Introductions were made.

"I apologize, my lord," he said to Ethan. "I would have arrived sooner, but I was delayed by a new development..."

He hesitated, clearly uncertain what he could say in present company.

"You may speak freely," Ethan said. "My family knows everything."

"It concerns Dobson Gill, my lord."

"You've found him?" Ethan said alertly.

"Yes." Rawlins glanced at Mama and Gigi. "The matter is somewhat, er, delicate—"

"There is no need to shilly-shally, sir," Mama said briskly. "Given that my son's well-being is at stake, the sooner we know Mr. Gill's whereabouts, the better."

"Very good, my lady." Rawlins cleared his throat. "However, Mr. Gill is no longer a threat to his lordship's, or anyone's, well-being. He was found this morning...drowned in a stream."

CHAPTER THIRTY

After touring the site of the fire, Rawlins conducted his interviews. He'd advised against Ethan being present as he thought that might intimidate the staff and prevent them from being entirely truthful. Ethan had relented, with the caveat that Rawlins apprise him of all findings. The constable did so, reporting that William and Fred had been asleep when the fire started, and as they shared quarters, they provided alibis for one another.

Mrs. Johnson had also been asleep, but she had her own room, and no one could confirm or deny her claim. Canning and Parkhurst claimed they'd stayed up playing cards, parting ways sometime after one. Having developed a megrim, Canning had requested willow bark from Brunswick, who verified that he'd brought the powder to the guest around two o'clock before heading to bed himself.

"If the fire started around two in the morning," Rawlins concluded, "then the whereabouts of Mrs. Johnson and Mr. Parkhurst during that time remain unconfirmed. I will delve deeper into your cook's background, my lord. As for Mr. Parkhurst..."

"Leave him to me," Ethan said starkly.

"As you wish. There is, er, one other matter."

The constable's hesitation caused Ethan's nape to prickle. "Yes?"

"It concerns Mrs. Wood." Rawlins cleared his throat. "I know she was with you at the time the fire started, but she seemed rather nervous when I spoke with her—"

"I did not give you leave to interview her," Ethan cut in.

"Yes, but she is, after all, a newer addition to your household. I would suggest taking the precaution—"

"Mrs. Wood is not involved," Ethan said firmly. "You are not to harass her further. Is that understood?"

"As you wish, my lord."

Afterward, Ethan found himself mulling over the constable's words. Xenia's nervousness did not surprise him; after all, he knew she had secrets. What bothered him was that he'd not yet won her trust, and he was getting tired of waiting. He had been forthright about wanting a future with her...hell, he'd introduced her to his family, and she'd more than held her own with them. He refused to hide her like some dirty secret. She was a part of his life—a permanent part once he could get her to discuss the future without wheezing—and those in his inner circle might as well get used to it.

Papa and James strode into the study together.

"Ready to go?" Papa asked. "I've had the carriage brought around."

Ethan nodded, and they headed out.

Ethan's gut had told him that Dobson Gill's demise was no accident. Since Rawlins had his hands full, Ethan had decided to make inquiries on his own. He wanted to search Gill's lodgings to see if he could turn up any clues. Papa and James had insisted on accompanying him, and he saw no reason to turn down their company. He was, however, relieved that Owen had decided not to join. While he and his younger brother had managed to be in the same room without succumbing to fisticuffs, he didn't want to push his luck.

Papa's well-sprung carriage bounced over the country road, the rolling hills and farms passing by in a blur of green and gold. Sitting across from him, Papa and James discussed land management, a topic the two had a shared passion for and which Ethan had once found soporific. Now that he was managing his own estate, the conversation held some interest for him. It felt good being in his family's company again. In fact, it felt almost like old times—before his injury and the falling-out with Owen. He felt lighter and better than he had in a long time.

He cleared his throat. "I am surprised you managed to convince Mama to stay home."

"You know better than that, lad." Beneath the brim of his hat, Papa's eyes gleamed with amusement. "No one convinces Mama to do anything she does not wish to do. She said she had other plans today."

"What sort of plans?"

"She did not inform me of the specifics," Papa replied.

"Maybe she is tending to Owen," Ethan said.

Instantly, he was embarrassed by his snide remark. Devil take it, he was no longer a child competing with his siblings for parental affection. Growing up, Owen had been the baby for years before Gigi came along, and he'd leveraged his position to his advantage, especially where Ethan was concerned. He'd instigated fights for which Ethan got blamed and acted like a daredevil without fear of reprisal. Once, he'd fallen out of a tree and nearly flattened Mama, who'd tried to catch him...but Owen, being Owen, escaped punishment.

Ethan was ashamed that he'd held on to the old, petty resentment. Rationally, he knew their parents loved him and his siblings equally. He also understood why Owen had needed the bulk of their parents' attention since his return from war.

"Owen is fine." Papa's tone held no judgment. "In fact, he is better than I've seen him in some time."

"Then why didn't he join us?" Ethan couldn't help but inquire.

After trading looks with Papa, James replied, "He was not certain that he would be welcome."

Ethan stiffened. "I never said or did anything to—"

"It is not you, son. It's Owen. After the price you paid for his mistakes..."

Papa drew a breath and looked at him squarely, and Ethan glimpsed the pain behind the stoicism. The pain of a father who knows that he cannot make things right between his sons, that they would either come to an understanding themselves...or they wouldn't.

"Owen understands that you have every right to your anger," Papa finished quietly. "For what it is worth, he is trying to do better. He has, for instance, given up spirits."

"How long has this lasted?" Ethan asked cynically.

"Longer than his previous attempts." James shrugged.

The battle between anger and forgiveness raged inside Ethan. Why was it so difficult to let go of the past? Why couldn't he move on?

"This is your home, Ethan," Papa said. "We—not just Owen, but all of us—are here to assist, in whatever fashion you see fit."

Ethan accepted his papa's acknowledgment with a gruff nod. "I am glad you came. The situation has grown worrisome."

Tacitly taking his cue, Papa shifted the topic of conversation. "Do you trust this fellow Rawlins to carry out the investigation?"

"Don't let Rawlins's manner fool you. He is sharper than he appears."

"My old friend Ambrose Kent, the retired investigator, lives in Chudleigh Crest," Papa said. "When I heard what was happening, I tried to contact him, but he is visiting the Continent with his family."

"There's no need to trouble Mr. Kent," Ethan said. "I can handle the matter."

"We will help," James stated. "*Ad Finem Fidelis.*"

For once, the invoking of the family motto didn't stir Ethan's antipathy. Instead, he felt...grateful. Tragedy had strained but not broken the Harrington bonds.

"I would appreciate the help," he said.

He saw his father and brother's surprised expressions.

"What is it?" he asked.

"Nothing. It's just that..." James smoothed a crease on his trousers. "You seem changed."

"Leaving London helped."

"I mean you've changed since I saw you last. It has been less than three weeks, and your state of mind seems improved." James gestured at him. "Your overall disposition as well."

"It is even more obvious to me," Papa said. "For I have not seen you since...well, it has been a few months."

"You were going to say since Constance jilted me," Ethan said.

Papa sighed. "My apologies. I did not mean to bring that up."

"It is all right."

"Is it, son?"

Before inheriting the marquessate, Papa had had a military career. As Lieutenant Colonel Blackwood, he'd been a hero who'd fought Bonaparte. To those under his command, he'd been known for his fairness, integrity, and insistence upon the truth. Growing up, Ethan and his brothers had been no match for the steely-blue gaze, which had led to many a boyhood confession.

In this instance, though, Ethan was glad to share the truth.

"Yes," he said. "I am fine. Better than fine, actually."

The taut line of Papa's mouth eased. "Your mama will be happy to hear it. She has been worried about you."

"As I recall, Mama was not the one who reminded me repeatedly of my brotherly duty to check up on Ethan," James said dryly.

"I was concerned, as any father would be," Papa said. "However, I had full confidence that Ethan would see that things turned out for the best."

Papa was a gentleman, and it would take a lot for him to say a word against a lady.

But Ethan read between the lines.

He arched a brow. "You didn't approve of Constance either?"

"I thought she was charming," Papa admitted. "Your mama, however, suspected all was not as it seemed with your former fiancée. She believed that you deserved better, and as usual, she was proved right."

"It seems like Ethan *has* found better," James said with a smirk.

Papa frowned. "There is no need to be crass, James."

Ethan didn't know if it was a lifelong habit or a flaw in his nature that made him enjoy the impeccable heir's chastened expression. His enjoyment proved short-lived, however, for he found himself under paternal scrutiny.

"However, I must ask." Papa fixed him with a severe look. "What are your intentions toward Mrs. Wood?"

"They are honorable, sir," Ethan said readily.

"I assumed as much." Papa's matter-of-fact response was that of a man who knows he has raised his sons to be gentlemen. "You have considered the consequences of such a match? Mrs. Wood, lovely though she may be, comes from a different world."

"That is not a problem for me. Is it for you?" Ethan asked.

Papa frowned. "I judge a person based on character and personal merit, not on factors beyond his or her control. When it comes to making a match, your mama and I care only for your happiness. I daresay we have been rather modern parents, encouraging our children to marry for love."

Ethan knew this, and he felt guilty for doubting his father for even an instant. He noted that James turned his head to stare out the window, his expression unreadable. Ethan wondered how James's wife Evie was faring; despite her reclusive tendencies, she usually made an effort to attend family gatherings. He hoped things were well between her and his brother.

"However, my view and that of society differs," Papa went on. "If you and Mrs. Wood marry, you must be prepared to face the consequences of what many in our sphere will label a *mésalliance*. It will be your duty as her husband to protect her and help her find her place in society."

"We haven't addressed the matter yet," he replied.

"I'm surprised to hear it. This is important, Ethan. You must consider how marriage will affect your future wife."

"The truth is...Xenia and I haven't discussed marriage yet."

Papa lowered his brows. "I thought you said your intentions were honorable."

"They are. I am not the one who is dragging her feet when it comes to marriage."

"I do not understand." His father looked genuinely baffled. "You are a gentleman of sound character, with excellent means and prospects. You come from a family who will welcome her into the fold. What is the cause of her prevarication?"

Ethan felt as if he'd entered a field of tarpits. Warily, he said, "There are things in Xenia's past that she fears will affect our future."

"What things?"

"I don't know," he admitted. "She will not tell me."

"Secrets are dangerous, son." Papa's expression turned grave, some dark emotion leaking through the steel of his gaze. "If they are allowed to fester, they can destroy a relationship. Take it from me: you must insist upon honesty *from the start*. Otherwise, you are gambling with your future happiness."

Ethan swallowed. "Yes, sir."

He was saved from further reply by the stopping of the carriage. It was just as well, for his papa's advice had shaken him more than he cared to acknowledge. As they alighted in front of a decrepit row of buildings, he saw that James looked somber too.

"Be vigilant, lads." Papa's military background was evident as he scanned the environs. "This is not a place to be caught unawares."

His father was not wrong. The narrow street was flanked by lodging houses, taverns, and other disreputable establishments. Men lounged in packs, some leaning against lampposts, others propped up against walls. Some had eyes that were red-rimmed by the excesses of the night before, and some continued tippling from flasks. Weapons glinted in the sunlight.

With the address provided by Rawlins, Ethan located the lodging house. The three-story edifice sagged with age, and he ducked to enter through the low-hanging doorway. The place had a sickly stench, ammonia masked with cheap scent. The proprietor, a fellow with side whiskers and twitchy movements, seemed in awe of the presence of gentlemen in his establishment, and Ethan used it to his advantage. In a lordly tone, he stated that he was Dobson Gill's former employer and demanded to see the fellow's quarters. The proprietor scrambled to fetch the key, bowing and scraping as he showed them to Gill's room.

After dismissing the proprietor, Ethan studied the cramped quarters.

"Not much to see here," James muttered.

There was a cot set against the wall, a chipped dresser, and a small washstand. The unmade bed was the only sign that the room had been occupied. Wordlessly, Ethan went to examine the dresser, a floorboard squeaking beneath his boot. The dresser wobbled as he opened the drawers and rifled through the contents.

"Find anything?" James inquired from the cot.

Ethan shook his head. "A few items of clothing. Nothing of note. You?"

Grimacing, James plucked a dirty pair of smalls from the sheets and held it up between pinched fingers. "I've discovered that hygiene was not a priority for Gill."

"The man had to have some personal effects," Papa said. "Unless they have already been purloined?"

"Living in a place like this, Gill would know to hide anything of value," Ethan said.

He took a step forward, pausing when the floorboard squeaked again. Crouching, he rapped his knuckles against the wood. The resulting resonance suggested a hollow space. He ran his fingertips along the perimeter of the plank, jiggling it until it came loose.

The others joined him.

"What did you find?" Papa asked.

One by one, Ethan removed the items from the hiding place. A battered purse with a few coins and some letters of reference extolling Gill's work as a footman, undoubtedly forged. His blood chilled as he fished out a set of chains and pots of white and red face paints.

"The first cook I hired thought she saw Bloody Thom," he muttered. "It could have been Gill in disguise...but I hadn't fired him at that point. He had no reason to retaliate against me."

"Unless Gill wasn't after revenge but something else." James crouched beside him. "Anything else in there?"

The space looked empty. Nonetheless, Ethan reached down.

"I don't think...wait, there's something stuck in a corner. Some sort of fabric..."

He tugged and felt the material tear free from whatever it was snagged on. He lifted it out, and his pulse quickened at the sight of the familiar orange stripes.

"Why the devil would he hide a neckcloth?" James curled his lip. "Although if I owned such an eyesore, perhaps I would conceal it too."

"It is not just a neckcloth," Ethan said. "It is a badge of membership worn by the Corrigans."

"Do you think Gill was a member of that gang?" Papa asked.

"This neckerchief would indicate so." Pieces of a puzzle jostled in Ethan's mind, and to his frustration, they did not quite fit. "But

Gill worked for me prior to my confrontation with Patrick Harlow, the leader. If Harlow sent him to infiltrate my household, the motive would not be one of revenge."

"Methinks it is time to consider other reasons why someone might want you gone from Bottoms House," James said. "Let's bring the evidence back and see what the others have to say. I'd wager the womenfolk are anxiously awaiting our return."

"I would hold on to my money if I were you, son." Papa's smile was wry. "By now, you ought to know that Mama is not one to wait on anyone. She finds ways to keep herself occupied."

Chapter Thirty-One

"I hope you do not mind that I invited myself along on your errands, Mrs. Wood," the Marchioness of Blackwood said lightly.

"Not at all, my lady."

Despite her apprehension at being alone with her lover's mama, Xenia managed a smile. She was already on edge after Rawlins cornered her in the stillroom, where she'd been preparing more ointment for Ethan's hand. The constable had seemed friendly, but his questions about her prior employment and history had spurred her heart into a panicked gallop. She'd told the truth where she could and replied vaguely at other times.

She didn't know if Rawlins was suspicious of her. Or if Ethan was aware that the constable had questioned her. What she did know was that she felt a strong impulse to flee the manor, and she'd almost made it out when Lady Blackwood intercepted her and requested to accompany her to Chuddums.

The carriage had deposited them at the village green. Xenia had a list of errands to run, and her first stop was at the draper's to acquire more linens for the guests. As she and Lady Blackwood strolled toward the shop, they were shadowed by a pair of footmen.

"My husband would have a fit if I did not bring an escort." Shaded by a ruffled parasol that matched her walking dress, the marchioness gave Xenia a knowing look. "The Harrington men tend to be overprotective."

Since Xenia couldn't think of a response that wouldn't give away too much, she said nothing.

"May I call you Xenia? It is a lovely name."

"Of course, my lady. Thank you," Xenia mumbled.

"In return, you may call me Pandora. Or Penny, if we are to become friends."

"Oh no, I couldn't, my lady."

Xenia glanced around nervously. She'd already waved at a few villagers who were watching her and the sophisticated lady with unabashed curiosity. The last thing she needed was to fuel the gossip mill by appearing overfamiliar with her employer's mama.

"Come, my dear. We are women of the world, are we not? As such, I hope we may speak frankly, without the pretensions of formality."

The marchioness, Xenia observed, had a talent for getting her way, but doing so in a fashion that was disarming and gracious. It was a talent that she had passed on to her daughter.

"Now, my son introduced you to us in a way that states his intentions quite clearly," Lady Blackwood said. "What remains less clear to me are *your* intentions."

Xenia knew the tattered brim of her bonnet didn't hide her flaming cheeks. Never in her life had she been so embarrassed—so caught in the act of wanting something beyond her reach. It was how she'd felt when Ethan noticed her eyeing the green dress, only this was a thousand times worse.

"I-I do not have any, ma'am. Intentions, I mean," she stammered. "His lordship is my employer—"

"Dukes have married shopgirls and ladies eloped with footmen." Lady Blackwood's shoulders moved in an eloquent shrug. "Since my son does not seem to care about such things, I do not see why you should. His father and I raised him—and all his siblings—to follow their hearts when it comes to making the most important decisions in their lives. My question to you is whether you return Ethan's affections. Whether you care for him...and not just the life that he can afford you."

At the marchioness's pointed words, indignation burst in Xenia's chest.

"I don't give a whit about his money or title," she said tightly. "I've been fending for myself since the age of sixteen and getting by just fine. I do not need anyone to give me what I can earn for myself. It's a simple, peaceful life I want—the kind of happiness that, no offense, my lady, money cannot buy."

"None taken, and I happen to agree," Lady Blackwood said easily. "If it is not my son's fortune that interests you, I hope it is not his fame. As much as it grieves me to say it, Ethan is unlikely to perform again. Although his former fiancée would deny it, she was never comfortable with his injury, and I believe it played a role in her ignoble ending of their engagement."

Xenia narrowed her eyes. "From what I understand, his fiancée ended things because Lord Ethan was getting better, and she could no longer play the role of nurse and martyr."

The marchioness arched her brows. "I take it that you have been talking to Gigi."

"No, ma'am. I have been talking to the person whom this concerns—the person whom *you* should be having this conversation with. Since you asked, however, I will say this: my only worry about Lord Ethan's injury is the pain that it causes him. Not the physical sort, which he has learned to cope with, but the emotional loss that comes from being deprived of one's art. Yet your son is strong, my lady, and he is not allowing his disability to define him. Did you know that he is now composing? Even if no one hears his beautiful piece, it will not matter because the important thing is that he is making music again. He is doing what he loves most, what he was born to do..."

Too late, Xenia realized she'd let her emotions get the better of her. Lady Blackwood was staring at her as if she'd suddenly sprouted two heads.

Blooming hell, did I just give a marchioness—and my lover's mama, no less—a blistering lecture? Must I ruin everything all the dashed time? What is wrong with me?

"I'm sorry." Xenia's chest constricted. "I shouldn't have—"

"It is all right, my dear."

To Xenia's shock, a faint smile played on Lady Blackwood's lips.

"To be candid, I was wondering what Ethan saw in you," the lady said thoughtfully. "Now I think I understand."

"There is nothing to understand, ma'am. Believe me." Xenia was desperately glad they'd arrived at Mr. Duffield's. "Here we are at the draper's. I'll just, um, pop in. There is a dress shop across the way, if you would care to browse. Or the Leaning House offers a fine cup of tea…"

"I will amuse myself." Lady Blackwood waved her on. "Attend to your business, my dear."

Not needing to be told twice, Xenia dashed into the shop.

Mr. Duffield, a dapper blond fellow in his thirties, was the genius behind the manor's new curtains and upholstery. As he was patient, kind, and handsome, he was popular among local matrons. Currently, he was besieged by a circle of women vying for his opinion on various decorating projects.

"Good day, Mrs. Wood," he said with a flustered smile. "I'm assisting other patrons at the moment, but if you wouldn't mind waiting—"

"I can manage on my own this time, sir," Xenia replied. "If you could direct me to the fabrics suitable for bed linens?"

He pointed her to the right section of the shop, and she took refuge among the bolts of white fabrics. Focusing on a mundane task was a relief after the tension-fraught day. She was stroking a fine Irish linen when she felt a presence behind her. She spun around.

"Alice?" She kept her voice low, thankful that the surrounding bolts provided shelter from curious eyes. "What are you...are you all right?"

Getting a closer look at her former colleague, she saw the bruising around Alice's right eye, which the artful application of paint did not completely conceal.

"The Abbess sent me to find you." Alice's voice had an uncharacteristic quiver. "She ain't happy and says she wants to discuss your future employ."

"I already sent her a message and returned her money—"

"You ain't got a choice, Mary. None o' us do." Shadows flitted through Alice's gaze. "The Abbess 'as found 'erself a new place 'ere in Chuddums. By the docks, wot used to be the Rope and Anchor. You're to meet 'er there tonight."

"And if I don't?" Xenia said coldly.

"She said to give you this." Alice took out an envelope, pressing it into Xenia's unwilling hands. "Be smart. You're a good girl, and I don't want to see you get hurt. Midnight—don't be late."

Then Alice was gone.

Xenia, casting a furtive look around, broke the seal, and her heart shot into her throat at the message scrawled in a spidery hand.

I know who your mother is...and the world will too unless you do as I say.

Dazed, Xenia stumbled out of the shop. She heard Mr. Duffield calling after her, asking if he could help, but she didn't reply because no one could help. Panic gripped her as she stepped into the street, the hustle and bustle of everyday life a jarring juxtaposition to her inner chaos. She'd imagined exposure so many times, yet somehow she was still unprepared. She didn't know what to do next.

You know what you must do. Run.

Yet how could she leave Ethan, the man she loved?

A commotion on the corner distracted her from her turmoil. It was Mr. Bailey, and he was surrounded by three ruffians in front of his shop. Xenia recognized the leader of the brutes immediately.

Patrick Harlow.

"I paid you back what I owe and plenty more besides!" Mr. Bailey shouted, his eyes wild and nose bleeding into his dark moustache. "Borrowing money from you was the most foolish thing I've ever done, but I'm finished. I ain't giving you another farthing, so if you want to take your pound o' flesh, you're welcome to bloody try."

He raised his fists, his face pale but determined.

"If it's a public lesson you're wanting," Harlow sneered, "then that's what you'll be getting."

He took out a cosh, metal studs gleaming on the wide head of the weapon.

Xenia's insides clenched. Members of her mama's gang used a similar instrument, and she knew the damage it could do. Spectators gathered, horror on their faces as they watched the unfolding violence. The cutthroats closed in on Mr. Bailey, who bravely stood his ground.

All Mr. Bailey had done was try to get by. To keep his business afloat and support his loved ones. Why did brutes and villains always win?

Why is life so blooming unfair?

A dull roar filled Xenia's head. It drove her to the nearest weapon she could find. Grabbing it, she let it fly, and her aim hit true.

Harlow jolted as the potato struck him between the shoulder blades. Onlookers gasped as he whirled around, his eyes glittering with menace when he saw her.

"You again," he snarled. "What do you think you're doing, you little bitch?"

"Leave Mr. Bailey alone." Xenia grabbed another potato from Mr. Pickleworth's cart. "He's paid you back, fair and square. You have no business with him any longer."

"My business ain't none o' yours. Lads," Harlow barked at his two comrades, "you take care o' the butcher while I put this stupid wench in 'er place."

The brutes smiled evilly as they cornered Mr. Bailey. But Xenia couldn't help him, her own focus on the rapidly advancing Harlow. She gripped her makeshift projectile, ready to pelt him again...

Splat.

A tomato caught him in the face, exploding with juicy red gusto.

Stunned, she turned and saw Mr. Pickleworth standing close by.

The greengrocer lifted his brows. "I told you the tomatoes were ripe."

Beside him, his wife Loretta held a cabbage the size of a cannonball. "Don't make me use this," she called.

Harlow bared his teeth, advancing.

"Stand back," Xenia said to the pair.

She threw the potato, and Harlow ducked. He grinned, then yelped as something slammed into his jaw, knocking him to the ground. A rock?

Turning, Xenia saw Mr. Khan, who gave her a nod of support...and he wasn't alone. Mrs. Pettigrew, Mrs. Sommers, Mr. Duffield, and a dozen other villagers were there, all armed with makeshift weapons. Mrs. Thornton wielded a cast-iron frying pan while her husband carried a cricket bat. Similarly equipped residents of Chuddums had gathered behind Mr. Bailey as well. The two brutes backed away, helping their leader to his feet. The Corrigans were surrounded.

Harlow looked wildly around the circle of resolute faces. "You are going to pay for this! No one crosses the Corrigans."

"Leave our village," someone shouted. "We don't welcome the likes o' you!"

The words became a war cry, and suddenly the crowd began to chant.

"*Leave Chuddums! Leave Chuddums!*"

Harlow's eyes darted, and like the bully he was, he knew when he was beaten. He fled, followed by his lackeys, the three of them stumbling and running as the townsfolk chased them out of the village green.

When the last Corrigan disappeared from sight, a wild cheer erupted.

"Well, my dear."

Xenia spun around to see Lady Blackwood. Her footmen had their weapons drawn, eyes scanning the square. But there was only the boisterous celebration of ordinary folk discovering their own power.

"Have you completed your errands?" the marchioness inquired. "Or do you have other villains to expunge?"

Now that the peril was over, Xenia felt dazed. "I'm done."

"Splendid. If the men return in time from Cookham, we can all reconvene for tea." Lady Blackwood looped an arm through Xenia's, adding in a confiding tone, "I must skip the scones, however, having overindulged in Mrs. Pettigrew's delectable pudding."

Chapter Thirty-Two

"He's here." Terror flooded her. "Please, you have to let me go—"

"No," her beloved said. "I will protect you."

"You can't," she said miserably. "No one can."

"Go and hide where I showed you. You know how to get in."

"I can't leave you." A sob hitched in her throat. "I'm scared... scared of the darkness."

"Don't be afraid, my love. Darkness can be a sanctuary."

"You *are* my sanctuary," she whispered. "I cannot lose you."

"Don't come out until I tell you it is safe." He kissed her. "Trust me, my darling Rose."

Shivering, she did as he asked. Even curled up in her hiding place, however, she didn't feel safe. Her enemy's footsteps made ashes rain from the walls, his rage reaching her through the bricks. She wanted to go to her beloved and fight by his side, but she'd given him her promise to stay safe and protect their future—

A shot blasted.

"Die knowing this," her enemy hissed. "The little whore is mine."

She stuffed her fist in her mouth to stifle her scream.

The run-in with Alice and the Corrigans and the lack of sleep the night before took their toll on Xenia. Exhausted, she'd nodded off during the short carriage ride home. Lady Blackwood insisted that she take a nap, and when Xenia protested that she had too much to do, the marchioness pointed out that she would be far more efficient rested. Relenting, Xenia decided to have a short lie-down and asked Mrs. Johnson to wake her in half an hour.

But the cook didn't need to; Xenia woke herself up screaming.

She didn't have a chance to speak with Ethan as he didn't return until suppertime. The nightmare lingered with her as she worked behind the scenes to help Brunswick and the staff serve the meal. She had other distractions too: namely, the Abbess's demand to meet this evening. The idea of running away—of leaving Ethan—was impossible to fathom. Thus, Xenia would have to deal with the problem head-on and confront the bawd.

After supper, she was in the stillroom, taking stock of her supplies, when Ethan entered. Her heart thumped when he closed the door and took her into his arms, kissing her until she was swoony.

"I missed you, pet," he murmured.

"I missed you too." She inhaled his scent, letting it soothe her ragged nerves. "But you shouldn't be here."

He nuzzled her neck. "I wanted to invite you to drinks in the drawing room."

While she liked his family very much, she couldn't imagine sitting through an evening pretending all was normal when she had a meeting with the Abbess looming. She still had to figure out a way to protect herself—and Ethan—from the bawd's extortion.

"Could you make excuses for me?" she asked. "While I would enjoy your family's company, I am rather tired."

"Understandably." He tucked a loose curl behind her ear, his eyes warm. "Mama shared your exploits over supper. While you and I are going to discuss your recklessness, you've certainly won Mama over. She called you a heroine."

Xenia was relieved that she hadn't ruined her chances with the marchioness.

"As it turns out," he added, "you were not the only ones to tangle with the Corrigans today."

Ethan told her about his discovery that Gill had likely been a member of the gang. He had also spoken to other lodgers who'd described Gill as a loner and not well-liked. Gill had been a braggart who thought he was better than everyone else, and this got worse when he was in his cups. The night before he died, he'd apparently boasted that he had valuable information that was going to make him richer than Croesus.

"Given the timeline of events, I no longer think that revenge is the motive behind these hoaxes," Ethan concluded somberly. "I think someone wants me to leave this place because there is something hidden here—something valuable."

"If there is some sort of treasure hidden in Bottoms House," she said, frowning, "surely we would have found it by now. We've cleaned the place top to bottom and done renovations."

"We shall have to conduct a thorough search." Ethan cupped her cheek. "In the morning, though, after you've rested. Sweet dreams, my love."

My love.

She didn't know if he meant anything by the endearment, but three words slipped from her heart, sticking in her throat. She was not yet free to say them. The dream from earlier constricted her chest and filled her with determination: unlike poor Rose, she wasn't going to hide while her beloved died trying to slay her demons.

Tonight, she would battle them herself.

From a nearby wingchair, Ethan watched as Papa and James got trounced in a game of whist by Mama and Gigi.

"Someone is cheating, lad," Papa said to James. "Obviously, it is not one of us."

"Perhaps Lady Fortune favors Gigi and me tonight," Mama said demurely.

"I cannot argue with that." Looking amused, Papa said, "You are my lucky Penny, after all."

He took Mama's hand, kissing it with enough warmth to make her blush and James and Gigi groan, Ethan along with them. Growing up, protesting parental displays of affection had been an act of solidarity amongst the siblings, and one was never too old to act like a child, he supposed. Owen had always objected the most theatrically, slapping his hands over his eyes...

However, Owen wasn't here. According to Gigi, he'd closeted himself in his room all day and opted to have supper delivered on a tray. Ethan couldn't quell a trickle of concern regarding his younger brother's behavior, but he wasn't sure what to do about it. Maybe he could extend an olive branch and ask Owen to help in the search for the valuables. With Parkhurst and Canning gone—they'd departed this morning for London, saying they didn't wish to be a fifth wheel to the family reunion—Ethan could say he needed more hands on deck.

He decided to talk it over with Xenia. She was a good listener, and he trusted her opinion. Moreover, she was getting to know his family and vice versa, and he wasn't surprised by how well they all got on. Xenia fit in like she was meant to be a Harrington...which was a good thing since he planned to make her one.

Around eleven, Ethan suggested it was time for bed. It was early, but everyone was tired from the day's events, and they had a day of treasure hunting ahead. Before parting ways, his mama pulled him aside for a *tête-à-tête*.

"Xenia is perfect for you," Mama declared. "She is different from the other ladies you've spent time with, dearest, and I mean that as a compliment."

"Truly, did no one like Constance?" Ethan muttered.

"Papa thought she was quite charming." Mama rolled her eyes. "If he has a flaw, it is that his honor blinds him to female machinations."

"An advantage for you, I'm sure."

He was teasing, but his mama's countenance grew troubled.

"The ability to hurt people you love is never an advantage," she said quietly.

Because he knew how much his parents adored each other and the unbreakable strength of their bond, he was surprised that she was taking his banter seriously.

He drew his brows together. "I didn't mean—"

"I know, my dear. But you have a lot of Papa in you, and by that I mean you are a man of honor whose instinct is to protect those you perceive as vulnerable. You are like a knight of old, dashing to the side of a damsel in distress."

"Xenia is no damsel," he said.

His minx was no wilting violet, and he admired her resilience, bravery, and pluck.

"She is not," Mama agreed. "Yet she has vulnerabilities all the same. For instance, I get the distinct feeling that she does not think herself worthy of you. While that might be due to your differences in station, I have a sense that there is more to it. Is there something in her past, perhaps, that might cause her to feel this way?"

"I don't know all the details," he was forced to admit. "She doesn't like to discuss her past."

"Oh, my dearest." Mama took his hand in hers, a strange note of urgency in her voice. "If you mean to marry her, you cannot allow that to stand. You *must* get her to speak openly about her past so that whatever ghosts she may be hiding do not have the power to interfere with your future happiness."

Ghosts.

After bidding his mama goodnight, the word lingered with him. He wondered if his mama had been affected by the talk of Bloody Thom...if they had all been. He'd intended to leave Xenia to her rest tonight, but he found himself heading to her room, driven by an inexplicable need to see her. An eerie feeling of *déjà vu* came over him. As if he'd walked this path before...not as himself but someone else. He felt as if he were retracing another's footsteps as he made his way to the servants' quarters. Eagerness, desire, and anxiety pounded in his chest like an echo of another's feelings.

He shook off the uncanny sensation. The curse nonsense had obviously gotten the better of him, and if he wasn't careful, he would succumb to the phantom mania that had besieged the general population. Anyway, Bloody Thom was a distraction that he didn't need. He had to focus on convincing Xenia to disclose her past.

His parents were right. Without trust, there was no hope of building a future together, and he knew that the only future he wanted was one with Xenia in it. He evaded the patrolling guards and made it to the servants' wing. He was in the kitchen, about to head up the stairs to Xenia's room when a voice came from the shadows.

"She's not there."

"What the devil?"

Ethan nearly jumped as Owen emerged from a dark corner. Once Ethan's heart stopped racing, he straightened his lapels, doing a creditable job of acting as if he hadn't been startled out of his skin.

"Why are you lurking about?" he said irritably.

Owen shrugged. "I couldn't sleep. There weren't any servants about, so I came here to rummage for a snack. That is when I saw Mrs. Wood head out."

"What do you mean, *head out*?" Ethan narrowed his eyes. "Have you been drinking?"

In the past, his question would have elicited a defensive, and likely belligerent, response from his brother. Now, Owen waved at a half-filled glass on the table.

"I've had milk," he said with a slight smirk. "Does that count?"

Bloody Owen. Annoying when he was drunk *and* when he was sober.

"Where would Mrs. Wood go this time of night?" Ethan bit out.

"I didn't ask. From the dark cloak she was wearing and the stealthy way she dodged the guards, I assumed she did not wish to be seen."

A chill spread in Ethan's gut. "Did you see where she was headed? How long ago was this?"

"Ten minutes, at most." Owen shrugged again. "I can show you where she went."

CHAPTER THIRTY-THREE

When Owen showed Ethan the path that Xenia had taken, it was obvious that she was headed to Chuddums. But what business did she have in the village at this time of night? Why did she pretend to be tired, then sneak out? Possible reasons for her deception crowded his head...the most obvious one being that she was playing him false.

The way Constance had.

Rage swelled, fed by an undertow of humiliation. He was certain that he wasn't going to like what he discovered this eve. Yet he had to know. He readied Legato and was surprised when Owen saddled a horse as well.

"What do you think you're doing?" he asked.

"Going with you," Owen said. "You're not riding alone this time of night."

As Ethan didn't have time to argue, he simply spurred Legato on. Owen followed, and they didn't encounter Xenia on the path to the village. Ethan suspected they were only a few minutes behind her since they made the journey to Chuddums at breakneck speed, and she was on foot. Upon arriving on High Street, he saw that he was correct: a familiar cloaked figure was at the end of the street, taking a turn east toward the docks.

"That's her," Owen said. "We can catch up—"

"No," Ethan said grimly. "I don't want her to know that I'm here. I want to see what she is up to. We'll stay close but out of her sight."

Owen raised his brows but said nothing.

They left the horses at the Briarbush Inn on the corner, then continued after Xenia on foot. She had widened her lead on them, but he tracked her easily enough. They reached the docklands, which were teeming with riffraff and the light-skirts who serviced them. Taverns, brothels, and gaming hells flanked the street, business spilling into the dark alleyways between the buildings. Guttural sounds came from the shadows, mingling with cheers of merriment and shouts of aggression.

Ethan's gut tightened when he spotted a cluster of brutes sporting orange-striped neckcloths. At least a dozen Corrigans stood in front of a dilapidated waterfront building, which looked to be their headquarters. He noted that Xenia steered clear of them, and he did the same, keeping the brim of his hat pulled low. Luckily, the ruffians were too inebriated to notice.

He and Owen followed Xenia another block, where she paused in front of a tall, narrow edifice. The windows were drawn, but the licentious glow emitted by their scarlet curtains advertised the nature of the trade. And if that didn't make the purpose of the place obvious, then the pair of whores at the entryway did. Their faces were masked, their skimpy dresses leaving little to the imagination.

Ethan's nape chilled when Xenia exchanged brief words with the pair. One of the prostitutes handed her a mask, and she slipped it on. Then she went inside.

Owen asked the obvious question. "What business does your housekeeper have in a brothel?"

"I am about to find out," Ethan said tersely. "Wait for me here."

"And let you have all the fun?" Owen replied. "I think not."

"I don't have time for your nonsense—"

"No one is sicker of my nonsense than me. You can count on me, Ethan. For what that is worth."

Seeing Owen's resolute expression, Ethan went against his better judgment. "Fine," he muttered. "But don't get in the way."

"Unless you need me, you won't even know I'm there," Owen promised.

The whores struck provocative poses as they approached.

"Welcome to the Nunnery, gents." The one with brassy curls held out a pair of masks. "You're in for a treat this eve. Sister Sirena, the Salacious Storyteller, will be taking confessions."

The realization came as swiftly as a blade in the back, making Ethan stagger. All the similarities he had ignored, the signs he'd obstinately refused to see. Her voice, her figure, the way she'd seemed to know his deepest fantasies—to know just how to embody them.

He was stunned by how obvious it was...by the extent of her deception.

Xenia was Sirena.

Why would she deceive me? Pain spread through the cracks of his soul, bewildered rage following in its wake. *Was this some sort of game to her...did she amuse herself at the expense of her crippled fool of an employer? While I was falling in love with her, was she laughing at me?*

"Are you certain you want to do this?" Owen asked.

Numbness took over, allowing Ethan to nod. He had to see this through. That was the one advantage of being broken: he was used to picking up the bloody pieces.

From the bawdy scene around her, Xenia saw that the Abbess's latest venture catered to a different class of clientele. Whereas previous incarnations of the masquerade had been built on the precept of exclusivity, this version brokered its success on cheap mass appeal. The patrons appeared to be men who worked by the docks. The entry fee was low, and the entertainment was conducted in a series of crowded public rooms for all to see.

Xenia didn't recognize many of the prostitutes, including the two performing fellatio on the sailor sprawled on a tattered sofa. Nor the one who was dancing naked on a table while a circle of men showered her with coins. Xenia's search for the Abbess took her into the next room, where a row of women knelt on all fours, saucily wriggling their bare rumps as patrons lined up to take their turn.

Feeling queasy, Xenia wondered if coming was a mistake. Yet for the first time, she had decided that she would not run—that she had something worth staying for. *Someone* worth fighting for. She would do everything in her power to be worthy of Ethan, and that began with confronting her past. For him, she would face her demons. She would face anything.

"There you are."

The Abbess approached. Beneath her mask, her mouth was curved in a gloating smile.

"You're late, dove," she admonished, as if Xenia were a naughty child. "I've customers waiting for the inimitable Sister Sirena, and we cannot keep them waiting, can we?"

"I no longer work for you," Xenia said boldly.

"We'll see about that."

The bawd's razor-sharp smile released a trickle of dread in Xenia.

"Come." The Abbess crooked a finger. "We shall discuss the terms upstairs."

Curling her fists, Xenia followed.

The Abbess led her upstairs to a corner room. Xenia saw that it had been set up to resemble a confessional, with a curtain dividing the chamber in two. Through the gauzy fabric, she spotted Sister Sirena's costume laid out on a battered sofa.

The Abbess closed the door. "Now, dove, we have business to discuss, don't we?"

"I will not play Sister Sirena tonight or any other," Xenia said fiercely. "I returned your ten pounds. There are no ties between us, and I owe you nothing."

"Now that you're a housekeeper for a fine lord, you think you are too good for this work?"

"My reasons are my own." Xenia met the madam's eyes squarely. "Your attempt to blackmail me will not change my decision."

"Are you certain, dove? You came tonight, after all."

"I came for one purpose: to tell you face-to-face that I will not be extorted."

"But I know who you are, Mary Smith. Or is it Jane Wood? Oh, that's right—it's *Bernice Wardell*."

It was strange how foreign the name she'd been born with sounded. Yet she drew strength from the fact that determination and hard work had put distance between who she'd been and who she was now: a woman who'd carved her own path. From the day she'd chosen to be Xenia Loveday, she'd made the decision to leave her old self behind. While some might sneer at how she'd gotten by, she was proud of doing honest work, from selling fantasies to managing a manor. Proud that she now had a lover who saw and brought out the best in her. Proud that she'd made friends and found a place where she belonged.

"Bernice Wardell ceased to exist years ago." She lifted her chin. "I left that despicable life behind me."

"You may have flown the coop, but others are still looking for you, dove. My sources tell me that authorities from London to Manchester remain on the lookout for Lady Jo and her gang, which includes her daughter Bernice." Malice gleamed in the bawd's eyes. "It's said Bernice has a singular ability to mimic accents, which she used to con more than a few people during her time. She's said to be a mistress o' disguises, and she takes after her mama with her bright-red hair and features as fine as any lady's. Her brown eyes are said to be her most valuable asset, for their guileless appearance allows her to manipulate and beguile."

Although Xenia's heart was pounding, she refused to be cowed. "What do you want?"

"The world is my oyster, ain't it?" The Abbess's mask didn't hide her smugness. "To begin, you will continue in my employ. Working for free, of course, in exchange for my silence."

"I'm done working for you," Xenia said through gritted teeth. "Go ahead and tell the constables. I'll tell them the truth: that my mother forced me into a life of crime from the time I was a child. That every time I tried to escape, she dragged me back and beat me until I couldn't walk. That she starved me, kept me chained like a dog." She balled her hands. "I'll tell them that she took away everyone I loved, but she still couldn't bend me to her will. The only way I'll go back to her and her stupid gang is in a *bloody box*."

"Now, there's no need for theatrics." The Abbess's tone turned cajoling. "You know I'm not a fan o' constables and other hypocrites who get in the way o' a person's God-given right to make a living. Besides, there ain't no advantage in giving you to them...their reward is a pittance compared to the blunt your clever tongue brings in. I need you, dove. Without Sister Sirena, I won't recover from these weeks o' lost income. Only you can lure back the toffs. If you don't help me, I'll be stuck selling three-penny uprights for the rest o' my life."

Xenia cut through the woman's self-pitying drivel. "If not the authorities, then who will you tell if I refuse to work for you?"

"The bloke you've fallen head over heels for," the Abbess said with equal bluntness. "Rumor has it the two o' you have gotten close. While he might be willing to overlook the fact that you're a servant, how would your master feel if he knew you worked in brothels? If he discovered that you'd brought off hundreds o' men with your talented tongue? And what if he knew that you weren't only a girl with a wicked imagination, but one who'd done unimaginable things? One who is the daughter of the infamous lady cutthroat Joanna Wardell?"

Despite her churning fear, Xenia set her shoulders back. "Go ahead. Tell him."

"Trying to call my bluff, are you?" The bawd gave her a cold look. "Well, it won't work, dearie. If you don't put on that bloody nun's costume right now and satisfy the patrons I've lined up for you, I *will* tell his lordship everything."

"It won't matter." In that instant, Xenia made her choice—the choice she would have made sooner if fear hadn't held her back. "Because *I* am going to tell him everything."

The instant she said the words, she felt the chains fall from her. Amazed, she realized that she'd held the key all this time. Freedom wasn't about getting away from her past but facing it.

"Please." The Abbess scoffed. "Only a fool would give up that golden goose, and you strike me as a female who's learned to live by her wits, Miss Wardell."

"He's not a golden goose to me. I love him," she said ardently. "He deserves to know the truth. I should have told him earlier, but I was trying to protect him."

"Protect *yourself*, you mean. From being tossed out on your arse."

"It's true that, at first, I didn't tell him I was Lady Jo's daughter because I needed the job and a place to stay. But once I got to know him, I didn't tell him about my mama because I knew he would try to protect me from her. I could not stand for him to be hurt because of me."

"No man will protect you once he knows you're a criminal and a whore," the Abbess sneered.

"He will." She spoke with confidence because she knew her beloved—his character and sense of honor. "After I explain everything and beg his forgiveness, he will stand by me because that is the kind of gentleman he is. That is why I love him."

Even though her knees were shaking, she headed to the door, her head held high.

"I made you, and I can unmake you," the Abbess fumed. "I'm going to report you to the Peelers. See how you like rotting behind bars, you ungrateful bitch—"

"I would reconsider that decision if I were you."

At the familiar male voice, Xenia whirled around. Her heart hurtled into her chest at the sight of Ethan standing on the other side of the curtain. Had he been in the room this entire time... hiding behind the sofa? He tore the material out of his way with a savage motion; without that barrier, she saw the full extent of his fury. His eyes blazed in the holes of his mask, incinerating her confidence. The enormity of her mistake struck her.

She'd trusted that love would shelter her...but she didn't know the extent of Ethan's feelings for her. They'd never exchanged words of love, even if she'd felt them in her heart. If he didn't love her, how could she expect him to take on the daughter of a notorious criminal, a woman who'd survived by performing in brothels, who'd been lying to him all along? It was asking a lot even if he *did* love her.

She had deceived him, just as his fiancée had. Though she hadn't betrayed him with another man, she'd done so with a ghost. The ghost of her past. Although Xenia had been knocked down time and again, she'd never felt defeated. Until now. When she saw the disgust and revulsion on the face of the man she loved and knew she deserved it.

Chapter Thirty-Four

Emotions roiled in Ethan, and he went with rage.

He faced the Abbess, letting her see the full extent of his wrath. "If you speak about my housekeeper to anyone, I will ruin you," he vowed.

"Please, my lord." The Abbess's voice held a tremor. "You, er, misunderstood."

Like any bully, she was weak, cowed by a show of greater strength. She was the opposite of Xenia, who'd had her power stripped from her time and again yet still stood up for what she believed in. Who was staring at him, her eyes wide with fear and trepidation...

I'll deal with her later. First I must ensure the bawd's silence.

"If her connection to Joanna Wardell becomes public, I will make it my personal mission to destroy you," he said. "Those wealthy patrons you're after are my peers. All it takes is a few words at one of the gentlemen's clubs: about how indiscreetly you run your business and how unclean your whores are. No one of any consequence will patronize your establishment again."

"Have mercy, my lord," the bawd said plaintively. "Upon my

mother's grave, I would never do anything to endanger Mrs. Wood. In fact, if anyone asks, I will say I don't know her."

"You had better." His gaze told her he meant it. "Now get out and lock the door behind you."

"Yes, my lord."

The bawd slithered out, leaving him alone with Xenia. The latter looked as if she were having difficulty breathing. He went up to her and yanked off her mask before removing his own.

"Now I see you clearly," he said coldly.

"I...I can explain," she said.

Her expression was anxious and uncertain, yet it was the desperate hope in her eyes that punched him in the gut.

"You've said that before," he bit out.

"You have every right to be angry—"

"Trust me, I am aware." He was angry...for so many reasons. His emotions were a vortex that threatened his self-control. "This is why you refused to commit to me? Because you're the daughter of a criminal?"

"My mother isn't an ordinary criminal." Her voice quivered. "She is vicious and cruel—a monster."

The storm in him raged as he recalled what she'd told the bawd. His Xenia—beaten, starved, *chained* by her own mother because she refused to participate in a life of felony. He'd always known that she was a survivor...he just hadn't realized the extent of what she'd survived.

"If she finds me, she'll destroy everything I care about. Everyone I love." Xenia's gaze turned distant and blank. "She murdered my papa when he tried to take me away. When I escaped again, she found me and killed my friend Mr. Trelawney. All he'd done was give me a job. I couldn't let that happen to you."

"Because you love me." He said it for her.

Her gaze snapped to his, and he saw the life coming back.

"Yes." Her face held painful longing. "Having an affair with you was wrong, and I knew it. I knew from the start that you deserved better. Yet I was selfish and fell in love with you anyway. I told myself I would leave at the first sign of trouble—"

"But you didn't. Why?"

He had to know.

"Because..." Her voice hitched, a tear spilling over. "Because you are worth fighting for."

"So are you, Xenia." He took her in his arms, feeling the sobs that racked her body. "I would lay down my life for you."

"That's what I am afraid of. If my mother finds me, she will try to take me back. And if you stand in her way—"

"I will handle your mother." He thumbed away a tear. "Trust me?"

"I do, Ethan." She bit her lip, her eyes searching his. "But can you trust *me*, after everything? I swear I was only trying to protect you."

He raised a brow. "From Sirena?"

"I was wrong to keep that from you," she said humbly. "I didn't realize it was you until your second visit, and by then I was so attracted to you that I was afraid to tell you how I earned my living. I was afraid that you would reject me. But I swear that I quit after that second time. Do you...do you still want me, knowing the work I've done?"

"I won't say I like it," he said with blunt honesty. "But I understand you had to do what you did to survive. All I want is your promise that I'm the only one you share your fantasies with from now on."

"I promise," she said fervently. "You're the only one with whom my fantasies were real. You're the only man I've ever loved."

"Then promise you'll be mine. Marry me, Xenia."

"I will, Ethan." Her voice cracked. "If you still want me."

"I want you," he said fiercely. "I love you."

A sob left her. "I love you. More than anything."

Triumph surged over him, and he closed his mouth over hers, sealing his claim.

Giddy with love, Xenia basked in Ethan's kiss.

Somehow, disaster had turned to victory, the heavy shackles of the past dropping from her. Even though the man of her dreams knew who she was and what she'd done, he still thought her worthy of his love. He accepted her and forgave the mistakes she'd made and those that had been forced upon her. There was no longer a need to pretend because her wildest dreams had come true.

Joy and gratitude flooded her. She was free at last. Free to love.

She kissed her beloved with all the passion singing in her veins. What began as a tender reunion soon turned into a wilder, darker need to claim. They ate at each other's mouths, their tongues swirling and tangling. She pressed up against him, reveling in his hard strength. Her nipples pulsed against his chest, and her pussy fluttered with yearning.

She wanted to be his in all ways. To belong to him irrevocably.

She slid her hand between them and cupped the thick ridge of his erection. "I want you, darling," she whispered. "Make love to me."

"Here?" Desire flashed in Ethan's gaze, his hunger barely held in check. "Are you certain, sweeting? We could wait—"

"We've waited too long already. I ache for you, Ethan, and want to belong to you fully."

Obviously, he felt that same desperate craving, for he swept her into his arms, their lips melding in the heat of their kiss. He laid her on the sofa. She felt Sirena's wimple crumpling beneath her, and she didn't care. Because all that mattered was Ethan and their love, which knew no boundaries but the ones they chose.

The urgency to be one possessed them both. They vied to get closer, not bothering with the nuisance of removing their clothes. There would be time for that later—after this initial, overwhelming hunger was appeased. Ethan tossed up her skirts, and she moaned when he touched the wet, needy core of her.

"Devil and damn." He groaned. "You're ready for me, love."

She was. When he unfastened his trousers, the sight of his huge, stiff cock told her he was just as ready for her. He fisted his rod, rubbing the wide head against her slit until she was panting, writhing to get closer, to impale herself on his thick offering.

"Make me yours, Ethan," she begged. "*I love you.*"

"You're mine, Xenia," he said savagely.

He pushed, the stretch of his possession stealing her breath. Locked in the safety of his gaze, she felt no fear, only the wonder of discovery. All the stories she'd told about this act vanished from her mind as the reality of it consumed her...the heat, intensity, and flood of sensations. His burning claim pushed her to her limits, yet she felt the primal satisfaction of being filled where she'd been empty...of being one with the man she adored.

When he seated himself that last inch, they both expelled a breath.

"All right, love?" he asked hoarsely.

"I am more than all right, darling." Drunk on happiness, she framed his hard, beautiful face in her hands. "I belong to you now, and you belong to me."

"Forever," he vowed.

He kissed her and began to move. With each thrust, discomfort blurred into new and intriguing sensations. Pleasure unfurled in the deep places where his body stroked hers, and she moved instinctively, seeking more of it.

"That's it," he said between harsh breaths. "Tilt your hips for me. Let me in deeper."

She did, and he nudged a spot that set off sparks of bliss. He did it again, harder and harder still, and the sparks built into a flame. Pain became a distant memory as she clung to his shoulders, arching up to meet his thrusts, moaning his name.

"I knew it would be like this for us," he gritted out. "Wild and hot, so bloody sweet. Can you take more, pet?"

"I want everything," she breathed. "All of you, Ethan."

With a growl, he slammed his hips, pushing her breath from her lips. She realized then that he'd been holding back. Now he drilled into her, his stones smacking heavily against her swollen folds. He found her pearl, strumming it while he plowed her with his massive shaft. She gasped as the fire at her center flared, spilling through her veins.

"That's it," he said thickly. "Come for me, love."

With a cry, she did. Blissful spasms rocked her body, and she heard him groan, his thrusts growing faster. Then he roared her name, shuddering and inundating her with his hot pleasure. They were gazing at each other with dazed and breathless joy when the door flew open.

The rest happened so suddenly that Xenia felt paralyzed. Stuck in a dream where everything happened in an altered version of time that was fast yet slow. People stormed into the room, and before Ethan could fasten his trousers, he was yanked off her by a pair of brutes. One of them slammed a fist into his jaw. When he tried to fight back, the ruffian hit him again and yanked out a pistol.

"No!" Xenia scrambled to her feet.

"There she is, like I said." The Abbess cowered as she addressed the leader of the gang. "You...you'll let me go, Lady Jo?"

"You'll go." Lady Jo moved as she always did, with lethal speed that belied her elegant looks. She caught the bawd from behind, her blade at the other's throat. "To hell, that is."

The menace in her eyes was brighter than the flash of steel.

"But you promised..." the Abbess gurgled.

Scarlet pulsed from the bawd's throat, her shocked gaze fixed on Xenia. Lady Jo wiped her blade on the dead woman's dress before letting the body thud to the ground. She smirked at Xenia's horrified expression.

"Miss me, daughter dearest?" she purred.

Gagged, restrained, and held at gunpoint, Ethan watched in helpless fury as Xenia was terrorized by her mother. Joanna "Lady Jo" Wardell's cruelty was worse than what he'd read about in the papers, worse even than Xenia's fear of her had implied. Lady Jo's beauty, the only thing Xenia had to thank her for, made her viciousness seem worse. If looks were a measure of character, she ought to be a hag. Instead, she was willowy and delicate-looking, her gleaming red hair styled in a coronet. She wore an expensive burgundy dress, and jewels sparkled on her fingers and at her throat.

"No greeting for your beloved mama?" Lady Jo taunted Xenia in a light, musical voice. "I taught you better manners than that. The Abbess left me no choice, you know. She was blackmailing you, dear heart. Threatening to turn us both in to the bleeding Peelers."

"There is no *us*," Xenia said hoarsely. "I am not a part of your gang. I haven't been for seven years."

"Oh, Bernice. Don't you remember what I told you?"

The steel in her mother's voice caused Ethan's muscles to bunch.

"No one leaves Lady Jo."

Lady Jo had ensured this was true. She had five brutes with her, all armed. Two held him, two were at the door, and one towered over Xenia. Even if Ethan could get free, he couldn't take all of them...even with Owen's help. Not that Owen was anywhere to be found.

"*You can count on me,*" he'd said.

What a joke. Knowing Owen, he was probably three sheets to

the wind by now or tupping some harlot. He was unreliable at best and self-destructive at worst.

With a rush of bitterness, Ethan shelved the hope of any assistance from that corner.

"Fine. You have me." Xenia balled her hands. "Let Ethan go."

Lady Jo strolled over, backhanding her daughter with stunning nonchalance. The force of it sent Xenia reeling, and Ethan bellowed through the gag, struggling to get to her, but the ruffians held him back.

Xenia staggered to her feet, her cheek splotchy and lower lip bleeding.

Her eyes remained defiant.

"That was a mere reminder, daughter mine, that you are in no position to make demands. If required, I shall be happy to furnish further correction." Lady Jo smiled thinly. "Since you were a child, you have responded better to a stick than a carrot...and what a large, fine stick Lord Ethan Harrington possesses."

To his shock and disgust, Lady Jo ran a lewd gaze over him, her light-brown eyes lingering on his unfastened trousers.

"You leave him alone," Xenia said in a trembling voice.

"I'm not going to hurt him. Not unless he begs me to." Lady Jo smirked. "But cocks are ten a penny, and if you haven't learned that by now, you're a bigger fool than I thought. I have more important uses for your lover: he is my insurance that you do what you're told."

"What do you want?" Xenia asked flatly.

"Listen up, girl." Lady Jo's tone turned brisk and businesslike. "If you want to see your lover alive again, you will deliver the treasure to me tomorrow night."

"What treasure? I don't know what you're talking about."

"A little bird told me that a local gang has loot stored in Bottoms House."

So I was right. There is something hidden in the manor. And the bird must be Dobson Gill.

"I haven't seen any treasure," Xenia said.

"That's because it is well hidden. The twist in the tale is that the Corrigans themselves don't know where the goods are hidden. They had a regime change, and their old leader, knowing his days were numbered, apparently nabbed the gang's cache of stolen jewels and stowed them somewhere in the manor. The new bloke in charge, Harlow, made the amateur mistake of killing his predecessor before learning the location of the loot. He and his gang have apparently searched everywhere for the jewels, to no avail. To throw another wrench in their plans, Lord Ethan here suddenly moved in. Harlow planted a spy to scare off his lordship and continue looking for the jewels, but the spy failed at both and got his arse tossed out instead."

After Gill's failure, he must have been afraid to return to the Corrigans. He'd gone into hiding, then realized that he had a commodity to sell: information about the so-called treasure.

"The manor has undergone significant renovation, and no jewels have turned up," Xenia argued. "Your source must be lying—"

"Oh, I doubt it. I paid for that information. Although"—Lady Jo's smile was sly—"not as dearly as my informant. But I couldn't have him selling that information to others as well, could I?"

That answers the cause of Gill's death.

"I haven't found any treasure. I swear it," Xenia pleaded.

"Then you'll have to look harder, won't you? Due to my generous nature, I'll give you until nightfall tomorrow, when I will come to collect. If you fail to meet my demands—if you breathe word of this to anyone—this handsome lord of yours will meet a painful end. Do you understand?"

Xenia looked at him with panic and misery and desperate love. He hated that he couldn't protect her. That he couldn't communicate the words burning inside him.

This is not your fault. But I know you can handle the situation. I believe in you—I love you.

He wanted to tell her that she could trust his family. And that she should, under no circumstances, trust Lady Jo to uphold her end of the bargain.

"There are people in the house," Xenia said, gnawing on her lip. "How can I look for treasure without them knowing what I'm doing?"

"Get rid of them. You'll find a way." The corners of Lady Jo's mouth tipped up with satisfaction. "You are my daughter, after all."

Chapter Thirty-Five

Xenia reached Bottoms House just before dawn. She'd run all the way back, stumbling through the darkness, desperate to get started on the Sisyphean task of finding the treasure. She had less than a day remaining; Lady Jo had made the terms of her "bargain" explicit.

"To ensure your compliance, my men will be keeping your lover in a secret location," her mother had said. *"If my treasure is not ready for me when I arrive, I will send word to my men, who will end your precious lord faster than you can shed a tear. However, if you are a good girl and do as your mama says, I will let your lover live."*

Experience had taught Xenia not to put faith in her mother's mercy.

This is my fault. Despair suffocated her. *Ethan's life is hanging in the balance because of me.*

She entered the manor through the kitchen. Lighting a lamp, she moved stealthily, for she didn't want anyone to hear her come in and start asking questions. Lady Jo had been clear that she was to tell no one...to do so would put Ethan in danger. Yet she couldn't quell her doubts: even if she succeeded in finding the treasure, Lady Jo was likely to kill Ethan anyway. Once he was no longer a bargaining chip, he would become a liability...and Xenia would be powerless to help him.

I cannot save Ethan on my own. Who can I trust? Would the Blackwoods believe me if I went to them...or would they think I'm in cahoots with Lady Jo and have me arrested?

If she went to Ethan's family and they didn't trust her—honestly, who could blame them?—she might lose what time she had to look for the valuables and barter for his life. On the other hand, if she followed her mama's instructions and managed to empty the house, she would have to find the treasure on her own.

What if I fail? What if I cannot save Ethan?

She agonized over the right course of action, wishing she had someone to advise her. Wishing she was not so alone. Suddenly, a sensation swept over her: the feeling of another presence nearby. She looked around the empty kitchen, and instead of feeling afraid, she was comforted, even if the company was ethereal. When a cool draft caressed her cheek, she turned her head in its direction, and her gaze caught a copperish gleam on the floor.

Going over, she picked up the object.

A penny.

Xenia clutched the gift to her chest.

"Thank you," she whispered.

Summoning her courage, Xenia knocked on Lady Blackwood's door. As the housekeeper, she knew from the state of the marchioness's bed in the morning that her husband spent the night with her, but this did not prepare her for the sight of a disheveled Lord Marcus Blackwood standing in the doorway. Clad in a navy dressing gown, his thick hair tousled, he seemed even more formidable than usual.

"What are you doing here at this early hour, Mrs. Wood?" He frowned. "What happened to your face?"

"I need to speak to Lady Blackwood," she said. "Please, it concerns Lord Ethan."

"Marcus, darling, who is it?" Lady Blackwood's sleepy voice drifted over.

"It's Mrs. Wood." His gaze alert now, the marquess stepped aside to let her in. "She says it's about Ethan."

Inside, Xenia was greeted by Lady Blackwood, who'd obviously just thrown on her robe and was lighting a lamp. Nonetheless, her violet eyes were sharp.

"Xenia, what's wrong?" she asked.

"Ethan is in danger," Xenia blurted. "I need your help."

She told them everything.

About her mama and the life she'd led before running away at sixteen. About the work she'd done. About getting a job as Ethan's housekeeper, turning a new leaf, and falling in love with him. About her mama's threat, the supposed treasure, and Ethan being taken as hostage. She didn't spare herself: this was *her* fault, all of it. She'd been too weak to stop her mother, but she would do anything—even turn herself in to the authorities—if they would help her find the stolen goods and get Ethan back.

"I'm s-sorry." Her voice hitched as she saw the Blackwoods' expressions, which had gone from astonished to grim. She didn't know what else to say.

They hate me...and I deserve it. But please let them believe me. Please let them believe that I am not working for my mother—that I want only to free Ethan.

Lady Blackwood came up to her, and when the marchioness raised her hand, Xenia instinctively flinched. Yet it wasn't a slap that landed on her cheek but a gentle touch.

"You are not to blame for this," Lady Blackwood said firmly. "And we *will* get Ethan back."

Relief rushed through Xenia, and she shut her eyes, willing

back the tears. Her body seemed to have lost its starch, however, and she swayed.

"Sit before you fall." The marchioness ushered her to a chair, then turned to the marquess. "What is the plan, darling?"

Lord Blackwood aimed a severe gaze at Xenia. "You have no idea where these jewels are supposedly hidden?"

"No, my lord." She shook her head helplessly. "And given that I oversaw much of the manor's renovation, I know every inch of the place."

"There must be a hiding place somewhere," the marquess said. "We'll comb the property."

"But Lady Jo told Xenia to get rid of everyone," Lady Blackwood pointed out. "She threatened to harm Ethan if Xenia breathed word of any of this. My guess is that she'll put eyes and ears on the property to make sure her orders are being followed."

Not for the first time, Xenia wondered about Lady Blackwood's uncommon acuity when it came to the darker side of life. Whatever the reason for the lady's knowledge, she was grateful for it. Humbled, in truth, by the marchioness's willingness to see beyond her shameful origins and give her the benefit of the doubt.

"You are right, my love," Lord Blackwood said. "Any search we conduct will have to be done with utmost discretion. As for the staff, do we know whom we can trust?"

"Other than Ethan's servants from London, everyone else is new." As much as Xenia hated to say it, she had to. "My mama could have bribed any one of them. Or, like Dobson Gill, they could be working for the Corrigans."

"Right. If we cannot trust them, then we need them gone—"

Lord Blackwood turned as the door opened. "Owen?"

He drew his brows together at the sight of his youngest son. Lord Owen looked as if he'd been dragged through the bushes. His brown hair was mussed, his cravat missing, and his gaze was wild.

"Dearest." His mama looked at him with concern. "Is everything all right? Did you have another bad dream—"

"They took Ethan," Lord Owen said hoarsely. "I was there with him...at the brothel. I was waiting for him and Mrs. Wood to, ahem, sort out their problems."

Cheeks flaming, Xenia realized he must have overheard her and Ethan's intimate interlude.

Sorting out our problems is one way of putting it.

"Out of nowhere, I saw a gang of cutthroats barge into their room. I went into the adjacent chamber and listened through the wall. I heard everything." He turned burning eyes on Xenia. "I heard your deranged mother beating you. I know she is holding Ethan ransom for the stolen goods. I wanted to intervene, but there were too many brutes to take on. So I decided to follow them instead."

Hope pierced Xenia to the quick.

"Do you know where Ethan is being held?" Lady Blackwood's trembling voice betrayed the fear she'd been holding in check.

Owen nodded. "Yes, Mama. It's not far from here."

"Good work, lad." Resolve hardened Lord Blackwood's features, and he issued commands like the military leader he'd been. "Go get James and be discreet about it. Penny, you fetch Gigi. Now that we have Ethan's location, we will work together and bring him home safely."

CHAPTER THIRTY-SIX

A little after dawn, Xenia stood with Gigi in the entrance hall. The Blackwoods' bags were packed and waiting in the carriage, and Gigi was dressed for travel.

"Are you certain I can't stay, Xenia?" Gigi's countenance was anxious. "I don't like the idea of leaving you alone."

Although Xenia was touched, she shook her head. "You must go with your family. Your job is to rescue Ethan."

Gigi slid a disgruntled look at the rest of her kin, who came to join them.

"My *job* will be to wait at the inn while the rest of them free my brother," she said sulkily. "I might as well be here and keep you company."

Xenia didn't want the young woman anywhere near the property when her mama came. "You need to be safe," she said firmly.

"Are you certain you will be all right, Mrs. Wood?" Lord Blackwood studied her. "I share Gigi's concerns, but in the event your mama is watching, we must give the appearance of following her instructions to the letter."

Earlier, Xenia had told the cook, footmen, and maids that, as a reward for their excellent service, the master had given them three days off. Everyone had seemed elated at the prospect and didn't waste time vacating the premises. In case the manor was being monitored, the guards had been instructed to depart as well. Half would meet up with the Blackwoods and assist in freeing Ethan; the other half was to monitor the manor discreetly from afar. At the first sign of trouble, they would swoop in and help to capture Lady Jo and her gang.

"Hopefully, Ethan's old retainers will have found the constable and conveyed our plan," Lady Blackwood added. "Help will be on the way."

Rawlins and his men were to serve as additional reinforcements. Like the guards, the constables were to surveil the manor while lying low.

"According to Owen's reconnaissance, the abandoned farmhouse where they are keeping Ethan is only a few miles away," Lord Blackwood said. "Once we free Ethan, we will return straightaway."

"I will be fine." Xenia managed a smile. "The only thing that matters is Ethan's well-being."

"That is not the only thing, my dear."

To her surprise, Lady Blackwood pulled her into a hug. The maternal gesture swelled Xenia's throat. She had to blink away tears as the other's warmth engulfed her.

Releasing her, the marchioness said softly, "You are more than your past, Xenia. You *chose* to be more—to be the woman my son fell in love with. Do not doubt yourself, for Ethan never would."

The Blackwoods left. Although she was alone, Xenia did not feel that way. Ethan's family had bolstered her courage, and as she looked around the empty manor, she felt the support of another presence as well. It reminded her that she was the housekeeper: she had given Bottoms House care and attention, and now it would give her what she needed.

She straightened her shoulders and nodded.

"You're right," she said. "This is *my* home. And I will not go down without a fight."

Xenia spent the day setting up reinforcements. She'd learned a thing or two from the years spent under her mama's thumb. Her knowledge of the house gave her an advantage, which she utilized to the fullest. She hated undoing the work that had been done, but the manor could be fixed up again whereas she had only one shot at survival. After she was done setting traps and compiling weapons, she tidied up and left everything looking as it had before. Her housekeeping skills had come a long way, after all.

She spent what extra time she had looking for the stolen goods. She checked all the attic rooms, including the one where the bats had been, and even went to look in the coal cellar. She found nothing. A feeling niggled at her...as if she was forgetting something, but for the life of her, she didn't know what it was.

By the time dusk was seeping through the windows, she still hadn't found anything resembling treasure. Thank heavens for the Blackwoods' plan. By now, Lady Jo ought to have left the farmhouse to come here. Knowing her, she would travel with most of her pack, leaving behind a few men to guard Ethan. If things were going as planned, the Blackwoods would have made their move, and Ethan might already be safe.

Xenia clung to that hope even as the doorbell rang.

Inhaling, she went to open it.

Lady Jo swept in like the mistress of the manor. She wore a frock of forest-green velvet, her braided hair wound like a crown on the top of her head. She'd brought eleven lackeys with her, all armed to the teeth...figuratively speaking, as the brutes were missing most of their pearly whites.

"Good evening, daughter mine," Lady Jo said grandly. "Do you have my jewels?"

"Yes, Mama." Xenia managed to keep her voice even. "If I show you where they are, what is my guarantee that you will set Ethan free?"

"There are no guarantees in life, dear heart." Lady Jo pulled a pistol from her skirts, pointing it at Xenia. "Except for the consequences if you cross me. Now show me the loot, girl, and be quick about it."

Her heart thumping, Xenia prayed that she could buy enough time for the reinforcements to arrive.

"Follow me," she said.

Taking cover behind a hedgerow, Ethan spotted the two waiting wagons parked outside the manor, each handled by a driver. At the farmhouse where he'd been held, he'd counted fifteen cutthroats in addition to Lady Jo. Even minus the two who'd been left to watch him—those bastards were in custody, thanks to his family's rescue efforts—that still left a sizeable number of enemies to deal with.

"In addition to the two parked out front, there are eleven brutes inside," Ethan said in a low voice. "Plus Lady Jo. Rawlins, take your men through the back. My team will take the front. The priority is finding Mrs. Wood and keeping her safe. Is that understood?"

"Yes, my lord," Rawlins replied. "Eyes sharp, men."

The constable and his team kept under the cover of hedges as they made their way behind the house.

Ethan addressed his group. "Papa and Mama, keep watch out here. If the enemy tries to escape with Xenia, stop them."

"You may depend upon us, dearest," Mama said.

A pistol glinted in her gloved hand. While she'd always been vague about how she'd acquired certain skills, Papa had once told him and his siblings in confidence that she was a wartime heroine.

"James, Owen, and the rest of the guards are with me," Ethan said tersely. "We'll subdue the drivers first to prevent them from alerting the others—"

The sound of gunfire jolted him. *Xenia*. His heart thudding, he sprinted toward the house. His approach startled the drivers, who raised their pistols, but he got a shot off first, catching one in the shoulder. Ferris picked off the other.

"I'll take care of these two," the guard shouted. "Go on, my lord."

Ethan ran to the house, shouldering open the door. His jaw slackened as he took in the chaos and destruction. A brute lay groaning on the cracked marble floor, trapped under the heavy chandelier. Another was holding on for dear life near the top of the stairs, having fallen through a collapsed step. Yet another ruffian was unconscious, sprawled near the base of the staircase. He looked like he'd slipped and taken a nasty tumble down the steps; the soles of his shoes looked slick...with butter?

"This is absolute mayhem," James muttered. "And what the devil is a chicken doing in here?"

The silver-grey hen that wandered by looked equally confused.

As the guards tied up the moaning villains, Ethan sprinted to the drawing room. The door was open, and when he entered, something wet dripped onto his cheek. He looked up and saw an empty bucket suspended by a pulley. He wiped off the droplet, sniffing it.

Linseed oil?

Terrified cries came from the corridor. Ethan and his brothers watched as two brutes *in flames* ran past the doorway, yelling at the top of their lungs. An instant later, a ruffian came running from the other direction, chased by a furious Brutus, who squawked angrily, attacking with his beak and spurs.

James raised his brows. "Is Mrs. Wood responsible for all this?"

They hurried into the morning room. There, a cutthroat lay unconscious: the large bump on his head looked to be caused by one of the round brown objects scattered around him.

When Owen picked up one of the lumpy projectiles, it looked oddly familiar.

"Where did Mrs. Wood find all these rocks?" he asked.

Recognition dawned. "Those aren't rocks," Ethan said. "Those are her buns."

"Well, she's creative," Owen murmured. "You have to grant her that."

Pride swelled in Ethan. "That's my housekeeper."

In case she needed rescuing, however, he dashed off to find her.

Panting, Xenia hurried through the servants' corridor. She could hear the mayhem on the other side of the wall; her traps were working. She'd managed to give her mama the slip—literally. The butter-coated floorboards had sent her parent crashing into a wall, giving her enough time to dash into Ethan's bedchamber. From there, she'd taken the hidden passageway. It wouldn't take long for her mama to figure out where she'd gone, but at least she had a head start.

On the ground floor, she thought she heard sounds of fighting, and hope knocked against her ribs. Had Rawlins's men arrived... was Ethan safe? She decided to take a risk and check. Arriving at the library, she pressed her ear against the panel. When the room seemed unoccupied, she tried to open the panel—one thing the Hirschfields hadn't gotten around to fixing—and succeeded after several jiggles.

The library remained untouched. She crossed the room to the door; taking a breath, she cracked it open and peered into the corridor. She saw figures grappling at the far end of the hallway...it looked like Rawlins and one of her mama's men.

Help is here.

With a surge of optimism, she looked around and grabbed a heavy volume, intending to throw it at Rawlins's attacker. Yet as she stepped into the hallway, a shot rang out. Rawlins crumpled to the ground. Her mother stood there, smoking pistol in hand.

"Enough games, daughter," Lady Jo hissed. "I'm going to make you pay for your misbehavior."

Xenia ducked back into the library. She managed to get the key in the door, locking it an instant before her mother started pounding on it. She dragged a chair in front of the door as well but knew she hadn't bought herself much time.

"Let me in, you ungrateful wretch!" her mama yelled.

Heart thrashing, Xenia dashed for the servants' corridor...but the panel wouldn't open. The dratted thing was jammed. She tried and tried and couldn't yank it free.

Blooming hell.

The door shook in its frame, Lady Jo ordering her lackeys to break it down. Xenia darted around the room, looking for an escape. There wasn't time to break one of the windows...

Go and hide where I showed you. The male voice from her dream filled her head. She held onto it like a lifeline as it gave her directions. *You know how to get in.* Ashes raining from walls, a voice coming through a wall of brick...

Suddenly, Xenia remembered.

She ran toward the mahogany cabinet. It was heavy, but she just needed to move it enough so that she could squeeze behind it and hide—in the fireplace. Grabbing one side of the cabinet, she nudged it a small distance from the wall. Dashing to the other side, she evened the distance so that the cabinet's placement would not betray her hiding place.

Exhaling, she squeezed herself into the narrow alley she'd created between the cabinet and the fireplace. She twisted, lowering herself into the fireplace opening and fitting herself inside the little cavern as the door yielded with a loud crack.

"Find her." Lady Jo's voice filled the library. "She's in here somewhere."

As boots thumped on the floor, Xenia curled deeper into her den.

Hurry, Ethan, she prayed. *Find me.*

The voice that answered was his but not his.

Don't be afraid, my love. Darkness can be a sanctuary.

She felt a ghostly touch against her hand. It guided her fingers over the brick surface of the firebox, fitting them to a subtle indentation. She pressed...and a faint click sounded. She felt something shift behind her...a new opening? A side of the firebox had swung open to reveal a hole just large enough for her to squeeze through. She slipped inside the secret refuge and closed the panel behind her, sealing herself in darkness.

Don't come out until I tell you it is safe.

Chapter Thirty-Seven

"I *saw* my bleeding daughter run in here. Keep looking, you bacon-brained fools!"

Ethan charged into the library, his brothers at his back. No sign of Xenia, but that was a good thing since Lady Jo was there with a pair of lackeys. The gang leader's face contorted with fury.

"How in blazes did you get free?" she snarled.

"It's over," Ethan said. "You're surrounded and outnumbered. Surrender now."

The two brutes flanking Lady Jo gave her questioning looks.

"Don't be idiots," she fumed. "*Attack.*"

The pair bared their teeth and lunged. James and Owen leapt forward to take them on, leaving Ethan to deal with Lady Jo.

"Set down your weapon," he said.

"Which one?"

She yanked a small pistol from her skirts, letting off a shot. Ethan dove, the bullet whizzing past his ear. He hit the ground rolling and was on his feet in a blink. A groan sounded behind him, and he twisted around, afraid she'd hit one of his brothers...

but no, she'd caught one of her own men. The cutthroat Owen had been grappling with lay writhing on the ground, clutching his side.

"Are you all right?" Ethan asked his brother.

Owen nodded, sprinting off to help James.

Ethan returned his focus to Lady Jo, who'd tossed aside her pistol and was now brandishing a dagger.

"Give up," Ethan said. "I don't want to hurt you."

Her laugh was derisive. "You couldn't hurt me even if you had two functioning hands."

The jibe sharpened Ethan's focus. His opponent was ruthless and lethal, but he had advantages: his greater size and his determination to see this villainess behind bars so that she could never hurt Xenia again.

Lady Jo came at him with the quickness of a cat. He dodged the swipe of her blade, trying to grab her weapon arm. She kept to his weak side, and while he had to fight his ingrained impulse not to hurt a female, she had no qualms about inflicting damage or fighting dirty. She stomped on his foot, and he barely evaded her attempt to knee him in the groin.

When he managed to grab her wrist, twisting it and forcing her to release the dagger, she smiled, another blade appearing as if by magic in her other hand. She struck out, and he moved but not quickly enough, steel slicing into his upper arm. As he retreated a step, she tripped him. He fell backward, nearly hitting his head on a cabinet.

Before he could recover, Lady Jo leapt atop him, her teeth bared and dagger flashing. He caught her wrist with his hand, the tip of her knife hovering inches from his throat. He grunted with effort, trying to keep the blade from sinking into him, while her eyes glowed with murderous triumph.

"I'm going to gut you like a fish," Lady Jo crooned.

"Go to hell," Ethan retorted.

He's here.

Hearing her beloved's voice, Xenia scrambled to open the secret panel in the fireplace. She activated the hidden mechanism, which made the side of the firebox swing open again. As she crawled out, her mother's voice rang with menace.

"Prepare to die, you bastard. As you bleed out in your fine manor, know this: I'm going to take my daughter back with me and make her suffer in ways you cannot begin to imagine."

I cannot let my mama hurt Ethan. I must get to him.

There was no time to squeeze through the tight alley between the cabinet and the wall. Terror gave Xenia strength, and she charged into the back of the cabinet. It swayed, rattling the objects inside. Putting her entire weight against the heavy mahogany, she pushed again. The cabinet tilted...and then it toppled.

The crash echoed through the room, the floor vibrating with the impact. Xenia spotted Ethan on the ground nearby and clambered over the cabinet to get to him.

"Ethan!" Kneeling beside him, she saw the blood on his sleeve. "Are you hurt? Did my mother—"

"I'm fine, love." He sat up, catching one of her hands. "Especially now that you're safe."

"Well done, Mrs. Wood."

This came from the Earl of Manderly, who was accompanied by Lord Owen. Both looked disheveled but unharmed, the cutthroats they'd defeated now being led away by the constable's men.

"Where is my mama?" Xenia asked. "Did she get away?"

"You, er, prevented that, pet." Ethan cleared his throat. "When you pushed the cabinet over, your mother was on top of me, trying to slit my throat. I saw the cabinet tilting and managed to push her off and roll away. Lady Jo, however..."

Whipping her head around, Xenia felt her jaw slacken. Her

mama was lying trapped beneath the cabinet, her legs poking out. One of her leather shoes had fallen off, revealing her clocked stockings.

"Odds bodkins," Xenia croaked. "Did I...did I kill her?"

Xenia had wanted to protect herself and defend the manor. But she'd never imagined killing anyone. Not even her monster of a mother.

"No, you worthless child, you couldn't even do that properly." Lady Jo groaned, her voice muffled by the wood. "But you've crushed my blooming arm."

Ethan and his brothers lifted the cabinet. Xenia saw that Lady Jo had been lucky: most of her body had been protected by the space between the narrower top section of the cabinet and the floor, thus avoiding any critical damage. Her right arm, however, had been pinned by the heavy base; it was bleeding and lay at an odd angle.

Just in case, Xenia kicked the dagger out of her mother's reach. "She needs a physician."

"I don't need a damned sawbones, you ungrateful bi—"

"Shut your mouth," Ethan growled. "Or we'll let you bleed to death where you are."

"My men will see that Mrs. Wardell is taken care of." Rawlins hobbled over.

"Are you all right, sir?" Xenia asked anxiously. "I saw my mama shoot you."

"Luckily for me, this stopped the bullet." The constable showed her his notebook, which now bore a large dent. "Now, I believe you and I have some things to discuss...Miss Bernice Wardell, is it?"

Xenia wanted to deny it. She'd fought with everything she had to leave that person behind. Truth be told, she was tired of running —of living in fear. It was time for her to face the consequences of being her mother's daughter, whatever those may be.

She was about to speak, but Ethan beat her to it.

"My fiancée's name is Xenia Loveday," he said. "Soon to be Xenia Harrington. If you wish to interrogate her, I must insist upon being present."

The miracle of this man swelled her throat. Hearing Lady Jo cursing and screaming as the constables carried her out, however, Xenia felt it was only fair to give him a choice. To make certain he still wanted to honor his proposal.

"Are you certain you want to marry me?" she asked. "After meeting my mother?"

"You are not your mother. You are *yourself*," Ethan said tenderly. "A brave, loving, and alarmingly resourceful woman, and the only one I've ever loved."

"I do love you so." Her voice hitched. "But your family—"

"We will welcome you with open arms."

This came from Lady Blackwood, who entered the room with her husband. They were both smiling at her...as were Ethan's brothers. If Xenia's heart got any fuller, she feared it might burst.

So this is what it feels like to belong. To be part of a family.

Rawlins cleared his throat. "I daresay an interrogation will not be necessary, my lord. It is obvious that Joanna Wardell was behind the nefarious schemes carried out this eve and was thwarted, thanks to the brave actions of Miss Loveday. However, I was hoping that Miss Loveday could furnish me with facts to solidify the case against Mrs. Wardell—"

"I nearly forgot!" Xenia exclaimed. "I found the stolen valuables. They are in a secret room behind the fireplace. It was dark so I couldn't see the items clearly, but I think there are at least three large chests full of jewelry."

"You defended the manor and found the treasure. How efficient of you, my love." Ethan laughed and pulled her close. "No more excuses. Will you be mine?"

Xenia's heart spoke for her. "Now that I am free from my past, all that I am is yours—my heart, body, and soul."

His eyes gleamed with proud recognition of the gift she was giving him. In front of everyone, he kissed her, and she kissed him back. The world faded to the beauty of being in her beloved's arms...of coming home at last.

CHAPTER THIRTY-EIGHT

With the turmoil over, Ethan wanted to marry Xenia as soon as possible. Yet his mama had insisted that everything be done right for Xenia's sake, and he'd relented...up to a point. He was willing to wait three weeks, sufficient time for the banns to be read and preparations to be made. Mama and Gigi, who'd taken charge of planning the affair, protested vociferously at the haste, but Xenia sided with him and offered to help expedite the arrangements however she could.

The wedding would take place in the village church, with a reception afterward at Bottoms House. Thus, fixing up the manor became a priority since it had sustained damage during the battle with Lady Jo. Fortunately, the Hirschfield brothers were up to the task...as were other residents of Chuddums. To Ethan's surprise and gratitude, the villagers came in droves to lend a hand.

Mr. Bailey and his sons helped rebuild the gazebo. Mr. Duffield brought over fabric samples and agonized with Mama, Gigi, and Xenia over the color scheme for the wedding. Mrs. O'Hara was supplying flowers from her garden (as long as Mrs. Elmwood's felonious feline hadn't dug them up), and Mrs.

Thornton and Mrs. Pettigrew offered to cook for the afternoon reception, with Mr. Khan bringing a selection of sweets. The catering came as a blessing because Ethan once again found himself without a cook.

The jewels Xenia had found matched those taken during a spate of house burglaries. The Corrigans had been the main suspects, but without the goods, the constables had lacked proof of wrongdoing. Now that the jewelry had been recovered—in chests that bore the Corrigans' insignia—Rawlins and his men went to make arrests and discovered Mrs. Johnson living in the gang's flash house.

Apparently, the cook was married to a gang member and had been sent to infiltrate Ethan's household and search for the stolen loot. Failing to find the jewels, she'd killed the chickens, staged the hoax with the piano, and set fire to the gazebo in hopes of scaring Ethan off the premises. Rawlins had taken her into custody and arrested Harlow and other gang members for burglary and extortion, as several villagers had come forward to bear witness. A few ruffians had escaped, but the constable wasn't concerned because the gang's power had dwindled since the village's revolt against them.

Peace settled over Bottoms House, and Ethan had never been happier. He was spending time with his family, including Owen. With Xenia's help, he was making progress on his sonata and discovering a passion for composition. Sitting at the piano, he felt a renewed sense of purpose and destiny, especially when he had his pretty fiancée by his side. During those intimate sessions, they worked on his pieces, their hands moving in perfect synchrony over the keyboard...and often over each other.

They had cozy talks, too.

Xenia finally felt free to tell him about her past. Tears had streamed down her cheeks as she'd shared how her mama had taken away the two men who'd protected and cared for her and her fear that Lady Jo would do the same to Ethan. She'd described a few happy memories, too: of her papa and how he'd given her a love of stories.

It was Ethan who suggested that Xenia find a new way to channel her storytelling talents now that she'd laid Sirena to rest. This had started gears turning in Xenia's head, and she'd eagerly started outlining a novel which included a forbidden romance, treasure hunt, and possible ghost. He couldn't wait to see what she came up with.

As for Xenia's mother, Lady Jo had been convicted of numerous offenses and put behind bars for the rest of her days. Rawlins had given Xenia credit for the capture of Lady Jo. Although the issue of Xenia's past involvement in the gang had arisen, the magistrates rightfully saw Xenia as a blameless victim of her mama's brutality, and no charges were pressed against her.

Xenia was free from her past. She no longer had to pretend to be anyone but herself—the brave and inventive little minx he'd fallen in love with. Freedom suited his bride-to-be. It was as if the burden of her history had been a disguise of its own, and she shed that entirely now. She radiated happiness, her peerless eyes bright with the promise of their future. She was so beautiful that he couldn't stick to his gentlemanly intention to wait until their wedding night.

During their rendezvous, they explored each other with ravenous delight. She'd been sore after their first time, but he'd discovered a creative use for her balm. The memory sizzled through him of pushing his ointment-covered fingers deep into his beloved's snug cunny, her eyes heavy-lidded as she watched. He'd spread the stuff thoroughly, stirring his digits until she'd begged him for more. He exhaled, recalling the tingling tightness of her pussy around his cock. When he showed her one of his favorite variations, turning her over and rubbing the ointment over her pearl as he plowed her from behind, she'd sung her Siren's song into a pillow, her rippling climax milking him dry.

Xenia entered the study, her expression quizzical. "What are you smiling about, darling?"

Her blush-colored frock set off her fiery hair perfectly. She was as delectable as a peach, and he couldn't wait to eat her. Tonight, hopefully.

"You." Reminding himself that their wedding night was only a few days away, he satisfied himself with a kiss on her cute, freckled nose. "Is that a new dress?"

"The garments keep arriving." She looked a little frazzled. "Your mama says I must have a proper trousseau, but at the risk of sounding ungrateful, she has ordered enough clothing for a dozen brides. Your parents have already been generous beyond words, and I don't know what to do."

Toying with a loose tendril at her temple, he suggested, "Let them spoil you."

His family adored Xenia, and he wasn't surprised that they recognized in her what she still sometimes had difficulty seeing in herself. Her humility was part of her charm. And he had a lifetime to cure her of it—to prove to her just how special she was.

"They are not the only ones spoiling me," she teased.

She wiggled the fingers of her left hand, causing her engagement ring to glitter. He'd chosen the large center ruby to match her hair and added a halo of diamonds for extra sparkle. Since she'd protested that the ring was too much, he couldn't wait to see her reaction to the matching necklace he planned to give her on their wedding day.

He lifted his brows. "Are you complaining?"

"No. I am wondering how I got so lucky."

Her adoring expression thickened his throat.

"I am the lucky one," he said huskily. "I love you, and my family does too. That is why they are welcoming you with open arms and why you should let them do so."

Her eyes shimmered. Cuddled in his arms last night, she'd shared how much she looked forward to becoming a Harrington—

to belonging to a loving family. He'd replied that he was happy to give that to her...and that, in her own way, she'd given him the same. Because of her, he was himself again and able to reconnect with the people he loved.

"Speaking of your family and fresh starts." She fiddled with a button on his waistcoat. "Have you spoken to your younger brother?"

He...hadn't. The truth was he was avoiding it. He and Owen now had civil conversations, and while the ability to tolerate one another wasn't the same as their past closeness, it was better than their prior hostilities. As he'd told Xenia during one of their talks, he wasn't as angry as he'd once been. He recognized the changes in Owen, whose actions had, after all, led to his rescue and foiled Lady Jo's scheme.

Ethan owed Owen...but he didn't know if he could forgive his brother completely.

Xenia's response had been the same then as it was now.

"Talk to your brother," she urged. "You will both feel better for it, and I say this as someone who has learned the importance of confronting the past. If you feel uncertain about what to say, just pretend that you know what you're doing and follow your instincts."

While he didn't share her optimism that talking would improve matters with his brother, he did want to clear the air. Thus, he went to look for Owen and found him outside. To his surprise, Owen was helping the gardener with the planting of rosebushes.

"You needn't bother with such work," Ethan said to his brother. "I have staff now."

"I know. I needed something to occupy myself with."

Rising, Owen dusted himself off. He was dressed to work in old trousers and a loose shirt, a cap jammed over his shaggy hair. His collar was open, the cloth tied around his neck darkened with sweat.

His grey eyes were wary in his tanned face. "Was there something you wanted?"

"Come walk with me," Ethan said.

Wordlessly, Owen strolled with him along the neatly cleared garden path. The walkway had been weeded and blanketed with new gravel, the flanking hedges neatly trimmed. The sun was bright, the sky blue, and birds and butterflies were in abundance. The setting had the makings of an idyllic late summer day...save for the brewing tension.

Ethan took the bull by its horns. "I haven't yet thanked you," he said.

Owen shot him a surprised glance. "For what?"

"For tracking me to Lady Jo's hideaway."

"It was nothing. Following someone is hardly heroic. It was not as if I took her and her men on single-handedly—" At his unfortunate choice of words, Owen paled, cutting himself off abruptly.

Ethan waited for the bitter anger to surface; when it didn't, he felt a sense of relief. Xenia was right. The more time he spent with Owen, the more normal it felt. Avoiding their conflict had only made things worse...at least for him. Seeing the guilt and self-revulsion on Owen's face, he had to say something.

"You acted wisely," he corrected. "You rescued me and helped defeat the villains who threatened Xenia. I am in your debt."

"You owe me nothing." Owen's gaze was locked on the path, his jaw clenched. "There is nothing I can do to make up for what I did to you, Ethan. You and I both know that. The others may try to gloss over the past, but the truth is I took *everything* away from you. *I* am responsible for ending your career as a virtuoso. *I* robbed you of your destiny and your future. There is no bloody going back."

Ethan's chest pounded at the truth laid bare. What Owen said was fact. Ethan had brooded over the exact same things—had used them to fuel his rage against his brother. Yet what had that accomplished? His fixation on the wrongs done to him hadn't helped him to heal. It had only made him angry and resentful, and he'd alternated between lashing out at the world and wanting to hide from it.

What *had* turned things around for him was finding love. Finding Xenia.

Awareness prickled through him as he recognized the truth. Xenia had freed herself by facing her demons. And he could do the same.

"You're right," he said. "There is no going back."

Owen's features tightened. "Mama and Papa wanted me to stay for the wedding, but if you want me to leave, I will."

Pretend until it's true. Follow your instincts.

"I forgive you."

The instant the words left him, Ethan didn't know why he'd held onto them so long. Letting them go, letting go of the resentment and rage, felt like a miracle. Like Atlas shedding the weight of the world. Lightness filled him, and now he knew what Xenia had meant when she said, *"Now that I am free, all that I am is yours—my heart, body, and soul."*

He felt the same way. Filled with love. With possibility.

"Don't."

He turned his attention to Owen, who looked agonized.

"Don't forgive me," Owen said hoarsely. "I don't deserve it. Not after everything I've done."

Ethan saw his brother's suffering with opened eyes, and his throat clogged. He reached out a hand, intending to clap his brother on the shoulder, but when he saw Owen trembling, he pulled him into a one-armed hug instead.

"It's all right, Owen." He spoke in the tones of the big brother he remembered he was. "Everything is water under the bridge."

Owen drew a shuddering breath. Then he wrenched away. "I'm sorry, Ethan." His eyes were bright and determined. "Sorrier than you'll ever know. And while you may forgive me, I will *never* forgive myself."

He strode off, and there was nothing Ethan could do to stop him.

Chapter Thirty-Nine

The wedding took place in Chuddums on a perfect, sunny day. The villagers flocked to the tiny All Saints Church, packing the pews. Xenia felt like a princess walking down the aisle in the beautiful white dress and veil Mrs. Sommers had made for her, a wreath of orange blossoms in her hair. She smiled at all her beaming friends, but her smile grew wobbly when she saw her groom waiting for her at the altar.

Even if she lived to be a hundred, she would never forget this moment.

Ethan Harrington was the prince of her dreams, and he looked every inch the part. He was magnificent: long, lean perfection in his dove-grey tailcoat and trousers, his blue waistcoat complementing his vibrant eyes. When he smiled, her heart threatened to soar from her chest.

In front of their family and friends, they exchanged the vows that would bind them forever. When he kissed her, she lost track of everything but the beauty of their connection. It took the reverend's clearing of his throat and Gigi's smothered giggle for Ethan to end the kiss, and even then Xenia had continued to gaze dreamily into her new husband's eyes.

Afterward, the reception was held at Bottoms House. The manor's reputation had once kept the villagers away, but now they explored the stylish abode and gardens with curiosity and admiration. More than one guest proclaimed that it was one of the finest homes in the county and would surely put Chuddums on the map.

If anyone had hoped to see a ghost, they were disappointed.

The wedding cake had been baked by Mrs. Pettigrew, and true to form, its tiers were slightly and charmingly askew. As the cake was being served, Xenia and Ethan circulated and chatted with guests, including Mr. Parkhurst and Mr. Canning, who'd come from London. When Xenia spotted Mr. Walford, she brought Ethan over and made the introductions.

"When did you get back from Manchester, Wally?" she asked.

"Just last night. I couldn't miss the grandest wedding Chuddums has ever seen." Wally beamed. "There aren't many occasions to wear my finest coat. I had to dig it out of the attic; for some reason, my granddaughter misplaced it there."

Since his finest coat was a bright, checkered chartreuse, Xenia had an inkling why Mrs. Sommers might have stowed it away.

"By the by, I apologize for not responding to your letter," Wally went on. "My rheumatism makes it difficult for me to hold a pen, and I thought it would be easier to talk in person. You had questions about Thomas Mulligan?"

Although the danger had passed, Xenia still had unanswered questions.

"Mrs. Sommers said that you once told her the story of Thomas Mulligan and the witch was a love story," she began.

"You've got it wrong already," Wally said. "Rosalinda wasn't a witch."

"Her name was Rosalinda?"

Xenia shot an *I-told-you-so* look at her new husband, who merely raised his brows.

"Did you know her, Mr. Walford?" Ethan asked.

"Only from afar. I used to see her by the stream." The nonagenarian's eyes had a faraway look. "I was only eight at the time, but I still remember how beautiful she was with her long, dark hair. She was part of a traveling family, and I wasn't supposed to go near them, but sometimes I would sneak away to the stream, just to hear her sing while she washed her clothes. She had a captivating voice."

Xenia canted her head. "If Rosalinda was so beautiful, why does the legend say she is a witch?"

"Because villagers can be small-minded," Wally said darkly. "They've never liked travelers, and Rosalinda's family was no exception. Their prejudice turned into gossip and talk of witchcraft because her family sold herbs—the normal, everyday kind you use in your own salve, my lady. But the villagers twisted the family's business into something evil...which says more about them than Rosalinda and her kin."

"Do you think Rosalinda murdered Thomas Mulligan?" Xenia asked.

"No, I do not," Wally said definitively. "I saw them together by the stream one day. I was a child and didn't yet know the ways of adults, but even then I knew they were in love. When Mr. Mulligan was found dead, and Rosalinda was accused of murdering him, I tried to tell my parents what I saw, but they had their prejudices too, I'm afraid. They made me keep my mouth shut, and I was too scared to disobey. To this day, I regret not defending her as I ought to have."

"You were a child," Xenia murmured. "If the villagers had made up their minds, they certainly would not have listened to you. Do you know what happened to Rosalinda?"

Wally shook his head. "When the accusations of witchcraft started flying, she and her family moved on. Can't say I blame them."

"It is interesting that none of this is referenced in the rhyme about the curse," Ethan said thoughtfully.

"Do you know the rhyme, my lord?" Wally peered at him. "In its entirety?"

"I've told it to him." Dutifully, Xenia recited,

> "Beware, beware the rattling chain
> The flapping robes stained red and bold
> Beware the moans and wails of pain
> For 'tis Bloody Thom they do herald.
>
> He brings death to all who cross his path
> Be they creatures with feathers, fur, or skin
> Green will wither and fortunes dwindle until his
>   wrath
> Is quenched by a true reckoning
>
> He plays a mournful ballad of blame
> Shaking the manor with his ire
> His cry for justice is like a flame
> Scorching all with unholy fire."

"You've omitted the last verse," Wally said.

Xenia widened her eyes. "There's another verse? No one's mentioned it."

"That is because folks these days have forgotten about it. The actual rhyme ends like this:

> Alone, alone in his manor of sadness
> Bloody Thom does howl, trapped by rage
> Alone, he curses the village in his madness
> Until love's seasons free them from their cage."

"I don't understand." Xenia furrowed her brow. "What are *love's seasons* and who does *them* refer to? Who is being freed and what is their cage?"

"It sounds like a riddle of some sort," Ethan said.

"I've mulled it over for years, and I don't have the answers." Wally smiled slowly. "But I do know this: I prefer a story that ends with love and hope, don't you?"

Chapter Forty

"I thought the guests would never leave," Ethan said.

"That is hardly a hospitable attitude."

Xenia's teasing voice came from behind the dressing screen. That was not the only thing teasing him. He could see the outline of his bride's nubile form as she finished getting dressed for bed. He didn't know why she bothered when he intended to divest her of her clothing at the first opportunity.

His blood heated as she bent over. Through the translucent silk screen, he could see the curvy silhouette of her bottom. Beneath his dressing gown, he was hard as granite, and when she smoothed her hands over her hips and waist, his cock wept a tear of lust. Devil and damn, he couldn't take much more of her provocative little show, which reminded him of...

Oh ho. He knew exactly what it reminded him of.

Sirena.

"You little minx." He narrowed his eyes. "You're teasing me on purpose."

"Is it working, my lord? Am I making you hard?"

Christ, she was using Sirena's voice, her sultry tones like a caress against his balls. Given who he'd married, he should have known that his wedding night would be far from ordinary. Anticipation simmered, and he praised God once again for giving him a naughty bride. A wife who liked to play passionate games—his perfect match in every way.

"You'll have to work harder than that." It was a lie, but he enjoyed pushing her. "Touch your tits for me like a good girl."

She did, cupping her full mounds in her hands. He could see the protruding tips, his pulse quickening as she teased them between her fingertips, plucking lightly.

"Harder," he ordered. "Pinch them like I would."

With a breathless whimper, she did.

"Did you like that?" he asked.

"Oh, yes. It makes me feel so needy."

"That is because you're a hot little vixen. Tell me, is that naughty cunny of yours wet?"

"I'm drenched, sir."

"We must make certain. My cock is huge for you, and I don't want to hurt your snug little pussy when I ram it in. Pet yourself and tell me when you're wet enough to take me."

Her hitched breaths told him she was as aroused by their filthy talk as he was. She didn't hesitate to follow his command, reaching between her thighs. He was glued to her shadowy movements, not wanting to miss a thing. How many grooms were lucky enough to have their bride give such a performance on their wedding night?

"I'm so wet and ready," she said with a sigh.

"That didn't take long. Prove it. Hold your fingers up against the screen."

She did, and the wet spot she left on the silk made his blood rush. He strode over, licking her fingers through the screen, and her husky moan was more than he could take. In the next instant, he yanked her from behind the barrier and into his arms. They kissed with wild abandon while he carried her to his bed.

There, he indulged in one of his favorite treats, coaxing her to sit atop his face—not that Xenia needed much coaxing. Her sleek thighs framing his head, she held onto the headboard as she rode his tongue like the darling wanton she was. When she spent, he gripped her bottom, savoring every delectable drop of her juice.

Only then did he roll atop her, entering with a deep thrust that sent bliss blazing up his spine. Her body held him as reverently as her eyes. The sense of rightness—of being where he was meant to be—overwhelmed him.

"You're mine," he said hoarsely. "Now and forever."

"Yes," she breathed. "Take me, Ethan."

She'd forgotten her sultry role, but he didn't mind. Sirena was just icing on the cake that was his Xenia. He drove into her, and she urged him on. They moved in perfect unison, attuned in body, mind, and heart. As primal need took over, he slung her knees over his shoulders, pounding her pussy at a fierce tempo, and his wife came again. Her rippling passion summoned his own crescendo. He roared with ecstasy, slamming into her as the climax seized him —a finale as hot, wild, and beautiful as their love.

He pressed his lips to her forehead, nose, and mouth. "I adore you, Lady Xenia Harrington."

Her smile was glowing. "And I you, my lord."

"By the by, thank you for the wedding gift." He waggled his brows. "I wasn't sure I would see Sister Sirena again."

"It's true that she has retired." His beloved's eyes had a naughty twinkle. "But you, my love, may book her for private performances."

Two weeks later, Xenia was in the drawing room, making preparations for the wedding trip. Ethan had surprised her with yet another gift: a tour of the Continent. They would be spending time in Italy, Austria, and France, and he'd planned an itinerary of concerts, sightseeing, and shopping. Her new husband was spoiling her rotten, and she adored him for it.

He came up behind her, wrapping his arms around her waist and nuzzling her ear.

"Did you complete everything on your list, pet?" he murmured.

Distracted by his embrace, she'd forgotten the paper in her hand.

"I still have to interview the candidate for the housekeeper position...stop that." She laughed breathlessly, twisting to look at him. "I can't think when you do that."

"You didn't complain last night." He smirked. "Or this morning."

"Someone tell me when the honeymoon is over," James drawled.

He entered the room with Owen. While Ethan's parents had

left to attend to their estate, the brothers and Gigi had stayed on, and Xenia was glad the siblings had more time together. Day by day, they were rediscovering their former closeness which, she noted, often took the form of good-natured ribbing.

"Ethan and Xenia are newlyweds." Owen sprawled into a chair, giving Xenia an apologetic half-smile. "We're the ones intruding upon them."

"When it comes to family, there is no such thing as intrusion," Xenia said firmly. "You are welcome to stay as long as you like."

James winked at her as he helped himself at the spirits cabinet. "Easy to say when you are escaping to the Continent."

The siblings' teasing had extended to Xenia, and it gave her a warm glow to be included.

"Don't you have your own wife to tease?" Ethan retorted.

"Evie has more important things to do than to be teased by me," James said.

Although the earl spoke with his usual affability, Xenia noted a flatness to his tone. Ethan had told her a bit about his older brother's marriage. Even though he liked James's wife, Evie, he wasn't sure how happy the two were together. Xenia wanted to meet Evie...but that would have to wait until after the wedding trip.

"Speaking of important things!" Gigi burst into the room, the petals on her bonnet fluttering. "Guess what just happened to me? No, you'll never guess. But do try anyway!"

Ethan raised his brows. "You've found a dress. And if I had to hazard a guess, it is blue."

"Please." Gigi huffed out a breath. "Would I be this excited over clothing?"

"You met a fellow," Owen speculated. "You're head over heels in love."

"Oh, no. This is much more interesting than love."

"Goes to show," Ethan murmured in Xenia's ear, "how much my sister has to learn about love."

Xenia nestled closer to him, but at the expression on Gigi's face, which was both exhilarated and resolute, she braced herself. Everyone did.

"I know I am going to regret asking." James sighed. "What has brought about this unholy level of excitement?"

Gigi's eyes sparkled with triumph. "I found a job!"

Author's Note

Ever since Marcus and Pandora, the Marquess and Marchioness of Blackwood, made their debut in *The Lady Who Came in from the Cold*, I knew there would be more stories to tell about this passionate, loyal, and loving family. I'm so thrilled to be able to share their children's stories in the Blackwood Legacy series.

Given Marcus's military background and Pandora's work in espionage, war has had an indelible impact on the family. It felt right that this legacy would continue with the next generation, with Owen being part of the 44th Regiment that made the disastrous retreat from Kabul in 1842, one of the worst military defeats in British history. During the withdrawal, over 4500 British and Indian troops and some 12,000 camp followers were killed. This was the infamous battle where Assistant Surgeon William Brydon arrived alone on horseback to a British garrison in Jalalabad, and when asked where the rest of the army was, he said, "I am the army."

In my story, as one of the few survivors, Owen was found alive a few years after the massacre...but of course, he was a changed man.

The trauma he experienced spilled over to the rest of the family, with particularly tragic consequences for Ethan. Yet what I love most about the Harringtons is their resilience in the face of adversity. Happiness does not always come easily for them: they must earn it...and they do. They find a way to work through life's challenges, and they do so with love, courage, and loyalty.

Or as they would put it, *Ad Finem Fidelis*.

Stay tuned for Gigi's story...

Two Secrets to Surrender

The only thing hotter than their animosity is their attraction...and the sizzling secret they share.

Spirited debutante Lady Gigi Harrington wants to help revive a fading business in the quaint village of Chudleigh Bottoms. The arrival of a ruthless industrialist jeopardizes her plans, especially since they share a sizzling secret. The pair lock horns, drawn together by scorching animosity and even hotter passion. As their conflict escalates and hidden identities are revealed, they cannot resist their hearts' deepest desires. Will their enemies to lovers romance lead to happily ever after...and unlock the secrets of the village's ancient prophecy?

Acknowledgments

Thank you to all the readers who have asked for more of the Blackwoods. They've been on my mind too. I hope you love the next generation as much as I do!

I'm so grateful to the readers who share their love of my books online and through word of mouth. I couldn't do this without you. From the bottom of my heart, thank you!

Thank you to my editor, Peter Senftleben, for his invaluable insights. And to my proofreaders Faith Williams and Alyssa Nazzaro for making my work shine. Also, thank you to my assistants Jill Glass and Cheryl Maddox for keeping me (somewhat) sane.

And to my dance community: you rock. Thank you for bringing joy to my life and for sharing in the magic that is movement.

And to my family: all my love, always.

ABOUT THE AUTHOR

USA Today & International Bestselling Author Grace Callaway writes hot and heart-melting historical romance filled with mystery and adventure. Her debut novel was a Romance Writers of America Golden Heart Finalist and a #1 National Regency Bestseller, and her subsequent novels have topped national and international bestselling lists. Her writing has also received critical acclaim. She is a three-time recipient of the Daphne du Maurier Award for Excellence in Mystery and Suspense, the Maggie Award for Excellence in Historical Romance, and the Passionate Plume. Her other awards include the National Excellence in Romance Fiction Award, the Golden Leaf, and the National Excellence in Storytelling Award.

Growing up on the Canadian prairies, Grace could often be found with her nose in a book—and not much has changed since. She set aside her favorite romance novels long enough to get her doctorate from the University of Michigan. A clinical psychologist, she lives with her family in Northern California. Her hobbies include dancing, dining in hole-in-the-wall restaurants, and going on adapted adventures with her special son.

Keep up with Grace's latest news!

Newsletter: gracecallaway.com/newsletter

facebook.com/GraceCallawayBooks

bookbub.com/authors/grace-callaway

instagram.com/gracecallawaybooks

amazon.com/author/gracecallaway

9 781960 956262